STORM
SPEAR

GENEVA
MONROE

PURPLE PHOENIX PRESS

CONTENT WARNING

Star Spear is a work of adult fantasy and not intended for minors. It contains scenes that may be distressing to some people, including strong language, graphic violence, death, themes of grief and loss, torture, attempted assault, discussion of rape, and explicit sexual content.

PLAYLIST

IRIS - THE GOO GOO DOLLS

SHIP IN A BOTTLE - CHLOE BREEZ

HEAT STROKE - BLACK MATH

YOUR CROSS TALK - EMERSON WARE, DEXTER FRENCH

STOP FIGHTING IT- APRIL JAI

FU IN MY HEAD - CLOUDY JUNE

REVOLUTION - BISHOP BRIGGS

CRAVIN' - STILETO, KENDYLE PAIGE

GOLDEN HOUR- JVKE

POWER - ISAK DANIELSON

BURN - 2WEI, EDDA HAYES

I'LL KEEP YOU SAFE - SLEEPING AT LAST

DANGEROUS HANDS - AUSTIN GIORGIO

PLAY WITH FIRE- SAM TINNESZ, YACHT MONEY

RUNNING UP THAT HILL - LOVELESS

IF YOU LOVE HER - FOREST BLAKK, MEGHAN TRAINOR

NO LEAF CLOVER - METALLICA, SFSO

LET IT BEGIN - SAYSH

BORN FOR THIS (EPIC MIX) - FOXXI

LEGENDS NEVER DIE - LEAGUE OF LEGENDS

Pronunciation Guide

CALLEN - cal-len

ELYRIA - eh-lee-ree-ah

XOC - schock

REIHANEH - ray-haan-ah

KAELIANA - Kay-lee-on-ah

ALESSIA - Ah-less-ee-ah

ELOAXIA - el-oh-asch-ah

LILANDRA - lie-lawn-dra

TROUPE SOLAIRE - troop sol-air

VENTERRA - ven-terra

SENESTERRA - sen-ess-terra

DESTERRA - des-terra

SUMAN - soo-mahn

OERWOOD - oar-wood

INNESVALE - in-ness-vail

INDEMIRA - in-deh-meer-ah

VENTERRA

EAST STRAIT

WEST STRAIT

The Isles

THE STEPS

CAMBERTINE

Laluna

LUNAR FOREST

The Bullseye

Basilica of Commerce

BONE ROAD

SENESTERRA

Sumenði University

Suman

THE PLAINS

Oerwood

MT. CARIN

This book is dedicated to everyone who
listened to my self-doubts,
and refused to accept them.

1

CALLEN

1 Year Ago

I swirled the amber liquid around my glass, watching it coat the rim.

"That's the ace to you, Cal."

Tilting my head to the side, I lifted the corner of my cards up. Of course, he had to lay a fucking ace when all I had were single digits and not a spade among them. Godsdamn him and his astounding luck. Whatever demon he struck a deal with to get his never-ending streak of good fortune needed to swing by my rooms sometime because Mal had an unbelievable ability to call all the right cards to him. All the right everything was always coming to him. The sour taste of envy coated the inside of my mouth, making my tongue thick and hard to swallow.

I flicked my gaze up to Mal giving him my best crooked smile. His corn silk blonde locks hung low, shielding his eyes from me and revealing nothing. Fucker.

"What's the matter?" he asked with a smug laugh. "You aren't folding your hand already, are you?"

"No. I didn't say that." I leaned forward, adding a golden coin to the growing pile at the center of the table. The crown pressed into its surface glinted in the lamplight, mocking me. I'd growl if it didn't give my hand away, opting instead to down the contents of my glass in one smooth swallow.

"Fine, I'll take your money." Mal threw back his head with a laugh, and leaned against the arm of his chair.

Bouncing red curls against a sea of mahogany skin made their way around the edge of the bar, catching my eye.

"Lucy!" I lifted my glass in acknowledgement, meeting the azure eyes of the barmaid. "Hit us up, darling. My glass is dryer than the Dead Lands."

She nodded, tossing the ringlets over her shoulder. She was pretty, in an ordinary way. Which was exactly what I was in the mood for after the night we'd had. Like many people from the Isles, her coloring reminded me of a cool autumn day. Light rolled off of her heaving breasts. Her corset was only loosely tied from her last hurriedly finished tryst.

She walked over to us, her bare thighs parting her skirts with every step. She sat the bottle on the table, then unnecessarily leaned over to pull the stopper. Amusement tugged up the corner of her lips. We'd dropped our finery before heading to this particular corner of Innesvale, but I was sure she knew who we were.

"I'm starting to think you're only drinking so much to get me to keep coming back here to refill your glass." Her watery blue eyes sparkled down at me.

I brushed my hand forward, slipping it along the slit in her skirt and drifting my fingertips across the back of her knees. She breathed a coquettish giggle that fooled no one. Gods, I was bored.

"And if I am?" Her playful smile shifted to something promising and wicked. In response, I lifted my hand further up the back of her leg.

Lucy draped an arm around my shoulder and leaned across my chest to my opposite ear. Her carefully calculated stance placed her décolletage in a position that was practically daring me to take a bite. At least this little apple wouldn't be trying to snag my crown from my pillow while I did. She might not be the most intriguing of women, but at least Lucy was upfront with her intentions.

"Then, I keep the good stuff upstairs." She drew my earlobe into her mouth and raked her teeth over its surface. Releasing me, she added, "There's a door to the upstairs apartment around the back."

I slid my hand over her ass, giving it a not so gentle squeeze, then removed my hand from under her skirt.

Walking her fingers along Mal's shoulder, she added, "You going to join us, too?"

Mal shifted uncomfortably in his seat, "No... No... not this time."

"Pity." Her ruby lips pouted, then, with a wink and a sashay of her hips, she walked back to the bar, leaving behind the bottle of brandy.

Mal picked it up and refilled my glass before topping off his own. "You're unbelievable."

I tipped back the brandy, rolling the burning liquid around my mouth. "How so?"

"You could have any of the ladies at court. At the Prophecy Ball, Lady Bernadette was literally throwing herself at your feet. The entire line of this year's debutantes were falling over themselves to get you to dance with them."

"I don't want them," I groaned. "I'm done with the court. All they do is try to please you."

Mal rolled his eyes. "Yeah, why would you want someone to please you?"

"No. Not like that. Every one of them is a complete fraud. They all act exactly how they think I want them to act. Not that anybody bothers enough to find out what I actually desire. They all know the expectation is for me to marry after I take the crown. The only thing those women want is a nice shiny tiara. The way they fawn over me is disgusting. Honestly, fucking them is only one step up from masturbation." I sighed and pinched the bridge of my nose to fight off the coming migraine that happened anytime I thought too long about my ascension.

"You know what you are?"

I raised my eyebrows at him. "I suppose you're about to tell me."

"You're the Calico Cat."

"Like, the children's rhyme?"

"You just can't be satisfied with the rat, so you spend your time chasing the mice."

I waved him off. "It's not like that."

"It is exactly like that, CALico."

"You don't get it. You can leave the Floating Palace *anytime*. You can choose

7

what you do and when. You don't have to worry about answering to anyone, except maybe Ferrus."

Mal's face drained of color at the mention of the old dragon. His eyes, which were just so full of joy, darkened completely.

"What is it?" I leaned forward in my chair, resting my arms on the table. "Mal?"

He shook his head, like trying to shake away whatever thought had just clouded his vision. Then he topped his glass to the brim with the remnants of the bottle and downed the lot in one long draft.

"It's nothing," he said with a cough, wiping at the corner of his mouth with the back of his sleeve.

"Ok... I'd believe that if you hadn't just drank a fifth of brandy before saying it."

"It's Ferrus."

"Ferrus?"

"I can't believe I'm telling you this." He ran his hands through his hair and then gripped the back of his neck. "He's been showing me some truly terrible things, Cal. It used to be that he'd only come to me once or twice a year. But... but ever since my last visit to Kraav, I keep having the same repeat dream. I've been having it for months. It's the *only* thing I've seen in my dreams since the last time I brought him our offerings."

"I mean. How bad can it be? They're just dreams."

Mal shook his head, refusing to look at me. "These aren't just dreams. He's planning something, something truly terrible."

I scoffed. "Who, the dragon? He hasn't left the mountain in over five thousand years. What can he possibly do from his lair?"

"He keeps showing me wave after wave of death. A thick cloud of smoke rolls out from Mt. Kraav and swallows Innesvale, then crosses the sea to Suman, the ice fields of the North, the Bullseye. It covers all of Venterra in a blanket of twisting shadows. It's so thick you can't breathe. You can't see. You can only choke. Then... the screaming starts. First, it's just a single woman. She wails in this pitch that sends lightning shooting through your head. Once the blood is pouring from your ears, she's joined by a chorus of cries. They raise and roar until the deafening sound rattles your bones and splits the earth. The entire world screaming at once." Mal's voice cracked, his hands beginning to tremble. "And when the shadow creeps back into the mountain once more, all that is left are bleached white bones. Bones of men and women, mothers holding their children, priests praying at altars... kings sitting on thrones." His eyes drilled into me like spears of ice. "All of Venterra, dead. Everyone."

I blinked at him. What did he expect me to say to that? Thank the gods it was just a dream. A wave that kills all of Venterra — is impossible. Nothing, not even a dragon, has that scope. If Mal thought there was any truth to these dreams, then it was because they'd driven him mad.

His stormy eyes were wide. They trembled with the fear I could see had shaken him to his core.

"Well fuck... at least I won't have to keep fending off Lady Bernadette's advances." I laughed, tipping back the remnants of my glass.

Mal's face went stark, then, just as quickly, twisted into a scowl. "You're a dick. You know that?"

"Come off it, Mal. It's just a dream, but extra points for creativity."

"You're not hearing me. This is *real*. Ferrus is a real threat to Venterra. If we don't do something, there will be nothing and no one left to mourn its remains."

I sighed, then leaned forward. "And what do you propose? That we kill Ferrus? We go running back to Mt. Kraav, and then what? Do you even know how to kill a dragon?"

"I'm not sure. There's this crystal shard. Maybe we could—"

A breathy, disbelieving laugh slipped from me, and Mal's brows furrowed with stern indignation.

"I will figure something out."

"Or perhaps your dreams are just *dreams*. Venterra has been at peace for centuries. The dragons have slept for millennia. There is no reason for one to come out of his slumber and wipe the world clean." Standing up, I threw my cards down, displaying my obviously losing hand. Then, gesturing at the pile of coins in the middle of the table, I added, "You win."

"Cal, wait." He stretched forward, grabbing at me.

I clapped him on the back. "Relax, Mal. Go get laid and try to remember that there's more to life than our nightmares."

I lifted my chin, catching Lucy's gaze. "Or at least that's my plan."

"That's not a solution."

"No, it's not. But it's better than the alternative."

2

ELYRIA

The Present

Wind whipped at the lines above us, and the spray of seawater misted my face. With the back of my hand, I brushed away the drops of water clinging to my lashes.

"Bein, take us out," Captain Morgan Sangrior called to the large man standing at the helm. She quickly ascended the stairs to join him. Bein dwarfed her petite form, looking even larger as he raised his hands to make a massive swell of water push up from the dock. The ship rocked, surfing the crest of the wave as it rolled out of the bay.

I lurched forward, reaching out my hand for something to steady myself. Cal wrapped his arms around me. I gave in to the sensation, letting his strength support me—if only for a second before pulling away. The tensing muscles pressed against me rebelled at letting go. Nevertheless, I stepped away from him. His fingers trailed down my arm as I moved from his grasp. I felt their longing presence hanging in the air between us, like the ghost of what might have been.

This was not something we were doing. Cal was not saving me, holding me, not going to be doing anything with me. He spent the past weeks feeding me lies and keeping the very core of who I was a secret. I'd wanted nothing more than knowing I wasn't alone in this world. One tiny flame to hold on to while I was drowning in the darkness of my grief. That was all I wanted, and he'd denied me that. No, he wouldn't get the satisfaction of feeling me pressed against him

The hiss of unfurling sails mingled with the sounds of sloshing water and the ship's crew. The sound of Rei's laughter drifted over the roar of the waves crashing against the sapphire hull. She stood with a single arm draped over Morgan's shoulder, her fingers dipping playfully beneath the hem of the captain's tunic.

Well, at least she's happy.

A blonde-haired man approached the helm beside Bein. He raised his hands, sending an intense rush of air to fill the sails. Immediately, the dragon shaped hull sliced through the moon-crested water. Two more Wind Singers joined the bridge. With a single push, the ship rocketed into the open ocean.

The sudden change in inertia threw me into Cal, the force toppling us both to the deck. As we fell, Cal wrapped his arms around me, letting his body cushion the blow. We ended up sprawled on the deck, our bodies tangled around each other. His amber eyes were bright with amusement. Our position was startlingly similar to how we met; on a different day, and a different time when he caught me stumbling. I never stumbled, but the universe, it would seem, had a sense of humor.

For one fraction of a moment, I forgot the pain of losing everything from my heart to my father. I ran my hand up his arm, taking advantage of the way circumstance had dropped me, once again, into his arms. Rei's shadow blotted out the moonlight bathing us.

"You know, they have cabins for that." She winked at me.

What was I doing? Why was I fondling the sexy curve of his arm when I should be sticking him with the pointy end of something sharp? Falling into our old rhythm was too easy, literally.

I scrambled away from him, but not before Cal trailed his hands down my legs. "You're not funny," I said, straightening my shirt and scowling at Rei.

"I dunno..." She flicked her eyes over to Cal. "It's a little funny. Besides, I told you, the moment you declared you were done with him, you'd fall right into his arms." She lifted her hand in a stage whisper. "And look, there you were—in his arms."

Heat spread up my neck, and despite the dark night, I knew I wasn't merely blushing anymore. My entire body felt like a bright red beacon of embarrassed light.

Cal ignored Rei, but his eyes trailed over me as he ambled to the railing. "Of course, Morgan has both sea and wind singers on board. That explains why her ship is always outrunning our patrols."

"I'd be willing to bet that her entire crew is one or the other." Xoc moved out of the shadow of the mast to take up a spot beside us at the railing.

The black ocean smoothed beneath the ship, quickly leaving the shores of Suman and the carnage we'd wrought far behind us. The wind tossed my hair, and I closed my eyes to the freedom of the open ocean. The chaos and heartache grew smaller by the second. Ahead of us laid only new possibilities.

One by one, the others drifted into the ship, leaving only Cal and I looking out over the wing carved into the dragon hull.

"There's nothing like the ocean at night."

Moonlight glistened off the waves of his auburn hair as the wind tousled them about. If not for the full moon, they would almost look black, nothing like the gold when he showed me the truth of who he was—what he was. His eyes, on the other hand, were ringed with it. They'd had that golden hue since we were at the university, never fully returning to their rich chocolate color. I wondered if that was because he was keeping his emotions open to me or if what had occurred between us had rattled his control.

"When I was a kid, whenever I was upset or had a nightmare, I would watch the moonlight reflect off of the water from my balcony, listening to the sounds of the water pouring from the spouts built into the palace walls. It always calmed me."

"The palace." Because he had a balcony as a child. I longed for a home with a picket fence, and Cal grew up with an entire castle as his playground. I shook my head with a silent laugh.

He nodded, and his eyebrows knit in what almost looked like pain. He was trying to share. This was an offering after all the lies, but all it did was make me realize I knew nothing about him.

"Tell me more," I said hesitantly. Whether I liked it or not, if I wanted to make Malvat pay, my fate was tied to his. It didn't mean I had to forgive him, even if that was what my treacherous heart was already begging me to do.

Cal's eyes were full of glassy emotion, making the gold in them more luminous. He gently tucked the errant strands of my hair behind my ear, letting the back of his hand drift down the lines of my neck. I deliberately pulled my hair over the opposite shoulder, ignoring how that simple gesture made my heart flip.

"Elyria, I-"

"If you tell me you're sorry again, I'm going to blacken that other eye," I snapped, cutting him off and removing his hand. Whatever followed him saying my name with such longing was not something I wanted to hear.

"You should know, the stories I've told you have all been true. It's killing me that I even have to say this, but the only lies I told you were my name and what we were doing in Laluna. Everything else was genuine." His eyes pleaded with mine for forgiveness. He wasn't going to get it.

"That should make me feel better?" I turned away, sparing myself from the mournful look of regret on his handsome face. I pressed a fist against the deep-seated ache that pulsed with each pump of my heart. Why did this hurt so much?

Cal's hand tugged on my shoulders, twisting me back to face him. Heat flowed from his palms in a current that I felt down to the swaying ship beneath my soles.

I sighed. My resolve was crumbling. Why couldn't he just let this be? "It was never the lies, Cal. It was not telling me things you damn well knew I needed to hear... and the manipulation. Gods, you made me fall-" I bit off that sentence, not willing to finish it. I wasn't about to admit to him the things I wasn't even ready to admit to myself. Tears blurred my vision. I hated how weak they made me feel. "You only told me what you wanted to and kept the rest for yourself."

"What do you want to know?"

"Everything," I said a bit too loudly, causing the people coiling the mooring ropes to look over at us. I took a deep breath, repeating myself in a more reasonable tone. "I once asked you for a secret. Your truth is all I've ever wanted from you." If he wanted to prove he was worthy of my trust, then this was how he did it. "It's several days to Innesvale. You owe it to me to show me who you really are."

"I owe you more than my truth. I promise, Sunshine, I *will never* deny you again."

His expression was so disarmingly serious; it made my chest tight and my knees weak. I grabbed the railing before I ended up stumbling into his arms...again.

"Okay, *Callen,* then *s*tart at the beginning."

"The beginning." He ran his hands through his hair and slid to the ground with a long exhale. Leaning against the hull, he patted the ground beside him, holding my gaze until I relented and sank to the floor.

"Well, let's do this properly..." He held out his hand to me, which I shook with a bemused grin. "Hello, my name is Callen Shadow. I'm a 525-year-old crowned prince of Innesvale with questionable morals and—"

"525?! Are you serious right now?"

"Yes." He smiled gently at me, and the sheer difference in our ages settled on me like a weight. If he really was so much older than me, then why was he interested in me at all? How could he possibly see anything but my naivety? It did explain how he was able to lock down his magic so completely that I hadn't known it was there until it was swirling around us—and merging with mine. Heat flooded down my spine, pooling in my stomach. Fusing our magic had felt so absolutely euphoric, creating a sense of completion that made my soul hum with pleasure from the mere memory of it.

Cal continued his explanation, snapping me back to the moment. "A new draken is born following the death of the previous one. Or, in the case of gold draken, there are two. In the Shadow line, the last draken was my Great Uncle, Toren Shadow. I was born about five months after his death. Twenty-five years ago, the Asche draken died, and the power was passed on to you. Her name was Allisandrea Asche; she was the Grandmother of the current queen."

I opened my mouth to speak, but Cal put a single finger to my lips, silencing me.

"Before you ask, I never met her. That is honestly all I know. There are probably fifty generations separating the Shadows and Asches, and Indemira has never been forthcoming with friendship or information. The borders of Indemira are heavily guarded, and its citizens rarely leave the shelter of the Blood Birches."

I fiddled with the torn edge of my soot-stained shirt, pulling at the fraying threads and trying to ignore the tingling sensation Cal'd left behind in my lips.

"When a child is born with Aurus's mark, that child is presented to him. Aurus only meets his progeny once, usually. When you were born, your parents probably brought you to him."

Your parents. The words echoed in my head, keeping me from being able to do anything but nod.

"After the birth of a draken, an emissary is sent between our two kingdoms. Twenty-five years ago, when Allisandrea died, we waited for a confirmation that never came. Nobody knew who the next was until I found you in Laluna."

My mind was spiraling. With each bit of information Cal revealed, two more questions took their place. If at least one of my parents was related to the Queens of Indemira, then why were they living in a nothing town near the Straits when Duke found me? Why didn't the Asches know of my birth? Why didn't anyone in Indemira try to find us?

"Malvat must have traced the line. It's why he targeted you and, before that, me."

Targeted him. I could almost still feel the heat of his fire wrapping around me while he made his confession. *We share more than scars.* In my grief, I hadn't taken the time to think about *his* pain.

"Tell me about that night." I placed my hand over the hidden scar on his chest. The color washed from his cheeks, his expression tightening until a tremor ran beneath my fingertips.

"Elle... Fuck, I don't know if I can." Throat bobbing with a hard swallow, he placed his hand over mine and lowered it to his lap. "I..." Cal squinted his eyes, his fingers tightening as he tried to fight between the painful memory and keeping the promise he'd just made. "I... haven't discussed this since the day I

18

awoke from my coma."

The raw agony in his expression echoed the ache that was a constant under-current in my heart, filling me with a sudden need to take that burden away. This must have been what he was feeling the entire time we were at the Solaire camp. How did he withstand seeing me weep and feeling powerless against it?

"My father was the first instance of the Shade." His voice sounded raspy, but he didn't stop. "My memory from that night, and the days before it, is blurry. The only solid memory I have was standing on the balcony. My father held this jagged dagger. The blade was how I knew the spider that bit Duke wasn't just a spider. They were both made from the same black-green crystal."

An unsolicited shiver ran down my spine. The bulbous body and spindly legs haunted me. Every time I closed my eyes, I saw the tiny insect scuttling up Duke's neck and the fangs piercing his flesh. Worst of all was the way it vanished into smoke like it had never existed, except for the black stain spreading along my father's throat.

The hand wound tightly around mine squeezed, bringing me back to the present. Even though he was sharing his worst trauma, Cal was still keeping me grounded.

"Elle, my father is... *was*—" He winced. Knowing the cost of his loss, and that he was sharing this with me despite it, strummed something deep in my heart.

"–nearly 800 years old. He suffered from a bone disease so advanced that the healers couldn't do more than slow its progression. He should never have been able to beat me, but he was impossibly fast and strong."

Andromeda, the assassin who attacked us in the library, had been inhuman. I'd dealt her quite a few deadly blows, and even with a broken knee, she'd managed to chase me down. No person should be able to move like that. Was that what his father had been like? It was almost too cruel to imagine.

"I tried everything I could to snap him out of it, but nothing worked. In the end, he drove the knife into my heart." He blinked slowly with unfocused eyes, like he was watching it play out on the deck before him. "and then I watched as it disintegrated into wisps of smoke."

He swallowed hard, his gaze drifting up to the moon. One thin trail of tears broke free. As I stared at his tear-streaked cheeks, the raw honesty of what he was doing slammed into me. This wasn't a show. He wasn't playing with my emotions to turn them back on me. We'd dipped a toe into the well of his pain, and he was giving me this vulnerability willingly.

"I lost consciousness staring at his face. What looked back at me was pure *wickedness*." He brushed away the tear trail with the heel of his hand. "I knew I was dying, and his malice would be the last thing I ever saw. I sometimes think things would have been easier if I had died that night. Then maybe Malvat would have been satisfied and left Innesvale alone. Maybe he would have left you alone." His head rolled against the unforgiving wood, meeting my eyes with his no longer hidden pain, but there was something else there, too. He reached up and traced the line of my jaw with his thumb. "I had nightmares about it. Almost every night, I would wake up screaming, drenched in sweat, with phantom pain lancing into my fingertips... every night until I held you in my arms."

Did I really calm him, the way being in his arms always soothed me? I swallowed around the lump forming in my throat. Even now, the heartbeat thrumming in my ears demanded I close the distance between us and replace the ache with something else altogether—But I didn't.

"The night in the forest, when I was screaming in my sleep, I dreamt Duke was trapped by the worm, and I had to watch as it devoured him." The memory of the way Cal had cradled me and never once judged me for my tears chased away the shiver trickling down my spine. "When you held me, it was the closest I've ever felt to being safe."

Cal leaned forward, hesitating so that he barely hovered above my lips. He whispered my name with a long, slow breath that brushed over my skin. The warmth of his palm against my cheek made my stomach twist into an aching knot. Our shared loss echoed around us. I desperately wanted to feel anything but this ache and to make his disappear.

My eyes dropped to his mouth. The split on his lip shined crimson in the moonlight, and remorse laced itself within the empathy. The reminder was too sharp to ignore. Every moment we'd shared was tainted by the cloud of his lies, even the bittersweet ones.

Closing my eyes, I turned my face to the side. If we lingered even a second longer, my weak self-control would break, and I would give in to the temptation sitting beside me. There had been too much of that already.

I needed more than a single moment of shared grief.

Cal's lips brushed my temple before sitting back. For several long minutes, it was quiet except for the rhythmic sound of the water against the side of the ship. Threading his fingers with mine, his thumb slid against the back of my hand in time with the waves.

"That night, my father took the knife that Xoc keeps at his hip, and–" Cal lifted our joined hands to his mouth. Closing his eyes, his lips pressed against the exact spot his thumb had been smoothing. "–slit his own throat with it. There was nothing Xoc could do." One heavy tear at a time, a fresh stream flowed from his eyes. "Malvat was controlling him. I'd loved him like a brother, and he repaid me by murdering my father."

The sadness shifted into something darker—sharper. I recognized that feeling too. The dragon in me wanted to burn it all to the ground, to release my power until every inch that lay between here and Mt. Kraav was nothing but ash. For Cal, for me, for Duke, I would see all that Malvat held dear incinerated.

"Innocent person after innocent person. He'd possess them. They'd throw themselves off the falls, before rushing carriages, or into a blazing fire." Cal shuddered. "All to punish me for not dying that night. We had to make special cells to hold those who had been infected because there's no way to stop it. There are hundreds of souls trapped in their own minds, and there is nothing I can do about it. The only way is to end him."

And just like that, we'd circled back to the beginning. "So that's why you went looking for me; because when we're near each other, our power is stronger."

"Yes."

He'd found me to stand beside him in the fight of his life. A fight that I was a part of, even before I met Cal.

"You can't blame yourself for what he's done. Malvat would have tried to kill me anyway," I said resolutely. "Even if you hadn't come looking for me."

"Probably. You really weren't that hard to track down. I mean, you called yourself The Golden Dragon and blew fire." He smiled, and I knew he was remembering my performance.

"I never breathed fire until the night you came to my show." I stood up. "Give me your hand."

He placed his hand in mine and stood.

I ran my finger over his palm, testing the sensation. A pulse moved from my hand to his. "This happens nearly every time you touch me. I don't know how I didn't realize what this feeling was. It's like I can feel the fire in your veins calling to me. The pull burns. It's intense."

"It is." Nodding, he turned my hand over in his. "Now, I want to see something. I've felt what it's like when you summon your power, but I've kept mine bottled tight this entire time." He traced a figure eight against my palm with his index finger. With each rotation, his finger grew hotter. "It's exhausting, especially when my emotions are running high. Which, with you, is all the time. You have a way of igniting my passions."

We placed our palms together. His eyes shifted to a brilliant gold. A wave of warmth ran from my fingertips to deep in my core, blazing to life with recognition. The world swayed in a way that had nothing to do with the movement of the ship.

"Woah."

He nodded and called a small flame between our hands. A second wave of power coursed into my veins and then back to him. The flame flickered brighter, nearly purple.

"Someday, when there are less eyes on us." He tilted his head towards Bein and the Wind Singers still casting on deck. "We will test this properly."

"ARE YOU SERIOUSLY PLAYING WITH FIRE ABOARD MY SHIP?" I jumped. How can such a loud and booming voice come from someone so small?

We immediately put our hands down, hiding them behind our backs like naughty children. I turned toward Morgan as the puff of extinguished flame lingered in the air before me.

I opened my mouth to apologize.

"Shut it. Whatever kinks you two have, keep fire out of it for as long as you are aboard my vessel." She leveled on me. "I catch you doing that again and you can enjoy the ride to Innesvale at the end of a rope off the back of my gallery."

Cal growled. Actually growled. I held up a hand to his chest.

"You're right, Morgan. I don't always think before I act. That was..." I looked up at Cal. The spell weaving between us cracked, and reality came rushing back. "Foolish."

She nodded, side-eyeing Cal. "I've had your quarters made up. Space is tight on my ship, so don't be expecting anything extravagant. Your cabin is below deck. Bein will show you where." She gestured to the large man behind the helm. A younger man took his place, and he swiftly made his way down to us. It was astonishing how she didn't need to say anything and everyone on the ship automatically responded. I thought of all the times I'd repeated instructions to the troupe; my voice was practically hoarse by the end of an average day. It made me weirdly homesick for those assholes.

Bein addressed Morgan with a rumbled, "Captain." It snapped me out of my memories and back to the moment.

"Sorry, did you say cabin? As in one?" Flashes of our night at Joseph's moved through my mind. I was not ready to relive that. Or at least, I was pretty sure that I wasn't.

Morgan smirked.

"Yes. I told you space is tight, so you three will have to share quarters."

"Three?" I looked across the deck to where Xoc was laid out on a long bench. His arm was draped over his eyes, already asleep.

"What about Rei? I can just bunk with her." I could feel Cal's gaze burning into me.

Morgan smiled, eyeing my body up and down. "She's already in my bed, but if you wanted to join us, I'm sure that's not something she would be opposed to — and I know I wouldn't be." Her sapphire eyes dropped over my chest and then back up in a slow appraisal.

I flushed bright red.

"Yeah, I didn't think so," she laughed, then gestured to Bein. "This is Bein Roskr, my first mate."

Bein was large, perhaps even taller than Xoc. He towered over Morgan's petite frame. Next to him, she looked like a child. He wore a slim sleeveless shirt that showed off rows of curving tattooed muscle. His skin, much like Morgan's, was dark like highly polished mahogany. The thin hatch mark of scars covering his body told of a history of conflict. Red hair threaded into long locks were tied on top of his head and held in place by a thin bone rod. He ran a large hand over his face, emphasizing the cropped beard that only strengthened his jawline. Blue eyes, not as dark as Morgan's but just as piercing, looked down on me in banal amusement. He was the portrait of intimidation. Who would win in a battle of stoicism, Bein or Xoc?

Morgan gave one last look at me and then walked back towards her quarters.

"Well–" Cal burst out laughing. "Who could turn down an offer like that?"

I backhanded him in the shoulder, but he only laughed harder. "You know, I think you like me kicking your ass."

"Oh, I definitely love watching you try."

"Are you two done?" Bein asked, seemingly annoyed by Cal's laughter.

We followed him down a narrow flight of stairs and into the galley of the ship. He pushed open the door to a plain cabin with a single narrow bed anchored to the wall. A porthole looked out at the water, nearly level to the window. Crates were stacked in the corner, taking nearly every inch of floor space save for a narrow path to the door. I was about to protest about the size when the door closed behind us, leaving Cal and me alone.

Heat radiated from him, making me very aware of just how close we were standing— of how close we would be as we slept in this comically small cabin. A sensation brushed over my shoulders, and I was sure that he was about to touch me. But as I turned, his hands were firmly plastered to his sides. As if a bit of linen could anchor them in place, the knuckles of his fingers were turning white from gripping the hem of the enormous shirt he'd borrowed from Xoc.

"How did you want to do this?" I could almost hear his hammering pulse.

Each muscle was tensed, and his careful, restrained expression looked like he was waiting for me to drop the ax and deliver him a killing blow.

I didn't know how to respond. What did I want? My angst wanted to pummel him into the wall so that a lasting imprint of his form was carved into the wood. But then every cell of my body was screaming to touch him, to have him touch me. There would be no keeping space between us in that tiny bed. He would spend the entire night pressed against me. The knowledge of him being that close was something that I both longed for and feared.

"Look," he said. "It's been a long night. I promise to face away from you and keep my hands to myself."

"Clothes on," I added, thinking of the last night we'd shared a bed with my shirt bunched around my waist.

"Agreed, while I would gladly sleep with you naked." His eyes roved over me for just a second. "I don't trust the crew enough to be caught in any state of undress."

He kicked off his boots and slid into the bed facing the wall, giving me a view of his broad shoulders and back. A faint outline of his dragon mark glowed through the thin fabric of the tunic. How had he kept that hidden from me all the times he'd been shirtless?

The mattress sank beneath my weight. I carefully turned to face the door, my back pressing against his. He was a beacon of warmth in an otherwise chilled room. The heat radiating from him seeped into my bones. I hated how comforting that was.

Reaching towards the small lantern, I was about to call the light to me when the flame zipped across the room and playfully sat against Cal's fingertips. I craned my neck over my shoulder to look at him, my mouth hanging open in shock. Around his fingers spun a small ball of fire. It tugged on an invisible cord that felt like it was tied directly to my heart.

"So this is what that feels like," I said breathlessly.

He looked over his shoulder, flashing me a knowing smile. "Goodnight, Elle." The fire extinguished into a poof of smoke.

In the dark, I listened to the creak of the boat rocking, keenly aware of how and where our bodies touched. One arm and half of my leg hung over the edge of the bed, close enough to the crates that my knee was shoved against the wood. This was absurd. Why was I fighting this so much? We'd already crossed this line. Did it matter what part of me was touching him? Especially when I knew how perfectly we fit together.

Turning, I spooned my body against his, just as he'd done to me so many nights. My cheek nestled between his shoulder blades, and my arm wrapped around his waist. I hated how much I loved this feeling. Cal laced his fingers into mine, bringing my palm to his lips for the lightest kiss before resting our joined hands against his chest.

This was going to be a long night.

3
CALLEN

For the first time, maybe ever, I slept soundly the entire night. No night-mares, no looming threats to force me awake, and no guilt weighing me down like a lead blanket.

I hated that telling her the truth shattered what had been built between us, but last night's confession was freeing. Elyria didn't trust me anymore. That much was clear, but I'd seen that flicker in her expression. A part of her wanted this as much as I did.

That was enough to give me hope.

Elyria slept snuggled behind me with her hand pressed against my heart. I twined my large fingers between her slender ones and silently vowed that I would do whatever it took to earn back her trust. Last night that meant falling asleep holding only her hand.

Now that I'd awoken, apparently, it hadn't stayed that way.

In our sleep, Elyria curled into me. Gold-tipped hair splayed across my chest. One leg linked through my own, allowing the perfect curve of her body to mold against me. Her head rested above my heart, sleeping to the rhythm of its beat.

The rhythmic rise and fall of her chest told me she was still asleep. Elyria's hair coiled between my fingers, and slowly I smoothed my thumb over the golden ends, careful not to wake her and shatter this moment of quiet contentment. I took a deep breath and soaked in her smokey scent. For a heartbreaking moment at the university, I thought I would never breathe in the floral and ember fragrance again. When I told her the truth of her father, the look of venom in her eyes tore me apart. Worse was the pain in her expression when she realized I had lied about being draken.

I feared I would never get her back again.

But then, here I was, drinking down this silent indulgence, relishing in the feel of her body pressed to mine. I didn't deserve her or the privilege of feeling her perfection curled in my arms. I was one lucky asshole. Fate graced me with a second chance, and I wasn't about to waste it.

The ship gently rocked beneath us. We'd be at sea for at least another day, and with nowhere to go and nothing to do, being able to simply lay in bed felt like a true luxury. To laze in bed with Elyria was a daydream I had toyed with for weeks now. Granted, my daydreams usually involved less clothing and a larger bed.

Elyria shifted slightly, nuzzling deeper against me with a tiny sound that made me think of a mewling kitten. Her body tensed as she slowly realized her surroundings. Lifting her head, she blinked at me with tired eyes. I placed a soft kiss on her hair. Even now, with her brow furrowed, she was still the most beautiful thing I had ever seen.

"Good morning, Sunshine." My voice was deep and rough from sleep. Entirely on its own, my hand began idly stroking her back. She instantly relaxed and hummed softly.

"I slept all night, no nightmares," she mumbled against my chest before sliding back onto the pillow and leaving behind a wave of cold emptiness.

"Me neither."

Squinting at the morning light peeking in from the porthole, she reached out and pulled the blanket over her face.

"Did I really spend the entire night draped over you like that? How embarrassing."

Smiling, I rolled onto my side and tugged the blanket down to reveal sparkling golden eyes. "Delightfully, yes. I think so."

She pulled the blanket back up, leaving only enough to peek out at me. I could just make out the slight blush to her cheeks. Adorable. She was absolutely fucking adorable.

"I slept so well that I forgot where we were for a second," she said over a yawn.

"It's the boat rocking. I always sleep deeply at sea," I replied. "Plus, the porthole is so small, it stays dark much longer in the morning than a typical bedroom."

She moved to get up, and I reached out. "Stay." I didn't want to get up and go out into the world, not when it was so perfect in here.

Elle blinked down at my hand on her arm. I could feel her hesitation.

"Just stay here. Be with me. Please." Elyria glanced uneasily back at the door. "There's nothing out there but grumpy sailors, salty air, and one very cantankerous Xoc."

Resolve cracking, she settled back into the pillow, facing me. Tucking her hands beneath her cheek, Elyria snuggled back down. Her foot slinked between my legs, wedging into what little space there was in the tiny bed. Before long, it wasn't just her foot laying claim, but her entire leg.

"I think maybe there's another inch in there somewhere... if you want to keep looking?" I said with a chuckle.

She innocently batted her lashes, not surrendering a fraction of the space she'd claimed.

"So what happens when we get to Innesvale?" she asked.

I swallowed. I was so consumed by the here and now that I hadn't thought of what our actual arrival would be like. Not in detail, anyway. "We'll have to take the long way into the city since we won't be arriving on an officially scheduled transport." Given her history with our fleet, the harbor patrol might actually give Morgan a bit of trouble. I was going to have to make sure her signalmen knew the royal codes to avoid being sunk by Innesvales' defense turrets.

"And then, I'll need to check in with my mother. There are official matters that I'll probably have to take care of, seeing as I've been gone for so long." I sighed. The bureaucracy and the more pragmatic parts of leadership were something I'd dreaded my entire life.

Her eyes opened wide with realization.

"If your father has–" she hesitated, "What I mean to say is, aren't you *king* now?" She scanned the room as if the absurdity of laying in a tiny cabin bed with a king was just dawning on her.

"I'm not king yet. Though I'm sure that day will be here sooner than I'd like."

"You don't want to be king?"

"It's not that I don't want to. It's just that being king is more than wearing a crown and making decisions. Being prince afforded me more liberty than I'll have once I ascend to the throne. That's all."

"But if you're here, then who's ruling right now? I mean, someone has to be."

"Trust me, I would much rather be here in this bed with you than sitting on any throne. Fuck, I'd rather be lying in bed with Xoc than sitting on that throne right now."

Elyria giggled. I reached out, wanting to drag the back of my hand down the smooth skin of her arm. Her sun-brightened, golden eyes followed the movement.

Realizing what I was doing, I lowered it back to the sheets. No matter how badly I wanted to sink my hands into her hair and draw her strawberry lips to mine, that was not what we were doing. This was about me opening up and showing her I was worthy of her trust.

Fuck, who was this man? The old Callen never cared about such things. He would have stripped her bare and laid her out like a ten-course meal. She would have been screaming my name before the door to the cabin even closed. Now, I was chastising myself for wanting to touch her arm.

"My mother is acting as regent." I groaned, not wanting to dwell on responsibilities, or how Elyria brought out parts of me I didn't know existed. "Elle, the kingdom doesn't know of my father's *death*." I hissed out the last word. Her eyes melted with empathy. "We've tried very hard to keep the information about the Shade as quiet as possible. If the people knew that even the king wasn't safe from it, there would be mass panic. For now, the public believes that because of his illness, he has been put on bed rest. As he is unable to attend public duties and functions, the normal progression of power would be for my mother to step in as regent. This also allows me the opportunity to handle matters with Malvat on a more... personal level."

I felt my soul darken just at the mention of his name. The stab of betrayal was there, the memory of the knife in my chest twisting every time I thought of him.

"Once the Shade is no longer a concern, we will tell the public that my father has passed because of his failing health, and then I'll proceed with the coronation. Or at least—" I closed my eyes. "--that was the plan that we all decided on after his death." I fell back onto my pillow. The heaviness of it all settled on my chest.

"Tell me more about your father." Elyria's voice stumbled over the sentence like she wasn't entirely certain she should ask it.

I cracked my eyes open, letting them drift down to her.

"Tell me something happy and good about him." A coaxing smile coated her words.

I put an arm behind my head. One corner of my mouth quirked upwards. "You first."

She looked like I'd struck her. Was this pushing her too far? I had much more time to process the death of my father than she had.

"Nooo." She poked at my chest. "You go first, and if your story is good enough, then I'll reward you with mine. But mine is really good, so you have to make it count." It was the first truly playful thing she'd done since the blowout in Suman.

"Ooo, no pressure."

"Extra points if it's embarrassing," she said, with a fiendish sort of laugh. I knew I was right to play this game with her.

"Embarrassing!" I joined in with her laughter. "Fine. I have plenty of embarrassing stories. Shall I tell you the story of Callen and The Bee?"

I loved the way her eyes crinkled when she laughed. The wrinkle at the bridge of her nose and the tiny dimples in her cheeks. She was practically cherubic. I swear time slowed around us. Or maybe, I just wanted to bask in the glow of that smile forever, and it made it feel like time stopped.

"Please." She gestured for me to continue.

"When I was young, very young, maybe ten?" My voice trailed off as I did some mental math. "Yeah, probably about that age. Kaeliana, my sister, before you ask, hadn't been born yet. My mother used to insist on these mid-day picnics in the gardens. You know, she's been with my father forever, but I think the true loves of her life are those flower beds."

Elyria smiled, and warmth blossomed inside me. I reached over and coiled a loose strand of her hair between my fingers. I played with it until the curl slipped free, and my hand fell back to the no-man's-land between us.

"A huge picnic would be laid out on soft blankets, and the three of us would sit under the sun and eat. Afterwards my mother and father would gaze at the clouds while I ran around the grass with a kite or some other toy."

"I bet you were an adorable child. I can picture it perfectly, the blue sky and the green grass, surrounded by flowers, your auburn hair catching in the wind as you flew your kite. It sounds idyllic and completely unlike anything from my childhood," she said wistfully. Elyria's eyes were luminous, and then, to my absolute delight, she scooted closer to me, her hand resting atop mine.

"I was flying a kite I'd designed to catch the wind and do dramatic loops in the air." I flipped her hand over and traced curling lines along her palm. "Kites can be especially thrilling when you can sing any air current into being."

"Mmm...thrilling," she said, biting down on her lip to suppress a laugh.

"Anyway..." I gave a mock scowl. "I was flying my kite when this big fat bumble bee flew right into my nose." I made a little flying motion with my hand and flicked her nose lightly.

"What?" she shrieked, full of disbelief, while waving in the air at my fingers.

"It's true. I don't know if the bee had a death wish, but it flew right into my nose." I pointed to my left nostril for emphasis. "Got his dumb ass stuck way up in there."

Covering her laugh with her hand, she squeaked, "Oh my gods! What did you do?"

"Screamed. A lot. But my father grabbed the ice bucket and ran over to me. My mother laid my head on her lap while he iced my nose. It reduced the swelling, and then, with some gentle coaxing of air, the bee flew out. He saved me. I was terrified, and the entire time it was his steady eyes that kept me calm."

The image of him staring down at me in contempt, a knife protruding from my chest, flashed before my eyes. I blinked it away before it could freeze over the warmth of that day in the garden.

Elyria smiled broadly at me. "Well, I guess we know where your fear of bugs comes from."

"Hey, you try having a bee shoved up your nose and then talk to me about being afraid of bugs."

I gave her a playful shove on her shoulder, misjudging how close to the edge of the bed she was. Elyria tipped over the side of the cot, landing with a hard *thud*.

"That was not intentional," I said, barely suppressing my laughter.

"Ow," came a strangled voice from the floor. Her head popped back up, and her face was bright red, but the expression was pure joy. She climbed back into the bed. Rather than return to her carefully distanced place, she slid into what felt entirely natural and rested her head on my shoulder. Unintentional or not, I was definitely winning.

"Okay, I told, now it's your turn. If a bee up my nose doesn't earn me a story, nothing will," I said, leaning in to nuzzle the top of her head. Smokey, floral tendrils drifted up to me as she gave a long sigh. Elyria toyed with the collar of my shirt, making my heart thump and a deep buzz hummed through my veins.

"When I was little, there were lots of times when I would get anxiety and not be able to fall asleep. My dreams have never been a particularly welcoming place. Rather than face them, I'd stay up all night, pacing."

I started running my fingers through the hair along her crown, sifting the long strands through my fingers before beginning again. It was for my benefit, a purely selfish indulgence. I loved her hair. I loved how it felt, how it smelled, the way it gleamed in even the lowest light. Then Elyria made a contented hum that made my chest feel tight. I committed the sound to memory and promised to do this every chance she'd let me.

"This was before he bought me and the girls our own wagon. Back then, I had a cot in Duke's. Sometimes the nightmares were about parents I never knew, or performances gone wrong with angry audiences, really anything. I'd be unable to lie in bed, so I'd pace back and forth...for hours. I'd try to be quiet, but Duke always woke up. One night, when my anxiety was particularly high, we tried something new. He cranked this old music box that had been Lila's."

"Who's Lila?" I interrupted. This was a new name she'd never mentioned before. She pulled the chain and rings out from under the collar of her shirt. They jingled in the air before me. I recognized them instantly. These were the rings Elyria took off of Duke at his funeral. The same rings she toyed with whenever she was nervous.

"She was his wife."

"Duke was married?" I had a hard time reconciling the flirt I'd met in Laluna with someone who could have committed himself to just one person.

"Lila passed away before Duke found me. They used to travel in a band of for-hires," then with realization, she added, "With Amos, the owner of the Crooked Crow. You remember him."

Now Amos was a name I recognized. The grizzled bartender was who I had to thank for coaxing Elyria to dine with me the day we met. "Yeah, he's pretty unforgettable."

"Duke gave Lila a music box when they were first together. It wasn't anything fancy. Just a small cedar box with a flower inlay. It played this pretty little waltz." Elyria closed her eyes and hummed. It was a sweet song, one I almost recognized.

Gods, I wanted to kiss her. My skin was nearly vibrating with the need to embrace her. The dragon inked along my spine burned.

"He would take me in his arms. With my child-sized feet placed on top of his enormous ones, he waltzed me around the wagon like it was our own tiny dance hall. We wouldn't stop until I was laughing, and then he tucked me back into bed. For years, whenever I had a nightmare or was too anxious to sleep, we would literally dance it away." Elyria peered up at me. She was smiling, but a small tear rolled over her cheek. I reached down and wiped it away with my thumb.

"That's not even a little embarrassing. I thought you said you had a really good one," I teased.

"That was. Of all my childhood memories, dancing with Duke is my favorite. It's the best one I've got."

36

She dipped her head down to my chest. I wrapped my arms around her in an echo of the way we'd been lying when we awoke. Wet tears slid over my skin and dampened my shirt. My heart ached for the stolen time with her father that she would never get back. I wanted so badly to take this pain from her.

Several quiet minutes passed, and then into my chest, she said, "Tell me about Malvat."

Heat plumed up from her. The surrounding air shimmered with it.

"Elle, I don't know that now is the—"

"The *only* thing I know about him is that he will die with my hand wrapped around his burning heart. Maybe *then* he will understand the heartache he has caused."

The air around us pulsed, her skin glowing with heat. I took a deep breath, stroking her back. Fuck, keeping my hands to myself, not when she needed comfort so badly. Like a ripple in the ocean, her breaths slowly fell in line with my own. Elyria relaxed into the touch, and the heat shimmer vanished.

"I know he's the Iron Draken, and Lord of the Floating Lands, but I really don't know anything else about him." She tilted her head and flashed hot eyes at me, the kind you couldn't broker with. "So, tell me about the man who took everything from me."

"Okay," I said, not entirely sure this was a good idea. "He...well..." How did I tell the woman I loved that the man who'd killed her father wasn't always a bad guy? How did I tell her that his betrayal sometimes hurt more than my father's death? "He wasn't always evil. In fact, until a year ago, I called him my friend."

She sat up to look at me clearly. Confusion etched lines into her perfect skin. "*Friend?*" She hissed the word with contempt.

"Let me explain." I eased her back down. Elyria settled into my chest, but the line of her shoulders never truly relaxed. Anxiety slowly poured into me. This conversation might go very wrong, and we were currently in the middle of the South Sea.

"I've known Mal since we were children. He was funny and wasn't afraid to get into some mischief. I trust no one in the world more than Xoc, but he never wanted to stir up trouble. Mal always did. If Xoc was the anchor that kept me steady, then Mal was the storm that rocked the seas to begin with." I laughed to myself at the memory of Xoc with chocolate cake plastered to the side of his face after he caught Mal and me eating all of Lord Bradley's wedding cake. When Xoc threatened to turn us in, Mal threw a piece of the sugary confection at him. Chocolate frosting smashed into his hair and streaked the corners of his face, making him look just as guilty as we were. It didn't matter that he wasn't culpable when the evidence was right there for all to see. He was so worried that we were going to get caught, and I'd never laughed more.

"I genuinely enjoyed his company, and I looked forward to his visits." The shadow of loss hung over us. How could he sink so deep into the darkness that he'd been able to throw away centuries of friendship? "Whenever he would come to Innesvale, I'd feel like I was a kid again. We'd sneak out of the palace at night to play cards. Sometimes he'd even jack an air skiff and fly over to the city. By air, it doesn't really take long to get from The Floating Lands to Innesvale. I'd slip him into the palace, and we'd be *free* for the night. He wasn't a lord, and I wasn't a prince. We were just two kids kicking up mischief."

I paused, and my face went slack. A memory rushed at me like a flood-gate being lifted. Images flashed in quick succession in my mind.

"What's wrong?"

I blinked slowly.

"Cal?"

Vaguely, I registered Elyria looking up at me. Concerned, she lifted a hand to my cheek.

"I just remembered something. Mal was there the night my father died. We slipped out to a den on the harbor." I spent the entire night distracted by the red-headed barmaid. "I lost all my money... and... when we were done, I slipped us back into the palace."

I sat up with a jerking motion, keeping her tucked into me like a child with a security blanket. "*Fuck*. FUCK."

"Cal. It's okay." She smoothed her hand across my chest.

The oxygen in the room disappeared. I couldn't breathe. A tremor snaked its way up my spine.

"It's okay," she whispered again. I tightened my arms and sank my face into her hair. Then, slowly, I lowered us back down to the pillow.

"That was how he got in. After I was stabbed, I couldn't remember the days leading up to being wounded. But now...Gods, Elle, it was me. *I did this*. I brought that evil into the palace."

I curled even deeper into her soft frame. A desperate need to feel anything good shook me. Maybe if I could just hold her tight enough, then I could lose myself in that feeling and not need to face the demon in the shadows of my own memory. It was my fault my father died that night.

I was distantly aware of her hand wrapping into mine.

"You want to hear the insane thing? He kept going on about this dream, some nightmare about a wave of death washing over Venterra. A black wave that turned everything it flowed over to bone. He said that it was all he ever dreamed about. Mal was absolutely petrified of it, sure that it was Ferrus — But, *he* was the wave all along. It was always him."

Elyria fought her way out of my grip, tugging me to my feet. "Let's get some air."

For the first time this morning, leaving felt like a good thing. I needed to look out onto the ocean and feel the wind in my face.

4
CALLEN

The sea air was cool and smelled of brine. Elyria spotted Rei and motioned that she was going that way. Scanning the deck, I spotted Xoc nose deep in yet another book on plants. How many books did he keep in the pocket fold? This had to be the third, during this trip alone, that I'd seen him reading.

"You two seemed cozy," Xoc said, snapping the book closed. "I tried coming down last night, only to find the two of you wrapped around each other in the smallest damn bed I've ever seen. So, I got the privilege of laying all night on this nice hard bench here." He patted the worn wood for emphasis. "Don't worry. It was as terrible as it looks."

I shrugged in a terrible attempt at nonchalance. But I couldn't keep from grinning. Waking up with her in my arms had been one of the most fulfilling moments of my life. It felt like, without the lie hanging between us, things were finally fitting into place as they should.

"I'm going to get some *actual* sleep now." He started walking towards the lower decks before turning around to say, "Don't wake me until supper, then you can have the room again tonight. Gods know I'm not going to try and squeeze into a room with the two of you." Xoc's eyebrows knit together so completely they looked like one giant, tattooed caterpillar. I was sure he was imagining being forced into a bed with us.

"That's fair. Unless-"

"No." Xoc's russet cheeks reddened, reminding me of the ochre-painted caves in Mt. Carin. There wasn't a chance in Kraav I would ever share my girl, but that didn't make teasing the giant prude any less fun.

My grin tugged up higher. "But I—"

"Sorry, I don't think I was being clear enough. Let me say it slower. FU-UUCK. NOOO." His giant finger flicked me in the center of my forehead, punctuating his point.

I rubbed the mark. "You don't have to be rude. I was just trying to-"

Xoc looked at the sky. "I hate you."

"--be kind..."

"Callen Shadow, pain in my ass, thorn in my side, Crowned Prince of Innesvale, go over there." He pointed to where Elyria was chatting with Rei. "Continue pretending you're not madly in love with your little draken."

I scowled at him.

"Or don't. Profess every dark secret. I don't care. Just leave me out of it."

"I'm not pretending anymore. I made her a promise."

He rubbed at the back of his neck. "Well, it's about damn time."

"Yeah, it is."

"Then why are you still here, badgering me? When you could be there, badgering her?"

Xoc pushed me away, directly towards my girl. Elyria laughed at something Rei was saying. My heart swelled and squeezed in turn, unsure if it wanted to gallop out of control or stop altogether. She was stunning at all times, but when she laughed, it felt like standing at the center of the sun. I scrubbed at the center of my chest to abate the pressure.

Rei spotted me first. I tried to ignore her smug expression, like she knew a secret no one else did. Elyria, seeing me approach, suddenly went quiet.

"Why do I get the sincere impression you two were discussing me?"

Rei looked like she might explode.

"I'm gonna go," she said hurriedly. Before leaving, Rei whispered something into Elyria's ear, making a pumping motion with her fist. I couldn't hear her, but I definitely heard Elyria tell her an emphatic "*No.*" The flush creeping up her neck was unmistakable and more than a little tempting.

I sidled behind Elyria, circling my arms around her waist and nuzzling into her neck. I probably shouldn't be invading her space like this, but a blushing Elle was too good to resist. My self-control only extended so far.

"What did she say?" I couldn't keep the amusement out of my voice. Elyria ruffled was almost as tempting as Elyria happy, almost.

"None of your damn business, is what she said."

"Fine, keep your secrets," I mocked, throwing her own words back at her with a laugh. Which was probably the wrong thing to say.

"Oh, I've got something you can have." She threw back an elbow. It sank deep into my gut, driving the air from my lungs. Before I could recover, she turned around and slugged me with every ounce of her draconic strength. The impact even forced me a tiny bit back. I was actually impressed that she could pack such a hit with no wind up.

"Ow." I mock rubbed at the bruise. Her face flamed a glorious shade of scarlet, and that made my smile even broader. She was so adorable when she was angry.

"Good morning, Ma'am, Sir." A bright-faced young man approached us holding a bundle of neatly folded clothing. He was young, probably not more than eighteen.

"Good morning, Banks."

Banks tipped his head in acknowledgement to Elyria. My eyebrows shot straight into my hairline.

"*Banks*? Why do you know his name?" Confusion and a tinge of unexpected jealousy peppered my words.

The young man, Banks, handed me the clothing. That jealousy must have been plastered on my face because he elbowed me in the shoulder.

"Don't worry, mate. Alls I did was show her the privies last night. That daisy ain't been plucked."

"Plucked?" Elyria remarked, part taken aback, part amused.

"Rei gaves us all strict instructions to leave the two of you alone. Said you needed to bond." Banks lifted his eyes to me as if there was some joke the two of us were in on together, but I was still reeling about Elyria somehow slipping out of our cabin in the middle of the night.

She lifted her chin at me. I met the challenge in those too-bright eyes.

"And do you always do what Rei says when she's on board?" I asked him without looking away from Elyria.

Banks snorted a laugh, jabbing me again with his elbow, forcing me to finally address him directly. "Look, anyone who can make the Captain *find god* as many times a night as she can is worth listening to. I swears if I could make honey scream the way she can, the women would be lining up for me at every port of call."

"Well, damn." Elyria looked up at me with barely restrained amusement. "You're making me think I should reconsider Morgan's offer to join them." Elyria swallowed a laugh, her eyes flicking over Bank's shoulder.

The clipped steps of the Captain came to a stop behind the young sailor. His eyes went wide with realization, mouthing "shit." He'd fucked up, and he knew it.

"Banks!"

Elyria's new friend slowly turned. The two of them shared a long stare, one Banks was most definitely on the losing end of.

"Those privies you mentioned, I believe they need scrubbing."

"Yes, Captain." He dipped his head low, then scurried off before Morgan could come up with a more creative punishment for his candor.

Shoving the clothing he gave me under my arm, I grabbed Elyria before she could squirm away. Her ass cradled neatly into the curve of my hips. I loved how easily I dwarfed her. I curled my thumb around her slender fingers, stroking a path against her palm and causing her breath to hitch. I loved that, too.

My lips brushing her ear, I whispered, "Is that what you want, a religious experience? Because that's the kind of bonding I can get behind." The muscles of her back tensed against my chest, but she didn't pull away. No, to my absolute delight, she pressed back into me, and her fingers tightened against mine. I couldn't keep my smile from breaking against her neck. She may still be putting up barriers, but the moment was coming when that wall was going to fall spectacularly down, and when that happened, I was going to be right there falling with her.

"Although–" We'd fallen back into this teasing rhythm so easily. I rubbed my nose along the shell of her ear, noting the way her pulse quickened, ticking the vein along her neck. "--I can't promise it will be god's name you call out."

She lifted her head, twisting so that her lips were barely an inch from mine.

"Cal..." Elyria ran the nails of her free hand up my thigh, a deep current of warmth trailing behind them.

"Mmm." The heat pooling in her gaze threatened to incinerate me.

"The only religious experience I plan on having for a long time is the kind you get from deep *self*-reflection."

Elyria simply extricated her hand from mine and stepped away, leaving my now too-empty palm to rest against my heated thigh.

Sitting back on my heels, I slipped my hands into my pockets and shrugged my shoulders.

"I have no problem with that, so long as I can watch." What a sight that would be. I let my mind roll over the feast of new imagery. Fuck, I was going to burn in Kraav, but it would be worth it.

She bit on her lip like she knew where my mind had just strayed. With a playful slap to my cheek, she added, "*Self*-reflection, Cal. You should try it sometime."

My jaw went slack, and Elyria's eyes sparkled with triumph.

Did she just tell me to go fuck myself? *Gods, this girl.* I was going to have to marry her. My eyes dropped to the way she was still chewing on that lower lip. If I kissed her right now, would she push me away or pull me in?

"I'm okay with that too if you'd rather be the spectator."

That gorgeous shade of scarlet returned to her face. She might actually hit me again. I tensed, ready for the blow because I definitely deserved it.

Morgan cleared her throat, "Cute."

Damn, I was so wrapped up in teasing Elyria that I'd forgotten the captain was here. My intent was to give Morgan my full attention, but I had the hardest time tearing my gaze away from the heat radiating off of my girl. She was so sexy when she was riled up.

"Good morning, Captain Sangrior."

The tattoo over Morgan's eye arched, adding emphasis to her expression of disinterest. She pursed her red lips and nodded at the bundle shoved under my arm. "I see you found the clothing I acquired for you. I assumed you were in need of them, or else I can't imagine why you'd still be wearing that absurd shirt. There's something for Elyria as well. At least one of you should look presentable when we arrive."

I held out the shirt Xoc lent me. She was right; it was absurd. "Oh, I don't know. I hear it's already a trend on the western shores. Pretty soon everyone will be wearing them five sizes too large." I could see a small crack in her veneer. She wanted to smile.

"Thank you, Captain," Elyria added with a cordial smile, doing nothing to dispel the awkwardness in the air.

"Could you tell us our current coordinates?" I asked, distractedly looking over to a young man mopping the quarter-deck. Her entire crew was perfectly organized, dedicated. I hadn't seen a single person out of place.

"Course," she replied flatly and glanced down at the water. "We're about 20 leagues west of Skoal Island. Don't worry, your *Highness*. At our current trajectory, you'll be back in your palace of stone just after mid-day tomorrow."

"Sorry, did you just look at the water to tell me where we were?" I asked, a bit confounded. I wasn't a sailor by any means, but I'd been on enough ships to know that you needed a chart and instruments to determine your location at sea.

Morgan stepped forward until the toes of our boots touched, head tipped back but still somehow looking down her nose at me. "Tell me something, can you feel the air? Do you need to see the people on this ship to know they are there?"

I didn't answer her. She was baiting me. Of course I could feel the air. If I wanted to, I could render her entire crew breathless with a mere flick of my fingers. But there was no way that I could track the sheer volume of air that would be comparable to reading the ocean. Rather than challenge her outright, I narrowed my eyes with the barest of expressions.

"This is my sea. I know these waters better than any sailor in the world. To me, those waves are as clear as any map. I can tell you the location of every landmass and reef. I know exactly how far it is to Skoal Island and how many leagues we are from the western mainland."

"The entire ocean?"

"It's not my attunement, not entirely." The corner of her ruby-painted lips lifted. "I know what you're thinking."

I had been thinking it but she didn't need to know that. Her water attunement would have to be intensely concentrated to be able to control a mass of this size. If it was true, then Morgan Sangrior was terrifying.

"It's a method of navigation that my people have been using for millennia. We don't need star charts or maps. I need one chart to read the waves, and I've had that memorized for well over a century. Trust me, when I say that we will be gazing at the shining white marble of Innesvale by *mid-day tomorrow*."

I looked up at the sky, trying to get my bearings.

Morgan sighed, "Save me from spoiled princes." She snapped her fingers in the air.

A man hurried over. "Captain?"

"Tormond, tell me our last recorded coordinates."

"56 degrees, 49 minutes and 20 seconds north; 95 degrees, 42 minutes and 12 seconds west, Captain."

"At our current speed, when should we be arriving at Innesvale?"

"Mid-day tomorrow, Captain."

Morgan leveled me with an annoyed look. Flicking her hand, the man walked away.

"Color me impressed, *Captain.*"

"You're all the same," she muttered under her breath, already walking away.

A man behind us shouted, "Captain, I think you should take a look at this."

Elyria was trying not to laugh. I think she actually enjoyed seeing me dismissed. I didn't care what it was, so long as she kept smiling at me like that.

Once again, we were alone. It was a trend that I was really starting to like.

"So, what do we do now?" With a wicked smile, she held up a hand to my chest. "Religious experiences aside."

I held my hand to the horizon, judging its distance to the sun. It was directly above us, blocked almost perfectly by the crow's nest. "It's already mid-day."

"We wasted the morning sleeping and talking."

I tucked the stray hairs blowing in the breeze behind her ear. "I wouldn't have spent it any other way." She bit down on her lip, hiding from me whatever it was she wanted to say. Eyeing the platform at the top of the mast, I said, "Let's get a better view." I pointed up. "I'll race you to the top."

5

CALLEN

E lyria's face lit up with the challenge. She took off at a run, knocking over the mop boy. With a single leap, she grabbed the rope and leveraged herself onto the lowest rung. She swung and flipped between lines, easily shimmying her way into the sky like she had been born to live among the clouds.

Morgan leaned on the upper railing, watching her. She nodded in approval at Elyria's fearless ascension. A warm feeling of pride washed over me.

I watched for as long as I dared, then summoned a gust to lift me to the top. Just as Elyria rolled into the compartment, I stepped effortlessly onto the platform beside her.

"Xoc's right. You always cheat," she said, a bit out of breath. She was laughing, and that was all that mattered to me. Elyria couldn't stay mad, not with a view like this.

Wind swirled around us. The long strands of her hair whipped in all directions while she battled against the current to keep them contained. I held up a hand, stilling the air.

"Thank you," she said with a relieved sigh.

"Don't thank me. I did it for purely selfish reasons." Her eyes narrowed. "It's easier to see your smile this way." I ran my thumb down her jaw, delighting in the way she fought so hard not to reward me by lifting those berry lips. Smacking my hand away, she rolled her eyes and turned her attention to the sea.

I scanned the infinite horizon. The flat expanse of dark turquoise water extended in every direction, met at the horizon by an equally blue sky. The only obstruction was a tiny boat in the distance.

"Wow." Elyria rested against the ledge. "This is—"

"I know," I said, cutting her off.

"But it's just—"

"I know." I circled around her, placing my hands beside her own on the railing until there was no option but to mold our bodies together. Whether intentional or not, she tilted her head, brushing her cheek against the short beard that I'd grown over the past few weeks.

Fuck, I loved this feeling. Nothing compared to it, not the heat, the passion, or the power. Nothing topped the feeling of completion I got from having her in my arms. It was like we were two magnets, inexplicably drawn to each other, and I was exhausted from fighting the pull. The velvet skin of her neck was barely an inch from my lips. I could already hear the breathy moan she would make when she arched back into me.

A loud, deep horn blared. Elyria jumped from the sudden bellowing sound. My eyes focused on the tiny ship along the horizon. It was bigger now, gaining on us. Which was surprising because, from where I stood, there were at least two attuned crew manning the boat's propulsion.

Below, people scattered. A man was quickly climbing up the rigging to meet us. He carried a crossbow strapped over his back and a line of blue orbs clinked at his hip.

"You two probably don't want to be up here," he warned, hurriedly throwing a leg over the railing.

Morgan stood on a platform, one booted foot propped on the railing. She held a long spyglass and was looking directly at the approaching ship. It was close enough now that I could see three masts, each with huge billowing white sails. So, not a tiny ship after all. The approaching vessel was quite large, an entire class bigger than Star Spear.

"What's going on?" I asked, trying to fully assess the situation.

"That ship isn't friendly, is it Brindley?" Elyria asked.

"You know his name too?" I gaped at her. "Exactly how much of the crew did you meet last night?"

"Are you jealous?" She bit down on her lip.

"Wildly."

She moved to walk over to him, but I kept her caged in my arms.

"Seriously? Are you that insecure?" She elbowed my ribs, then smiled sweetly at me before ducking under my arm.

I groaned at the pain throbbing in my side, "You could have asked."

Brindley made a questioning look between us as he started setting up along the railing.

"That barque" – he nodded towards the advancing ship – "is the Kilmaine. He's been dogging Captain Sangrior for the past year. Usually, he keeps his distance or fires a couple of shots in warning to stay out of his waters. Star Spear is faster than most boats, though, so we usually outrun him. What he hasn't figured out is that all waters are actually hers." He pointed toward Morgan.

I nodded, appreciating the respect he had for his captain. She was small but commanded her men better than captains I'd known three times her size.

"It's unusual for him to engage us directly like this, though. I think that's why the Captain has ordered everyone to post."

Elyria held her hand up to shield her view from the sun. "I don't see any identifying flags. Does that mean it doesn't have a nationality or claim?"

"Usually," I explained. "It means that whoever is on that ship will take whatever business they can get, and they aren't beholden to any one country's laws or policies."

Elyria opened her mouth to ask another question, but I knew what it was before she said it. "No, that isn't legal. And, yes, that probably means that whatever is waiting on that boat is not friendly."

The ship rotated to face us, exposing the two rows of guns pushing from tiny hatches along the hull.

"So many guns," she whispered. "There must be two dozen gun ports on that ship."

"Don't you worry. Captain Sangrior has more than one surprise up her sleeve. If they decide to engage, they'll be regretting it come sundown."

A gut-shaking boom echoed across the water. A puff of smoke streamed out of a hatch along the waterline.

"That's a long gun!" exclaimed Brindley.

A black ball soared towards us. With a whoosh of whistling air, it zinged just past the mast. The explosive force of the cannonball splashed into the sea, causing a plume of water to fountain up. From below, Morgan yelled, "Come about! Bein, ready the guns."

The ship rotated, and shuttering vibrated up the wood as our cannons rolled and locked into place.

I ran my hands over Elyria's shoulders. A slight tremor moved along them. She flinched when two more concussive blasts echoed over the water.

Below us, a line of attuned crew stood in formation at the bow. Hands raised to the sky, they performed in unison, a movement that looked more like a dance than an attack. A cyclone formed in the water beside the ship. With a combined upward thrust, the funnel flew high.

BOOM! A third long gun fired in the distance.

The cyclone snatched the first two cannonballs from the air, and with a swirl, it redirected them toward the water on the starboard bow of the ship. Great waves of water sprayed into the air. Mist caught on the wind, peppering my face with the tang of salt water.

The third ball continued zooming towards us. I held up my hands, ground my feet into the decking of the nest, and flung out as much power as I could muster. I wasn't entirely certain I could counter the momentum of something with such little surface area, but the ball of iron was flying straight for us. Gritting my teeth against the force, the cannonball spun harmlessly in place, several feet from the upper rigging of the mainmast.

I let out a long slow breath.

"Fucking brilliant!" Morgan shouted from below. "Maybe you're not worthless after all."

"You're welcome," I shouted down to her. I flung my arms wide, reversing the projectile's trajectory. With a crack, the cannonball ripped open the side of the opposing ship. Morgan's crew whooped with excitement. The Captain's blood-thirsty grin was all the approval I needed. Maybe now she would start treating me with the respect my rank deserved and less like an annoying child.

"They aren't firing all the cannons, but they outgun us. Why wouldn't they press that advantage?" Elyria questioned.

"Because they plan to board us," I answered resolutely. That ship was coming for something specific, and there was only one thing loaded on this ship right now—us.

"Board us? But why? You don't think this could be Malvat do you?"

"It's definitely Malvat. It's not exactly a secret where we're headed, and nobody else would be so reckless."

I tamped down the impulse to shiver. Malvat was coming for Elyria. Even in the middle of the ocean, he was still trying to take her from me. I briefly tried to determine exactly how much fire I would have to summon to burn down a vessel of that size. Could I manage it surrounded by so much water? I wasn't sure. But I did know that I would be damned before one of his possessed minions stepped foot on this ship.

"Fire!" Morgan yelled. Five guns went off in quick succession. The sound was deafening, the force of the cannons sending a shudder up the mast and trembling the platform beneath our feet. Nearly a dozen black streaks cut through the thick smoke billowing around us. Thick chains connected between balls, designed to cut through anything they made contact with.

"Speed!" Morgan bellowed. In unison, she and Bein raised their arms. In time with them, the crew of singers to their right joined in. A wall of water rose along the port side of the ship. Soundlessly, Star Spear rotated. With a single thrust, the ship hurtled toward the opposing barque. The wall of smoke left from the cannons trailed along with us, cloaking our sudden increase in speed. There was no way the other vessel would be able to gauge distance and prepare for Morgan's next attack.

A tinny version of Morgan's voice filtered around us. *Brindley! On my command.*

The gunner glanced for a second at the flared opening of the long metal tube affixed to the mast. The captain's voice was being relayed via a tube. "That's brilliant."

Brindley nodded in agreement, reaching forward and pulling back a large wooden arm that I hadn't even realized was there. "It's so there is no delay because of the distance." With a click, the arm locked into place. "It ensures my timing is on point with the men below." He quickly eyed the ship, then began cranking to tighten the spring further.

The contraption looked like a miniature version of the catapults we used in siege fare. I squatted down to examine the inner workings. "I've never seen this technology employed on a ship before."

Brindley unhooked one of the orbs from his belt. Each ball of blue glass was filled with powder and small bits of iron. He inserted a long fuze into the top, feeding it down into the mixture. When that exploded, it would take out everything around it with devastating efficiency. Gently, the marksman placed the shining orb of destruction into the hand of the lever.

"*Light.*" Morgan's ability to manage so many different elements of the attack at once was amazing. She was commanding Brindley in the crow's nest while coordinating the cannons, the movement of the ship, and elemental singers in both attack and defense. I knew Sangrior was a captain of legend. I just never expected the legends to be true.

Brindley pulled out a flint stick and began sparking at the fuse.

"Need a light." Elyria extended a single lit finger to the fuze. It crackled to life.

The ship rounded on the Kilmaine, just as the volley of cannon fire hit. Waves of splinters flew into the air.

"Grenado!" Morgan yelled, and Brindley pulled the pin. The beautiful blue glass flew into the center of the Kilmaine's rigging before exploding in a brilliant array of sparks and color. There was a crack, and the mizzenmast of the Kilmaine toppled over. The man perched in the crow's nest fell into the water with a loud yell.

Not pausing to see the destruction his strike had wrought, Brindley cocked back the arm. I watched the tiny man below flail in the water and considered if Brindley was right. Perhaps we shouldn't be up here. It did, however, afford us a perfect view of the action.

"Let down the deck ports," Bein's voice boomed.

"Deck ports?" Elyria asked, leaning over to look at the doors dropping along the hull in quick succession.

Brindley loaded another blue ball. "That's so we can't be boarded from below."

Elyria nodded. "Makes sense. It'd take nothing to cast a line and crawl in through one."

"Plus, we can't use the long guns anymore anyway," I added.

"*Light top guns and grenado.*"

The ship crackled with the sound of a dozen lit fuzes.

"Fire!"

Six more concussive blasts sounded, and an answering blast from the Kilmaine came in response as the entire row of their top guns exploded.

I grabbed Elyria and braced for the impact, ready to catch us in the air the second we were launched into it. Instead of splintering wood and tattered sails, a wall of water rose in a protective cocoon around the ship. Seven Sea Singers stood on the starboard bow, Bein at the head of the formation. Their hands were all raised into the same form, one fisted arm lifted high, the second cocked straight back from their shoulder.

"Push!" bellowed Bein.

The crew of Sea Singers pulled their fisted arms back, making the water bend toward us, curling higher. With an intense, full-body release, they punched forward. The tidal wave rolled down, drowning the chorus of shouts coming from the Kilmaine. Crashing water rocked the ship to its side. Broken masts and tattered sails dipped below the surface.

I held my breath. For ten heart-stopping seconds, the ship hovered, perched on its side. With the groan of shifting wood, the Kilmaine rolled back upright, nothing but wreckage remaining of her upper decks. The crew members that managed to hold on scrambled about, several jumping into the sea before the next attack could come.

"Hard to port. ready the STING!" Came Morgan's command. She stomped off of her platform and took the helm, carefully aiming Star Spear. The ship spun a full 180 degrees. I looked away from the horizon to try and stave off the dizziness from spinning so abruptly. Elyria's hand gripped into my arm. "Woah, a little warning, Morgan." When we looked up again, the aft of the ship was facing the Kilmaine.

"Are we running?" I asked, not believing that Morgan would back down during a fight she was so obviously winning.

Brindley swiveled the catapult arm, keeping the sights trained on the enemy.

"No, that's the sting." He pointed towards the rudder.

Elyria and I walked around to the other side of the nest.

The grinding of metal and gears clanged loudly, each turn of a massive wheel causing the mast to shake. Four men slowly walked in circles, pushing a massive wheel around the center mast.

"Gods," I whispered. "She's going to fire that thing."

The tail of the ship wasn't purely ornamental, as I had originally assumed. The barbed end of the dragon's tail rotated out of its upright position. Now that it was horizontal, it was obvious that it was actually a giant spiked harpoon.

"It's a ship-breaker," replied Brindley. "It will rip that ship in two."

Elyria sucked in a breath.

"This fight was over the moment they set their sights on blue sails," Brindley remarked with a nod of his head. "The Captain has never lost a challenge ship to ship before—not one."

A flash of light redirected my attention to the main deck of the Kilmaine. A silver-haired man stared up at the crow's nest where we were standing. His long, silken hair billowed behind him in the wind. The man flicked his wrist, sending a spear of ice straight at us.

Elyria raised her hand to counter it, but fast as a scorpion's sting, Brindley slipped the crossbow off his back and fired. A bolt sank deep into the man's chest, and the spear of ice halted its progression.

"Wow," Elyria said, eyes wide with astonishment. We weren't exactly close, and his accuracy was perfect, especially with how quickly he'd fired the weapon.

Star Spear listed to one side, averting the ice spike.

"RELEASE!"

Chains roared with a deafening rattle. A trail of shining light flew from the tail of the ship, highlighting each highly polished spike before plunging deep into the Kilmaine's side. The sound of breaking wood crackled over the water, peppered by the screaming shouts of the few remaining crew members.

"RECOIL!"

"Hya—*Ho!* Hya—*Ho!*" The men chorused, moving and pushing the wheel as one. The chain slowly recoiled around the central mast.

Like the earth breaking open, the harpoon ripped through the core of the ship. Wood splintered as each spike broke free of the hull. The back of the Kilmaine tilted up. Water flooded into the ship, frothing around the broken edges. With a final crack, the parts of the ship separated. The tail end of the ship sank, taking on water at an impressive speed before the front half followed. Sailors, abandoning the wreckage, jumped into the churning water.

Morgan cranked hard on the wheel. Like a dragon circling its prey for the killing blow, Star Spear came about the floundering debris that was once an attack barque.

Brindley moved to the other side of the nest, tracking the desperate people screaming in the water.

We followed around with him to where a grinding sound echoed from the iron jaws of the figurehead. The maw of the dragon slowly opened, shifting the muzzle from a growl to an attacking roar. The sharp teeth dripped sea water and gleamed in the sunlight.

There was a scrambling sound from below. A moment later, Morgan climbed over the side of the crow's nest. A gleam of devilish pride shone in her intense blue eyes. In only a few brief attacks, Morgan had rendered the Kilmaine dead in the water. She knew it. I knew it. The men treading water beside the wreckage knew it.

"Nicely done, Captain," I said with a mock salute.

She smiled, and it was chilling.

"I'm not done yet. That bastard has been nothing but a thorn in my side for months now. This time he was stupid enough to actually *fire* on me. I'd say he's about to learn his lesson, but he won't live long enough to learn anything."

Churning water rolled against the side of the boat, as the remaining air bubbled up from inside the Kilmaine. Morgan gripped the railing, raising a single hand. Bein and the entire crew stared up at her, all waiting for the command.

She looked up at me over her shoulder, a ruby smile stretching across her face. "Are you paying attention, *Your Majesty*?" The over-annunciated way she drew out the word majesty put my teeth on edge. Morgan was using this entire battle as a demonstration; should my forces ever decide to come after her, they would never win. She'd climbed all the way up here to ensure that the message wasn't lost on me.

"I haven't missed a second of it," I replied coldly.

"Good." She lowered her hand.

Bein bellowed, "Oil!"

Men stationed behind the figurehead began pumping. A green oil sprayed from the mouth of the dragon, dousing what remained of the Kilmaine. A circular current in the water kept the oil from spreading and ensured that everything within the barrier was coated with a rainbow sheen. The men clinging to the wreckage feverishly wiped the slippery substance from their eyes.

Morgan raised her hand again.

My heart rate quickened with anticipation. Beside me, Elyria grabbed my arm, her nails anxiously cutting into my bicep.

The entire crew waited silently. The only sounds were the panicked cries of alarm coming from the water. All eyes trained on Morgan's raised arm.

Maintaining eye contact with me, Morgan lowered her hand.

There was a clicking sound followed by a burst of bright white light that blotted out my vision. I lifted my hand to shield my eyes from the torrent of fire that roared from the jaws of the dragon. It rolled over the two remaining sections of the Kilmaine. The ship lit up, and what was once floating splinters of wood and sinking wreckage was now a rocking bonfire.

Heat radiated up to us, circled by thick black smoke. The power within me jumped to the surface, demanding control. I looked over to Elyria, who looked just as hungry to claim and summon that inferno. But her face had turned white, and she looked like, at any second, she might be sick.

Morgan spun around to face me, silhouetted by the raging fire behind her.

"That is what happens to those who are dumb enough to fire upon me." Her voice was low, the viciousness harmonized by the men still screaming in the water.

Smoke drifted over the ocean like a blanket of destruction.

"That was brutal," Elyria said, swallowing hard. "Those men didn't need to die." I could see her trying to hide it, but this had been her limit. Slaying a foe in open combat was one thing, but watching dozens of men slaughtered mercilessly was something else entirely. I ran a hand down Elyria's still trembling shoulder.

As Elyria tucked into me, I shifted my attention to Morgan. I never wanted Sangrior to cross the Shadow Crown again. More importantly, there was untapped genius lying behind those sapphire eyes, and it could give us the edge against Malvat that Innesvale sorely needed.

"We need to discuss having you under a permanent retainer. Your crew is flawless."

I expected her to be pleased. A royal commission was no small honor, but Morgan only tightened her gaze at me. "No, we need to discuss why the Kilmaine was so direct in engaging us and who might be responsible for sending an attack barque." She said it in clipped words. Morgan pursed her lips. I shifted on my feet uncomfortably. When was the last time anyone had made me feel like a child being scolded?

While maintaining a side eye with me, Morgan added, "Excellent shot with that crossbow, Brindley. I knew having you take the tops was the correct call."

"Thank you, Captain," he replied with a polite nod.

Without another word to any of us, Morgan started climbing back down the rigging. Elyria and I followed her down while the ship smoothly pulled away, leaving only a wake, embers, and smoke behind us. At least the screaming had stopped.

Elyria leapt from the last crossbar to the deck, forgoing the rope ladder entirely. I didn't miss the admiring way Morgan assessed her dismount.

"So, that's why you call the ship Star Spear. It's the harpoon in the tail," Elyria said a bit breathlessly.

Morgan readjusted the saber on her hip. "No, I call her Star Spear because nothing is out of my reach."

"Not even the stars," added Bein as he approached, the deep timber of his voice seeming to rattle the surrounding air.

"Report," Morgan commanded.

"Superficial damage only. Thanks to the prince deflecting that stray cannon-ball." He gestured to me. I gave a small wave of supplication.

"We didn't sustain anything serious. Addams could use some work on the timing of his movements. He was a half-second off sync with the other Sea Singers during the push. But, all in all, the crew performed perfectly on cue."

A half-second. They seemed pretty damn close to being on cue to me.

"Very well. Store the arms, and open a cask at dinner with my compliments. Addams can spend the night scrubbing down the oil ports. I want double lookouts doing rotations in the tops and another on either end of the ship. Someone hired him to come after us, and I won't be having any surprises while we're in the black."

A door swung open. Xoc walked up the steps from the lower decks. His dark hair hung limply on his shoulders, and he rubbed sleep from the corners of his eyes. "What in the hells was going on up here?"

6

ELYRIA

Bang! Bang! Bang!

Solid, hard warmth wrapped tighter behind me. I smiled into my pillow and refused to open my eyes or acknowledge the person behind the door.

BANG! BANG! BANG!

Again, a fist slamming into the door pounded through my head. Or maybe it was just the blood pulsing in my veins.

An irritated and rough voice filtered through the thick wood. "Captain says we'll be approaching Innesvale within the hour!" Heavy footsteps carried whoever it was away from the door.

I opened my eyes, taking in the tiny cabin. Light filtered through dust, landing in a single stream on a tall stack of crates. Cal's arms pulled me in tighter, his inhale making the back of my neck tingle with awareness. He exhaled with a low groan.

"Remind me to murder whoever disturbed the perfection of this moment," he groaned.

I giggled under my breath. *Giggled? Mother of demons, who was I?* I wasn't the kind of woman who giggled at things.

"It's nearly mid-day. Someone was bound to come down here, eventually. You'd think after last night, no one would blame us for sleeping in."

After the battle with the Kilmaine, everyone's blood was pumping. A cask of rum was uncorked, and we settled down with the remainder of the crew in the galley. Rei spent the night challenging one sailor after another to a drinking game that involved correctly predicting cards as they were turned over. She was uncannily good at it. At least two men had passed out on the floor after challenging her. Later, she confessed her tattoos worked to keep her sober, healing her as she continued to imbibe. It was devious and exceptionally fun to watch. "I'll heal them all in the morning," she promised after the last burly man fell beneath the table.

Cal spent the entire night at my side, some part of him in constant contact with me. A hand on my arm or a leg brushing mine, small touches as if he couldn't stand being apart for more than a second.

Damn me to Kraav, but I loved knowing he couldn't help himself. For the first time in my life, I craved the endless attention. Every time I laughed, Cal's entire face would light up like he'd just heard his favorite song. Pure adoration lined every look and touch. Not the lustful heat I'd get from an adoring crowd or the rakish smiles he'd thrown me in the past, but something deeper that was completely disarming in its honesty.

The sun was already beginning to lighten the horizon by the time we made our way back to the tiny cabin. As soon as we entered the room, Cal rounded on me, the hard length of his body as unrelenting as the wood at my back. I don't know if it was the lingering adrenaline surge from the attack or the general merriment of the evening, but whatever restraint he'd put in place snapped. The building tension of the night had mine snapping right along with him.

His large hand circled my wrists, pulling them over my head and slamming them into the freshly closed door. The other fisted into my hair, gripping my neck to angle my head exactly how he wanted me. Cal's lips were hot on mine, deep and all-consuming. He tasted so sinfully good, like whiskey and every desire I'd been denying myself.

Sparks jumped from his skin to mine, lighting up my veins and making my head spin. His hands released the hair he had fisted, sliding down the slope of my body to settle on my hips. Second, after indulgent second, I drew him deeper. If I never breathed again, I wouldn't care so long as I died feeling his lips on mine.

Cal's fingers slipped beneath the loose hem of my shirt, making my sanity melt the moment they connected with the sensitive flesh above my waistband.

His fingers tightened with a pulse of heat, the searing energy making my soul sing. All at once, he shoved himself away from me like the fire drifting between us had burned him. He ran both hands through his hair while scanning my features. I'm sure my shock was all over them.

I brought my fingertips to my lips. Their puffy, abused surface throbbed with a longing to reconnect with his. The simple movement forced a glimmer of unease to flash across Cal's expression.

"Elle..." The single syllable of my name sounded like every one of his morals was being tortured. He'd promised to prove that there was more between us than the physical, but right now, physical was exactly what I wanted. "I shouldn-"

Before he could vocalize any of that concern, I hooked my fingers into his waistband and yanked until his hips were fitted perfectly into mine. He didn't get to be chivalrous, not when I was drowning in reckless need. After a night of endless touching and flirting, I wasn't about to be denied. I rolled against him, making sure all of my welled-up desire was properly communicated with each press of my lips.

Cal groaned with longing so potent his entire body shook from the effort of holding back. I skimmed my hands up his torso, popping open the buttons of his shirt as I went. The light shifted along the lines of his abdomen, shadowed and perfect, before disappearing beneath the band of his leather slacks. I wanted to taste him, to feel my skin sliding against his as I drew my tongue over each band of muscle. My nails raked their curves, trying to determine exactly where I wanted to take my first bite.

I dragged my tongue over my teeth, meeting the uncertainty in his eyes with the fire in my own. "Don't ever say my name like that again." I leaned in, pressing my lips to the center of his throat. It flexed with a hard swallow as I pushed up on my tiptoes to whisper in his ear, "If you're going to say it, then it better damn well sound like a prayer."

"Fuck, Sunshine." His hesitation disappeared like smoke on the wind. Gripping my ass, he lifted me so my legs wrapped around his waist. This, gods, this was exactly what I'd been wanting for weeks. Our bodies fused together, separated only by scraps of leather and cotton. My fingers sank into his dark auburn locks, anchoring those kisses to me before his conscience could interrupt us again.

We remained intertwined against the door for several perfect, mind-altering minutes. Power coiled around my heart, linking with his until they pounded as one. Exhilarating warmth bled through me, making every inch of my skin tingle.

When I finally came up for air, my gaze snagged on my fingers threaded in his hair. The wavy strands were shining golden in the morning twilight, no longer auburn. It was his draken power I'd felt flooding through me, recognizing my own. The gleaming strands might as well have slapped me in the face, and the revelation stung. In the frenzy of passion, it was too easy to forget how I'd been deceived. Every moment we'd shared was tainted by the truths he'd kept from me, the very truth still wrapped around my fingers.

I grew up feeling like I was a singular fluke, one who never should have existed and didn't belong. I'd told him as much, divulged my deepest secrets. Yet, when I asked him to tell me his, he'd chosen to use my grief to manipulate me over giving me the only thing that I had ever wanted.

"Wait." I flattened my hand against his chest and forced space between us. I needed a second to breathe and to let my whiskey-addled brain catch up to what was happening.

Could I allow myself to fall for him, again? The war of emotion and need was enough to make my head spin. I craved the euphoria of his flames circling mine, but could I allow myself the vulnerability of loving someone who had lied to my face when I told him I was draken? Could I give myself over to the man who held me in my most desperate moment, knowing that he would use my need for vengeance to drive me to the exact spot I was currently standing?

Cal registered my emotions, eyes reading mine and understanding this was out of control. How was I supposed to make sense of how I felt when I could still feel his power coursing through me? Cal nodded with a slight tilt of a forced smile.

"This is... you're... I..." Goddess slay me. Apparently, I'd lost my ability to speak along with my common sense. I didn't regret kissing him. I just wasn't ready for whatever this was.

I eased my feet back onto the ground, wavering for only a second. My hand still rested against his chest, and the beat of his heart galloped like a wild beast against my fingertips.

Cal kicked off his boots and extended a hand to me. "It's late, or I guess it's actually early," he joked, giving me a kind smile that made all of him seem warmer. "Either way, with arriving home tomorrow, we both need some rest."

"Home, right," I whispered with a tiny nod of understanding. Now there was a strange sentiment. To me, home was never really a place and was more about the people you were with.

Cal settled on the mattress. Strong arms curled around me in a familiar and comforting position that both claimed and protected. I closed my eyes, trying to imagine if a life with Cal could be one that felt like home. Even more unnerving was that I was pretty sure it already was.

We stayed like that until the pounding in my brain echoed the pounding at the door.

I blinked my eyes, trying to force the blurriness of sleep from them.

Cal ran a hand down my arm. Rolling onto his back, he exhaled long and hard.

"Are you nervous?" I asked, trying to puzzle out the mass of emotions he was displaying. This was him. No mask. No agenda. No deception. It was the man he'd shown me from the second we stepped onto this ship. I could ask him anything, and I knew he'd say it without hesitation.

"There's a lot going through my mind right now." He smiled. "Not the least of which being all the things I can think of doing with you in the hour before we dock at the harbor."

Heat rolled up the back of my neck from deep in my core. The flecks in his irises shifted, turning from their usual brown into a warm, honeyed gold. Those gilded pools pulled me in like quicksand.

This voyage had changed something between us. I wasn't sure what it was, but I felt like the entire axis of the world had tilted. This new perspective had me seeing everything, feeling everything differently. It would be so easy to crawl on top of him.

A very real part of me wanted that.

It'd be too easy, which was why it was time to get up. Either get up now, or there was no getting out of this bed. Not when he was looking at me like that. Not when my skin tingled from the press of the fingertips gliding over my arm.

I rolled over, letting my feet slide to the ground.

"Come on," I reached for a boot. "I want to see Innesvale as we approach."

He nodded, then grabbed my wrist, his thumb ghosting over my pulse.

"Kiss me."

"What?"

"To give me strength."

I tucked a stray hair behind my ear, and he smiled when it immediately slipped free. I swear, that smile tugged on an invisible thread, making my heart beat in my throat.

He continued, "Because for the first time in a long time, I've remembered what it felt like to simply be myself. These past couple of days with you have felt like a gift, one that I don't deserve. I know that when we walk through that door, I have to go back to being Callen Magnus Shadow, Crowned Prince of Innesvale. So, before things begin to be complicated again, just kiss me. I want one last pure moment with you that I can hold on to."

Pure moment.

"Oh." Well, when he put it like that, it'd be cruel to deny him. Right?

I leaned in to place a kiss on the top of his head, but he grabbed me around the waist and threw me down onto the mattress. I squealed with the unexpected twist.

His weight settled on top of me, my body opening to him in a way that felt entirely too natural. He brushed the hair from my face and placed the softest kiss to my lips. His mouth moved gently against mine. Every movement tugged at my chest, those invisible threads between us vibrating with so much emotion that I couldn't tell if they were my thoughts or Cal's buzzing around my mind. When he pulled back, he scanned my eyes as if he was memorizing each golden fleck of light.

Cal took a deep breath and brought his forehead to mine. "You are my undoing, Elyria." This time when he breathed my name, it *was* a prayer. "In fact, I'm pretty sure I've been undone for a long time." Then, with a quick movement, he crawled off the bed and scooped up his boots.

Emotion rose in a vicious wave. I pressed my hand to my chest, trying to slow the rapid drumming against my ribs.

"Come on, Sunshine."

I tilted my head to look at him. Was he serious right now?

"You can't just kiss a girl like that–" My lips were still tingling. "--say those words, and then jump away like nothing happened." I propped myself up on one elbow.

"I want to see Innesvale as we approach." Cal winked, then nodded his head towards the door. A fat smile stretched across his face. He'd won. He knew it. Whatever walls I'd built between us were ash blowing away on the wind. If I was being honest with myself, I'd never really erected them in the first place.

I reached down and chucked the pillow at him.

7

ELYRIA

"There's already land!"

I shot Cal a scornful glare. Green rolling hills hovered along the horizon.

"I regret nothing," he said, hand on his heart.

"What is it you don't regret?" asked Rei, beaming. Her eyes flicked to where Cal's other hand lingered against my lower back. "I, personally, have never had regrets. Life is for living. There's no point in living it saddled by regret."

I didn't doubt that even a little bit. Rei seemed very unbothered by most things, except when something impeded her from getting what she wanted.

In the distance, a glittering black mountain came into view. From its peak ran a massive, bright blue waterfall.

"That's the Vanfald." Cal reached out his hand to me, slipping his fingers between mine. He led me to the bow of the ship. A knowing chuckle came from Rei as she took up position next to me against the railing.

"Remember when I said I grew up in the shadow of a waterfall like the one we...swam in."

I nodded, feeling heat flush my cheeks from the memory. Rei looked at me, wide-eyed, and mouthed, "*What waterfall?*" I waved her off.

"The mountain and the cliffs are made from the same black mica as our waterfall, so the waters in this area have that same glittering quality." He lifted our joined hands, pointing with an extended index finger to where the shoreline curved. "It's the water from the Vanfald that flows through Castle

As if on cue, the ship rounded a bend in the peninsula, and a shining white castle standing atop a high black bluff came into view. Obsidian sparkling cliffs ran the length of the coast, making the white marble of the castle that much more striking. Uninterrupted, polished marble spires soared into the sky. Blue water flowed through archways carved into the castle, pouring from spouts into the roil and foam of the dark sea below. The sunlight filtered through the spray casting dozens of sparkling rainbows.

I sucked in a breath. The absolute beauty was staggering. It was the perfect blending of man's craftsmanship and nature's majesty. I thought of Cal's offer to show me Innesvale that night in the bar. *The best view is from the ocean, as you approach from the south, where falls frame the crystal windows.* That had felt like such a fantasy, and yet, here we were.

Cal leaned into me and pointed. "See that balcony, flanked by large windows." I nodded. Ornately scalloped windows and carved balconies reflected the midday sun, making them nearly glow against the black cliffs. One sat separate from the rest, pointing north towards the harbor. "Those are my chambers. That's my balcony."

I tilted my head to look up at his inviting smile. Cal leaned in further, placing a hand on my hip and gently pulling me into him. His jaw brushed against my cheekbone. Goddess above, the feel of his beard against my skin did something to me. Speaking low enough that only I could hear him, he added, "There are adjoining apartments. They're yours, Elle... if you want them." I felt my blood heat, small beads of sweat cooled in the breeze against the back of my neck.

Rei whistled. "Damn. What happened in that cabin last night? Do I get to have my own apartment in the *palace* too?"

Ok, so maybe not low enough that only I could hear him.

Cal laughed. "I didn't think you usually had trouble finding somewhere to sleep."

She opened her mouth to protest but then closed it again.

"I do alright," she said with a wink and flipped her tousled hair.

"But, yes, we'll find you somewhere of your own," he added with an amused grin.

Rei squealed and clapped her hands together lightly.

Star Spear angled into the harbor towards a giant marble bridge that extended from the docks up to the castle. Two statues, the size of buildings, stood sentry at the end of the bridge. They were Innesvalen knights standing with swords crossed high in the air. Water channeled down the edges of the bridge, culminating in two large, cascading waves. I turned over our joined hands so that the sigil on Cal's cuff glinted in the light. Silver and sapphire waves, with crossed swords, over a shield--exactly like the guardians on the bridge.

Xoc's broad shadow fell over us.

"I will never tire of seeing these walls," he said with his eyes locked on the guardians as we drifted along.

It was undeniably an impressive sight. The ship silently passed under the bridge, the shadow of the knights momentarily darkening the deck.

"What have you been up to, brother?" Cal asked.

"I've been around, although I doubt you noticed." Xoc's eyes pointedly drifted down to me. "You've been preoccupied."

"I can't think of anything I'd rather be occupied with." The hand on my waist tightened in emphasis.

Xoc raised his eyebrows at Cal, then returned his gaze to the bridge. "Bein and I were discussing naval tactics. He was telling me about some of their encounters. It's been enlightening. If you and Morgan could stop posturing long enough to have a conversation, I think you might find what she has to offer of real value."

Cal gave a thoughtful hum, resting his chin atop my head.

The harbor was full of ships, every type, from galleons to schooners, both anchored and docked. The sails rolled upwards, and our speed slowed. Star Spear slipped easily into an empty berth, coming gently to a stop. Sailors jumped onto the docks, quickly tying down the mooring and lowering the gangplank.

We had arrived.

The harbor was at the edge of the city. It was a comfortably long walk past the multicolored buildings lining every inch of space along the water. They looked like an artist had spilled his palette over the city, staining Innesvale with the bright and welcoming hues of summer. The stacked buildings extended up the hillside, stretching far beyond the shoreline.

Framing the end of the city streets were the flags and canopies of a giant market. A huge canvas cover provided shade over dozens of stalls. Fresh fish, vegetables, and other imported goods were available at tiny shops. As we walked through the market, we were approached by several merchants, each holding a tray of different goods. My head spun with the presentation of silk scarves, cosmetics, and jewelry, each more beautiful than the last.

Rei gobbled down the visual feast before us. She ran a strand of glittering purple beads through her fingers.

"If you'd like for me to set up a line of credit for you, I can," Cal said, glancing over at Rei. "Although, I don't feel terribly confident about the safety outside of the castle walls at the moment."

Rei looked longingly at a tray of pearls. "I think I could brave it. I'll take a few of those muscle-bound guards with me." She pointed to the line of guards who had joined us the moment we arrived in port. Morgan's ship hadn't exactly arrived unnoticed.

The stalls we passed were adorned with blue and white streamers. Flower petals were scattered along the ground. Across the square, similar pennants and banners fluttered festively in the sea breeze.

"Is there a holiday approaching?" I asked, pointing to a thread of flowers hanging overhead.

Cal groaned, "I really hoped we missed it."

"Missed what?"

From behind me, Xoc answered with a sneer, "Prophecy Day."

"Prophecy Day," confirmed Cal.

I looked over my shoulder at him, incredulous. "What's Prophecy Day?"

"It's the celebration of the founding of the Shadow Crown," Cal said with a placating sigh. "Every year, Innesvale celebrates the coming of Ariyn Shadow. It's a week-long event with nightly parties all throughout the city."

"And a ball," growled Xoc.

"A ball, really?" Rei asked brightly. "Do we get gowns? I want mine to be slinky and silver."

Cal nodded, doing a double take at Rei while she held up an extra large set of earrings to her ears.

"Too much?"

"Rei, everything about you is too much," I quipped.

"Aww, I knew you liked me, fire girl."

"The Prophecy Ball is an Innesvalen tradition. It's held at the palace every year." Cal grimaced. "What it really is, is a reason for my mother to parade my sister and me around like some sort of badge of achievement. *'Oh, look at my son so strong and handsome.'*" He waggled his brows.

I couldn't help but laugh. The man was insufferable, and why did that make him more attractive? It shouldn't. It really shouldn't. My common sense and I were going to have to sit down and have a long talk.

Cal's expression completely changed, doing that look of adoration he'd done so much the night before. It made my skin tingle, and the air between us sparked.

Ahead of us, a decorative arch of ornately carved marble stretched over the entryway to the bridge. The eyes of the sentries at the gatehouse went wide with sudden recognition, swiftly bending to one knee and fanning a hand over their hearts.

The moment their eyes fell on him, Cal's entire demeanor transformed. His form seemed to grow, his shoulders rolled back, and his spine lengthened. It struck something in me that made the muscles of my stomach clench.

Xoc stepped beside Cal, hands folded behind his back in a practiced position of command. Seeing the two of them standing so formally was a bit unnerving. Were these really the men I'd seen racing on bikes? They were barely recognizable, entirely rigid and unyielding in their expressions. The soft playfulness of Cal was gone, and Xoc's look of quiet contemplation had shifted into one of judgment.

I don't know why it had taken me seeing them in these roles to realize that I'd been granted the rare insight to who they really were. Those days spent walking in Laluna, climbing the steps, and racing cycle rigs through Suman, that was real. I wasn't sure how to process that information. Despite all the lies and secrecy, Cal'd been more honest with me during those weeks than he probably was daily with anyone at court.

I want one last pure moment.

I hadn't really understood what he meant when he'd told me he wanted to hold on to something, but now I did. Palace life was all about calculation and image. If this performance was any indication, then there was probably very little reality on the surface.

"Rise." Cal strode past the guards, not bothering to slow or give them a second glance.

The formation of men rose to their feet but remained at attention. While Cal continued through the gate, Xoc stopped to inspect the men. He tugged on the lapels of one man, straightening an appellate.

"Elle?" Cal looked down at me with a flash of softness to his expression, something I realized now was reserved only for me. "Are you coming?"

He held his arm out to me in invitation. I linked my own through his letting him guide me onto the bridge. This was something that was actually happening. I had just arrived at the palace, on the literal arm of the prince. The idea was practically surreal.

Cal gave my hand a gentle squeeze. "Welcome to Castle Shadowhaven."

I stopped to take in the overwhelming view. The bridge was made of white marble, with tiny purple veins that sparkled in the sunlight. The palace was framed perfectly by the walls of the bridge. It stood proudly shining in the mid-day sun, with the glittering black mountain of the Vanfald behind it.

My jaw hung open. Cal leaned in low. "I told you Innesvale was the most beautiful city in Venterra." His lips grazed just below my ear, forcing goose-bumps down my arms. I wanted to look up at him, but I couldn't tear my eyes away from the bridge towers. Affixed to each turret were giant stone knights, each just as large and imposing as the guardians.

"You should see the bridge at–"

"Sunset, It looks like it's on fire," I interrupted him, remembering how he described this view and the fantasy that I briefly entertained. Yet here I was. I had blown off his description as mere flirtation, but this bridge left me awestruck.

I turned, looking back at the viewing platform on the end of the bridge, where the Guardians watched over the harbor. It was hard to fully appreciate their immense size from the water. Now that we were level with them, each of these behemoths loomed over us, reminding me of how very small I was in this world. Nearly a dozen more of the stone giants stood at attention, hands resting atop equally massive swords. The sound of rushing water filtered from the small rivers that flowed in the channels along the edge of the bridge.

Movement caught my eye, redirecting my attention. Archers were stationed along the ramparts. I hadn't seen them from the ship. I'd also missed the defensive cannons mounted at the tops of each tower. The bridge was a deceptively strategic fortification.

"So beautiful," I murmured under my breath. It was like I'd been hypnotized.

"The most beautiful thing I've ever seen," he said, breaking my trance. I glanced up to see him studying my reactions. Then flashed hot when I realized he was talking about me. Not about my gold-tipped hair or my unusual eye color— but about the way I was absorbing the view. It was a realization that made my heart feel both heavy and weightless.

Cal laced his hand into mine, bringing it up to brush a gentle kiss to my palm. I tried to play off being unaffected but was finding it hard to speak.

"I..." My heart fluttered in the cage of my chest like a trapped bird. The way he was looking at me, it was... I didn't even have words to describe it. My fingertips brushed over the stubble of his cheek as he lowered my hand but didn't release it.

I cleared my throat, swallowing against the parched, breathless feeling creeping up it. "I've been called that so many times the word beautiful lost it's meaning."

Cal tilted his head, but I could tell he didn't understand.

"I've had sonnets recited to me about the color of my hair, lecherous men slinging compliments while secretly plotting to steal a kiss, ardent fools who thought that telling me of how my eyes sparkle might earn them a chance at my affection."

Cal's expression tightened, jealousy flaring his nostrils.

"My father told me countless times how my beauty will earn the troupe piles of gold. While I know he loved me, Duke capitalized on it, patented it, and put it on posters. I've known how people looked at me, known what they see, and I've used that against them to get what I wanted. But I've never in my life actually felt beautiful. Not truly."

The furrowed brow of Cal's face softened. He stepped in closer, making the air between us that much harder to breathe. His hand raised to stroke the curve of my jaw, his thumb ending on my lips, but his eyes didn't stray from mine.

I could feel fate sitting up and taking notice.

"Never in my life until you looked at me." I swallowed the hesitation and sucked in a small breath. "The way you are looking at me right now. The way you've always looked at me. Like you're looking past the shimmer straight to my soul, and that is where you believe my beauty lies."

Cal's lips parted, at first, I thought he was going to say something, but then, his gaze dropped to where his thumb still rested against my lips.

The world around us narrowed to that single point of contact. I don't think I'd ever wanted him to kiss me the way I did at this moment. This was more than simple lust. My heart was burning to feel his lips on mine. My soul screamed to connect with his.

Just as his chin began to lower, Rei and Xoc pushed past us. She eyed our joined hands, one eyebrow raised at the palm cradling my cheek. Yes, she was going to have some questions for me later. How would I ever explain this?

The sound of their steps echoed off the smooth stone as they walked towards the castle. With those echoing steps, the bubble of emotion that was forming around us popped, allowing the air to rush back in. I took a step back, and Cal's hand slipped into the emptiness between us.

"Sorry," I mumbled, shaking my head in an attempt to clear it. "What were we talking about... before I was thoroughly distracted by the... bridge?"

I swallowed hard, still struggling to take a breath. Okay, maybe the moment hadn't completely broken. I could still feel the brush of his fingers on my lips, the sensation radiating out to make my skin hum. It felt like I wasn't on solid ground anymore, which was a problem. I wasn't ready to start free-falling.

Cal's eyes crinkled with amusement. "The prophecy."

"Right, Ariyn Shadow." I started walking. My strides were longer than they needed to be, putting distance between myself and whatever that moment was. "I'm guessing this is the same Ariyn who was the son of Elyria The First?"

It took nothing for Cal to catch up to me. It also took nothing for him to take my hand and slow me down. There was something seriously wrong with me. Why was I allowing myself to fall for this man— again?

"The same. She bore two children, Selina Asche and Ariyn Shadow. One to the Aschen Queens ,and the other was given to a barren lord and lady who lived in these lands."

"Wait." I pushed a hand to his chest, a truly alarming thought racing to the forefront of my mind. "That doesn't mean we're... Gods, tell me we're not actually like cousins or something."

Cal's eye twinkled with amusement. "Hardly. It's been thousands of years, Elyria. There are so many branches to those trees. The only thing left connecting us is the magic."

I heaved a sigh of relief. Cal lowered his voice so only I could hear. "The people don't know Ariyn Shadow was draken, only that Aurus brought him and that his coming was foretold. Many years later, he established the citadel of Innesvale and made the city a sanctuary to all in need. As the population grew, he was named king, and thus began the Shadow line of kings. It was his dying wish that Innesvale remain a city of acceptance and peace. He declared the gates should always remain open, a haven for all who seek to live here. Every king since has honored that. One day, I'll honor it, too."

Cal gestured towards the city, and I felt the honest sincerity in his voice. He genuinely loved Innesvale and the people living in it. Cal may not want to be king yet, but he had all the makings of a great one.

Following his arm, I walked over to the wall and looked down at the winding streets, at the people below who went about their business like ants. Boats moved in and out of the docks. The blue dragon silhouette of Star Spear stood out amid the sea of brown ships. I imagined Morgan and Bein commanding their crew to prepare for some new adventure.

Cal draped an arm around my shoulders, his fingers toying with my hair.

"I thought you'd been to Innesvale before?" he asked. I could sense the smile on his lips, even without looking at him.

"I was so young then, and we were never invited to the castle. We performed at the theater." I pointed down to a black glittering hemisphere carved into the cliffside. Of the theaters Troupe Solaire has performed in, Innesvale's was by far the most beautiful. It featured a large stage and a lavish orchestra pit for the band. I glanced over my shoulder. "We camped just outside the city. I've never approached from the sea, and the castle and bridge were only ever blips in the distance."

"Blips?"

"Yes, blips," I held up my fingers to show just how small they appeared from the other side of the city.

"How do you do that?"

"Do what?" I said, looking at him through my pinched fingers and repeatedly squishing his head between them.

"Make even the most mundane things seem wondrous. I've always loved this city, but what I love most is seeing it through your eyes."

Gently cupping the nape of my neck, he drew me in and kissed my temple tenderly. I don't think I've ever felt so cherished. It was very possible my swelling heart might burst, and I'd never make it off this bridge.

From behind us a voice cleared his throat, his heels clicking to a close on the marble. I tensed. We weren't alone, but for a moment, I'd forgotten about everyone but Cal.

A gray-haired man in a simple trimmed suit stood behind us. A small folio was tucked under his arm. His back was ridged, and his expression bland in refined neutrality.

"Mattias," Cal said, warmly addressing the man. I glanced back to where the guards were waiting for us. On a whim, I walked to look at the view from the bridge, and yet half a dozen men were standing at attention waiting for us to continue our stroll. Cal didn't even seem to notice. Xoc and Rei had continued on, but the guards had waited. It made me think of what Cal said about a throne and the liberty he had without one. Suddenly, pretending to be a cosmetics merchant made a lot more sense.

I glanced back up, seeing him for what felt like the first time. A rough beard had grown in during our trip. Gold rimmed his warm brown eyes, and the shadows gracing his sun-kissed complexion accentuated the handsome line of his jaw. His eyes flicked over to me and caught me studying his face. His head cocked to the side, and then he winked.

Ass. Shit, why did my stomach feel like I was flying on a trapeze without a net?

Cal gestured for Mattias to join our walk towards the castle. He held his hand back to me. Taking his arm, I fell into position beside him.

"Your Highness. We received news of your arrival moments ago. I already have the staff preparing rooms for you and your guests." Mattias glanced at me, eyes lingering over my knives.

Cal smirked. Pride shimmered off of him, unlike the scowl burning a path down Mattias's long nose. I realized what Mattias must see, the sheer contrast of my appearance to that of the other ladies walking along the bridge. They had swirling skirts and parasols, while I had leather and knives. It couldn't have been more obvious that I wasn't a courtier. If the look Cal was giving me was any indication, that was what he loved most about me. Mattias's judgment, however, had me tripping over my steps.

That single assessing look suddenly had so many questions swirling about my head. Had Cal ever given rooms to a woman before? Heat rushed up the back of my neck. *Why did I suddenly care if he'd ever had an official partner?* Three days in a cabin on a ship, and I was practically falling over myself for him. Had a few quiet moments really smoothed over all my hard edges? But, as I took in the easy way his hand wrapped over mine, I realized that I wasn't all that angry anymore.

If anything, these past couple of days had given me something I didn't realize I needed— perspective.

"I've also taken the liberty of alerting your mother of your arrival," Mattias continued.

And then I tripped. Again. Me, the acrobat capable of walking high wires, kept literally tumbling from one shocking revelation after another.

Cal chuckled, tightening his grip on my arm to keep me upright.

The queen. I sucked in a breath and tried to regain my steps.

"Of course." Cal gazed up at the castle with an unreadable expression.

"Is there anything else you require, sire?" Mattias asked.

Cal looked over at me, and a wide grin pulled at his lips. "Mattias Amberly, may I introduce Miss Elyria Solaris." He gestured to me. Mattias took my hand in his and dipped in to a small bow.

"Hello, sir," I said, doing a polite dip in return. From the look on Cal's face, he knew this formality was making me uncomfortable, and I could swear he was enjoying seeing me squirm.

"Mattias is the personal secretary to the crown. He is the mastermind who keeps the palace functioning. He handles all of our daily affairs, as well as managing the staff to the royal family." Cal gestured ahead. "The girl walking with Commander Xoc is Reihaneh Almont. She and Miss Solaris will each need to have quarters outfitted for their stay. We had to leave with very few supplies on hand. They are to be afforded every luxury while in Innesvale, all of their expenses are to be handled by the crown. Be prepared for Miss Almont to make some outlandish requests. Appease her," Cal slowed a step, then added, "within reason. Both women will also need a protective detail...Oh, and..."

Cal's eyes searched mine, looking for the answer to a question I didn't know he was asking. He hesitated for a moment before his hand came over the one I had clinging to the crook of his arm. His thumb smoothed over my wrist. "Miss Solaris will be using my personal adjoining quarters."

Mattias looked at me but didn't reveal any kind of opinion. Would it be a scandal for Cal to allow a girl of my standing to share an apartment with him?

"Of course. I will inform the staff."

I shifted uneasily.

"Mattias, I seem to have lost track of my days. When does the festival start?" Cal winced slightly.

"I'm sorry to tell you that you've missed nearly the entire festival. Tomorrow is the ball."

Drifting my eyes over Cal's shoulders, my mind wandered to imagining what his trim form would look like in a well-cut jacket or how we would glide across a floor. Dancing with Cal at a ball felt like the kind of stories Duke would tell me when I was young and still starry-eyed. It was a fantasy; princes didn't just sweep girls like me off our feet. I had only ever attended fancy parties as the entertainment, never as a guest, and certainly never on the arm of a prince.

"Elyria?" as if from a distant place, I heard Cal's voice drifting to me. He came into focus, making me realize that I was well and truly lost in that daydream.

"Sorry. What was the question?" I said, blushing. Or rather, *still* blushing, since it seemed every look from Cal since we'd woken this morning had my skin flushing.

"I asked if there was anything specific you wanted," Cal replied, holding back a smile.

Wanted. Now there was a concept. What did I want? My mind wandered back to last night and the press of my back against the wooden door. I swallowed, hard.

"No, I don't need anything."

"I didn't ask what you needed. I asked what you wanted."

What do you want, Elyria?

"Just maybe a change of clothing and a bath. I would do nearly anything for a warm bath at this point."

"I'll have to remember that," Cal said with a barely noticible wink.

Mattias cleared his throat again. "Well, if there is anything else you desire-"

Cal raised an eyebrow at me. Was it getting hotter? The leather of my halter felt too tight.

"Please just call, and I'll see it is done. Welcome to Castle Shadowhaven, Miss Solaris. "

With that, Mattias took off with a quick clip towards the castle.

Anything I desired. I looked at Cal, who was biting back a laugh and grinning. That fleeting moment of heat died on the edges of that stupid grin, quickly replaced by annoyance.

I smacked him hard on the shoulder.

"Careful," he chided. "Striking a prince is a punishable offense."

"Then I better make the hit worth it," I said, laughing. "Don't worry, I'll try harder next time."

"You can certainly try."

I growled at the anticipatory gleam in his eyes, baiting me to play with him. Well, I wouldn't give him that satisfaction. By this point, Xoc and Rei were already to the end of the bridge.

"We should catch up."

Cal snatched my wrist as I turned. His grip was tight and halted any ideas I had on running away. I looked back, expecting to see a laughing grin, but his expression was serious.

"What is it?" I asked, confused. But he only stood there, arm extended, thumb stroking my inner wrist. Cal slowly reeled me back until my hand rested lightly against his chest, directly over the scar I knew was hidden there. With a single finger, he tilted my chin up so that our eyes met.

"This is one of my favorite places in the capital." As power slowly bled into them, the rings of gold enveloped Cal's dark irises. "--and I've-" He brought my fingers to his lips. "I've imagined walking with you along this bridge, showing you my home, bringing you here." He swallowed, and I watched as his throat bobbed. "I don't want to rush it. Please, Elle. Do this for me."

Fuck, he looked so vulnerable like this. He said, please. When did Cal ever say please?

"You imagined this?"

He nodded his head slowly. "Many times, Sunshine. So many times."

I turned, looking back over my shoulder towards the castle. Every single person on the bridge was watching us. It was the only time I wasn't on stage, yet everyone's eyes were on me. It was a different kind of gaze, one I wasn't certain I was comfortable with.

8

ELYRIA

A black stone road weaved up to the castle, flanked on either side by sprawling gardens. Flowers from every season and part of Venterra bloomed on meticulously cared for bushes. There were even Ice Lilies, which I knew only grew on the northern shores of the continent. They were beautiful, adding a honey scent to the bouquet perfuming the air.

"My mother grows them."

I ran my fingers over the waxy petals. They bled from nearly clear to the deepest shade of crimson like they were frostbitten. At the center, glittery stamens shimmered in the light like ice crystals.

"It's her attunement. Like Xoc, she moved here from the Oerwood."

I spun to face him, the petal of the flower coming unexpectedly with me.

Cal chuckled, seeing my expression of surprise. "What, you just assumed that my mother was from Innesvale like my father?"

"Yeah, kind of," I said, realizing that was a very closed-minded way of looking at things. It explained his bronzed complexion and the way he sometimes made his vowels sound rounder than you'd expect from a Desterran.

"My father met my mother while fighting in the Covenant Wars."

His entire tone changed. The volume became softer, almost loving. Even the tilt to the corners of his eyes had changed, just as they had when he told me of his childhood picnics. He loved his parents, loved what they represented. What must it have been like to grow up seeing that level of adoration every day?

"Wait, that would mean–" I stopped abruptly, my history lessons and Duke's stories catching up to me. "But Innesvale and the Oers were opposed in that

"She was a captain of the vanguard for the Oers. Mother was taken down by an archer and later brought as a prisoner of war to the Innesvalen infirmary."

The entire image I had of his mother changed. I figured she was a proper lady, lounging in massive gowns and doing needlework to pass the time. Now I was picturing a battle-clad warrior. I guess I knew where Cal inherited his attraction to violence from.

"My father, then only a prince, would visit the wounded at the end of every day. It didn't matter that he was royalty; he offered aid to anyone who needed it. There were very few Oers ever captured in battle. So my mother was special and was kept in a wing just for her. My father believed in showing kindness to all, especially your enemies."

"I can't imagine ever being kind to my enemies." Without meaning to the memory of my hand crushing Andromeda's throat forced its way into my mind. I could feel the resistance of her windpipe flexing beneath my grip. I remembered every second of that fight, every sensation as if I was there. I'd do it again, and if I could ever get my hands on Malvat's throat—

The hand squeezing mine proved Cal knew exactly how dark my thoughts had gone, bringing me back from the shadows. "Diplomacy is tricky. As he saw it, how could your enemy ever become a friend if you always treated them like an enemy?"

I blinked away the memory. "That makes sense, actually. *If* you actually want them to be a friend." I had no such plans for my enemies. Malvat would know my flames, not friendship.

"Treat someone as you wish them to be, and let them rise to the occasion. Why do you think I've always treated you as someone to love?"

I inhaled, but I was fairly certain I hadn't taken in any air because I felt breathless and my heart raced like I was sprinting—not casually strolling arm-in-arm with a prince on the way to his palace. Gods, how was this reality and not a dream?

"My mother refused to take water from him, or speak to him for that matter. The more she refused, the harder he tried. After a week of trying, he told her he wasn't coming back, and for the first time she spoke to him, *"Don't."* It was only one syllable. But for them, it might as well have been a sonnet."

"That's really sweet."

"See, my mother saw indulging in his kindness as a betrayal to her kingdom. But, as far as the Oers were concerned, she was dead. Falling in battle and surviving was a disgrace. Should she fall, the expectation was to take the enemy with you; only then would Belhameth bless you to die in honor."

"That's terrible," I said, disbelief coating my words. "They would expect their own people to die over being wounded?"

"Yes. To the Oers, there's no disgrace higher than to fall and be healed by the enemy."

I tried to imagine what this intense and proud woman was like, grim-faced, staring down death.

"Even after the war was over, she was disowned by everyone in the Wood, except for one fellow outcast, who would later become my mentor."

"Master Rith!" I said. Proud to have drawn the connection. Cal looked at me with complete surprise, so much so that he stopped walking.

"Oh." Realization dawned on me. "That's why you studied there. At the time, I wondered why you would travel halfway around the world when Innesvale would have high-caliber tutors of their own. But when Xoc told me about Master Rith, I hadn't realized you were..." I hesitated, not wanting to blurt out his biggest secret while the eyes of everyone on the bridge were on us.

"Half-Oerish?" He shot me a not-at-all-subtle wink. "Apparently, you and Xoc talked more than I realized."

I shrugged. "Careful, Cal, your jealous side is showing again."

Flames danced in his eyes. I knew he wasn't entirely joking, and for some reason, that delighted me.

"So how does it end? The story of your parents?"

"While my mother convalesced, my father brought her food and water every day. She would eat, and he would tell her of his world." He gestured towards the city. "She sat in silence, never commenting but always listening. Even after she was healed, my father continued to visit. Somehow, despite the conflict she felt in her heart, my mother went from quiet defiance to yearning for the time they spent together."

The tightness in my chest returned. My heart knew far too intimately what it meant to war with your emotions.

"Then, one day, the war was over. The opposing nations signed a new Covenant, and once again, there was peace. It was on that day that she told my father she loved him. The first four words she ever spoke to him were, 'Don't' and 'I love you'."

I sighed. "That's terribly romantic."

"It runs in the blood." Cal grinned one of those trademark white smiles.

"These are her gardens." He stopped, the charming smile sinking into something far more serious. The look made my heart stutter with alternating beats of anticipation and trepidation.

"What?" I asked warily.

Abruptly, he turned off the path and pushed into the garden, dragging me behind him. Brambles caught in my hair as we fought past the bushes and into a clearing.

A sprawling lawn was flanked by rows of gardenia flowers. I scanned the sudden change in landscape, and then the air ripped from my lungs. My eyes were unable to look away from the tree standing on the far end of the green. I gripped at my chest, feeling the barely healed scars surrounding my heart split wide open. It drove me to my knees.

A willow tree wrapped in rich purple wisteria vines swayed in the breeze. This tree was a twin to the one that grew over Duke's ashes. The only difference being that this one lived in sunshine. Blood rushed in my veins, and I could barely see through my tear-blurred vision.

Cal knelt on the ground before me. "This is where we would have our luncheons." He pointed to the grass. "Over there is where my parents would watch the clouds, where I would fly kites." He took my hands in his. "This is where I learned what love looked like."

He'd given that to me. I thought he was a lying ass using my grief to manipulate me, and he'd given me a piece of that memory—a piece of what he loved most.

"Cal," I whispered, choking on the sob that threatened to escape.

"When I held you that day..." His golden eyes bored into me. "You were so hurt. I knew that ache intimately."

I closed my eyes. I couldn't look into his intense gaze and not feel every single emotion from the terrible morning. Cal leaned forward, resting his hands on either side of my legs and pressing his forehead to my own.

"Elle, I felt your sadness. It echoed in my blood with every sorrow-filled beat of your heart. Each golden tear that fell from your eyes felt like a knife slicing me open. All I wanted was to give you some happiness, and this place was all I could think of."

I couldn't speak. My throat closed around a hard lump. Unable to contain it any longer, the dam of emotion overflowed, hot tears finally rolled down my cheeks.

"Elle, I—"

The bushes behind me rustled.

"Your Highness," came the timid voice of a boy. Cal glared up at him, still kneeling before me. The sight this must be, his prince kneeling before a common dancer. The boy's voice shook. "I'm sorry to intrude, sire."

"You most definitely are," Cal snarled.

"Yes. I'm sorry. Please forgive me." The boy's voice cracked. I almost felt bad for him. I don't think I'd ever seen Cal look so murderous. "Her Majesty, The Queen, has requested you and Miss Solaris join her on the southern terrace."

Cal sighed, then looked up. It was so unexpected that I followed his gaze. Standing on a balcony overlooking the gardens was a stunning woman. Long auburn hair draped over rich tawny skin, the same unmistakable shade of Cal's. The cascade of luxurious hair was interrupted by a single long streak of white that made her that much more dignified. Even from here, her gaze cut into us.

Had she seen this entire moment? Did she know how raw my heart was, what that tree meant, what Cal was about to confess?

"I guess that means it's time to go." Before rising to his feet, Cal brushed away the tears clinging to my cheeks with the back of his hand and pressed a kiss to the center of my brow.

"Please tell my mother that we will join her once we've freshened up," he said, addressing the boy with the same stern command he'd given at the gate.

Cal reached down a hand to help me up.

"We'll have to finish this later." Disappointment and irritation hung unspoken around us.

He lifted me gently and placed me back down on shaky legs. Brushing the hair from my face, he placed a kiss on my temple. It was just the softest brush of his lips, but it made the ache in my chest abate.

This is where I learned what love looked like.

"Later, I want to show you the entire palace. But, I think first we should probably start with where you can take a bath, and then regrettably, my mother's balcony."

I resisted the urge to look up again.

We walked through the gardens to a pair of massive glass doors. They were ornately carved and lined in highly polished brass. I barely had time to admire all the intricate details before we were walking through them and into the darkened interior of the palace.

Cal led me through a labyrinth of white marble staircases and corridors. Crystal chandeliers hung before each window, painting the hallway with streams of rainbow-colored light. Tapestries and frescoed ceilings adorned nearly every surface, giving new meaning to the word palatial. I was sure that I'd never be able to navigate the maze of passageways on my own. Eventually, we stopped at a solid wooden door painted Innesvalen Blue.

"These are your rooms."

"Rooms?" I ran a hand over the simple craftsmanship of the carved wood. I got rooms, plural. Before Cal, I'd shared a caravan with two other women, but here I got rooms. The crest, gilded and inlaid in the center, gleamed brightly over the contrasting cobalt door.

Cal followed me into the room, closing the door behind him. For the first time, the contingent of guards that followed us from the dock were gone. Leaving us blissfully alone. A heavy weight that I didn't realize I was carrying lifted from my shoulders, allowing me to take my first fully unrestrained breath since leaving the security of our tiny cabin.

Cal flicked his wrist and the sconces lit, flooding the apartment with warm light. Several paintings decorated the white marble walls wrapping around us. Ornately cut arches separated the different living spaces. We stood in what looked like a sitting room, a place to receive guests – I snorted to myself – if I ever had any.

There were several lounges and couches. An inviting window seat at the far end of the room looked out at the sparkling ocean. It was easy to imagine sitting on the velvet cushion with a steaming cup of tea and a good book. At the center of the room, there was a large white fur rug. It looked soft and luxurious, though I had no idea what pelt it was made from.

I walked through the first arch into a study that held an oak desk with a high-back chair. Continuing past the desk and an absurdly large vanity, I stopped in front of a picture window. Next to it was an overstuffed bed covered in silk sheets and pillows. Heavy velvet curtains, in midnight blue, hung neatly. I ran the soft fabric through my fingers.

"It's to keep out the light. In the morning, the sunlight can be brutal against the white marble," Cal said, a bit too quietly, like he was afraid all this opulence would spook me and I'd bolt for the door.

I looked at him and gave him my most reassuring smile. My heart might be confused at the moment, but I knew I wasn't leaving.

I pointed at a glass door in the far wall. "What's in there?"

"Open it and find out."

I walked to the door, turning the delicate handle. There was a soft click, and the door swung silently open. Inside was a washroom twice the size of the wagon I'd shared with Macie and Violet. In the center, a stone bath was set into the floor, hot steam already rising from the basin.

"This is where I should remind you that you said you'd do anything for a hot bath." The wolfish smile spreading on his lips forced heat to pulse at my core.

"But it would seem there was already one drawn for you. So, I think it's probably best to let you enjoy this while it's hot."

He walked from the washroom towards a blue door on the far end of the bedchamber. "This connects to my rooms. So, if you need me, I'm just right on the other side." He pulled the door open. I glimpsed more white marble as he disappeared into his room.

I let out a long breath and ambled back into the washroom. I unbuckled my knives and slipped them from my waist.

"Oh."

I jumped, screeching in surprise, seeing Cal poking his head back into the room.

"I recommend the little pink bottle. It's an oil. Just pour it in the water." He pointed at the shelf lined with tiny pots and bottles.

"Thanks." I dropped my knives onto a bench for emphasis.

Cal raised an eyebrow. "I can't tell if that was a threat or an invitation."

"Go away," I said, picking up a towel and throwing it at him.

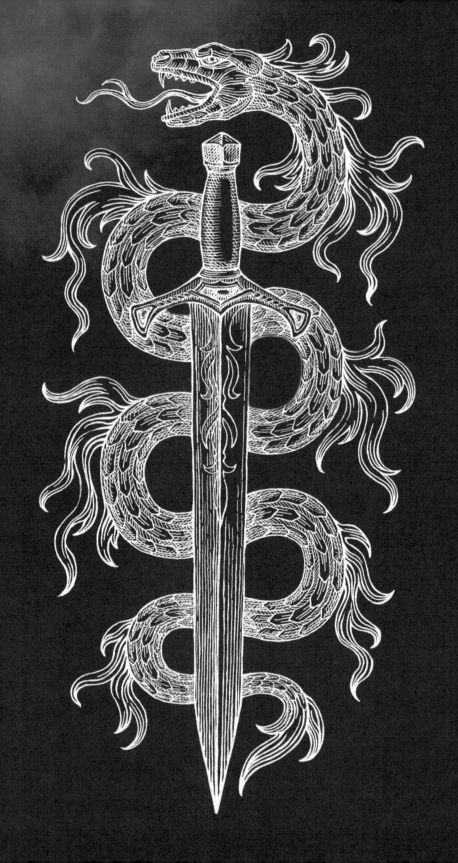

9
ELYRIA

The water in the tub was divine. Heat seeped into every inch of my body. Something in the water fizzed and made my muscles tingle in a euphoric relaxation. Palace life could definitely have its perks.

I had, in fact, tried the pink bottle. The oil smelled of roses and thick exotic spices. It gave a faint blue hue to the tub. Then, out of pure curiosity, I started pouring other random bottles in. One container held giant salt crystals that smelled of lavender and vanilla. Another contained a paste made from what smelled like sugar. The water bubbled and frothed, creating a milky layer of rainbow-colored suds.

Letting my head fall back, I closed my eyes. The golden burn in Cal's gaze as he kneeled before me floated around and around in my vision. *Elyria, I...*

What had he been about to say before the boy interrupted him? What did I want him to say? *Elyria, I like pancakes. Elyria, I've been an ass. Elyria, I can't live another moment without you wrapped around my cock.* Definitely not, *Elyria, I love you.* Because that fantasy tempted a part of me I couldn't reconcile with.

Flashes of him over the past few weeks reeled against my closed lids. Cal with glowberry juice streaked across his face, the look of desperation in his eyes the morning after I fell on the cliff, the expression he'd had after I flattened that fool at the bar, the strength of his hand in mine at the basilica, the shock when I emerged from the woods on fire, the dejected way he had looked when I left him in the harbor, the water crashing over my body as he kissed me in the falls, the feel of him curled into me as we slept, the heat of his fire wrapping around my own, and finally coming back to Cal kneeling before me.

"Goddess slay me." I moaned and let myself slip beneath the water.

Coming back up for air, I smoothed the suds from my face, scrambling for a cloth. All the things I added to the water served only to make my eyes burn.

Patting my face dry, I said to the void, "What am I doing here?"

Silence.

"How is this even my life?"

A little more than a month ago, I was an overworked performer, trying to wrangle a pack of misfits and my cavalier father into putting on a nightly show. Now, I was bathing in what could honestly be mistaken for a swimming pool while a literal prince waited for me on the other side of our adjoining doors. And all I could think about was what it would feel like to lie in that massive bed with his weight pressing into me.

It was too much to handle, too much for any person to process. Death, love, family, loss, belonging. My confused emotions spilled from me in a chaotic mess that perfectly matched how I felt. Tears mixed with the bathwater, and I choked on my laughter as I accidentally slipped beneath the surface.

With a strangled cry, I struggled to regain control. I'd let the dam break, and it took everything I had to patch it back together.

A knock rapped against the door.

Doing my best to keep from screaming, I looked at the shadow on the other side of the glass. "Cal, if that's you thinking you can make good on that deal. Know that I have an entire array of bottles here that I will hurl at your dick. We both know my aim is excellent." The threat sounded flat, even to my ears. Probably because the idea of him coming in here to join me wasn't one I was entirely opposed to.

"Ma'am, sorry. I'm here to assist you in dressing," came a small voice from behind the door.

Ugh. Mortification burned through me. Of course that wasn't him. Here I was shouting about hitting Cal in the dick and taking baths with their prince to some stranger. Perfect first impression, Elyria.

"Oh, sorry." I cringed at the awkwardness in my tone. "Hold on, give me just a moment." I glanced around the room, spying a stand that held fluffy white towels. Next to it, a white satin robe hung from a hook.

I clambered from the tub, rainbow clumps of soap bubbles clinging to my body.

"Ma'am, I can assist you," called the voice again.

"NO," I yelled a bit too emphatically. "No, that's not necessary. I can manage," I added, trying to be polite. Gods, I was truly terrible at this.

I toweled myself off and slipped the softest fabric of my life around my shoulders. A small and entirely too sexual moan came from me the moment the robe hit my skin. Seriously, did they spin the thread from clouds?

Tying the belt at my waist, I pulled the door open. On the other side was a woman, nearly my age, standing straight with her hands folded before her. Her brown hair was neatly pinned back, revealing her soft, pretty features. Dark brown eyes were cast down in submission.

"Hello," I said awkwardly, "I'm Elyria."

"Yes, Ma'am."

We stood in an uncomfortable silence until I realized that she was waiting for me to say something. A command, or a question.

"What's your name?" I asked, a timidity to my voice that I didn't recognize. Never in my life had I felt timid, but this place made me feel small.

"Alessia, as you please, Miss."

Miss. I sighed and ran a hand through the ends of my damp hair.

"Look, I'm new to this, and to be honest, the formality of everything here is a bit unnerving. Can we just pretend you and I are old friends? You call me Elyria, and I'll call you Alessia?"

Alessia tucked her hands into the pockets of her apron, relaxing her stance and meeting my eyes for the first time since I opened the door.

"Seriously, what I need more than a servant is a friend," I added. Trying to give my best "be my friend" smile. Why was I always so terrible at this? Most people assumed because I was comfortable on a stage, that meant meeting people came naturally to me. I could pretend well enough until strangers became friends, but internally, I was cringing at every single word that left my mouth.

"Okay," she said, returning my smile. "Just, I can't be your friend outside of this room. If Mattias saw me being so informal with the—" she bit off the end of that sentence.

"With what?" I asked, raising my eyes at the question.

"Well, you know. You're the prince's…" she said, looking at the door that led into Cal's rooms.

"*His what?* What exactly does everybody seem to think I am?"

Alessia gave me a pleading, uneasy look.

"Alessia, do not say 'whore'. Because that isn't even close to what's happening here." I waved my hand between me and the door. Anger rose in me, and I swallowed down flames before they could spill from my mouth. "That bastard put me in these rooms and now, what? Everyone thinks I'm here to serve at the prince's pleasure, just a pussy waiting for his royal cock?" I took a step towards Cal's room. He and I were about to have words.

Shock flitted across Alessia's face. " NO. No. Ma'am." She held out her hands.

I spun on her.

"Elyria," I clipped back.

"Elyria…" She corrected herself.

"Out with it, Alessia!" I said, trying to pull the answer from her with my hands.

"You don't know." She shook her head. "Maybe I shouldn't be the one to tell you this information."

"Oh no. You're going to tell me. Right. Now." I said, standing tall.

She swallowed hard, trying to look anywhere but at me. So much for being friendly. First thing I did was snap at her.

"Elyria," She folded and unfolded her hands, nervousness turning the knuckles white. "These apartments. They are for the future *princess*. Until this morning, they were covered and packed. No one has used these rooms since the queen was engaged to the king."

My heart stopped beating. It just stopped. A rushing sound filled my ears until her voice sounded like I was hearing her speak through a tunnel.

"Elyria?" she said, scanning my sudden onset paralysis. "I'm sorry. I shouldn't have spoken out of turn."

I shooed away her self-deprivations.

"Did...did you just say these were the queen's former quarters?" I choked out. I'd forgotten how to speak. Each syllable felt foreign on my tongue.

"Yes. Although, after their wedding and coronation—"

"Wedding and coronation?" I gripped at the wall for support. I was going to faint.

"—they were moved to the king's wing of the palace," Alessia added. She was speaking with such nonchalance. As if she hadn't just told me that Cal had effectively proposed to me by putting me in this bedroom.

I swallowed against my sandpaper tongue. My entire mouth had just gone dryer than the Dead Lands. I looked back at his stupid, blue door. I had to curl my hand into a fist to prevent myself from burning the damn thing down. Yeah, this was something we were going to have to discuss later.

Several heartbeats pounded in my chest before Alessia eased to me and placed a hand on my arm. Less like she was approaching a woman and more like someone daring to pet a tiger.

"Elyria, would you like to select something to wear? I assume you don't plan on meeting the queen wearing a robe." She laughed nervously.

"The queen..." I echoed back to her.

I felt lightheaded and leaned my head against the doorframe to the washroom.

"Yes. Let's do that." Clothing. I could handle clothing.

Alessia guided me to the sitting room where a dozen trunks had been brought up and opened. Well, hells, how long was my bathtub emotional breakdown? Maybe handling clothing was going to be asking too much after all. There must be a hundred dresses here.

"I still need to air most of these. They're in several sizes. Mattias wasn't sure about your exact measurements. But he actually has a pretty good eye for these things. There is also a variety for different occasions. And I'm to take down your sizing to have a gown fitted for tomorrow's ball."

I nodded. "Right. The ball." Loosing a long sigh, I turned back to her. Alessia pulled a long strip of measuring tape from a pocket. She began running it down each of my limbs. I felt a pang of homesickness, thinking of Jess, Troupe Solaire's costumer. He'd fitted me my entire life. From my first show costume when I was five to the magnificent gold skirt I'd worn the night of Duke's death. I could still hear him lamenting how much I'd grown after each of my childhood growth spurts. He would have loved to make something for a ball.

"Elyria, life at court isn't really all that different than life out there." She gestured to the window. My eyes flitted back to her, bringing me back into the moment. "Things are a bit more formal, and people are just more willing to give you what you need. That's all. You're going to be fine."

"Fine," I repeated, gazing around the room. Hours. We had been in port for hours, at the most, and an entire clothiers shop had already been laid before me, and apparently — now, I'm to be the next queen. Gods, what will happen by the end of tomorrow?

"So, what would you like to wear? I can help you dress in anything." She was trying so hard to be kind. I'd bit her head off and shoved it down her throat, but she was still being compassionate.

Alessia gestured at everything from simple shifts to elegant gowns. There was nothing like the leather trousers that I was used to. In fact, many of these fabrics looked quite flammable.

"Can you pick out something appropriate for me?" I asked, unsure if I should meet the queen looking the part of a princess or more myself. I thought of the woman in the jail cell refusing to speak. That woman would never dress up as something she wasn't.

"Actually. Do you have anything casual, leather preferably?"

"Leather?"

"Sometimes things get hot around me." I summoned a fireball in my hand.

"Woah." Alessia's eyes went wide.

I half smiled. "Flammable fabrics and I don't really mix well."

"Um... I don't have leather." She looked around the room at the crates, "But, I will see about having something made up for you."

She walked over to a crate and pulled out a beautiful dress-pant set. "How about this? It's appropriate for the season."

Stunning sea green silk caught the light, reminding me of the waters that surrounded the city. It looked like a marriage of a skirt and pants. From the front, you saw the silhouette of short pants, but then a soft skirt hung down the sides. A matching cropped top hung above them.

Alessia added, "Informal, but still stylish."

"Okay," I said. "This reminds me more of a show costume than functional clothing, but I like it."

"Life at court is always a performance. You just have to decide what part you want to play." She smiled, pleased with herself that she had picked well.

What part did I want to play? My head spun with the possibilities. I had no idea how to answer that question. In truth, I wasn't sure I wanted to play at all.

Brightening, she added, "This green will look beautiful against your coloring. Especially your hair. I have never seen anything so stunning. I can't wait to style it."

I nodded. The black and gold combo always drew comments from people when they first met me. Of course, no one seemed as drawn to it as Cal. He was always running his fingers through my hair and sighing at the way it felt. Sometimes, when he thought I wasn't paying attention, I would catch him inhaling the way it smelled, and it made me smile every damn time.

"Thank you," I said politely.

Alessia pulled the piece from the hanger and laid them on the settee before us.

"Did you want to style it up or down? I can do either." Alessia looked so happy and excited.

"Alessia?" I questioned. "What was your position at the palace before we arrived today?"

"I was the second handmaid to Princess Kaeliana." She held up the bottoms. "Did you need help with the lacing?"

"Maybe just up the back," I said. "So, is this posting a promotion? I mean, why you?"

"Mattias came to me specifically. He said you weren't like other courtiers and that I would suit you." Her eyes glittered, and she bit down on her lip. "I can be... a bit rebellious." I smiled at that. It was like I was a chaos magnet that attracted every troublemaker within a mile radius. "The princess and I have raised a bit of hell in the past."

"If she's anything like Cal, then that's not very hard to believe."

"Kaeliana has an affinity for sneaking out of the palace and masquerading in the city. Mattias hates that I enable her and has been looking for a suitable reason to take me off her staff for months." She smiled guiltily. "But my job was to serve *her*, so the stuffy old man can shove his rules on decorum right up his ass."

I snorted. Yep, I liked her.

I slipped on the silk short pants, discovering that the skirt parts were a separately wrapped piece of cloth that could easily be removed.

"You'll like the princess too. Or rather, I think she'll like you."

"Oh? Why's that?" I slid the top over my shoulders.

"She dislikes the court. They always preen over her, trying to curry favors. She hates how agreeable everyone is all the time."

I thought of Cal lamenting having to return to being a prince. Apparently, this was a common complaint among royalty.

"It's why she leaves and pretends not to be noble. I think she's been waiting for someone like you to join the palace. When you meet her, just be yourself, and she'll instantly like you. She's funny... and more than decent at cards. So whatever you do, don't bet any money against her."

I took a deep breath. Fortifying myself for my next question.

"And what about the queen? What is she like?"

Alessia circled behind me and began pulling on the straps of my blouse. I grunted at the sudden inability to breathe until I realized my laces weren't the thing making my chest tight.

"Stern, but fair," Alessia said as she heaved on the satin cording. "She's not afraid to fight for something if she believes it is right. Her strength is something most Innesvalen girls look up to."

So, exactly how I pictured her to be.

"She'll never admit it, but the prince is clearly her favorite. She was racked with worry the entire time he was gone, especially after he almost died last year."

My mind flashed to what Cal had told me about his father attacking him. I felt my face darken as I thought of the demons he fought when he closed his eyes. The ones he never let the world see. I turned quickly, forcing the laces to slip from her hands. "You know about that? I thought it was a secret."

Alessia's face turned sullen. "There's very little the princess doesn't share with me." She spun me back around and began refastening my blouse. "The King's death hit her hard. She's excellent at hiding her emotions, so you'd never know to look at her. While Cal was in his coma, she didn't leave his room. Mattias had to have all her meals sent up. We had a lot of wine and a lot of cake in those weeks. His mother, too. There is a unique kind of bonding that happens when you grieve with someone."

She came back around to the front with the skirt pieces in her hands. "Arms up." She reached around my midsection and tied the silk fabric to the hidden strings inside the waistband of the shorts. She stepped back and did a tiny clap of her hands. "Perfect. Now, how about your hair."

Alessia held her hands up and winked. A swirl of air rolled around me, sucking my hair into a tiny cyclone. It siphoned away every drop of water, leaving my strands smooth and bright. Whatever was in the bottles from my bath gave my hair an incredible luster.

"That is very handy."

Alessia smiled with pride, then waved off my praise. "It's not that impressive. Two-thirds of Innesvale are Wind Singers."

There was a knock at the main door of the apartment. I moved to answer it, but she put her hand on my shoulder, stopping me.

"You should let me. If it's anyone of importance, it would be bad if you were opening your own door, especially when your handmaid is present."

With each step Alessia took to the door, her casual demeanor morphed into something more subservient. The moment the door cracked open, Rei busted into the room. A tall guard grabbed her by the shoulders.

Rei kicked a hip out and pouted. "Don't worry, big guy, you can have your turn later."

The man smiled before meeting the eyes of the guard across from him and immediately returning to the impassive expression all the guards carried. He cleared his throat. "Miss, you can't enter the royal apartments without an invitation."

"Elyria, you hear this nonsense?" Rei looked the guard up and down, stroking the man's arm. "Invite me in before I have to find more entertaining things to do around here."

"**S**he can come in," I said to the guard in my most authoritative voice.

Batting her lashes, Rei rubbed a hand over his chest. "Don't worry, baby. Find me later. I often find myself in need of...protection."

The guard gulped loudly, his eyes following each swishing dip of her skirts as she strutted into the room. Rei gave a long look at Alessia as she walked past.

Rei scanned the room, whistling in appreciation. She peeked her head into every room before flopping into the middle of a pile of dresses.

"Are you still holding out on him? Cause I gotta say, it's working." She smoothed her hands over the lush variety of fabrics. Then, focused her eyes on Alessia. I watched uncomfortably as Rei let her eyes rove over my new handmaid's curves.

"Yeah. That's a bit much." I walked between them, interrupting her gaze.

"Bit much? Fuck, Elyria, you could get pregnant from the way Cal looks at you."

I scoffed.

She narrowed her eyes. "Yeah, exactly. Last night, he pretty much stripped you down and railed you hard over the table. So, I think I should be allowed to drink in a pretty form at my leisure." Rei laughed, twiddling her fingers at Alessia.

"I don't think she's your type," I added protectively.

"Who said I have a type?" Alessia sauntered over, leaning an arm on my shoulder and staring down Rei. "Gonna introduce yourself, or just keep molesting me with your eyes?"

"Alessia is my handmaid. Apparently, I get one of those. Alessia, this is Reihaneh Almont. Rei is a friend who I unwittingly put into the path of a killer assassin and now probably has a price on her head, so she's stuck with me."

There was a long second of silence.

"Yeah, that sums it up." Rei stretched both arms over the back of the settee. "I like to say we were just destined to be friends, but your way works, too."

"Sounds like you have an interesting story to tell," Alessia remarked.

"You have no idea," I quipped back.

"Well... I want to know what's going on with you and princey hot pants. Because three days ago, you were hurling fireballs at him, and today..." She rolled her eyes towards the door. "Let's just say what I saw on the bridge this afternoon wasn't lust."

I dropped into the overstuffed armchair, huffing a loud sigh.

Alessia grabbed my hands before I ran them through my hair. "I just styled that." She gave me a surprisingly strong yank, pulling me off of the seat. "And I don't need you getting all wrinkly before we head out to the southern veranda."

"Right, the queen," I groaned again and looked at Rei. "She saw something. Or rather, something happened, sort of." Fuck, the anxiety ratcheting up in my body was nearly unbearable. I needed something to do with my hands.

Her eyebrows rose in question.

"What do you mean by, *sort of?*" Alessia asked, slowly sitting and nibbling on a nail while I tried to find the coin I always kept tucked away for moments just like these.

"What do you mean by, *something?*" Rei added.

"Cal, he kneeled before me, and I think he was about to profess–" I paused, not willing to admit that he was about to profess love. Just saying it aloud felt like putting something I wasn't ready for in motion. "--something really important, but we were interrupted. When I looked up, she was watching us, The queen. She commanded us to come to her. And, fuck, Rei, what am I supposed to say to her? *Hi, I'm the girl your son has been putting the moves on for weeks, but he lied to me, and I don't know that I can ever trust him again.*" The words spilled out of me like verbal vomit.

112

Rei nodded. "I'd work on the delivery a bit."

Alessia leaned in. "Cal was kneeling?" Alessia asked. Shock made her mouth go slack. I nodded.

"That is really hot," Rei added, sitting up and taking my hands to calm me down.

"But now, I've got to go meet her. And, did you know that, apparently, these apartments are for the future *QUEEN*?!" I flung my arm wide, smacking it into a vase on a side table. The crystal shattered on the ground sending the spray of roses across the floor.

"Princess," Alessia corrected, already moving to pick up my mess. "Technically, you aren't a queen until after the coronation."

I stared at the ceiling and counted to ten. "That asshole put me in these rooms without even explaining what they were. And now, apparently, the entire palace is buzzing about who the mysterious girl is that he came home with."

Alessia snorted again. Rei and I looked at her.

"Sorry. It's just really funny to hear someone other than Kaeli call him an asshole."

"And that little display you gave on the bridge doesn't help anything either," Rei added.

"What do you mean display?"

Rei just laughed before bouncing up. "That man hasn't taken a hand off of you in two days." She slid her index finger down my arm for emphasis. "Don't think I didn't notice. He's got that "*she's mine*" stance down cold." Rei's voice dropped deep and growly before breaking into laughter. "Trust me. That man has fallen hard for you. And from where I'm standing, the only thing keeping the two of you apart is your own stubbornness."

Alessia leaned against the desk, taking everything in.

I opened my mouth to protest.

"Don't you argue with me, Elyria Solaris." Rei poked a finger on my shoulder with each syllable.

I smoldered, looking down at her hand. Was she really poking me?

"He lied to keep you safe, and it pissed you off. Because gods forbid anybody protect you—but you."

"It was more than that, and you know it."

"Get over it. You've already forgiven him. You just haven't admitted it to yourself."

I went to object. It was more complicated than she was making it sound. But, before I could so much as breathe, she pounced. "You know I'm right. You love him. He loves you. Stop fighting it. The sooner you do, the sooner you can eat you some of that sweet prince ass... and you'll be happier for it."

"Well, that's an image," Alessia said.

Rei winked at her. "Oh sweetness, you have no idea the images I could give you."

I shook my head, my pulse hammering behind my eyes. This was all too much.

There was a knock at the door. We all looked at it.

"I think I'm really going to like this posting," Alessia straightened her apron. "It's about time the palace had a little life to it."

Before she pulled on the handle, energy buzzed in my veins. I knew who was behind that knock. The hum was stronger than I remembered it feeling. Or maybe after all the time we spent together, I was just becoming more attuned to the feel of his power, making it easier to recognize. Worse, that restless need to fidget was instantly sated the moment I felt the current of energy drawing near.

Cal smiled at Alessia. "Good afternoon, Ms. Thorne." Did he know the names of the entire staff? How did he always manage to remember the names of everyone?

She bowed to him, and he stepped into the light of the room.

I sucked in a breath. Goddess slay me here and now. The grime of the road and the stress of our trip were gone from his features. His beard was shaved, making his firm jawline more pronounced than before. The usually unruly auburn hair was combed back from his face in a way that looked effortlessly refined. He wore a well cut white shirt with the sleeves partially rolled. Forearms shouldn't be sexy, but damn if I wasn't transfixed by them right now. The white of his shirt contrasted exquisitely with his tanned skin, making the golden hue look perfectly sun-kissed.

My lingering gaze dipped lower, and I shouldn't have done that. My toes curled, and my stomach clenched. A pair of linen pants hung expertly from his hips, hugging all the right places. He was casual but still somehow regal. I brought my hand to my lips to check that I wasn't drooling. Cal was always handsome, unfairly so most days, but this version of him was criminally beautiful. His dark eyes roamed over me, taking just as much time to linger as mine had.

Rei leaned in to me and, from the corner of her mouth, quipped, "I'm just saying..."

I slapped her shoulder. "Don't you have some guards to go harass or something?"

"No, this is far more entertaining."

I turned to Alessia. "Can you take Rei with you to figure out something for the ball for us to wear? She'll need a dress too."

Cal stepped forward. "Actually, I've given some ideas about that already. Your dress is being made as we speak."

"R-really?" I said, completely surprised. Since when did Cal think about dresses and ballgowns?

"You shouldn't look so shocked." Cal stepped forward, his hand slipping around my lower back and brushing the exposed skin there. Leaning down, his lips brushed my ear as he added, "I imagine you in... and out of all sorts of things." His eyes dipped, feeling as real as if he'd just cosseted his hands along my curves. I couldn't suppress the resulting shiver. The words *in and out* repeated on a loop in my stupid, sex-starved, forearm-obsessed mind.

Rei fanned her face. "Fuck, that was hot." She looked over at Alessia. "See what I mean? You could practically eat the sexual tension with a spoon; it's so thick."

"So, you've been talking about me?" Cal's lips tilted up into a playful smile.

"She was." I pointed to Rei. "I kinda forgot about you, to be honest."

"I guess I'll just have to try harder to be *memorable*." He lowered his lips to below my ear, barely brushing the skin and making me gasp.

Rei started walking toward the door. "I've gotta go get laid."

I pushed Cal out of the way. "No, you need a dress for the ball." I looked at Alessia, hoping for backup.

Rei looked at Alessia while saying, "Who says I can't do both?"

Cal raised his eyebrows at the handmaid.

She shrugged. "Come on, Rei, I'll take you to my favorite tailor. She makes all of Kaeli's dresses." The two girls walked out the door. Rei threw a very pointed look between me and Cal before stepping out the door. She dragged her hand over one of the guards. I heard her whisper something but could only make out the word "coming." He smiled a toothy grin at her, and then the girls and Rei's guards disappeared around the corner.

Cal looked at the remaining guards. "Give us a minute, please."

The man nodded and closed the door, leaving us alone.

Cal turned back to me, his eyes once again roving over my body. "You look positively edible," he said, the hand still on my lower back pulling me toward him. Cal leaned in to kiss me but met only my hand.

I sprang it between us before that confusing passion could spark again.

"When were you going to tell me that these apartments are supposed to be for your future *princess*?" I said coolly, keeping my voice level. Although I could already feel my ire rising.

"Oh," he said, stepping back and slipping his hand from my body. That delicious buzz I felt whenever we connected winked out.

"Oh?!" I let some venom into the end of the word. "Do you have any idea what people will be thinking about me now?"

"I don't really give a fuck what people think."

I scowled at him. He took a step forward, and I took an equal step back. Cal looked like this was all a game.

"What *I* think...," he continued.

Step. Step. We moved like it was a choreographed dance. His smile turned into a dark, almost feral grin.

"What I think is that I can't bear the idea of you being five feet from me?"

116

His hand reached out to my arm, and I slid back just out of his reach. Another, step-step.

"I think, the idea of you sleeping anywhere but in my arms makes my chest ache."

We stepped again, and I tripped over the settee, landing solidly atop a pile of dresses. Cal prowled on top of me, leaning in so that his chest brushed mine with each breath. "And I think that you having these rooms is the only logical thing to make that ache more bearable."

"Oh," I said. He smelled of salt and something citrusy... and smoke. Fuck, he smelled delicious. "You could have led with that." I tried saying it flatly, but I was sure I was doing a terrible job hiding how affected I was.

Cal dragged his nose up the inside of my neck, taking a deep inhale and groaning low enough that the rumble in his chest vibrated against my stomach. "The things I would do to you if we had more time."

My hands curled into the silk piled beneath me. I was melting. When Alessia returned to the room, she'd find nothing left to wait on but a puddle.

"As much as I would love to linger here" –He placed a far too gentle kiss to my jaw before standing up and extending a hand down to me– "I wouldn't want to sully all these pretty dresses." With a wink, he added, "Yet."

Infuriating. Sexy haired. Muscley. Ass.

Ignoring the way my core throbbed, I batted his hand away and pushed up. "Don't sound so sure of yourself." Ripping open the door, six guardsmen all stood at attention. "Six, Cal? A security detail of SIX."

I pushed uselessly at the impenetrable line of guards.

"You're right, Sunshine. There should be more." Cal nodded at the men, and they moved aside.

I growled low enough to make my dragon blood proud. Teal chiffon from my skirt flowed around my legs with every annoyed stomp.

Cal snagged my shoulder and pulled me into him. "Need I remind you." His voice was dangerously low. "I was stabbed in the heart on that balcony over there." He pointed back toward his room. "And there is literally nothing I wouldn't do to keep you safe."

"Fine," I said reluctantly. "But I still hate you."

"No, you don't." He held his arm out to me, and with a scowl I wrapped my own around it.

No, I didn't.

"You want me to step up and act like a king, but you seemed to think it was appropriate to withhold vital information before I sailed to the other godsdamn side of Venterra," I seethed. The bomb of my mother's words still hung in the air around us.

"*I'm surprised Dukant never told you about the draken.*"

Where did she get off keeping this kind of information from me? This whole time, she'd known about Elyria, the girl whose heart I could sense beating in time with my own. It was bad enough that every word has been dripping in judgment since I introduced her to Elle. But to have purposely kept us apart— it was almost unforgivable. How long had I searched for a sense of completion? How many years did I spend drowning that void with every vice I could find? Too long.

"I provided you with everything you needed." My mother waved her hand airily like my anger wasn't the slightest concern to her.

"How exactly are you defining 'need'?" I was going to be *king*. It was infuriating. Guilt had me flicking my eyes over to Elyria. This was exactly what I'd done to her. No wonder she didn't trust me.

I thought fate had put me on the path to Laluna. Remembering the day my mother handed me the pamphlet for Troupe Solaire, I laced my fingers through Elle's. In the dark days following my father's death, the only thing that kept me going was the hope that there was someone out there whose power would save this kingdom. But, somehow, during all of our preparations, Mother failed to mention that she personally knew Dukant Solaris and precisely where the

"Wait." Elyria pushed her lunch plate away. Despite not eating this morning, she'd barely touched the meal piled high before her. "I'm sorry, Your Majes-"

"Axia, or Eloaxia," my mother clipped. There was absolutely no kindness in her tone, proving that when my father died, he took whatever softness she'd had with him. "I think the moment my son decided for himself to give you a place in this palace, we moved past formalities." She was still looking at Elyria, but I knew who her cutting expression was actually for.

"I'm sorry, Axia," Elyria corrected. There was a timidness to her voice I'd never heard before. Godsdamn my mother for making Elyria shrink. She deserved better than to have her fiery spirit smothered.

For the fifth time this meal, I stared at the empty seat beside the queen, trying to ignore the pang of sorrow that came with it. He would have loved Elyria and the endless way she pushed me. My father would have wrapped his long arms around her and welcomed the girl I loved as a daughter.

Fuck, I missed him. I didn't realize how hard it would be to come home and see his ghost lingering in the emptiness he'd left behind. He was there in the field beyond the balcony, and in the hand I didn't feel clapping my back on our return. I closed my eyes, pushing the grief and guilt back into its cage, focusing instead on Elyria's hand in mine.

"I don't understand," she continued. I could hear Elyria trying to steel herself, her tone becoming stronger. I squeezed her hand in encouragement. This meal was simply another performance, albeit before the world's most judgmental audience, but Elle had spent her entire life under the scrutinizing eyes of Venterra. She could handle my mother. "How did you know my father? When we performed at the jubilee, the closest we came to the royal family was the box at the theater. We never even visited the palace."

My mother's cheek twitched with a memory, one I was sure she'd never share with us. "I had the pleasure of meeting your father once or twice. Dukant Solaris is the kind of man that is impossible to forget. I fully expected him to return with you. He knows the dangers in Venterra better than most. I'm surprised he let you go alone, especially after learning about The Shade."

"She isn't alone," I bit back, turning my attention fully on Elyria. "She has me." Her free hand, the one that wasn't tightening on mine, wrapped defensively around her middle. The mere mention of Duke's death was making the blood drain from her face.

"We don't need to discuss this now," I said protectively. Saving Elle from having to relive this pain was an easy choice to make. "Mother, a lot has happened in the past few weeks. You can interrogate me tomorrow."

"It's fine, Cal. Just tell her." Elyria's voice was quiet. It made my heart ache.

"You're sure?"

"Whether you tell her now or later, it won't change what happened."

Mother sat back, setting down her wine and gripping the arms of the chair in preparation for what was obviously bad news.

"Malvat tracked us to Laluna."

"Were you attacked?" Her fingers traced the grooves carved into the end of each arm. After losing Father, I knew she was worried about me traveling, but she rarely showed concern outwardly. Even this small tell was atypical of her, especially with Elyria watching.

"A few times," I said, clearing my throat. "But, I wasn't his target. The assassination attempt aimed at Elyria ended up killing Duke instead."

Elle flinched, her gaze traveling to the tree beyond the balcony. I hated that anything I said made her react like that. I would make it up to her. For every frown, I would elicit twice as many smiles.

"I'm so very sorry to hear that." For the first time since we'd entered this terrace, my mother's eyes softened, finally resembling the woman who'd raised me and not the cold warrior grief had shaped her into. "Venterra is worse for the loss."

"Thank you," Elyria whispered. I needed to move the discussion away from her father. Then tomorrow, my mother and I were going to have a long conversation about all the things she's been withholding.

"Malvat sent the Fasmas after us, courtesy of The Shade." I loathed that it was *our* top assassins that came for her, but not as much as I hated that it was my own stupidity that allowed her to be placed in danger to begin with. I should have been with her that night, not moping at the docks. Xoc was right. I should have been honest with her from the beginning. I'd give anything to take back that decision.

"Elyria took down Andros and nearly took out Andromeda as well."

The queen's eyebrows rose in surprise, flicking her discerning gaze back on Elyria. "Formidable opponents, especially if they were under the influence of The Shade."

"Elyria is very skilled, Mother. Her training might even rival your own."

"That is... useful," she said, looking Elyria up and down again. "Of course, Dukant would've kno-"

The glass doors to the terrace flung open, interrupting whatever she was about to disclose.

"CAL!"

Kaeliana jumped enthusiastically in the doorway. Kaeli was only ten years my junior, but you'd never know it from the youthful way she approached life. She was wearing black trousers with a matching lace top. I glanced at my mother to see her frowning. She was generally displeased with everything Kaeli did, which only endeared her to me more. Never mind the fact that my mother was ten times wilder when she was young, and that my sister had inherited more than her proficiency for growing unique flowers.

Kaeliana sprinted towards me. I managed to stand up just as she flung herself into the air, knocking me back a step.

"I ran into Xoc earlier," she said breathlessly,

"Xoc came to see you?"

She acted like she didn't hear me and kept rambling on, "I just knew the first place you'd come would be-" Kaeli's eyes locked on Elyria, interrupting herself. "My gods, is this her?"

Immediately forgetting about me, Kaeli rushed over to Elyria. Without hesitation, my sister wrapped her arms around Elle in an awkward half-standing embrace. Which, from the look on Elyria's face, was completely unexpected.

"Hello," rasped Elyria as she struggled to fully get to her feet with my sister's arms wrapped around her. "You must be the princess."

The absurdity of this entire scene, in contrast to the frigidity my mother was giving off, drove a hearty laugh from the center of my chest. Gods, I'd missed her unique brand of chaos.

"The palace is positively buzzing." Stepping back in appraisal, Kaeli said, "You're gorgeous." A blush crept up Elyria's neck. My sister looked back at me, smiling broadly. "You don't deserve her."

"Well, you've got that right."

Elyria brushed down her skirt, saying, "Alessia had lots of good things to say about you, er..." She stumbled over her words, adding an awkward, "Your Highness."

"Oh, Elyria, please call me Kaeli. Everyone does. Les is just about my favorite person in all of Venterra. I wanted to raid the kitchens earlier and wondered where she got to. I'm guessing Mattias put her with you. He's always droning on about how she enables my bad ideas."

"It wouldn't be a problem if you didn't have them in the first place," Mother responded cooly.

Kaeli walked over and plucked some grapes from an overfilled plate. She threw one high in the air, catching it in her mouth. Mother scoffed in displeasure.

"If Cal's allowed to traverse two whole continents, then I should be allowed to spend a few hours running around the city," Kaeli said, pointing at me and then my mother. "Who knows, maybe I'll come home with some dashing lad and put him up in my *adjoining apartments* too."

I could feel Elyria bristling next to me sending a plume of heat shimmering in my direction. She was definitely still upset about that.

"Nothing gets by you, baby sister." I tried distracting myself by toying with the food still on my plate.

My sister slid into the chair across from me, throwing her slippered feet on the table and knocking over a salt dish in the process.

Mother slapped her soles, swatting at her like she was a child. "Seriously, Kaeliana. Have you lost all common sense? In front of a guest, no less."

Kae dropped another grape into her mouth, shoving them into her cheeks like a squirrel and batting her eyes innocently. "So, Elyria, what has my brother shown you of Innesvale?" Kaeli asked around a mouth full of grapes. Swallowing hard, she added, "Did he give you a tour of the palace yet? Or the grottos?"

"I saw the gardens. They're very beautiful, and I can tell they're a work of love."

"Thank you," Mother and Kaeliana said in unison, to which my sister looked absolutely horrified.

"We took back hallways up to our quarters, so I haven't really seen much besides white marble corridors."

"What a travesty." Kaeli tsked at me, "Seriously, big brother, you bring this magnificent creature to the most beautiful place in the world, and all you show her is some dusty corridor?"

I shrugged. "We spent weeks on the road. Mother had already sent one of her minions to collect us; all we wanted was to get cleaned up. There wasn't time for anything else."

Kaeli ignored me. "Elyria, I'll show you around."

"I'd like that."

"We can start in the kitchens and have Mags sneak us some pastries for our walk. They've already started cooking for tomorrow. There's bound to be something good down there."

Elyria looked at the giant spread of food on the table, eyes going wide at the idea of being given more to eat.

Mother gave Kaeli a stern look, ready to reprimand her... again.

I held up my hand to her. "I'm showing her the palace." To which she pursed her lips. Five hundred years old, and my sister still pouted like a toddler.

"But, you can come along... for some of it," I added. "Which brings me to my next point. Kaeliana, I don't want you sneaking out of the palace anymore. It's not safe."

"Not you, too." She rolled her eyes at me. "I know all about your nightly journeys into the city to play in the gambling dens."

I sighed. I knew she wouldn't take this well.

"Kae, The Shade..." I pinched the bridge of my nose, feeling a headache beginning to pulse in my temples. "Malvat has increased his attacks. He's coming for me specifically, and he knows I care for you. You're a natural target."

Kalieana made a sound of disgust.

"Your brother's right. You need to be—"

"Careful," I said, finishing my mother's sentence before any more animosity formed between them. "When was the last time you trained? I could get Xoc to—"

"Annnnnd, that's my cue." Kaeliana jumped up. "I'd rather get an acid enema than endure the two of you giving me a lecture in both ears at the same time. So..." She held out a hand to Elyria. "Want to go do something that's actually fun?"

Elyria looked uncomfortably around the room. Kaeliana didn't wait for an answer. She tugged on Elle's arm, pulling her from the chair.

"Kaeli." Elyria anchored her foot against Kaeliana's pull, causing her to rubberband backwards. "Cal is trying to protect you. I know because he's always trying to protect everyone." Something warm pulsed in my chest. "But in this case, the boogeyman *is* real. Have you ever seen The Shade in person? It's terrifying, and those infected are nearly impossible to kill."

"And for whatever reason, Malvat's out to hurt me by striking at my weak points, the people I love." I glanced for a second at Elyria. It was quick, but I knew that my mother had picked up on it. I suppose it didn't matter, though, not after she saw the declarations I was making in the garden. "So for once, Kae, just do what you're told and stay in the palace."

Kaeli opened her mouth to complain, but I cut her off, "And don't go anywhere without a guard." She rolled her eyes at me.

"What I don't understand is why. Mal was a friend. Why would he suddenly target our kingdom?" she asked.

"Maybe because we're closest to the Floating Lands. Or, maybe, he's angry that the first assassination attempt failed, and now he's punishing me for not dying that night."

Mother visibly flinched.

"He knows I care for this kingdom, and this is as good as driving another blade into my chest."

The terrace had a warm breeze, but there was an icy chill surrounding our table. I stood, scooping up Elyria's arm in the process. "Thank you for lunch, Mother. I'm happy to be home. As Kaeliana so wonderfully pointed out, I have a palace to show off." With a bitter edge to my tone, I added, "Unless you have some more potentially life-altering information to share?"

She looked away, taking a sip of wine and refusing to address my comment.

"Heh." Elyria tilted her chin up in smug satisfaction. "It's good to see miscommunication runs in the family."

K aeliana crashed between us with an arm around each shoulder. "You said I could come along."

"Where should we go first?" I asked.

"Show her the ocean and the grottos. It's so beautiful," Kaeli said, then lowered her voice to whisper into my ear, "and romantic."

Elyria pushed out of our hold, stretching her arms and doing a small spin. "I'm sure it's beautiful, but let's do something fun. After whatever that was..." She waved at the glass doors to the balcony. "I think we're all sorely in need of some."

"I know all kinds of fun things we could get up to." I raised my eyebrows at her.

"Not that."

Faster than I had expected, her hand flew out, almost managing to slap me in the face before I caught it. Almost, but the heat in her eyes when I did was worth it.

"I like you." Kaeli hooked her arm in Elle's, spinning her away from me. "Cal, you can't have her anymore. She's mine now."

Elyria flashed me a mischievous grin. "Let's go to the armory."

"Ooo," Kae said, "Unexpected."

I shook my head but couldn't keep my smile down. "Beautiful marble palace, cascading waterfalls, endless gardens... and you want to see the armory."

"Hells yes I do. I've never been able to get access to anywhere as cool as a royal armory before."

I drew the knuckle of a fist slowly over my lower lip in contemplation. "Fine but every weapon you touch, you have to fight me with."

"Even better. I've been looking for an opportunity to kick your ass all day."

"How about you, baby sis? Still want to come?"

"I get to see a woman kick your ass, and you have to ask?" Kaeli draped an arm around Elyria's shoulders.

"First," I said, holding up a finger. "She's not going to kick my ass."

Elyria scoffed. "Okay."

"Sure, Elyria's deadly with knives and can more than decently fight. But there are a whole lot of things in that armory I'm more than proficient with."

"I guess we'll see," Elyria said, winking at Kaeli.

"What's second?" My sister asked.

"Second, introducing the two of you was a terrible idea." I groaned, already picturing a lifetime of them ganging up on me.

We walked out of the main palace and across a courtyard to a large windowless building. Its large, heavy bronze doors were guarded by two men. The dark patina of the metal added a fitting twist of danger to the usually bright Innesvalen crest.

The guards snapped to attention, hands fanning their chest in salute.

"Good afternoon, gentlemen. At ease." The men relaxed their stance.

Elyria glanced in my direction, still not used to seeing me command anyone. If the glimmer in her expression was anything, I think she liked it. I filed that information away for later.

A stick-like guard unlocked the Armory doors, which swung inward on squealing hinges. Elyria turned to him. "If you hear crying, don't be alarmed. I'm about to beat down more than the prince's pride."

Kaeliana snorted.

"See, I was going to take it easy on you, but now..."

"But now you've realized it's hopeless?" she said in an infuriatingly mocking tone.

"You better run, Sunshine," I growled.

Elyria squealed and took off, disappearing down the corridor.

I was about to give chase, but I caught Kaeli's expression. "What?"

"Nothing," she said behind a big toothy grin. "Just, damn. You've really fallen for this girl, haven't you?"

"Is it that obvious?"

"Oh yeah. You might as well just say 'I love you' with every breath you take. It'd be less work than all this absurd flirtation you're doing."

We started walking down the corridor, allowing Elyria a more than decent head start. "Plus, you put her in *the* apartments. You basically declared to the entire palace that you intend to marry the girl."

"They're the safest place I could think of to put her."

Kaeli raised a disbelieving eyebrow at me. Yeah, I wouldn't believe me either.

"You don't get it Kae. Elyria, she..." How could I explain something so massive? "She ignited something within me I didn't think I was capable of feeling. It's like my heart has always been connected to hers. As if she held a part of me that had been locked away, and now that I've found her, I'm whole."

"Wow."

"I know. I don't even recognize the words coming from my mouth right now." I scrubbed a hand over my face.

"No, I was just thinking, you sound like Father and all that sappy shit he'd always say about Mother."

"Shut up." I shoved her into the wall. But that was probably the nicest thing she'd ever said to me. I flashed her a smile and began running down the hall in search of my girl.

The armory was separated into categories based on the type of armament. I bypassed all of them and made straight for the last door. Above it hung two crossed sabers, indicating this was the chamber for blades.

Cautiously, I slid into the room. I wouldn't put it past Elyria to pull a sneak attack from the shadows. Rows of polished sword hilts glittered in the light. At the far end of the room, Elyria was bent over an open drawer, like a pirate gazing into a treasure chest. Her eyes sparkled with delight as she gazed at the gold and silver daggers lying nestled in their velvet beds. Reverently, she dragged a finger over them.

"Ah ah ah... no touching," I said mockingly.

Elyria jumped, her surprise instantly morphing into annoyance.

"These are gorgeous, more works of art than weapons. The poor things just sit here, tucked into a forgotten drawer." She shook her head. "It's a crime."

She leaned in until her rose-petal lips almost brushed the polished steel. In a voice more appropriate for speaking to an infant than to weapons of death, she cooed, "Are you lonely, baby? Do you need someone to come and play with you?"

"You're talking to a bunch of daggers."

Elle shrugged. "Just because something is sharp around the edges doesn't make it less worthy of love."

She had no idea. This girl had softened every one of my edges and turned me into something downright squishy.

"Pick one."

"Seriously? Cal, some of these knives must be priceless."

"You're right, and they aren't being appreciated in a drawer."

"Wait, can you say that bit about being right again?" She bit down on her lip, knowing exactly what that tone did to me. The second we hit that training floor, I was going to spank that sass right out of her.

"Pick one, breathe new life into it. Think of it as a gift to replace the knife you lost on the steps when it went hurtling past my face."

She pulled open another drawer and sucked in a deep breath.

A pair of wide silver blades lay amid black velvet.

"Those are called Butterfly Swords," I said.

Her golden eyes glittered, and a corresponding wave of heat rolled off of her, bringing with it her exotic smokey scent. It was utterly distracting.

"They were a gift from the Oers, to celebrate the anniversary of the new Covenant. They've been in here for centuries."

"They look too short to be a sword."

"It's because of the shape. It has a sword blade, but shorter. More lethal and fluid than your typical dagger." Each highly polished blade showed a perfect reflection of Elyria's awestruck expression. She ran a finger down a small ridge beveled into the center. Unlike most daggers and knives, these were thin but wide.

She picked up the sword, holding it like it was a baby bird. Seeing her touching a weapon with such love and care was so godsdamn sexy. I tried and then consequently failed to take my eyes off the loving strokes of her fingers.

Forcing focus to come back to my voice, I continued, "When used together, the swords create the look of a butterfly dancing in the air. Not unlike you, they form a beautiful but deadly display, cutting down foes with lethal delicacy."

Her deft fingers skated along the leather-wrapped handle. The truly breathtaking part of the weapon were the guards. A silver dragon looped over the handle, arcing into a knuckle bow. It formed the unmistakable silhouette of a charging dragon. The outer edge of scales were sharpened, forming an extra serrated blade.

Elyria bit down on her lip, claws slipping from her fingertips. She ran a taloned nail over the ridges of each dragon scale. A silver tinkling sound echoed in the room, setting my heart thumping.

They were perfect for her. Twin blades, each so thin they could share a single scabbard. In the hands of someone of her frame and skill set, they would be deadly. Not to mention how damn alluring she would be spinning them. About a dozen inappropriate scenarios flashed through my mind.

I glanced at the door. Kaeli hadn't found us yet. She wouldn't have known that Elyria would go straight for the knives, not like I did. She'd have to search each wing of the armory before finding her way here. How much time did I have before she flounced her way into the room? I gritted my teeth. Not long enough.

Elyria looked at the swords with such longing. She smiled bashfully at me, asking without words. It was almost laughable. I could deny her nothing and wanted to give her everything. If I was being honest, everything I had was already hers. She just hadn't realized it, yet.

"Take them."

"No. Cal, these..." She gestured down, her eyes drifting back to the shine of each gorgeous blade. She chewed on her lip. I could practically taste her lust. There was a flash in her eyes, like the one she had given me in those falls. The memory warmed my blood, calling my fire to the surface.

"There's no way I could ever take them," she continued.

Thinking of a brilliant idea, I said, "Fine, fight me for them. If you win, you can have them both." I slipped my hands into my pockets, hiding the slight tremor of anticipation.

"You can't beat me." She puffed up her chest and looked at me in disbelief. "Duke had me playing with knives before I could walk."

"Then you have no reason to turn down my offer. Of course, you've never really seen me fight besides that day in the woods."

"What day in the woods?" Kae said as she walked into the room.

Not taking her eyes off the swords, Elyria replied, "We were attacked by bandits. Cal became feral. You should have seen him, he-" Her eyes widened in understanding. "OHHH. That's why your hands were bloody. You used claws to tear into them, didn't you?"

I summoned claws to my fingertips and slowly ran them down the slope of her neck. "Afraid?"

"Of you? Never." Heat radiated from her in floral-scented waves. Yeah, that definitely wasn't fear she was giving off. A low growl rumbled in my chest, remembering the way she'd looked standing at the edge of the glade seconds after killing a man. "Maybe you should be."

She waved lazily in the air, dismissing my comment.

"What's to stop you from throwing the fight? We both know you're not above cheating."

I scoffed. "I have honor."

"Sure you do," laughed Kaeliana.

I pushed open the doors that led to the adjacent practice ring. "Bring those. I'll use a set from in here."

She gingerly picked up the blades. I could almost feel her shiver of excitement, could hear it in the way she exhaled.

I kicked off my boots and stepped onto the mat. "If you're really worried about my integrity." I glanced a side eye at her. "Then how about we make this match have something in it for me, an incentive to win?"

"And what exactly do you mean by that?"

She was rightfully skeptical. I walked directly to her and ran my index finger inside the collar of her shirt, smoothing the soft silk between my fingers and relishing the caress of her skin as her breathing deepened. "For every strike that lands, I get to remove an article of clothing."

Her eyes narrowed. Gently she pried my fingers from her shirt. "So, that goes both ways?"

"Fair is fair."

"And when I win, I still get the swords."

I smiled victoriously. Turning on my heel, I approached the far wall where practice blades hung, waiting for use. I took a set of butterfly swords down and spun the grips in my hands, feeling their perfect weight and balance.

Elyria's eyes widened, watching me as I spun each sword expertly and took up a fighting stance. I gave a little shrug. She was definitely underestimating my abilities.

"Come on, Golden Dragon," I said. "Let's see if your body can keep up with that mouth you keep running."

She looked down at my boots and toed off her slippers, laying them neatly next to mine. Kaeli climbed on a stack of practice mats, letting her legs swing beneath her.

Elyria picked up her blades, cradling them in her arms like she was holding an infant. As she walked toward me, my eyes locked onto the strip of ivory skin that peaked out at her waist.

"I'm going to enjoy slicing that gorgeous fabric off your body."

Elyria looked over her shoulder at Kaeli. "I don't know if you want to stay for this— It probably won't be long before your brother is wearing nothing but that arrogance of his."

I smirked. Kaeli just laughed.

Elyria went through some stances and practice movements, swinging and rotating each blade independently, then testing their movements together in tandem.

"These—Are—Fucking—Smooth," she said, each word punctuated with a slow and purposeful movement. Elyria gracefully slid across the floor, the swords nothing more than an extension of her body. Streaks of metallic light curled around her lithe form with each spin. It was mesmerizing to watch. "It's like my dagger, but fuck... so much better." She did a quick turn and jab. Her smile was pure joy.

With a flick of her wrist, one of the blades flew high into the air. The revolution was fast, looking more like an exploding star than a sword. On the release, Elyria twisted, snatching the shining steel from the air with the back of her hand.

Kaeli whistled and clapped.

A second rotation had Elyria sliding back into a readied fighting stance. As if she was executing a perfectly choreographed routine and not improvising with a new weapon. For the first time this evening, I wondered if the one underestimating skills had actually been me.

"Let's do this." She clanged the blades together. The metal sang with a clear tone that resonated in the small space. "I can't wait to look down at your face after I lay your stripped ass flat on the ground."

"Sunshine, I'll lay on the ground for you, and we don't need to fight to get me out of these clothes. All you have to do is ask nicely," I cooed, knowing it would piss her off.

"KICK HIS ASS!" Cheered Kaeli from the back of the room.

Elyria shifted her fighting stance, stepping back and coiling the front blade to mask her arm.

"First, scales. I'm not sparring with real blades without them." My voice was deep with authority, and I gave her a look that left no room to argue.

"Oh, Cal, you won't land a blow," she said, standing up.

I shook my head. Letting my own scales free. Her eyes followed them. They cascaded in a shower of gold down my arms. I paused. Then coated my legs as well. Knowing Elyria, she wouldn't hesitate to strike a low blow.

Elyria's eyes shimmered. I knew she felt the energy coming from me. The shift was a magnetic beacon calling to the draconic power coursing through her. I smiled in smug satisfaction. I'd been fighting that pull for weeks now. It was about time that she knew the agony of restraint.

"Scales. Now."

Elyria sighed, "Fine."

She rolled her neck. Brilliant scales slid over her shoulders, smoothing over the curve of her breasts before peeking out under her top and disappearing beneath the band of her shorts. Shimmering light highlighted the gold and black flecks.

Fuck me. She was positively resplendent. I hadn't thought this through. Had I ever sparred with a hard-on before? Of course, I'm wearing linen pants that provide zero compression.

Adjusting my waistband and thinking of every not-arousing thing I could, I added, "Arms and legs too. I'm not risking anything."

She rolled her eyes at me, and with a sigh, scales extended down to her fingertips. My heart rate sped up, and I glanced over at Kaeli. It was probably a good thing she was here. Elyria was so fucking sexy right now that my sister's presence was the only thing keeping me from mounting her to the padded walls and devouring her whole.

"Happy?" she drawled, but her face was bright with anticipation.

"You have no idea." I stepped back into a holding stance. I would let her make the first strike. Then, once the opportunity presented itself, I was going to pin her to the ground and watch her squirm.

Elyria did a slow prowling walk to me, arms relaxed at her sides.

Licking my lips, I narrowed my gaze on the ties at her hips. I'd start there. That skirt was going to be the first thing to go.

This was going to be fun.

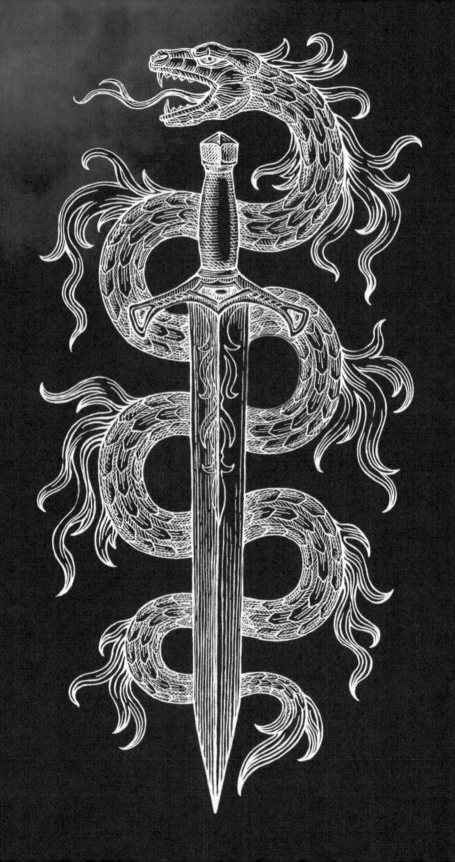

"**G**round yourself, feel the elasticity of the earth, and let it guide you. Read your opponent, Ellie. Make them second guess their instincts." It was like I could hear Duke's ghost whispering in my ears.

My sweet prince was a slave to his instincts. I pulled my right hand and sword into my hip, preparing to spin to the left for an upper attack.

Cal's lips turned up into a smile. He actually thought he knew how I planned to move. How adorable.

Rather than thrust or swing with the sword ready at my hip, I rolled the opposite blade. Catching in the handguard, the sword flipped back along the length of my arm. I kicked my elbow forward, bringing it down in a diagonal slash. It drove my body into his, close enough that he couldn't maneuver around me and was forced to engage.

His fiery eyes went wide. He hopped backwards, avoiding my slashing hand, but was unprepared for the spin and low thrust of my right arm. Cal threw up a hasty block, and the blades slid off of each other with a tingling sound that rang more like chimes than weapons of death.

Demon's below, this was fun. Cal countered, but I dropped and swung in a low swirling motion, straight at knee level. The tip of my blade sliced into his billowing pant leg. A scrap of linen fluttered to the ground, revealing shiny scales. Bastard knew I would strike low and had extended the scales all the way to his ankles.

I popped back up, eye to eye with Cal's thoroughly shocked expression.

"Point to me." I grinned wildly and took a step back to appraise the prize I'd just won. Eying him up and down, I said, "What should I claim first?"

Behind me, the light sounds of Kaeliana's laughter filled the room.

The cavalier smile was gone, replaced by grinding teeth and flaring nostrils. He really thought he was going to win this fight?

I sauntered up to him, tucking my swords under one arm. "Hope you're wearing undergarments." I pulled on the tie of his waistband.

"Tell me again where you learned to fight like this?"

"Duke, mostly, and Joseph." I released the cord, and the linen slipped free of his hips. I glanced down at the undershorts and firm thighs I'd just revealed. Gods, I wasn't going to make it through this fight. I couldn't help myself. Reaching forward, I raked my nails up the curve of muscle. "You know, I quite like this game."

"We're not nearly done yet." Cal kicked the pants to the wall. "Duke did his job, but I've worked daily at this for the past five hundred years. That pretty little blouse is mine, Sunshine."

"Yeah, well, I trained *twice* a day. Physical combat in the mornings before breakfast—" I took a step back and assumed a defensive position. Now that I'd nicked his pride, Cal wouldn't hold back. "—And weapons in the evenings before showtime."

"Don't you think it was strange that Duke trained you so aggressively?" Cal asked between volleys. "I understand wanting your daughter to be able to protect herself, but it feels unnecessary when you can literally burn anyone who gets too close."

I'd never really questioned it before. How many times had I heard him say, "*When your fire fails you, Ellie, what will you do then?*"

"He didn't want me to be vulnerable if I ever tapped the bottom of my magic. Or if I was ever attacked somewhere it would be unwise to use fire."

"Like in the middle of an ancient library?"

I shot him a scowl. "That was an accident."

His leg flew out in a roundhouse, one arm dropping as he turned.

"You're lucky reports out of Suman don't point at our party. Yet."

Spinning an arm above him, his blade swung out at me faster and harder than before. This was what I was waiting for; him unleashed and pouncing.

I slid on a diagonal into the space he'd created. That sorry fool left a wide-open hole in his defenses. My swords moved as one. A smooth slashing motion both deflected his counterattack and drove him backwards.

Kaeli whooped with excitement.

But I'd missed–and he was smiling. The realization slammed into me. I had let him bait me right into a trap. *Fuck.*

Cal didn't give me time to recover. He positioned one sword horizontally and swung the remaining blade in a downward arc. Tricky, but not impossible to defend against. If I had been smarter, then I wouldn't have had to in the first place.

I windmilled my arms, the serrated edges of the guards ringing out as they deflected each of his attacks.

"You didn't think it would be that easy, did you?" I panted. Why wasn't he out of breath, too?

"Nothing about you has ever been easy, Sunshine."

Curling the end of the handguard, I hooked his sword. Heat flashed around us in surprise. I was a heartbeat away from disarming him, and he knew it. Pity this fight would be over so quickly. I was actually enjoying myself.

A goading remark was perched on my lips when Cal stepped forward, forcing my own blade against my chest—effectively rendering my trick useless. Rather than admit defeat, I swung low. His golden arm blocked, and the blade harmlessly slid over the surface of his forearm.

"That shouldn't count," he said indignantly. "I struck your chest before you clipped my arm."

"With my own blade."

"I don't see how that matters." He prowled towards me, backing me all the way against the wall.

Cal's eyes dipped to my hips.

I rolled my eyes. "Make it good because it's your last."

His thumbs caressed my ribs, raising the hem of my shirt until they were brushing the under-swell of my breast. Cold metal slid against my exposed stomach.

"Don't move, beautiful."

My heart raced faster the longer he lingered. The sword slipped beneath the tie at my waist, and with a quick snick the silk fluttered to the ground.

"It's easier to maneuver without the skirts anyway," I said, raising my chin defiantly and pushing away from the wall.

"Keep telling yourself that, Sunshine. There's no part of you I won't enjoy unwrapping."

"Les is going to kill you for cutting that beautiful set," Kaeli remarked. She was kicking her feet against the mats like this was the best day of her life. It was actually really adorable.

"Well, Miss Thorne better get used to shredded clothing because I've never been a patient man."

"You... What?" I said, bringing my attention back to Cal. Goddess slay me. The idea of him tearing my clothes off made muscles I didn't even know I had clench, but if he really thought that was happening, then—

I moved to take up my stance, but before I could even raise my arms, Cal was hurtling toward me.

"Cheating!" I shouted in startled surprise. I kicked one foot against his chest and used it to propel myself into a backflip. I dropped to the ground gracefully, with one leg extended behind me like a cat.

Kaeli cheered at the unexpected acrobatics. Cal, on the other hand, was ready for it, and while I was flipping, he was moving forward into position. The sound of steel on scales rang out, and the vibration radiated across my hip just as my feet touched the ground.

Fuck.

Tongue pushed into the side of his cheek, Cal was already assessing what he'd won.

"Do you ever fight fair?"

"Not when it suits me." He moved in and examined the tattered fabric at my hip. Heat bloomed over my chest. His fingers slipped into the folds of my shorts, grabbing my now very exposed upper thigh.

Cal leaned close, his lips brushing the outer shell of my ear. "Now, what was that you were saying earlier about undergarments?" His thumb traced the lace trim of my underwear. Shivers rippled out from his touch.

"I wonder," he purred. "I really can't think of anything sexier than you topless, with swords in your hands. But that might be... distracting." Cal's hand slid further into the cut. Reaching around to grip the back of my thigh, he pulled my hips to meet his. A soft moan escaped me as I fought the temptation to rub against him like a cat.

Kaeliana, faked clearing her throat.

Cal turned his head to look at her, a purely demonic smile curling his lips. "Nobody said you had to stay."

Kaeli crossed her legs and arms. "I was promised ass *kicking*, not ass fondling."

"True." He rocked my hips so that I rubbed against the erection he wasn't even trying to hide. His eyes dropped to my torn shorts, and he nipped at my lower lip. "Do you yield, or should we keep fighting?"

My jaw dropped. Like I would ever fucking yield.

"I did promise her I'd kick your ass." I pushed hard against his chest. Of course, Cal was solid and barely moved. Which was both infuriating and did nothing to assuage my raging libido.

"Not before I get my prize." His sword slid up my thigh, slowly cutting away the shorts. In a whisper of fabric, they fell to the ground, leaving me in only underwear and a blouse. I looked down at the pool of sea-green silk. Another loss, and I would be showing Kaeli a whole lot more of me.

"Here, let me," Cal said, bending low. He dropped to one knee. His hands slid along my legs, trailing with it a coursing river of energy. He placed a single kiss to my inner thigh before standing and handing me what was left of my shorts.

I would have cursed at him if I wasn't so busy trying to catch my breath.

"Shall we continue? I think I'm really going to enjoy removing the next layer."

Swallowing my desire, I said, "See, I thought I'd just cut your shirt off myself. I don't know that I need help. " I stepped back, lifting my swords.

Cal lazily swung the knives. He wasn't even trying. That would be his last mistake.

I stepped forward with an overhead chop to where his neck and shoulder joined. It was a blow that could sever an arm. Cal easily deflected my strike and countered by scissoring his blades.

My block exposed my side, allowing Cal to go for the kill shot. Not fucking likely. I turned into him, flipping my blade backwards and dragging it across his chest.

"That's two," I said, elated by the shock that flooded his smug expression. He really thought he had me. He was close enough I could smell his salt and citrus scent, made sweeter by the frustration that was radiating from him.

I coiled my fingers around the hem of his white linen shirt and used my sword to pop the buttons. One by one, they fell away, exposing the rolling muscles of his torso.

He shrugged off the shirt and tossed it on top of the growing pile of linen and silk.

Biting down on my lip, I took in the gorgeous, armored skin. I longed to run my hands over each golden scale. Later. *Damn it, bad Elyria, we're still angry. Stop thinking about... licking things.*

"Stop looking at me like that, Sunshine. Or my next move will be pinning you to the mat and making you forget all about finishing this fight."

I huffed, either in disbelief or pent-up desire it could have been both.

"You'd have to catch me first." I gave the swords a lazy spin at my hip in a mockery of the way he'd done earlier. The room was definitely getting hotter, or maybe the air was getting thinner. The look he was giving me now made me feel like I was about to combust.

"Challenge accepted." Cal spiraled down on me.

I leapt to the side, thrusting both swords on an upward diagonal. Cal easily blocked me and the next several that followed.

I needed to do something unexpected.

A slight tremor shifted Cal's foot. He was transferring his weight, a tell that he was about to advance. I knew exactly how to play this.

As expected, he lunged towards me. I dipped, using my momentum to rotate my body across his back. The new transfer of weight threw him off center, tipping him forward. With one last rotation of my hips, Cal landed flat on his back.

"Ow, that hurt," he wheezed. I kneeled over him with my joined blades at his throat. They really did look like a butterfly.

Kaeli was cackling uncontrollably. I flicked my eyes up at her in amusement. I'd been waiting this whole fight to be able to do that. She fell over the edge and onto the ground.

"Wait, did you mean to say that I'd be pinning you to the mat? I think this means I win. If I take your shorts, then you don't really have anything else to give me."

"Sunshine, I have everything to give you." He reached up to my neck and pulled me down to kiss him.

He wasn't going to distract me from my victory, with another one of those mind-altering kisses. I somersaulted over him and sprang to my feet.

Cal moved at the same time, managing to somehow beat me to his feet. He used my surprise to spin around me, smacking the flat of his blade hard on my ass.

I howled from the stinging burn that radiated across my cheek.

"That's the one area I didn't fortify with scales, you asshole."

"Oh, I bet there are others," he mused.

My blood boiled. That son of a bitch. I won. This was over.

Cal laughed, and I launched myself at him. Soon, we were a cyclone of flying blades. The clang of metal on metal rang its glorious music into the quiet room. I pushed myself harder than I've pushed in a very long time. It became abundantly clear Cal had been going easy on me. Even now, he didn't seem the least bit unnerved by the sheer speed or strength of the volley.

With one final spin, our blades interlocked. Cal rotated, and the crossguard of each sword hooked into one another, forming a deadly star.

I tugged, but they didn't release. I tried twisting my hand, and still, they didn't release.

Cal laughed. That fucker planned this.

He pulled on the swords, forcing me to stumble forward. Leaning between the blades, his mouth crashed into mine. The razor edge of *my* sword scraped my jaw and settled against my neck.

Lips brushing mine, he said, "I win."

There was no way I was walking out of this room letting Cal win anything.

"You sure about that?" I purred, pushing deeper into the kiss before arching back. Breaking away, my teeth raked over his lower lip, causing the faint coppery taste of blood to splash against my tongue.

I dipped under his arm. The tangled mass of blades pushed up as I forced Cal's weight over my shoulder. In one smooth movement, I flipped Cal's body. He soared into the air, and with a grunt, he landed flat on his back—again.

Each of his weapons skittered away from him.

I tapped his chest with my sword. "See, I win."

Kaeli leapt to her feet, jumping and cheering.

Cal's expression darkened into something predatory. It was the only warning I had, but not enough to be prepared for the quick spin of his legs. Before I could even register what had happened, I was pinned beneath his weight. I pulled on each of my limbs, but he had them firmly planted.

Cal leaned in, close enough that I could almost taste the salt on his skin. The entire long line of his body pressed me into the mat. "No, I win."

I struggled again, trying to find leverage in any way possible. Elbows, knees, anything that I could use to shift his impossibly hard weight. Nothing moved, not even a little. It was pathetic how easily I'd been immobilized.

I let out a groan of frustration and then begrudgingly gave up. "Fine, you win."

Cal's honeyed eyes sparkled with delight. Still straddling me, he eased his grip and sat back on his knees. Golden strands of messy hair hung over his brow. He tossed his head, pushing them out of the way. Between the hair and the scales, he was almost too bright and beautiful to look at, like staring at the sun.

My heart pounded, each beat filling my body with need. I extended my arms over my head in offering.

"Take what you want."

"Oh, Sunshine..."

His hands smoothed along my sides, thumbing the texture of my scales in the space between my cropped shirt and the band of my underwear. Gods damn, the lava current that followed his fingertips felt good. My spine bowed, pushing my hips into his hands.

"What if I want everything?"

If he wanted all of me, he could damn well take it. I didn't care what he did, so long as he did it right now. Fire rose from within my core, and the lamps along the walls flamed brightly in answer. With a side eye, he looked at them, then grinned back down.

The tips of Kaeliana's toes came into my periphery. "That was *brilliant*. You moved like you'd been born to wield those swords. And when you laid Cal out, that was absolutely the best thing I've ever seen."

Realization that she was still here rocked me. The training room suddenly came back into focus. I'd been so singularly consumed by Cal that I'd forgotten about her entirely. Good thing, too; another second, and I'm pretty sure I would have started begging for more.

I craned my head to look over my shoulder at her. "Which time?"

Cal huffed, shifting my attention back to him. How much of that fight had been him giving me the advantage? He obviously didn't have any trouble restraining me when he tried. A fact I would not forget any time soon.

Cal stood up, effortlessly bringing me with him.

"You can still keep the swords, and the shirt, for now. I wouldn't want the guards to get any ideas." With a wink, he added, "I'll just claim my winnings later."

14
ELYRIA

"**W**hat in the name of all the gods? Where are your clothes?"

We all turned as one to see Xoc standing in the doorway of the practice room. He took in our general state of undress, opening his mouth to speak three times with nothing coming out.

Deciding to save him, I said, "Sparring practice. You missed all the fun. We're done here."

Cal trailed a finger over my exposed shoulder. "I wouldn't say we're *done*. There are many... many things I still plan on doing."

Kaeli fake wretched.

I stepped out of his reach. "We're done here."

Xoc looked like he might melt from embarrassment, trying to direct his attention anywhere but at the very exposed areas of my body. "Elyria, I've walked in on you naked too many times. If you're staying in the palace, then we're going to have to develop a code or something. I can't keep doing this."

"Times, as in more than once?" Kaeliana said in what almost sounded like outrage.

"It was only one time–"

"One time too many."

"--and seriously, not that big of a deal," I said, wrapping the remnants of my clothing into a makeshift skirt. "Xoc, all the important bits are covered. You don't have to keep staring at the ceiling."

"In case you were wondering, I didn't come down here so that I could have my daily dose of feeling uncomfortable." Xoc waved at Cal's bare chest. "So, put on a shirt...and, Belhameth save me, some pants, because Captain Sangrior is here, and the queen sent me to fetch you."

"Sangrior? Like the pirate?" Kaeli jumped up, tugging on Xoc's arm. "What is she doing in the palace? Can I meet her?"

"No," Cal said before she'd even finished the sentence, like he knew what she was going to ask the second she popped up.

"Apparently, a certain future king made her an offer, and she's here to collect. Your mother is not pleased."

"Ooo, nevermind," Kaeliana took a slow step away, locking the hand that was squeezing Xoc's bicep behind her back. "Mother is already angry that I stole a horse from the stables this morning, and I don't need that woman lecturing me for a third time today."

"How can you steal a horse? Your family already owns them all?" I asked while puzzling over why Xoc was still staring at his bicep like Kaeli had left behind scorch marks.

"I didn't say they were our stables."

Cal gave me a withering expression. I knew the last thing he wanted to do with his evening was spend it verbally sparring with Morgan and his Mother.

"I'll meet with them as soon as I've changed," he replied with a relenting sigh. Then Cal gave another long look at me. "Take the swords with you. They're yours."

"I can't—"

"You can and you will. Those blades were made for you, and they're doing no good locked up in here."

Kaeli bounded over to me. "Forget the knives. Want to go raid the kitchens with me? I'm starving. I never really got to eat. A few grapes and a stolen apple tart don't really count as lunch."

My stomach rumbled its answer for me.

"Go. I'll see you later tonight." Cal said, pulling on his shorts. "Keep your guards." Pointedly looking at Kaeliana, he added, "Both of you. And don't go creating too much trouble."

I gave him a look of indignation. "I'd never."

An hour later, we each had plates piled high with pilfered food. Kaeli mostly filled hers with sticky buns and danishes. My plates, the near opposite to hers, held a variety of cheeses, some type of salami, and knotted breads. Kaeliana tucked two bottles of wine under her arm, and we rushed from the kitchens before being noticed by anyone of importance.

We hurried like naughty children through the halls, giggling all the way back to my rooms. As I opened the door, I saw a surprisingly tidy room. The massive wardrobe from earlier was cleared. At the far end, Alessia and Rei were talking animatedly, lounging on cushions beside the fireplace.

"Hey!" they said in unison.

"We've been waiting for you," Alessia replied, taking my plates from me. "I see you've met the princess."

"Les, you're going to love this girl," Kaeliana replied.

Alessia laughed, looking at Kaeli's over-filled arms. "Did you leave anything for the banquet? Mattias'll be seeing red. You know he's going to find a way to blame me, right?" Alessia gently took the bottles from under Kaeli's arms. "I'll pop these and let them breathe while you go clean up."

She wrinkled her nose at me. "Why are you all sweaty, and what in the fires of Kraav happened to your skirt?"

"I was sparring with Cal in the Armory," I said around the hunk of cheese I shoved in my mouth.

Rei popped up. "Damn! And I missed it? Tell me you at least kicked his arrogant ass."

Before I could so much as open my mouth Kaeli jumped in.

"She was AMAZING. Twirling and flying, blow after blow." Kaeli choked on a bit of laughter. "Cal could barely keep up. She laid him flat on his back, flipped him right over— twice."

Rei lifted her brows in appreciation. "I bet that was satisfying."

The girls were all laughing, their bodies shaking with glee, but I didn't see any of it. The only thing filling my vision was an image of Cal hovering over my pinned body and the word *satisfying*. What had he said? *You've never really been satisfied.*

"In so many words," I murmured, shaking the image from my mind.

"Watching them fight was the most fun I've had in months," Kaeli mimicked my fighting moves, pantomiming each hit. Little bits of food flew from her plate as she spun. "Even if it did end with the two of them mostly naked. I don't *ever* need to see so much of my brother again."

"Naked?" Rei asked, full of amusement and meeting my guilty eyes.

"It was a bet. Which I won... almost, sort of."

"What, like strip sparring? Hmmm..." Rei took a long sip of wine. "Sorry, just pausing to imagine the two of you fighting naked."

Kaeli made a gagging sound. "And who are you exactly?"

"Oh," I swallowed down the cucumber spear I'd just bitten. "I forgot you two haven't met yet. Princess Kaeliana, meet Reihaneh Almont. She's a friend, and thanks to helping us, has a target on her back."

After quickly cleaning up, I plopped down on the cushion between Alessia and Rei, laying my plate of cheese on the floor. Alessia poured us each a glass of wine. It tasted dark and sensuous, with hints of vanilla and cinnamon. The heat of the drink was smooth going down. Exactly what I needed. I could already feel the tension leaving my muscles.

"You should have nicked more wine," Rei said, looking at the two bottles that sat on the table, one of which was already empty. "Two bottles will never be enough."

Alessia smiled. "Not necessary." She walked to the corner of the room and spun a tall cabinet. "I stocked this to the brim this morning." The sound of clinking glass drifted over to us, revealing a rack of wine and half a dozen hanging goblets.

Rei, whistled. "That's been here this whole time. Damn, Les, we could have broken into that an hour ago.

Walking back to the fire, Alessia snatched up her glass from the table.

"Did you get a dress for tomorrow?" I asked, looking between Rei and Alessia.

Rei chirped with elation. "Yes, and... I got to see your dress, too. The tailor wasn't finished with it yet, but damn. You are going to look heart-achingly, kill them where they stand, gorgeous. My money says you don't even make it five minutes without Cal ripping it off you."

"I don't know about all that," I said, feeling heat rise up my throat that had nothing to do with the wine.

"Yeah, how about you tell us what's going on between you and my brother," Kaeli said, smiling into her glass.

"Oh, yes! I want to know what you two have been up to these past couple of days. Seeing as you went from trying to burn him to ashes to melting the moment he looks at you."

"I-"

"And don't leave out any of the salacious details," Rei interrupted. "Be specific."

"Yeah, that's my brother. I don't need too many details," Kaeli countered, and we all laughed.

"I don't melt when he looks at me."

The girls all scoffed.

Rei looked like she was going to choke on her wine from disbelief. "Spare me the lies."

Hiding behind my drink, I added, "And besides, there's nothing to tell. Nothing happened."

Rei pointed an accusatory finger at me. "You expect me to believe that the two of you spent two nights and one *entire* day in that tiny ship cabin without something going down."

"Or someone," Les said under a cough.

Rei lifted her glass in a mini-cheers. "Please, I got off six times before breakfast, and you're telling me *nothing happened*?"

My heart rate sped up, and for a moment, I could still feel my legs wrapped around his waist, smell the musty wood crates. "Yeah, basically." I took another sip, hoping they'd read the flush in my cheeks as being from the wine.

"Six times?" Kaeli said, raising an eyebrow. "Is that even possible?"

"What I mean is we've kissed a few times. But, honestly, we'd talk all night until one of us fell asleep."

Rei let out the breath she was holding. "Well, that's just boring. You seriously haven't leapt on that chariot? Because if it was me, I'd be doing laps around the arena. Forwards, backwards, leaping those little hurdle things."

Kaeli spluttered the sip she had just been taking into her glass.

"Chariots don't leap hurdles." Les tilted her head to the side in confusion.

"Mine do." Rei winked.

"Honestly, I could count the number of times we've seriously kissed on one hand." I began ticking them on my fingers. "Once on The Steps."

"The Steps? Like step-steps, or like THE STEPS?" Kaeli said, sitting up and halting everything with the giant waving of her arms.

"*The* Steps. Not one of my better ideas. When Cal found me, we were in Laluna."

"Ohhh, Laluna! I've always wanted to go there," Alessia crooned, then looked at Kaeliana. "Why can't we ever go anywhere fun, like a land of perpetual night?"

"Because Mattias and my mother are determined to make sure I die unfulfilled and miserable. Laluna would be pretty fantastic to see, though. I hear there's a liquor that makes your eyes glow."

I nodded. I had fond memories of the first time Macie and I drank glowberberry wine. "And your lips, for at least a little while."

"Excellent."

"Anyway, I had this absurd notion that we should take The Steps instead of sailing around the Horn. In my head, it was only a few stairs, and we'd be saving weeks on a ship. I'll save you the trip. It was more than a few stairs, and the horrors on them... let's just say it's not a mistake I'll ever make again. I'm going to have nightmares about that climb for the rest of my life."

"Well, that's understandable if you were kissing my brother."

I chuckled. "But he was sweet, caring, and tender... and in a moment of concussion-induced weakness, I might have given in to him." I closed my eyes, the memory of Cal's hands sliding up my spine so tangible that I could have sworn he was in the room with us.

"Get on with it. When else? What about this waterfall Cal mentioned?" Rei said, licking her lips in greedy anticipation. "I've been waiting all day to ask you about it."

The fantasy shifted in my mind from the cliff to the feel of the water crashing down on us, contrasting with the heat of his body pressing me into that cold stone wall. Goosebumps prickled up my arms. I buried my face in my hands. "You seriously want to hear all of this?"

I hadn't been able to talk about Cal with anyone. At least when I was in the troupe, Macie was around for this sort of thing when she stopped speaking long enough to listen to what I had to say. For some reason, I felt like I could tell these girls each of my very confusing thoughts. Maybe if we laid them out, they would make more sense than the jumble currently rattling around my brain.

"There's this oasis at the top of The Steps. It had a big waterfall, with beautiful glittering water, and a sparkly black stone mountain. Cal showed me a small cave hiding behind the water, and we kissed under, or in it... twice." I smiled sheepishly.

"Twice? Only kissed twice?"

I slowly nodded. My cheeks were so warm I could feel the heat pulsing in them. "Twice was intense enough. I was naked, and he might as well have been."

"Fuck, that's sexy. Gimme a second while I run my mind over the two of you naked in a waterfall." Rei said, draining what was left in her glass.

"I was naked. Cal was not."

"Shh. You're ruining my daydream."

Alessia slapped Rei's shoulder, "Okay, that's three times."

"And then the night we spent in Joseph's house. "

Rei's face brightened. "Joey! I forgot he was the one who sent you to me. Did he make you drink that swill he brews? Because the last time I drank his shit, I nearly mounted a horse."

I choked on my wine, and Alessia spit hers across the rug.

"Fuck, I'm going to have to scrub that tomorrow," she groaned.

"I've had it before, so I knew well enough not to," I said, flashing Alessia a sympathetic glance. "But Xoc got hammered on just three glasses and spent the night sleeping on the floor."

Kaeli reached out, grabbing my arm. "Xoc was drunk? Gods, I'd have given anything to see that."

"Yep. It was glorious." I swallowed the last of my wine, licking the dregs that dribbled down the side.

"Stop distracting her," Rei chided.

"Cal and I got the loft. That night was..." Fuck. How do I describe the chaotic emotions I'd felt that night? "...frustrating."

Every one of them sat up, gawking at me like I'd just spoken another language.

"Elaborate." Alessia snatched a triangle of cheese and popped it into her mouth.

"Well...," I hesitated, not knowing where to start. "We messed around a little, but Cal stopped it."

"What?!" Kaeli said in disbelief. "You're lying. My brother has never stopped anything he wanted to do, *ever*. There isn't an ounce of self-control in his bones. He's always been a sprint to the finish line, damn the consequences, kind of person." I gave her a sideways glance the number of times that man had denied me. "I'm serious. The only restraint he knows is a rope."

Rei gave an unexpected chortle, sloshing her wine glass. "Shit, if he tied you up. Mmm, that's a fantasy worth exploring."

"I didn't mean like that... although, probably like that too. Man has a serious control complex. I wonder–" Kaeli drew the last word out as if trying to puzzle the pieces together. "---where did this newly found sense of honor come from?"

Honor. I laughed under my breath. He lied to me for weeks, and yet... all those times he'd pulled himself back. He could have taken advantage of me easily. I practically begged him to. What if it *was* honor? Some part of him didn't want to take the affection he'd won through deceit. The revelation made butterflies start doing acrobatics in my stomach. If he'd already changed for me, back then, what did that mean about now?

I'll prove myself worthy.

Kaeli continued, but her voice sounded far away beneath the memory of Cal's voice whispering into my ear as we laid in bed, telling me stories and giving me subtle praise while running his fingers through my hair.

"Are you sure you weren't confusing Cal with Xoc? That man is nothing but restraint, and trust me, I've tested it."

Alessia barked out a laugh.

"Don't judge me," Kaeli protested. "Xoc is burn in Kraav hot. You could bounce a whole bag of coins off that ass." She hummed into her glass. They were laughing, but it all seemed so distant.

Rei leaned forward and tapped my hand, her eyes seeming to know exactly where my thoughts had been. The sudden movement jolted me from my thoughts. Those ghosts disappeared as fast as they manifested.

I shook off her discerning gaze. "It wasn't honor," I blurted out. Why did my voice sound so unconvinced? "Maybe some part of it was, but I'm pretty sure he was teasing me, trying to prove that he could... and did turn me on. Fuck, I practically started begging."

Rei laughed. "Now, that's what I'm talking about. The chemistry between the two of you zings of bottled-up sexual frustration."

I rolled my eyes.

"Then, the next day, we met you," I said, pointing to Rei. "And you saw how well that night went for us."

Alessia and Kaeli shared confused expressions. When I didn't say anything they looked, pleadingly to Rei.

"Your brother lied to her to get her to come here. Cal told her he was a cosmetics salesman."

"Gods, he's a terrible liar. Always has been," Kaeli said.

Rei continued, "She put a dagger to his throat and demanded the truth. When he finally came clean, Elyria here nearly burned down the entire university."

"You forgot about his dick. I had my dagger at his throat, and a throwing knife pointed straight at the part he loved most."

"Ew. I just pictured Cal's dick." Alessia scrunched her nose while tearing apart a pastry.

"No wonder he's crazy for you." Kaeli leaned her head against the cushion. "I'll bet he has never met a woman who could match him blow for blow." I'm not sure what my expression must have said, but she went on, "It's true. I've never seen him look at anyone the way he looks at you."

"Like how exactly?"

Alessia spoke up, "Like he's been slowly suffocating, and you're a cool breeze of fresh air."

I sighed, deciding there was no point in holding back now. "He vowed to make himself worthy of my trust, and I think that's exactly what he's been trying to do. On Morgan's ship, we had lots of time to just talk. It was like he let down all of his walls and showed me who he really was, no posturing, no pretending. I guess...." I rubbed at the tingling in my cheeks, the wine making me brave enough to acknowledge what I'd been denying this entire time. "I realized that, for the most part, he'd been truthful with me. I'm still pissed as hell that he thought it was okay to keep important information, but I think... I think I've made peace with it."

The truth of that sentence settled into me. Without the resentment, there was just this warm feeling, like sinking into a bath. My eyes flicked over to the door that connected our rooms. If I walked through that door, would he be there?

I fell backwards into the cushions. My now empty glass rolled along the ground. "Now someone else has to share."

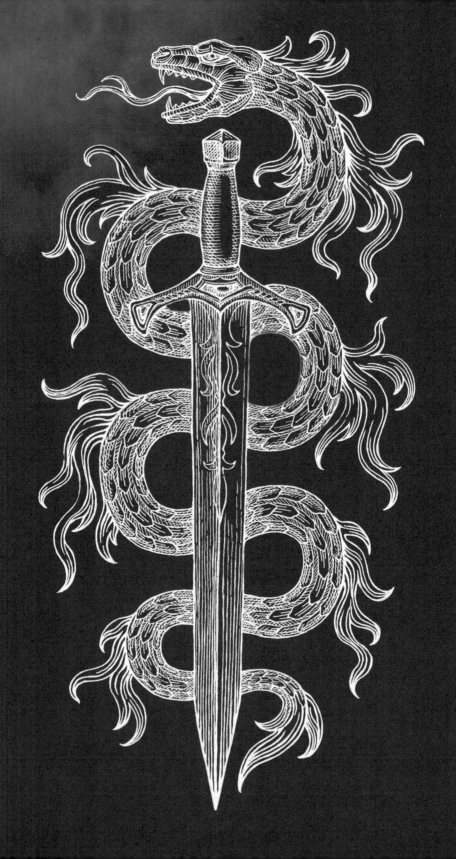

15

I opened my groggy eyes to see Cal standing above me. Sunlight poured through the open drapes, silhouetting his form. It was so bright I couldn't see, or maybe he was just so beautiful that it was hard to look at him.

Next to me, Alessia groaned.

"Sure looks like you had fun," Cal laughed, tapping a discarded wine bottle with the toe of his boot. "After a grueling evening of meetings, I came back to wish Elyria goodnight–"

"Sure, that's definitely why you'd be coming to her room in the middle of the night. To wish her sweet dreams." Rei rolled her eyes. "You aren't fooling anyone."

Cal flashed her a quick smile. "Imagine my surprise to find you four drooling on cushions."

"Shut up." I pushed the heels of my hands into my eyes in a feeble attempt to stop the pounding behind them. "We stayed in the palace. That's what you wanted. Right?"

Kaeliana sat up. "Did you seriously tell her you were a cosmetics salesman?" she said, throwing a pillow at him. He caught it effortlessly and chucked it back down at her.

"Not something I'm terribly proud of," he replied with what looked like genuine remorse.

"You're the *worst*. Seriously, big brother, that's worse than the time you tried to convince Father a stray cat knocked the ceremonial swords down and stabbed them into Mother's chaise five times."

Rei walked behind me and placed her hands on either side of my head. "Take a deep breath."

The tattoos circling her wrists glowed. A cold, tingling sensation swirled around my temples. Slowly, the pounding smoothed away, and the turning in my gut ceased. I let out a slow breath.

"Thanks. That's amazing." My mind and body felt full of energy, ready for anything.

Rei did a little bow, then went to the other two and repeated the trick.

"Can I keep you?" Kaeli said to Rei while poking at her cheeks. "Is my face supposed to feel this tingly?"

"I hate to be the bearer of bad news," Cal said, suppressing a chuckle. "but we have a ball to prepare for, and you four have already slept past lunch. Guests will be arriving in a couple of hours, and I doubt any of you want to go dressed like that." He gestured down at us.

Alessia began gathering the empty bottles and straightening the pillows. "He's right. Prophecy Day means lots to be done. Kaeli, you need to go back to your room and get dressed. Marcella is probably having a whole litter of kittens right about now."

"Ugh. She'll probably insist I wear the stockings too. Elyria, you stole the best handmaiden in this palace."

"Go," Alessia repeated, more firmly this time.

"I hope you appreciate the sacrifices I'm making for you," Kaeliana said, stomping out the door.

"I'll be back in a couple of hours to escort you," Cal pressed a casual kiss to my temple like it was the most natural thing in the world. It made something in me melt. With one last lingering look, he added, "Oh, and, Leopold, the tailor is here with your dress."

A tall man with a neatly cut suit came into the room. A large garment bag draped over his arm.

"Good morning, ma'am," he said, bowing his head to me. "His Highness gave me a good deal of liberty in the design. I hope you will like it. If it's alright, I'd like you to try it on so that I can make any necessary adjustments. I've also bought Ms. Almont's gown with me."

"Ok," I said, looking around for an ideal place to try the gown on.

Alessia wheeled a tall rod with a hook into the middle of the room. The tailor hung the dress on the hook and slid the bag away.

An audible hush went over the room as we took it in.

"This is for me?" I whispered. It was finer than anything I'd ever seen. I ran my fingers over the different surfaces.

Rei poked at my arm. "Don't just fondle it, Elyria. Put it on."

Cool satin slipped over my body. I ran my hands up my thighs to feel it smooth against my skin. It shined in the late evening sun. After two hours of Leopold altering the dress to make it match his vision and another hour of Alessia fussing over every detail from my hair to my toes, I was finally dressed. Never in my life had getting dressed been such an ordeal; not even before our largest shows had I been adorned to this extent.

Alessia pulled a golden medallion from a small velvet pouch. "Lift your arms for me. There's a belt, too."

In her fingers rested a delicate circle shaped into an image I knew better than any other, a dragon eating its tail wrapped around a sun, The Sun Serpent. I sucked in a breath, reaching for the shimmering bit of gold in her hands.

"Can I see that?" I asked, trying to swallow down the tremor shaking my voice.

"Sure." While eyeing me wearily, Alessia placed the cool metal into my out-stretched palm. "Is everything okay?"

"Yes, it's... This is my family's sigil. Or at least the one that Duke, my father, made after he adopted me." I ran my thumbs over the ridges of the dragon's scales. The first time my father unveiled the Solaire Sun Serpent, I hated it. It was around the same time he made my act the headliner. Duke put it on everything, from the side of our wagons to our posters. I loathed the way it drew even more attention to me. Now, this singular image signified everything that made me strong, and it was the one thing I had that still linked me to him. Cal knew, and he gave that to me.

I looked up at her through blurry eyes, the tears threatening to spill over the makeup she'd just spent an hour so carefully applying. "He... died shortly after I met Cal. He must have asked for it specifically."

"Smooth, Callen, very smooth," she said, laying the chain over my hips. "Cal has a surprisingly sentimental side to him. He remembers everything, tucks it away, and always manages to bring it back when it will matter most. For somebody who acts like very little matters, he cares more deeply than almost anyone I know. There are worse things than being the center of that man's attention."

Alessia connected the ends of the chain to the medallion, then reached up and gathered the single tear at the corner of my eye before it could track over my cheek. "Perfection. Come on, let's get you before the mirror." She took my hand, dragging me around the screen.

Rei sucked in a breath. "Slap my ass and tell me I'm a good girl because you are stunning. Fuck, your tits look amazing. Mr. Tailor Man, you've really outdone yourself. I'm completely jealous."

"Oh my gods, Rei," I spluttered.

"What? There's nothing wrong with a little healthy sexual exploration. Not that you'd know. Those thighs are closed tighter than the Basilica's vaults."

I looked at the beautiful ornate ceiling and tried not to die of mortification. Thankfully, Leopold didn't look like he'd even registered her comment. If anything, he seemed singularly focused on the long velvet box he just pulled from the bottom of his satchel.

"There's more," he said proudly.

"More? But this dress is already the most magnificent thing I've ever worn," I ran my fingers over the thousands of tiny black rhinestones adorning the slit of my skirt. Coupled with the golden silk peeking from beneath the black satin, it was like the dress was emanating its own light. It gave me a pang of homesickness for Jess, the troupe's costumer. The last several hours had made

166

me think of him more times than I could count. He would have fainted at least twice from the fabric alone.

The tailor steepled his fingers, hiding a feline grin. "Oh yes, there's more."

We all watched as he lifted two golden shoulder pauldrons from a bed of black velvet. Each was made from rows of dragonesque scales rather than the plating of traditional armor. When they swayed, the individual pieces reflected the light like facets in a diamond.

Leopold laid the first golden piece over my shoulder. It molded perfectly to the curve of my form, a tiny hidden fabric loop connecting it to the strap running behind my neck. The gold scaling spilled over my shoulders and along the low-dipping hemline of my back. With a gentle twist of my shoulders, he turned me to face the large mirror.

I barely recognized the girl looking back at me. It was such a startling difference from the reflection that used to stare out at me from my polished bit of tin. My hair was braided in alternating layers, leaving pieces to artfully hang down in golden spirals. I squinted at my reflection. The roots were still midnight black, but the gold in my hair seemed to have grown. The metallic tips had crept at least several inches higher. I marveled at the transformation, then my heart rate quickened when I realized that the gold started to grow at the same time Cal came into my life. Whatever the connection between us was, it was more than just attraction.

The tailor's deft fingers quickly draped several golden chains between the two sides of my gown, the longest brushing the base of my spine. When he was done, Leopold stepped back, clutching his hands like he was praying. I looked between him and Rei, who was biting on the nail of her forefinger.

"Well?" I looked between the three of them. They were being oddly quiet. "How does it look?"

"Five minutes," Rei said, nodding her head. "Ten gold crowns says he's got his hands on you within five minutes."

I twisted my body to see the chains that dangled down my back. Each delicate strand gently caressed the skin of my lower back. The dragon mark beneath them roared against its elegant cage.

"Ten, because the ass won't know how to undo everything," countered Alessia.

"You two are the worst," I laughed, imagining Cal trying to unfasten dozens of clasps and ties, then, just for fun, said, "I say he waits until there's a dark corner somewhere during the ball, or some secret room only he knows about." I shimmied my shoulders and watched in the reflection as the chains danced across my back.

"You shake like that, and you'll lose the bet for sure," laughed Rei. "Your breasts look magnificent, the way the satin clings to them, and just the right hint of under swell." She kissed into the air, then laughed. "Actually, go ahead and just give them a little shake."

Leopold sat back, pride beaming from beneath his smile. "This dress is my Magnum Opus, my great symphony, a masterpiece in satin and silk. I don't know that I will ever top it."

I did a spin before the full-length mirror, making the layered skirt fan out in an elegant swirl of black and gold.

"Leopold, what exactly did the prince ask you to make?"

An internal debate tightened the tailor's features, but eventually, he said, "He said it should be a dress that looked both violent as a dagger and as sweet as strawberries."

I sucked in a breath, hearing Cal whisper, *"you taste like strawberries and violence."* The tailor continued. "Then, I was to design a suit for him that matched your gown."

"Interesting." I absentmindedly ran my fingers over the Sun Serpent resting at my navel. The woman staring back at me in the mirror was radiant. If there was such a thing as a goddess of the sun, I was doing a hell of a job pretending to be her. Was this what Cal saw when he looked at me?

"Thank you, Leopold. I'm honored to be wearing this dress tonight."

Alessia bit down on her lip, obviously suppressing something.

"What?"

"Nothing, it's just. Nevermind," she said, brushing it off.

"What?" I prodded again. "Out with it. It can't be that bad. I mean, you were okay last night telling us about when you let the—"

"I think you would make an excellent queen."

"Oh." I shook my head on instinct. "Les, you barely know me. I'm probably the least noble person in all of Venterra."

"That's not true. You're gracious and kind to everyone you meet, even those beneath your station. Which is rare, before you ask." She gave me a gentle smile.

"I don't have a station. I'm a circus performer."

"You're staying in the palace at the invitation of the Crowned Prince. You have a station now, whether you like it or not. And, I know you aren't sure where things lie between you and Cal, but Innesvale would be lucky to have you wear the crown."

My heart rate picked up. Queen. Crown. The words hung suspended in the air between us.

Leopold cleared his throat, inclining his head towards Alessia in agreement.

Rei stepped out from behind the dressing screen with a dramatic sweeping entrance, interrupting the moment. "Well, what do we think?"

She was head to toe in a sparkling white dress. It hung along each curve and bend of her body before pooling at her feet. The color was stunning, seeming to glow even more brightly in contrast to her chestnut skin. As she moved, I could see that while the dress was white, something in the material gave a slight purple iridescence to it, matching the ethereal glow inking her arms.

Rei pinned her usually wild brown hair back on one side, holding it in place with an ornate comb. A dainty silver chain looped her neck before dipping low between her breasts, with a single pink diamond glittering at the end. If I was darkness and the dawn, then Rei was living starlight.

"Are you coming to the ball too?" I asked Alessia.

While Leopold said his goodbyes, Les walked to a wardrobe, pulling from it a deep blue gown. With a kick of her heel, she disappeared behind the partition. When she emerged minutes later, she no longer looked like a servant but could pass for any noble lady.

"Normally, staff are not permitted to partake in the events. However, for the Prophecy Ball, the entire palace is invited to attend. This is an older dress of

Kaeliana's. She never wears the same dress twice, and it would be criminal to discard it, so now it's mine."

She walked to the mirror and applied a bit of pale pink tint to her cheeks and lips. Then in one fluid movement, pinned her hair into a flawless chignon.

"What now?" asked Rei, hands on her hips. I could tell that she was itching to get to the party.

"You can go," I said, motioning to the door. "You don't have to wait for me."

Rei tilted her head to the side, frowning.

"Seriously, both of you, go have fun. I'm sure Cal will be here soon to collect me. He'd lose his mind if I went down without him." I picked up the masks from the table and handed them over. "I'll see you there."

Rei slipped the ornate silver one over her eyes, and Alessia took a simple black mask. The guards waiting outside the door all smiled at Rei as she walked, eyes dipping to the diamond nestled between her breasts. "Come on, boys. Which one of you is going to give me a spin? Don't worry. You can each get a turn. I have excellent stamina." In a second, they were all enthusiastically trailing behind them.

The door closed with a click, leaving me alone. It was an odd feeling. Alone wasn't something that ever happened with the troupe. The empty room felt heavy.

To calm my nerves, I began pacing. The luxurious dress rolled and caressed my legs as I walked. The gentle kiss of fabric did little to keep my mind off Cal. It brought back memories of lips on skin and hands brushing sensitive flesh.

My eyes drifted to the bright blue door connecting our apartments. It stood in the middle of the white wall like a beacon. Cal. My memory spooled through random times we'd spent together, ending with him in the garden, on his knees, about to profess... what? That he loves me? Everyone else seems convinced that he does, and hadn't he basically said as much that night on the dock.

Hasn't he shown me over and over again the man he truly is? It's that man who fills all of my waking thoughts, who makes an ache bloom in my chest whenever we're apart. My heart rate galloped out of control, fully acknowledging for the first time what the longing really was.

There was no pretending anymore. Cal hadn't for a while now, and it was about time I stopped, too. Propelled by my heart alone, I walked to the door that adjoined my room to Cal's.

I was done waiting.

16

CALLEN

Trying to be respectable was exhausting.

I barely recognized this version of myself. When did I become the person who cared about decorum... or boundaries? I never cared about these things before. Yet here I am, pacing outside her door like some love-addled fool.

Because you are a love-addled fool, Callen.

From the moment I met Elyria, there was this constant nagging in the back of my mind. It demanded that I do better, try harder, put my dick away, and strive to be a better man. Despite that, I don't think I'll ever truly be worthy of her.

All I know is that when she smiles, my heart stops—and I would do anything to ensure she does it again. So here I am, pacing and counting the seconds before this respectable version of myself can call on her.

I shuffled to a stop before the door separating our rooms. My eyes bored into the wood, as if I might be able to see through it if I only looked hard enough. A low growl rumbled deep in my chest. I hated feeling like this. I should just walk in there, pull her into my arms, and kiss her until she forgets how to breathe.

I clenched my hands into tight fists in a desperate attempt to keep myself from grabbing the handle. My nails lengthened into clawed tips, scraping my palms. Even that sting wasn't enough of a distraction.

It was bad enough that I had to listen all afternoon to the girls laughing. I wanted to bust through that damnable door every time Elyria's musical laughter rang out. But now, the room had gone silent. I leaned against the wood, trying to discern if they'd all left. Was Elyria in there waiting for me? Or did she decide to leave with my sister and forego my escort? Fuck, I hated this.

The tight waistcoat chafed at my neck. Resuming my pacing, I pulled against the dragon appellate that Leopold had sewn in. I gave him free rein on the suit, telling him all I wanted was for there to be no misunderstanding with the court. She was mine, and I was hers.

I was five steps from the door that connected our rooms when it slowly swung open.

The air vanished in a blink. Her trailing curls shifted, brushing along her jaw and making me realize I'd unconsciously pulled the air back. Gods, that was embarrassing. When was the last time I lost control of my magic? Never, I've never lost control. Releasing the tether on my power, air flooded back around us, fluttering her skirts in a mesmerizing display of black and gold.

"Sorry." My voice sounded rough and foreign. "You are quite literally breathtaking."

"Thank you." Elyria smiled softly, running her hands over her dress like she didn't know what to do with them. An adorable blush spilled across her cheeks. I'd seen this woman stand confidently naked before me. Yet now, dressed like a goddess, she was nervous. Worse, I think I was too. Were my palms sweating?

The glittering marble reflected the sky outside. Thanks to the sun setting over the balcony, the room was awash in shades of pale purple and orange. It was my favorite time of day for this very reason. But, despite the beauty all around us, all I saw was Elle.

I couldn't tell where to settle my eyes. Every inch of her was almost too stunning to look at. I committed every shining dip and curve of her body to memory. On frosty nights this image alone could keep me warm.

Elyria circled the room, dragging her hand along each surface. Her lean legs parted the skirts, exposing the peachy skin of her upper thigh. The layered fabric looked like sunlight masked by shadows, seeming to demand attention. I followed her leg up, over the practically indecent coverage of her breasts.

Fucking hells, I was going straight to the bottom of Kraav and back. The slightest shadow from the underswell of her chest was visible where the glittering edge of the fabric split. It was so intimate, and yet, on display, beckoning me to come and explore. I had to put my hands in my pockets just to keep from doing something rash.

Elyria gave me a sly smile over her shoulder as she turned toward the balcony. Her dragon mark was on full display, caged in by glittering delicate chains. As if anything so beautiful could ever be caged.

I felt myself moving towards her before I even registered that I was walking.

She looked out at the ocean. "The water rushing on either side of the balcony is unlike anything I've ever seen," she said a bit breathlessly. "How does so much water flow through the palace?"

I skimmed my fingers over the chains hanging against her shoulder blades. In the failing light, they shimmered in the most exotic and enticing way. The longest one dipped against the small of her back.

Elyria shivered. A slight tilt to her head and the goosebumps running down her arms were the only visible recognition of how close I was to her. "It's so beautiful. I understand why you said being here calms you."

Leaning in, I ran my hands down the skin exposed at her sides. My lips grazed the gentle slope of her neck, settling just below her ear. "There is nothing calming about what I see before me."

For emphasis, I let some heat flow into the palms of my hands. A soft hum, almost a purr, came from in her chest. I slid my hands around to her stomach, toying with the satin of her bodice. Energy pulsed with each press of my lips as I trailed a line from her ear to her collarbone.

"Oh my gods." She brought her hand over her mouth to cover her choked laughter. "That was barely two minutes."

I paused. "What?" With my lips against her skin, laughter was just about the last sound I expected to hear.

Elyria rotated, leaning back against the railing. "Just, I'm going to owe Rei a lot of money."

"What?" I repeated, even more confused.

"We had a bet on how long you would last before touching me. She said within five minutes. You didn't even last two."

"If you've lost the bet, I might as well make sure you get your money's worth." I hooked my fingers into the edges of her skirt and pulled her body flush to my own. "I'd hate to underperform." Tilting her face up to mine, I wanted nothing more than to taste those perfectly painted lips.

She threw up a hand, and my kiss bounced off her palm. I scowled at the unexpected barrier between us.

"Don't you dare mess up this masterpiece. Alessia spent hours making me look like this." She gestured to herself, adding, "And we *still* have a ball to go to."

I coiled one of her golden locks around my finger. "I don't know," I said, drawing out the last word. "Taking this masterpiece apart, piece by piece, could be quite fun." I pulled on the coil and let it spring back up for emphasis.

The flush from her cheeks spilled down her chest in the most delicious way. The fire at my core pulsed in response. I let my gaze dip to where her breasts rose and fell erratically. Her skin glowed with the setting rays of light. No, it shimmered. Had she been dusted with actual gold? I ran a single finger down her sternum, letting it slide all the way to where it met the belted waist of her skirts.

Sparks of energy glowed around us like fireflies.

"Besides," I said, dipping down to kiss the hollow of her throat. She arched into me, and I reciprocated by placing another kiss an inch below the first. Her breathing hitched. *Fuck*, I loved when she made that sound. My eyes lifted to meet a gaze that churned with heat.

"I could do wonders with what you've already provided me." I slid my hand into the slit of her skirt, grazing the soft skin of her upper thigh until I found the waiting band of lace circling her hip.

Her teeth sank into her ruby-painted lower lip. I wanted to claim them as mine. I wanted it to be my teeth and my tongue dragging over their plump surface.

The horizon flashed green, and the setting sun disappeared, leaving only streaks of purple reflecting off the water. Darkness quickly settled over the ocean, and with it, my darkening desire rose, as insatiable as the horizon was infinite. How many times had I fantasized about having her in this exact spot?

Elyria's hands lifted to the lapels of my jacket, studying the dragon embroidered there. "We look like we were made for each other."

Palming her cheek, she tilted her face into my touch while my other hand traced the lines of the only bit of fabric keeping us apart. "Who says we weren't?"

I slipped beneath the soft band, relishing the velvet feeling of her skin against my palm and the slick heat sliding over my fingers. She was so wet, so warm. Her lips parted on an exhale, and the pupils of her eyes dilated, completely eclipsing the gold in them until they were wide black saucers.

"Elle, we fit together in a way that's too perfect to be a coincidence." To prove my point, I pulled my power to the surface and let it course down to the fingertips that caressed her. Elyria's entire body trembled against me, clenching the lapels of my jacket to keep from collapsing.

Not being able to kiss her was a slow kind of torture. All I wanted was to peel this dress from her body and worship every glorious inch until she was crying out my name to the rising stars. Which...

I eyed the balcony.

"Do you trust me?" I whispered, my eyes locked with hers.

She held her breath, and I tried not to hold mine as she weighed that question. I'd hurt her, and she might very well tell me that she'll never trust me again.

Exhaling, she said, "I probably shouldn't, but I do."

"You can." Lowering my hand to her waist, I lifted her onto the railing. She squealed with surprise. Her hands latched on to my shoulders, but her face was alight with anticipation. "Let me prove it to you, Sunshine." I nodded to the space behind her. "Trust me."

Tentatively, she ran a hand along the hard wall of air that braced her. "This is insanity," she said, looking over the edge of the railing to where the water of the falls crashed into the black ocean cliffs far below.

"No, the way you make me feel is insane." I parted her skirts exposing the leg beneath the slit. A gold sandal laced around her ankle and snaked up her calf. Each golden band shimmered like a welcome invitation. "This is how I feel every second I'm near you, like I'm hovering between flying and falling. Sometimes, those seconds stretch into eternity."

Lowering to one knee, I bowed as I should have the moment I met her. With a coy smile, her eyes flicked to the leg that I cradled in my hands, silently challenging me to see what I would do next.

I pressed my lips to the delicate skin just above the last golden band. Her hands coiled around the railing as I skated my lips higher before placing another kiss to the sensitive spot behind her knee. She sucked in a breath, and I was rewarded by the tremor running up her leg.

Keeping my eyes connected to the gaze boring into me, I moved my kisses higher along her inner thigh. That purring sound came again, and I hummed back in approval, knowing she could feel the vibration through my lips.

"Cal…," she breathed my name so softly it was barely audible over the rushing water. Was it a plea? A warning? A benediction? Soft black satin fluttered in the wind, brushing against my face and neck. I ran a hand beneath the fabric, hooking her leg over my shoulder.

Elyria rocked on the railing, gasping when she leaned further over the edge.

"Trust me," I repeated, stroking the decadently soft fabric that spread across her stomach before pushing her to recline over the abyss.

Her scream of surprise was swallowed by the rumble of the crashing water around us.

"Cal! Oh my gods. *Cal!*"

Still keeping her pinned against that wall of air, I used my other hand to push her skirts higher. Baring her lower hip, I lightly nipped at the hollow. Her shrieks of protest faded into a low responsive moan of pleasure, one that made the blood in my veins crackle.

I looked up at her for permission to continue, but Elyria's head hung back, and her eyes were closed. She was utterly lost in the feel of my lips on her skin and the power wrapping around her. Her spine arched, stretching the satin taut over her breasts, her hardened nipples gilt by the moonlight reflecting off the shining fabric.

I was momentarily stunned by the sheer erotic bliss of the vision before me.

17

ELYRIA

My skin was on fire.

Every place Cal's fingers skimmed seemed to excite a maelstrom within me. I moved to sit up, needing to feel more of him, but his palm was firm against my stomach, forcing me to remain suspended over the chasm of rushing water. Which only made my already erratic heart beat faster. *This is how I feel every second I'm near you.*

My back pressed into his power. It pulsed and tingled against my exposed skin. He held me completely at his mercy, leaving me no option but to hold on.

"Trust me," Cal murmured again, his breath caressing my inner thigh.

His remaining hand slid higher, looping into the lace ties at my hip. Cal went still, his eyes searching mine. Was he asking permission? Because fuck me, every inch of my skin was begging to be touched. I dug my heel into the back of his neck and pulled him closer. His irises flared, the fire in my veins instantly responding.

Dipping his head to my inner thigh, he nipped lightly. From his lips, energy pulsed into me—and I *lit* up. Molten lava coursed through me, making my hands burn, and white streaks shot across my vision.

"What the fuck was that?" I breathed, my mind spiraling.

"The beginning," Cal replied, giving a dark chuckle that made my toes curl. With a quick pull, the tie at my hip released, and the scrap of lace fell into his hand.

I tried to rise, forcibly this time. Sinking my fingers into his now golden locks

I pulled him closer. Enough of the teasing, I was about to... about to...

Cal gave one slow lick, starting low and not stopping until the flat of his tongue flicked my clit. Suddenly, I couldn't remember what I was doing.

He pushed me back down and tsked, "Stay there."

A band of cool air wrapped across my chest. I groaned at the sudden restraint, craning my head to look at him. "You aren't playing fair."

"I never do."

Cal tossed the remaining fabric of my skirts over the railing. Baring me fully, and I was certain that I would ignite from the heat in his gaze alone. He looked like a predator in the night preparing to feast. Even his eyes were glowing.

I laid my head back, a light spray of water misting over my eyelids and steaming off my cheeks. Heat radiated from his fingertips, making me acutely aware of every place they hovered.

"Cal," I warned, writhing against the stone railing. I was desperate to feel the hand he kept posed tortuously out of reach. If he didn't do something soon, I was going to start hurling fireballs.

"Gods Elle, you are so fucking beautiful."

With one torturously light caress of his thumb over my center, I bowed against the wall of air, the bands strapping my chest forcing me to endure his exploration.

"More," I panted. But instead of giving me what I asked for, he brought his thumb up to his mouth savoring the taste.

"More what?" He circled my clit, never applying the pressure I was aching for, simply testing my limits.

"Everything." I pulled against the invisible bindings, my command transforming into a whimper. If he would just let me go, I would show him exactly what I wanted.

"Do you have any idea how many times I've fantasized about doing this?"

I tried to look at him, but as I lifted my head, lancing heat flared deep within me. Cal flicked his tongue, causing every nerve in my body to ignite. Power and stars spiraled across my vision. Then he did it again, repeating the action over and over, obliterating my senses.

I might have been screaming. Beneath me, there was nothing but air, above me, the stars, and Cal kept me teetering between them both. I lifted my hips but was contained by the buzz of his power. Each time I bucked against it, the power expanded, enveloping me. He was barely touching me, and I already didn't think I could endure anymore.

"Cal," I moaned, barely able to form coherent speech. "I... I..."

Before I could finish that thought, he slid a finger into me and hooked it back, stroking a point of pressure I didn't know existed. Energy flowed through his hand and straight into the core of my own power. It lit my veins with fire. Not my fire, but his, mingling and playing with my own in a rush of pure bliss.

I cried out, tipping over the edge into the release I'd been aching for.

"There she is," he said, sending a new tidal wave straight to the center of my being before I'd even come down from the last one.

This wasn't the torrent I was used to taming. I didn't know how to comprehend the intensity building within me. I couldn't control it, and so, that power carried me away on a wave of ecstasy.

He added a second finger and everything I'd been feeling doubled. I careened back into my body. I would die from this. If I thought the buzz of contact we normally shared felt like a storm, then this was the lightning strike. With it, Cal was searing into my soul. I cried out and pressed hard against him, chasing the high that followed each stroke of his fingers.

When he took me back into his mouth, the entire world vibrated. Purple flames crackled in the air. Waves of energy fought between us with each thrust of his hand and brush of his tongue.

Until finally, I was breaking under the force of it all. I exploded over and over again, the world disintegrating beneath a shower of purple sparks.

Slowly, he brought me down from the stars. Cal stood up, the wall of air pushing me upright. I was fairly certain that I was seeing double, needing to grab his lapels to keep from pitching back over the railing. There wasn't a word invented yet to describe what I'd just experienced.

Cal chuckled that dark laugh that made my muscles clench, already hungry for more of him. He grazed a warm kiss against my cheekbone.

I glanced over the railing, then up to the sky. "It's like I can't remember which way is up," I said, still trying to regain my breath. Where had the oxygen gone? Had I stopped breathing? Was that why I was so lightheaded? Or was it all the power being channeled into me? The marble railing I'd been gripping was hot.

Cal ran his finger down the light sheen of sweat that glistened on my chest, appraising how thoroughly he unraveled me.

"You taste like you were made for me too." He drew the lobe of my ear into his mouth, letting his teeth rake the surface. My heart stopped beating. "And having that fire, power, and violence wrapped around me is the only thing I'm going to be able to think about all night."

I mewed, a tiny sound of protest. Goddess slay me. How was I supposed to go to a ball after I'd just been so thoroughly shattered and reassembled?

"For the record, I will never play fair if your moans are what I earn as my reward." Cal lowered me to the ground. I swayed the moment my feet hit marble.

Smoothing the edges of my skirt, he added, "You still look like a masterpiece, even more beautiful than before, because now I know exactly what caused those perfect cheeks to flush." He licked his lips, and I couldn't help but track the movement. Gods, I wanted to kiss him. Taste him. Climb on top and ride him until the sun came up.

He extended a hand to me, every inch the perfect gentleman. As if his tongue hadn't just tied me in knots. "I believe you said we had a ball to go to, my lady."

Fucker.

Cal guided me across the room before pausing and looking behind us. "Forgetting something?"

I followed his gaze to the strip of lace that still sat on the floor of the balcony. "I don't know that I have much use for it anymore."

Cal sucked in a breath and slid his hand over the satin to caress my ass in a way that had me doubling down on that wish to cancel our appearance at the ball.

Cal flicked open a small box containing two masks. "For you."

I leaned over the table to peer into the box. Two ornate masks sat in a bed of

184

black velvet. One was more petite, more feminine in its curves. The other had heavier lines and more masculine features.

"These are beautiful." I breathed. For a party mask, this was finer than anything I'd ever known.

Thin spun gold formed the outline of a dragon. The beautiful beast bent over the bridge of the nose, his tail curling to form one eye hole and his long legs and roaring jaws creating the other. The scales were made from a spider web of gold wire. They rolled in waves that reminded me of the crest donning the doorways of the palace. Tiny black diamonds that matched my dress, sparkled around the eyes.

"You're exquisite." Cal's hand slid up my back, tracing the lines of my dragon mark and making the chains sway. "Did you know this shimmers? The dragon is practically writhing along your spine."

I picked up my mask and glanced over my shoulder at him. "No, but then again, there are a lot of new experiences happening here tonight." I slipped the gold filigree over my eyes.

Enveloping me in his dark scent, Cal kissed the base of my neck before helping me tie the mask in place. It took everything in me not to swoon. Why hadn't we done this sooner? Being with him felt so easy.

I lingered on that feeling for several long moments before rotating, taking the other mask with me. I placed it against his perfectly shaped cheekbones. "It could be the high of power that I feel like I'm riding on. You wouldn't know anything about that, would you?" I brushed the golden locks of hair off his face.

The filigreed edges of the dragon curled over his molten eyes. It matched mine perfectly. There was no doubt that these two works of art belonged together, that we belonged together. Realizing the declaration he was making to the kingdom, my heart rate sped up.

"I might," he said, pulling back on his draken abilities until the gold in his eyes vanished. The buzz against my spine retreated, making it easier to breathe.

Cal laced his fingers into mine and raised my hand to place a gentle kiss against it. "For once, I might actually enjoy this ball."

18

CALLEN

Music filtered through the ornate ballroom doors. Elyria took a deep breath, her grip on my hand tightening.

"We only have to stay for as long as you want. Say the word, and we can leave," I said.

Her eyes flashed to me. "Would you believe that this is what I'm like before every show?"

"Truly? You'd never know with how heart-stompingly confident you look."

"I'll be fine. I've just never been good at knowing all eyes are about to be on me."

"Then that dress was not the correct choice. Because, Sunshine, you will be all anyone sees tonight." Drawing her closer, I added, "You've always been all I see. Nobody else matters."

There would only ever be her.

I nodded to the men at the doors, and they pulled them open. I stepped forward to enter the ballroom, but Elyria didn't move. She was looking at the decorative stone scroll that separated the entryway.

"What is this?" she asked, moving closer to examine it.

"That's the prophecy. The one about the coming of Ariyn Shadow. The plaque was unveiled during the first Prophecy Day celebration. I'd forgotten it was even there."

She whispered the words, reading them aloud.

From golden scale and blackened talon,
Within the valley and among the fall,
Cast under by ash and shadow,
Twin lights burn to banish all.
When the ruins rise, a new age comes,
A silver shield to end the thrall.
From two swords crossed, the waves will calm,
A new king crowned to head the call.

"Cal?" she asked, running her fingers over the words "ash and shadow."

"Are you sure this is about Ariyn Shadow?"

I walked behind her, putting my hand to her lower back.

"I mean, it makes sense. In the valley and among the falls is Innesvale, and Aurus had twins, ash and shadow. And after Ariyn was crowned, Innesvale found new prosperity. It seems right."

"It's just... What if this is about us? Asche and Shadow." She pointed between us. "What if this is about the fight that lies ahead? "End the thrall" could be The Shade."

I kissed her forehead. "Then it looks like fate is on our side."

She smiled hesitantly, giving the carved words one last uneasy look. Elyria wrapped her arm into mine. A thrill filled me with each step we took into the ballroom. There would be no mistaking this entrance, and I couldn't wait for all of Innesvale's gentry to see her by my side. Elyria was mine, and by morning, all of Venterra would know it.

Standing at the top of the tall double staircase, we surveyed the party below us. Dozens of colorful couples spun in time with the music. At the edge sat tables laden with food from around the kingdom. Courtiers gossiped with one another. Lady Bernadette, wearing a garishly bright gown, slapped a man before stomping back to her tittering group of friends. The young man laughed, catcalling after her.

I squeezed Elyria's arm, surprisingly pleased to realize that chasing women was something that didn't appeal to me even a little anymore. Most years,

I would be spinning woman after woman around the floor before deciding which to seduce into my bed. Now there was only one woman I wanted, in my bed and anywhere else she would have me.

The delicate lines of Elyria's features tipped up with wide-eyed wonder. Gods, I truly was in love with her. She changed me. I left Innesvale consumed by wrath and returned—content, despite the horrors that awaited us and the trauma of my past. I shouldn't be this lucky. I didn't deserve this kind of happiness.

Elyria's eyes drifted over to meet mine. Realizing that I'd been studying her, she gave a tiny smile of recognition. "What is it?"

I ran my thumb in circles over the back of her hand. "I'll tell you later. Right now, let's go enjoy the party."

A smile quirked up at the edges of her lips. "You're up to something. I can feel it."

"No, I'm just pleased to have such a devastatingly beautiful woman on my arm. I'm about to make every courtier in the kingdom jealous."

Elyria's eyes glittered. I looked away only long enough to nod to the attendant standing at the top of the stairs. I wasn't lying when I said I had only eyes for her. She was all I ever wanted to see again.

The man moved into position heralding our arrival, "His Highness, Callen Magnus Shadow, Crowned Prince of Innesvale and Miss Elyria Solaris."

As we descended the stairs, the entire kingdom paused. The music stopped and, an audible hush fell over the ballroom, then just as quickly, it was replaced by murmurs. As they should be, all eyes were focused on the goddess beside me. Mouths hung agape at her beauty, or perhaps they were marveling at how seamlessly we fit together. Elyria played her part perfectly. She smiled down at them and commanded their eyes as if this was her nightly performance. The woman certainly knew how to make an entrance. The entire display gave me a deep feeling of satisfaction.

I waved them on, and the party resumed.

"Callie!" Kaeliana came rushing over to us. She wore a pale pink gown. Tiny pastel roses were woven into the auburn hair cascading over her shoulder.

Elyria covered her mouth to suppress a laugh, then snickered, "Callie."

"Don't call me that," I groaned, giving Kaeliana a light peck on the cheek. "You know I hate that name."

"You look beautiful," Elyria said, running her fingers over the roses.

Kaeli waved off the compliment, moving on to juicier topics. "You two sure took your time getting here."

Elyria's cheeks turned a delightful shade of pink. "Yeah, well, we were watching the moon rise."

Kaeli snorted. "I'm not the least bit surprised. You look even more stunning than I imagined. I think the entire kingdom held its breath when you entered. Did you see Lady Bernadette? She just about choked on her drink. That snake has been after my brother for years, and your entrance was perfection." Kaeli looked down to Elyria's and my intertwined fingers and rose an eyebrow at me. I pretended not to notice and scanned the room looking for Xoc. I've been so consumed by Elyria that I hadn't seen him since we left our discussions with Morgan the night before.

"Have you seen Rei?" Elyria asked, "Or Alessia?"

"Les is sitting at a table in the back of the room with a couple of other handmaidens. Rei has been flirting with everything on two legs for hours. She's probably spinning on the dance floor right now." She scanned the room. "There she is, dancing with that man with the brown coat. She's been twirling on and off of his arm all night."

I looked at Elyria. "Would you like to dance?"

She nodded her head. I knew she would. She had a natural grace that demanded to be on display.

The music slowed and changed key as we stepped onto the dance floor. As is to be expected anytime a royal arrives to a ball, the floor cleared and we took the center.

"Cal?" Elyria whispered. I could feel her anxiety, the fear of making some social misstep while in the spotlight.

"Eyes on me, Sunshine." I took her face in my hands and lifted her lips to mine. A murmur rippled through the crowd. This girl was all mine and now the entire kingdom would have no doubts about my intentions. "Let's give them a show."

"That, I know how to do." She smiled and gracefully dipped into a low curtsy before me. Gods, but if this woman didn't steal my breath away every time I looked at her.

Elyria took my hand. I spun her back to standing, and the glory of her beauty showered the onlookers. All eyes in the room were definitely on us, but she didn't falter. Quite the opposite, a new energy took over. She was in her element, performing before an adoring audience. By the time we were done here tonight, she will have stolen more hearts than just mine.

We glided across the floor. With each movement, her skirts flared, making Elyria look like she was floating. With the way my heart was beating, she very well might have been. She was stunning, and I found myself lost in the look of her hanging off of my hand. With every dip and turn, the light hit the sun at her waist, and it shone back in split rays of resplendent light. I forgot entirely about the other people in the room. There was only her and the pure joy on her face. It wasn't until others joined again that I remembered there was an entire ballroom watching us.

My mother stood to the side, drumming her fingers against her crossed arms. Her expression gave nothing away, but I knew she didn't like the way I had just made a clear statement to Venterra. However, I didn't care. This wasn't her choice to make. With Elyria by my side, I felt whole; a lost piece of my soul fitted perfectly back in its place. She could scowl, protest, and judge all she liked. It wasn't going to change my decision.

The music slowed, and with a smile, I led her from the floor to an attendant holding glasses of sparkling wine.

Xoc stopped beside us. "I think this might be the happiest I've ever seen you at one of these things, *Callie.*" Xoc snickered.

"*Callie.* Oh my gods. I can't breathe." Elyria grabbed his arm to slow the laughter overtaking her. "I'm never calling you Callen again."

"Fucking, Kaeliana. You heard that?"

Xoc's eyes lifted to the dance floor, immediately finding my sister. "Of course I did." He looked uncomfortable with a deep emerald suit, his normally tied-back hair hanging loosely at his shoulders.

"Gods, the entire room probably heard her." I scrubbed my face. "You'd think after all these years, she'd give up that insufferable nickname. That girl is impossible to love sometimes."

Xoc cleared his throat, then clapped me on the shoulder. "The two of you seem... closer. I'm glad you've worked out whatever it was holding you back."

Elyria opened her mouth to protest but then stopped. She looked up at me and beamed. "I wouldn't say we've worked it out so much as moved past it." With a laugh, she added, "He's still an arrogant bastard that I want to stab most of the time. Right, *Callie*?"

I tightened my hand in warning, then, with a wink, added, "You can try that later."

"You know what," Xoc said, looking between us. "I'm leaving. I was waiting for you to arrive. But, if all tonight is going to be is shameless flirting, then I don't need to be in the middle of it." He rolled his eyes. "I'm going back to my sad little quarters and not the nice big bed that I rightfully won."

"Rightfully?" I thought of our race through Bullseye to the edge of Suman and the web of vines he used to snare my cycle-rig. "Okay, if cheating gives you the right to claim that win, then go ahead. But I expect that bed to be fully occupied tonight, and it might be a bit tight with you in there, too."

Xoc looked at Elyria. She just preened, looking at her nails innocently. But she didn't protest, and that had heat rising within me. Fuck, I couldn't wait to strip her down and make her pay for that Callie comment.

"I'm going to check in with the commander of the guard, then head back to the barracks. I've been in this absurd costume for long enough. Not all of us had the luxury of showing up late." He clapped me on the back, then leaned in and said, "Enjoy yourself. You deserve a bit of happiness. You both do."

"Thank you, brother."

Xoc strode away, cutting a path directly through the center of the room. The people on the dance floor parted around him. His pace slowed as he slipped by Kaeli, giving her spinning pink skirts a long glance before continuing on.

I could have sworn she smiled as she watched him make his way back up the stairs. That girl was trouble wrapped in roses. I just needed to be sure she didn't snare my closest friend in her thorns. What was I thinking—nothing stopped that man, even my not-so-sweet, not-so-little sister.

"There should be fireworks soon." I was itching to have Elyria to myself and away from the eyes of the court. I pointed out the large glass windows towards the sea. "I can take you to a terrace that has an amazing view of the harbor. The best part is that most people don't know about it."

Elyria gave me a grateful smile. "Gods, yes. If I have one more woman try to touch my hair, I might faint." She glanced over her shoulder at the dance floor. "I hoped to see Rei some more tonight, but it would seem she's found other ways to occupy her time. I don't know why I'm surprised." She sighed. "Still, it would be nice to find somewhere that I don't feel like I'm under constant scrutiny."

"Now you understand why I hate these things," I said, taking her hand. We stepped onto a long terrace that circled the edge of the gardens.

"No guards?"

"I'm an expert at knowing just where to slip away from them." I placed a kiss against her cheek. "Also, there are guards at each of the entrances, so they aren't exactly far away."

She nodded, and I led her along the narrow corridor.

"There are old defensive walkways built into the outer walls of the palace. They connect each of the terraces," I explained, snaking our way to a corner of the palace that had a perfect view of the harbor.

"This is thrilling. I've only seen fireworks a handful of times. Those were mostly small displays during our stay in The Isles."

I scanned the terrace. Blissfully, we had the entire place to ourselves. "I promise this display won't be small. Every year the merchants try to outdo one another. So the shows continue to grow bigger and more creative."

Moonlight shone off the gold powder dusting Elyria's skin, making it glitter in the low light. But it was only half as luminous as the excited smile beaming back at me. I pulled the mask from her face, trailing my finger along her jaw and down the long line of her neck.

"You're a vision. I had to touch you just to be certain I wasn't dreaming."

"That's such a line." The satin over her hips shifted with each step she took to the railing, reminding me there was nothing beneath those layers of decadent fabric other than pure, smooth skin.

"That doesn't make it less true."

I slid my hands around her waist, my thumb gliding over the surface of the Sun Serpent on her belt. The goldsmith had done an even better job than I imagined, especially for how rushed the order had been.

Elyria looked down at the emblem.

"I don't think I've told you thank you yet," she said, turning to face me.

"You don't have to thank me, Sunshine. You deserve everything I can give you and more."

"No, thank you for this." She tapped on the sigil, making it catch the moonlight. "I don't know if you realize how much The Sun Serpent means to me."

"Only as much as you mean to me."

She shook her head in disbelief. After everything, she still didn't understand the depth of how I felt. I shared more of myself with her than I had ever shown anyone, and yet she still couldn't see the truth plainly before her.

"Do you know why I call you Sunshine?" I asked, taking her hand in mine.

"Because of the way I fawned over the sun at the top of the cliffs that day?"

I smiled at the memory of her elated face and that tiny strip of sunshine.

"No, Elyria." I paused and gazed into her sparkling eyes, studying the way those golden orbs looked back at me in question. There needed to be no doubts about the honesty of everything I was about to divulge. "It's because *you* are my sunshine at the end of a very long night."

She sucked in a breath, holding it. I knew she was remembering her words to me that day. *"That's how you should go through life, Cal. With your eyes on the sunshine at the end of the night."*

I moved closer still, placing her hand over my heart.

"Before I met you, I was in a dark place, shrouded by walls of wrath and grief. The day I met you, cracks formed along those walls, letting the light in. Being with you has reminded me that the night is not eternal, and as long as we're together, it will always have a dawn."

A streak of light arced across the blue-black sky, and with a pop, it exploded into a fiery star. A second and third streak took off in its wake, filling the sky with sparkling light. Each tiny burst of fire echoed within me.

The explosive display of lights illuminated her delicate features. Music from an orchestra in the distance floated to us over the sound of the falls and the crackle of fireworks. More colorful bursts of fire lit up, blanketing the sky in a rainbow of sparks.

She glanced back, her expression overflowing with joy.

I took her face in my hands, brushing a gentle kiss against her lips. Her fingers curled into my shirt. Dazzling light flashed in my periphery, the resounding beat of each explosion echoing off the marble walls. The energy of each fiery burst flared against my power, the same power that connected me to her.

I deepened the kiss, drawing on that connection, feeling it flood my system with incendiary warmth. Tonight I would open my heart to Elyria, and I wasn't about to let anything else get in the way of giving it to her. Not this time.

Breaking the kiss, I rested my forehead against hers. Elle's body rocked with each breath against my own. Mirroring the way she stood, I lowered my hand and connected to her own rapid pulse. Our hearts hammered in tandem, an undeniable truth residing in each beat.

I breathed her in. "I love you." The next words tumbled out of me in a rush. "I think my heart has always been seeking yours. There was this void at my center, a chasm that only seemed to grow no matter how hard I tried to fill it. When I found you, I realized what that ache actually was. It was you. I didn't know what it meant to be complete until I held you in my arms. Now that I know the truth, I need you to know it, too. I love you, Elyria. I always have. I always will."

The sky around us exploded in another shower of sparks.

The pound of her heart mixed with the pulsing fire in my fingertips, the tether on my power quickly slipping as all of my heart was laid bare before her.

I tilted her head to look into her eyes. They were warm, and in them, I could see the gold of my own reflected. She lifted a slender hand to my hair and ran her fingers through the now golden strands.

The shadow of conflict drifted over her features. It was the exact look she'd given me on Morgan's ship. She stepped back, her hand slipping from my chest. The cold space she put between us hurt more than any knife to my heart ever had.

An ache pulsed in my throat, sinking deeper with each passing second. It settled like a weight into my stomach. I'd felt the pull towards Elyria and known in a second that I was made for her. But I'd never slowed down long enough to consider that she might not feel that draw as intensely as I did. Or perhaps she might have, if I hadn't ruined any chance of her ever trusting me. My dishonesty had destroyed the possibility of her surrendering to it. I could see it in the way her hands trembled, in the tears glossing her eyes, and in the way she still hadn't said anything. The silence was deafening, stretching on and on in that space she'd put between us.

I was a fool and ruined the one good thing the universe had ever given me.

"The ball..." I swallowed, trying to keep the hurt from my voice, and forced my usual cavalier bravado to the surface, "We should probably be returning. I'm sure by now they've noticed we've left." My hands felt numb. Everything felt numb except the pounding ache of my heart.

I turned to walk back towards the ballroom, taking two steps before she said, "Don't."

Stopping instantly in place, I held my breath. I shouldn't let it but hope flared in my chest. Slowly, I turned back to face the woman I'd just bared my soul to.

Elyria grasped my hand, lacing her fingers into mine. With a gentle tug, she reeled me back. Her eyes were glassy with emotion, and her voice shook as she said, "I love you, too."

My heart stopped beating. The glittering fireworks in the sky froze as that one second seemed to continue forever, echoing her words over and over in my mind. *I love you, too.*

I lifted her in my arms, wrapping her tight. With all the intensity and emotion of the past weeks, I claimed her. Every moment shared between us flashed through my mind, every second of connection, every smile she'd ever gifted me, every moment of laughter, every spark of anger, every kiss and sigh. They each rolled through me. I held on, riding the wave, as emotion rocked over us.

When I finally released her lips, we breathed together as one.

"It's always been you, too, Cal." The words broke as her lips met mine between each breath like she couldn't decide which she needed more to confess her truth, breathe, or taste the purity of my mouth on hers. "I fought it for so long. You hurt me. I loved you, fell for you, trusted you, and you hurt me."

"I know. Gods, Elle, if I could take it back. You are all I've ever wanted from this life. You're all I'll ever need in the next, and seeing the way you broke beneath my confession that night tore me apart. There is no kingdom without you, no world for me without you in it. I don't exist without you. You are a part of me. Give me the chance, and I will spend my last breath proving it to you."

"Beneath everything, I've known the entire time, and denying that hurts more. I love you, Cal, and I don't want to keep fighting it. I want to stop hovering, suspended between the stars and the rocks. I want to fall, and I want it to be you who catches me."

Elyria's body melted against mine, and I cradled her to me, intent on never letting her go. I closed my eyes, reveling in the sense of completion. No matter what happened next, this could never be undone.

"Well, *that*... was really touching," said a smooth voice from behind us. "Really had me going there. For a second, I thought she might actually turn you down, again."

Icy dread slithered down my spine. I knew that voice.

With Elyria still in my arms, we turned together to face the figure emerging from the shadows. He swaggered into the light, a thin and ornate iron mask dangling from his fingers. He wore an impeccably tailored dark brown velvet suit with brass buttons and a fine copper filigree embroidered along the cuffs and collar. The dark color of his ensemble was in stark contrast to his pale skin and cornsilk hair. All of it paled in comparison to the menace dripping from him.

"Malvat," I growled and tightened my hold on Elyria.

"Malvat?" Slowly recognition and understanding tightened her muscles. There was a pulse beneath my palm as power flared within her.

"You vile bastard," she hissed. "You're dead."

She lunged toward him, but I dug in my fingers, holding her to me. I would not lose her. Not now that she was finally mine.

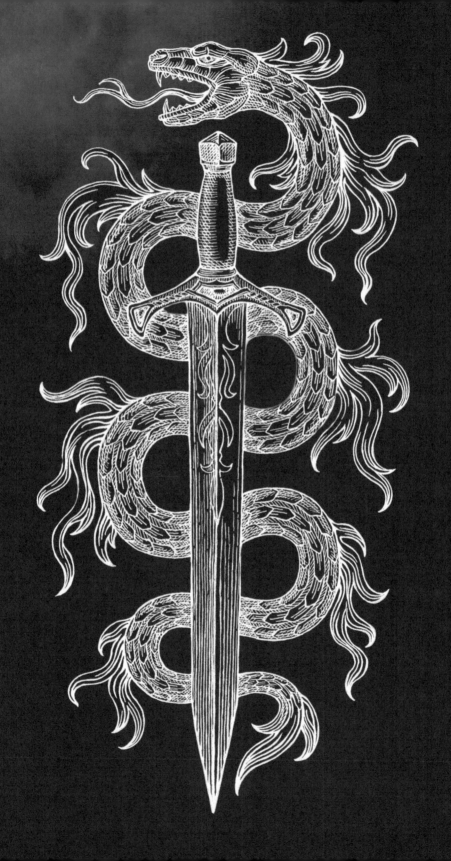

19
ELYRIA

"Let me go," I snarled. "I'm going to claw his fucking face off."

Cal's fingers dug into my arms as I pulled against his grip.

Malvat walked leisurely toward us as if the rage that was rolling off of me wasn't a tangible energy in the air. "I missed you too, little mouse."

Flames lit my fingertips, throwing slashes of light across his face.

Tiny bronze buttons stamped with a dragon head glowed brightly in the fire coiling around my hands. They contrasted with the deep brown of his jacket and the white blonde of his hair. Under other circumstances, he'd be handsome. But, beneath the shadows that clung to his high cheekbones and angular jawline prowled something dark. I could feel the malice in the eyes peering back at me. The skin around them was black and veined, resembling Duke's poisoned flesh in a way that made my stomach flip.

"Elyria," he drew out my name like he was savoring its taste.

Cal's eyes flamed golden, and through gritted teeth, he hissed, "Get her name out of your mouth if you want to keep your teeth in it."

Malvat tsked at him. With a long, languid look, those black eyes cast over my body. "Oh, her name isn't the only thing I plan to put in my mouth."

Cal stepped forward, throwing me behind him. I tripped, landing hard against the marble, and looked up just in time to see a fiery fist fly forward.

Malvat slid easily to the side, leaving Cal's punch to slam into a hard wall of inky darkness.

Cold laughter filled the terrace.

"Calico. You always were so predictable."

Maybe he was predictable, but I was a wildcat, savage and ready for blood. He had no idea what I was capable of.

I sprang to my feet. Cal was quick to arc a wall of protective flames. The fire was white and laced with more powerful energy than I had ever seen him loose.

My own ramped up inside of me. I dug my feet into the ground and readied myself to jump the barrier. I would explode, and that evil smile would be all that was left of Malvat.

"Elle," Cal said in a deadly serious tone. "Do not charge at him. That's exactly what he wants. I don't know why, but he's obviously here for you."

Black smoke formed around Malvat. It curled against the edges of the flame, testing its surface. The inferno flared, forcing the smoke to recoil. Malvat prowled around the arc of light. For every step Malvat took, Cal kept pace, ensuring he remained between us.

Anger and hatred roiled inside me, warring to the surface. My revenge was right there, mere feet away. I longed to burn those black eyes from his skull. Waiting for him to make a move was pointless. I fisted my hands, flames singing the delicate fabric of my dress. The golden scales on my shoulders flashed like armor.

"Elle, please," Cal whispered, sensing my intent. "For once, Sunshine, just listen to me."

He was right. If Malvat was here, he was here with a purpose. It wouldn't do any good to play into his hands, but this vile monster needed to die, and I would be the one to deliver his death.

Unfazed by the display of power before him, Malvat continued, "Thank you, Callen, for fetching my little mouse. Laluna was much farther than I could have ever traveled in this form." He turned, the full brunt of his gaze feeling like a knife to my throat. "Has he taken good care of you for me? I think so. I can smell you all over him. Does my little mouse purr or scream, I wonder."

"She isn't your anything," Cal said firmly.

"No bother. I'll find out soon enough." Malvat waved him off like Cal was nothing more than a bothersome fly. "Did Cal show you the delightful network of caves that reach far below the palace. They make it so easy to slip in and out. All I had to do was whisper in a few ears, and I walked right in. They practically escorted me. Just like old times." Malvat laughed, an inhuman sound like iron nails on stone. "It's been a lovely party. I quite enjoyed the night's entertainment. Of course, he was so wrapped up in you he never even noticed I was here. And look at you; I can hardly blame him for being blinded by your beauty. You *are* tantalizing. Although I quite prefer you like this, all ruffled by rage."

Malvat smiled, revealing rows of grotesque, pointed iron teeth. Why would anyone do that to themselves?

Cal stepped back, connecting his body to mine, grabbing hold of my hand.

"Oh, Calico, she and I are going to have such fun playing." His mask spun absently on a long iron claw. Because Malvat was draken. With all the demonic power he was flexing, I'd forgotten he was like us. I would never doubt Cal's motivations for finding me again. How could anyone fight this?

Cal tightened his grip on my hand and protectively pulled me towards him.

"What's the matter, Cal? Don't feel like sharing anymore?" Malvat gave a playful tilt to his head. "Ask him to tell you about the time they shared those twins from The Isles. All midnight skin and sweetness."

Malvat sucked in a breath through his teeth, lingering on a memory. His eyes glittered as they tracked up the length of my legs. "Aurus's child will taste even sweeter, wrapped up in five millennia of retribution. I bet your blood tastes like fire."

He wasn't even making sense anymore.

"What happened to you, Malvat? What poison did you drink to make evil drip from you like blood from a wound?" The surrounding fire burned brighter with Cal's rage. "You don't even resemble the friend I trusted. No, I think that man drowned in whatever malevolence took his place."

Malvat flickered into shadow before re-solidifying against the wall closest to me. The instantaneous change in location made me jolt. The speed was so much faster than Andromeda had been, practically instantaneous. He must have seen me flinch because the evil draken grinned.

"What a way to speak to your guests. What happened to that famous Innesvalen hospitality?"

"You're no friend of Innesvale," Cal said back coldly.

"Perhaps. I only came to collect what's mine, and then I'll be going." Malvat looked pointedly at me.

I would rip his heart out before he could ever lay a finger on me. The flames around us flared hotter, shifting in color as mine joined Cal's. Scales formed over my skin. The air shimmered with the billowing wave of heat.

"You will die before I let you touch her," Cal growled at him.

"Oh, I wasn't talking about Elyria. I'll let you keep her for a little while longer."

"Let him?"

Malvat's eyes shifted to me. "No, I was talking about my new pet," he cooed. "Would you like to meet her?"

I tensed, not knowing what manner of beast was about to prowl from the darkness. Malvat raised a finger and crooked it playfully towards him. "Come here, pet."

Next to me, black-green smoke gathered in a cloud. Cal and I jumped away from it, nearly falling into our own flames.

"You didn't actually think that pathetic wall of fire could keep me out, did you?"

I raised my arms into a defensive stance. Cal angled himself between me and the mist.

Malvat laughed, "The two of you are positively adorable. Look how hard he tries to keep you safe, but you can see from the panic in his eyes that he knows he can't protect you. If I wanted to mount you to this wall, then there's nothing either of you could do to stop me."

Materializing from within the cloud emerged a figure all in white. A glittering gown that glowed purple in contrast to her beautiful chestnut skin and trademark tattoos.

"Rei," I sobbed. The word pulled from me like it was tethered at the end of a hook.

She stood with a blank expression. Her shaggy hair had fallen loose from its comb and hung low over white eyes.

I reached for her, but Cal grabbed my hand. "That's not Rei. Not anymore."

"You would know, Callen. Reihaneh, here, has been much more fun to play with than your father was. Although, it was delightful the way you begged for your life and how sweetly my knife sank into your flesh."

Cal roared in anger.

I couldn't tell where to look, at Rei's white eyes or at Malvat's black ones? Each word from his mouth was more horrific than the last. The anger in me was so potent that nausea rolled in my stomach. I didn't know what to do. Save her? Kill him? How did you kill something that could become mist and smoke? Killing Andromeda had been impossibly hard, but it felt like child's play when I looked at the demon standing before me.

Malvat spoke, and as he did, it echoed from Rei's lips. "What's the matter, little mouse? Don't you like my new toy?" His ink-stained tongue slithered over those hideous teeth. "She was such a delicious mind to crack, too. Put up a real fight. But in the end, I always get what I want. I just have to be patient, and I have eons of patience."

"She's not some doll for you to play with. Release her, you bastard," I shouted, flames licking past my lips.

"No," he said coolly. Rei disappeared, materializing directly in front of me with her hands wrapped around my throat. She crushed my windpipe with a strength she shouldn't be capable of, cutting off my air entirely with a single squeeze. I scrabbled my hands, clawing at her.

Cal moved to strike Rei.

"Ah ha ha, Callen. You move, and I will snap her neck," said the dark voice that issued from Rei's lips. "The spinal column is such a fragile thing." To prove his point, her hand tightened further, and a miserable hiss forced its way past my lips.

Rei lifted me into the air, my gold sandals barely brushing the ground. She looked up at me with blank, white eyes. I thought of what Cal said about fearing his father's eyes would be the last thing he ever saw. This wasn't Rei, not really. She was more like some kind of automaton. My friend might be locked in there

205

somewhere, but I couldn't help her if I was dead.

Slamming my hands down into her arm, I kicked at her torso, but she didn't move. Instead, as punishment, her freshly manicured nails cut into my neck. The edges of my vision closed in.

Cal lunged toward Rei, throwing up a wall of air between us and blasting her back into the balustrade. The impact forced her to release my neck, long gouges carving into my throat from her nails as I crumpled to the ground.

Malvat laughed.

Cal kneeled down and wrapped me in his arms. His eyes searched mine, checking to see that I was okay. "I've got you, Sunshine."

"Stop worrying about me and kill that bastard," I croaked. Cal gently placed me on the ground and then rose to all six feet of his height, every inch lit by golden flames.

"That's the last time you ever touch her. It will be the last time you ever touch anything." Cal stalked towards Malvat. The beautiful black and gold jacket crumbled away to ash, leaving only his body covered by golden scales.

"You want to play with fire, Calico? Shall we see what we can burn?" Malvat's velvet voice echoed off the stone.

Rei stepped toward the flames, and Cal froze. His eyes flashed to her, only for an instant, before returning his attention fully to Malvat. He hurled a blade of glowing air that could have leveled a building.

The blast ricocheted off the shadow wall, feeding the flames and sending a wave of scalding heat back at us. My power surged at the same time Rei's tattoos glowed defensively against the looming peril, but she hadn't slowed her pace.

"NO." I reached out my mind to the barrier. When Cal's flames wouldn't answer me, I tried to scream, tearing the already raw muscles of my throat further. "CAL." All I could do was rasp. Despite my desperation, my voice was barely louder than a whisper. He was too focused on hurtling as much magic as he could at Malvat. Blades and cyclones of air exploded against whips of shadow.

He didn't see her.

I grabbed Rei's arms. I would not let her burn. Rei swung her elbow back, striking me hard in the temple. The earth somersaulted around my vision as I tumbled back to the marble ground. My vision righted itself just in time to see her step into the flames. The light fabric of her dress crackled in the heat, the magic instantly engulfing her. Rei's blazing form flooded the balcony with light.

Cal extinguished the flames, sending smoke billowing around us. Malvat had proved his point. The fire that should have protected us had done its damage. Rei walked to Malvat. Her dress, having disintegrated into barely more than tatters, hung indecently from her. Her tattoos pulsed as they healed the burns along her feet and ankles.

She draped herself over his shoulder, running a hand down his chest, then lower stroking the noticeable erection in his pants. She leaned in and licked the side of his face before turning to smile at me.

"Marvelous ability, being able to instantly heal yourself. I'm so glad you showed her to me. The things I can make her do. The possibilities for endless play. She will make a lovely toy, and it won't even matter how many times I break it. Did you know I can hear her screaming? Even now, she's fighting against my control. Of course, I can choose which sensations she feels or how much control I wish her to have."

The white clouding Rei's eyes pulled back, revealing their caramel color once more. Her brows tightened, the pupils blowing wide with pure panic as she realized what was happening.

"Elyria, hel-" Her voice instantly cut off as the swirling white and black filled her vision once more, but not before I heard the terror lacing those five syllables. Her facial features, which had just been twisted with fear, relaxed, returning to the mindless automaton. Except she wasn't. He'd proven that much.

As if watching her mutilate herself wasn't cruel enough, Rei's hand dipped into his pants, gripping him beneath the fabric. Malvat's iron teeth glinted in the moonlight as he sneered up at me.

Bile rose in my throat.

"I will kill you," I snarled.

"Yes, you keep saying that."

I pushed past Cal. Flames poured from my hands. The torrent of fire crashed against the marble of the terrace, spilling around Malvat's wall of shadow crystal. As soon as the barrage of flames ended, the crystal dissolved into wisps that floated in the air.

Malvat opened his mouth to say something, but before he could, I shot a second volley of flames. I was done listening to whatever toxic lies he was going to spew.

He would die—tonight.

This wave was hotter than the last. The metal on my shoulders heated, making the pauldrons glow red. Damning the consequences, fire rocketed from me, fueled on by pure wrath.

A wave of black shadow crested over my flames, snuffing them out. My back slammed against the marble ground, an explosion of stars filling my vision. Immediately, Cal was at my side. A barely visible shimmer surrounded me. The slight distortion was the only indication that he'd thrown a shield around my prone form.

"This is boring me, little mouse. I really thought you could do better than this." Malvat brushed a stray bit of ash from his lapel. That was the closest I'd come to singeing him.

"I'll give you boring, you iron toothed son of a bitch," I roared.

With a whistle, a streak of blue light shot through the air, a glittering trail behind it.

I held up my hand to the firework, commanding the blaze to come to me. Intense power coursed through my hand. I connected to the pure force behind the explosive, arcing the glittering orb towards the balcony.

"Fuck, Elle!" Cal shouted.

The bright blue streak rocketed directly at where Malvat stood. Fuck him. This ended now.

Cal threw himself on top of me just as an explosion blasted out in every direction. A shower of stars skittered over the marble balcony. The concussive blast slammed into the shield Cal erected around us, pushing us into the wall of the terrace. Branches of the nearby trees smoldered. The flower pots decorating the columns were little more than charcoal.

I scanned the smoke-choked balcony. Black glittering dust dropped in a curtain around Malvat and Rei. My heart sank. That blast should have killed him. It would have killed Rei too, but I knew in my heart she would rather die than remain his puppet.

"Now, that's better," Malvat smiled. "I'll be seeing you soon, little mouse. Then, we can really play."

I flipped off the ground, swinging a kick that should have been powerful enough to snap his neck. To my disbelief, my foot passed through him. Mist curled around my ankle, showing only the ghostly imprint of a metallic smile before disappearing before me.

"NO!" I screamed. "YOU COWARD, COME BACK AND FIGHT ME."

I looked at Cal. Hot, angry tears poured down my cheeks.

Rage boiled in me. I saw it reflected in his gaze.

They were gone.

They were gone, and he had Rei.

20

ELYRIA

It didn't take long to find one of the stationed guards. The trademark blank expression of a guard, turning to wide disbelief as he took in our disheveled state. The tattered bits of my dress fluttered against my knees, echoing what my sense of reality felt like.

"Your jacket. Give it to me," Cal commanded.

The guard immediately stripped, handing him the uniform.

"Find Commander Xoc. He should be in the barracks." Cal pulled the jacket on, the form too tight to properly fit over his broad shoulders. "Tell him to meet me in the War Room. He is to come immediately." The man looked baffled. "Go!"

We followed the sound of the orchestra back to the ballroom. The Captain of the Guard stood on the balcony, surveying the party.

"Belmont!"

"Your Highness-" he began.

"Malvat is in the palace." The Captain's entire demeanor immediately shifted. "I'm instituting Raven Protocol. Lock it down. Lock everything down. Anything that takes to the air is to be shot down. I don't care what it is. He'll be leaving on an airship from one of the grottos along the coastline. I want guards on my mother and sister immediately. The party is over." He waved his hands at the party guests below us. "Every guest is to be checked for signs of the Shade before they are permitted to leave."

Heat bloomed in my chest. Commanding Cal was hot. It was a side I hadn't seen before. The set of his jaw and the ferocity behind his eyes, the way the men around him all heeled to his control; it was sexy as sin. The partially dressed and battle-worn state only adding to the appeal.

Cal continued. "That metal bastard is *never* to step foot in this kingdom again unless it's with a sword plunging through his chest. Is that clear?"

"Yes, sir." the Captain said, before turning and walking at a hurried clip down the hall.

Cal looked at me. His lips quirked, and I was sure he saw the heat in my eyes, that was until they drifted down to my throat. His hands grazed over my neck, causing a sting against the cuts and bruises. The fleeting sense of desire was quickly banished by the rush of horrific memories.

The helplessness returned, stronger than before. I fought the lingering feeling of my toes scraping over the marble as I hung from Rei's hand. I closed my eyes, only to see black ones in their place. A tremor snaked up my spine, leaving every part of me trembling.

"I will kill him," he growled before leaning in to gently kiss my wounds. I clung to him. The shock of the evening finally settling into me. I felt so cold. Cal ran his hands up and down my arms, concern tilting his handsome features. He walked up to a woman with a white fur stole wrapped around her shoulders. I was fairly certain this was Lady Bernadette, the courtier who had been trying to ensnare Cal.

"Madam," he said, showing zero familiarity or warmth.

The woman bristled for a second before realizing it was the prince addressing her. Immediately, her expression softened into a placating smile.

"Your Highness," she said with a deep curtsy. When she stood, she ran her hand up the side of his arm in a way that was entirely too familiar. "I didn't recognize you."

I'm sure she thought she was being seductive as if a woman like her knew the meaning of the word. You actually had to care enough to learn what a person wanted to be able to seduce them.

Cal shook her hand off of him and stepped back so that she couldn't do it again, sending a surprised flood of satisfaction through me.

"I require your stole. The crown will reimburse you for whatever its cost," he said matter of factly, a hand extended to her.

"Of course," she cooed, handing it over to him. Then she gave me an uneasy look. "Consider it a gift."

Cal didn't give the woman a second glance. He walked directly to me and wrapped the plush fur around my shoulders. "Come on," he said, kissing the top of my head. "The War Room is this way."

"Until next time, your Highness," Lady Bernadette called after us.

Cal made a sound of disgust under his breath. "That woman is insufferable. If I could banish her and the rest of her ilk from the palace, I would."

Cal pushed open a thick set of oak doors, holding it for me. I stepped past him to see Xoc standing at a window, looking down to the central courtyard and main gate.

Behind us, the door closed with a heavy and ominous thunk. Cal's reassuring hand was at the small of my back, ushering me toward one of the many chairs that circled a long table.

Xoc turned to face us. "Fuck. Look at the two of you."

I looked at Cal, really looked at him, and saw what Xoc must have seen. Cal was wearing clothes in tatters and a random guard's jacket. Soot streaked across his chest and face. And then there was me. The stunning gown was torn, singed, and melted alternately in places. My throat was probably a mess of bruises pebbled by the deep gauges left by Rei's nails. My makeup was undoubtedly streaked across my face.

"Tell me everything," he said, looking between us.

Cal peeled off the ill-fitting jacket and threw it to the ground with a roar of frustration. Then he gripped the back of my chair. Pent up energy and emotion pulsated around him.

"Elyria and I were..." Cal's voice dropped off as he looked down at me, and the memory of his confession and mine came back in a flood emotion. Cal loves me, and I... I love him, too. How had it taken me so long to come to that conclusion? Now, as I thought about it, it felt blindingly clear.

"On the western terrace, watching the fireworks," he continued.

"Watching the fireworks?" Xoc asked, his lips quirking into an uncharacteristic smile.

"Malvat walked out of the adjoining drawing room," Cal continued.

"Malvat?"

"He was dancing with Rei during the ball," I murmured, almost dazed. Cal and Xoc looked at me. A memory, standing on the staircase and seeing her white dress glitter as she spun around a man in a brown velvet suit.

"My gods, Cal, I fucking saw him." My heart kicked into high speed. "In the ballroom." I held a hand out to Cal, twisting to grab his arm. "Kaeliana said 'she's been twirling on his arm all night.'"

"That means he was in the ballroom, and none of our staff noticed," Xoc concluded. "I didn't notice. Fucking hells, Kaeliana was in that room."

"Or, they did, and he infected them. Malvat said he 'whispered into the ears of a few guards'."

Cal placed a hand over my own. "That's why I wanted the staff checked. I think we may have more affected guardsmen than we previously realized. He came into the palace through the cave network that connects to the grottos. I've been so damn preoccupied by my own emotions that I never considered putting a detail down there."

I knitted my hands together, letting guilt wash over me.

"Don't. Don't you dare." Cal reached down and lifted my chin to meet his fierce gaze. "My love for you is *not* why Rei is gone."

If Xoc was surprised by Cal's casual profession of love, he didn't show it.

"Wait, Rei's gone?" Xoc asked, focusing on the real cause for concern.

"I'm getting to that." A shadow passed over Cal's eyes. "Malvat has some kind of plan. He intends to take Elyria. I'm sure of it."

I nodded in confirmation. It certainly seemed like he had sordid plans for me. The things he'd implied flipped my stomach, making my nausea resurface.

"Probably because he knows losing Elyria would be the worst kind of torture for me," Cal said.

"Where does Rei come in?" Xoc asked.

"She materialized out of black smoke."

"Fuck, he didn't just take her." Xoc sat down at the table across from me.

With a bang, the door opened. The queen strode in, her black gown billowing around her. She walked directly to me, taking my jaw in her hand and tilting my head to either side.

"Tell me you at least gave that bastard as good as you took."

"I tried, but I didn't even scratch him," I replied bitterly, then winced at the throbbing in my throat.

The queen turned to a guard, snapping to get his attention. "Fetch me the healer."

"She didn't just try, Mother. She threw a fucking rocket at him." Pride coated his words, which then promptly shifted to something much more bitter. "Which was reckless," he added, looking down at me. "If I hadn't been there to shield you, you would have blown yourself up."

"But you *were* there to shield me."

The Queen smirked in approval. The first she'd ever given me.

"We were just filling in Xoc on the events of tonight," I said, trying not to be intimidated by her commanding presence.

"Continue." She pulled out a seat at the end of the table.

Cal nodded, saying, "Rei was infected with the shade. The display of power he showed us, as he manipulated her was... sickening."

"Tell me about the fight. I assume, you didn't do that to yourself." She pointed to the tattered remains of Cal's suit.

"Actually I did." Cal quickly filled her in on all we'd learned about Malvat's newly acquired skills. Xoc nodded his head, making notes and calculating how to work offensively against it.

The healer entered with a quiet knock. The crystal hanging from his neck reminded me too much of the man who had tried to heal Duke. Luckily, it didn't take long for the pain in my throat to ease and the bruises to fade. All the while, Cal paced behind us, watching the man like a tiger in a cage.

"I don't think Malvat is entirely himself, almost as if he's being controlled by something," He said, stopping to look at us. "His eyes have that same black veining that happened after I was pierced by the knife." He looked at me.

"And after Duke was bitten by the spider." I nodded in confirmation.

Cal sat down in the seat beside me.

"Some of what he says and knows are things that only Mal would know. Things like calling me Calico."

"And the twins," I interjected bitterly.

"Yes," he answered cautiously. "But he said other things, conflicting things, as if Malvat was arguing against himself. And sometimes he was talking about himself in the third person... He mentioned 'five thousand years' as if he's been planning this entire attack for that long. But, Malvat isn't any older than I am."

"And Aurus," I added. "He mentioned Aurus, like he hated him."

Cal snapped. "You're right. I think it's time that I give you what you've been asking for all along."

"And what is that?"

He looked at his mother. "We need to talk to Aurus. We're missing something, something big."

"In the morning," she agreed with a nod to both of us.

My heart raced. This time tomorrow I would be face to face with The Ancient Gold Dragon. I would finally get answers about who I am... about my parents. And maybe Aurus would be able to tell us what we needed to do to defeat Malvat for good.

Xoc stood. "I'm going to check in with Captain Belmont. I want to read the reports from tonight. Then, tomorrow I will ride with you to the Vanfald."

21

ELYRIA

Cal opened the blue door, drawing an arm around me as we entered.

I looked up at him with a kind of vulnerability I'd never felt before. No part of me wanted to be alone.

Reading my mind, he said, "I plan to have you safely in my arms the entire night." Tucking me close, he added, "It's going to be a very long time before I let you out of arms' reach."

He guided me through the connecting rooms to where a large white bathtub was sunken into the ground, nearly identical to the one in my washroom. Warm water filled the basin, sending a blanket of eucalyptus and mint-scented steam into the air.

"I'm going to remove every trace of him from your skin and replace each touch of malice with ones of love," he said, pulling the stole away from my shoulders.

Cal lifted a damp cloth to my cheeks, swiping away the streaked cosmetics that had once been so artfully applied. The tenderness made tears blur my vision. Clean of tint and kohl, he ghosted his lips over each eyelid before placing a last gentle kiss to my mouth.

"Beautiful."

"Cal... I..." My voice dropped off, and my head dropped to his chest. I needed the tremor in my body to go away. I needed to feel his warmth wrapped around me, the stability I only ever felt in his arms. I needed him.

"I know, Sunshine."

He kissed me again, thick emotion lining each of his movements. It swathed his embrace, and for the first time, I recognized the emotion for what it truly was—love.

Cal gently twisted my shoulders, turning my back to him so that he could begin unfastening my dress. One by one, the tiny chains dropped against my back. He dragged a finger over my newly freed dragon mark, warmth following his trailing touch. When I began to squirm, his hands gripped my hips to keep me still.

"I love this," Cal said, dropping to one knee. "The first time I saw your mark, all I wanted to do was draw you close–" His nose skimmed the base of my spine before the warmth of his mouth closed over where I knew the dragon's tail curled. "--and study the beast until I'd memorized every single scale." He moved higher, tracing each bend and curve. With each press of his lips, the tattoo burned. By the time he made it between my shoulder blades, the chills that had wracked my system since leaving the balcony were nothing more than a forgotten nightmare.

Cal tugged at the scaled epaulettes and laughed. "You fused the shoulder pieces to the satin."

I looked down at my hands, curling them into fists. I could still see them burning white hot. My rage may have been supplanted by grief, but it took nothing to feel it rush back to the surface.

I hadn't been able to kill him.

My father's murderer had been right before me, and I wasn't strong enough to so much as mark him.

"No matter." Cal kissed the back of my neck, drawing me back to the present. "I think we don't need to worry about the integrity of this dress anymore, anyway."

He reached around my collar and tore at the fabric, letting it fall down to my waist. Behind me, the golden armor thunked to the ground. Humid air from the tub kissed at my exposed breasts, causing goosebumps to pebble down my arms.

Cal ran the back of his hand from my shoulder to my wrist, chasing them away. It did nothing to ease the sensitivity of my skin. If anything, the longer we were in contact, the more intense that connection felt.

His hands disappeared. I felt their absence, missing their warmth like the sun disappearing behind the clouds. The belt at my waist released. The swinging sigil sent a stream of golden light around the room. My eyes followed Cal as he laid the Sun Serpent reverently on the stand beside the tub.

He walked back to me, inhaling slowly as his eyes traced over my exposed breasts. "I am not worthy," he said on an exhale. My heart lurched, squeezing until I was sure I couldn't breathe. How could Cal believe he wasn't worthy? Nobody could ever compare to the way he made me feel. When we were together, my soul preened. I was a fool for denying it as long as I did.

Circling behind me, Cal released the few remaining hooks along my lower back. The fabric at my hips released, and the ravaged remains of silk and satin pooled at my feet.

His hands followed the silhouette of my torso, coasting along my sides and settling at my hips. "Gods, Sunshine..." He pulled me back against him, the hardened ridge of his cock pressing into my lower back. "You... are.... everything." Head dropping to my shoulder, his long exhalation drifted over my collarbone. Despite the obvious arousal, there was very little sexual tension lingering between us. Somehow, in the quiet of the bathing chamber, what was happening felt like so much more than pent up sexual desire.

"Let's get in the water," I said, slipping my sandals off and dropping them beside me. I heard the slide and fall of fabric as Cal removed what little remained of his own clothing.

He scooped me into his arms, cradling me against him exactly as he had in our lake. The soothing warmth of the water seeped into my bones, eclipsed by the strength and security of Cal's body wrapped around mine. When he'd held me in the falls, I'd been afraid of losing myself in him. Now, all I wanted was to disappear into that embrace and never emerge.

Cal leaned forward, soaking a large sponge in the frothy water. Soot and streaks of blood sloughed away from my skin with each slow drag. He tilted my head against his shoulder and tenderly wiped away the dried blood caking my throat. His lips grazed my neck, kissing away my already healed wounds and erasing the ghost of their ache.

Carefully, he removed the pins in my hair. Black and golden locks tumbled onto my shoulders. Cal buried his face in the mess of curls, inhaling deeply. Finally, the tension in his muscles eased. He wrapped tightly around me, while I circled my arms over his until we were holding each other in unmoving silence, listening to the faint sound of the falls outside the balcony.

Cal heaved a breath, and his arm at my hip tightened. "The first time I saw you, you were balancing on a chair, hanging a poster in the square at Laluna. I saw a flash of light and knew you were who I'd been waiting my whole life to find."

I remembered that day. Life was so much simpler then.

"I couldn't help but follow you into that patisserie. But, do you know when I realized I loved you?" he said in a low and hushed tone. Cal's heart pounded against my back.

"No," I replied softly, certain my heart was just as frantic.

I tilted my face, leaning into the crook of his neck. I fit perfectly against him. Cal was right on the balcony earlier, two people shouldn't fit so seamlessly together without fate being involved. His fingers drifted aimlessly up and down my arm.

"When you fell from the cliff. When you screamed my name, and I couldn't stop you..." The rush of stone against a night sky flashed through my mind, followed by the relief when he'd pulled me against him. It was the first time I'd acknowledged how right being with him felt. "In that moment, I knew. I held you in my arms, thinking it over and over again, the entire damn night. If I lost you, I would never recover from it..."

His hand stilled.

"For one terrifying moment, I thought he might actually kill you." His voice cracked over the words. Cal's arms closed around me, his face pressing into my neck. He pretended this bath was to comfort me, but he needed this. Just like he needed to hold me that night on the cliff. He needed to know he could protect me. Because feeling like he couldn't keep me safe was his worst nightmare.

Twisting, I lifted my hand to his face. "I'm still here."

Raw emotion turned his eyes bright gold. I caught the single tear rolling over his cheek with my thumb, brushing it away. I never thought I'd see it, but Cal's composure was breaking. Beneath it, there was so much fear.

I turned to straddle him. My legs wrapped around his waist and I settled my hips into his.

"Elle...I can't..." He closed his eyes tight, dropping his forehead to mine.

"I will always be here." I lifted one of his hands and placed it between my breasts. The other, I placed over his scar, being sure that he could feel how our hearts beat in tandem. "In this life, and the next."

The entirety of his raw emotion flooded through that touch, and when his mouth met mine, I surrendered to it. I would give him whatever he needed. My body, my heart, my soul. It was his.

Cal held me like he was trying to fuse together the essence of who we were. My power sang in answer, calling out to merge with his soul. The rightness of being with him was overwhelming, and I needed more. I didn't want to be able to tell where he ended and I began.

"I love you," I whispered, reaching between us. Cal shuddered when I took him in my hand, luxuriating in the feel of his silken skin against my palm with long, slow strokes. Beneath my body, each of his muscles tensed. The cage of his arms turned into a bowstring drawn tight as I aligned our bodies. I trembled at the promise of all that energy releasing into me.

"I love you too, Sunshine." Cal's fingers dug into my hips, pulling me down. I descended in one devastating slide. With each aching inch, heat pounded at my veins, embers filled my vision, and in my ears I heard only the pulsing of his power.

"This feels..." A vibrating energy snaked down my spine as we connected, and in response I arched back, forcing him deeper. "Nothing feels like this. Goddess above."

He leaned forward, kissing the center of my chest, rocking me backward, and shifting against something deep inside of me that forced a long moan.

Lips still hovering over the rapid beat of my heart, he murmured, "This is really mine?" There was so much disbelief and awe behind those words.

"Yes," I breathed, rocking my hips again. "It was always yours."

With each kiss, the fire that coiled deep within me wrapped around his own power, binding us together. A knot that tightened with each slow push and pull of our bodies.

More. More. More. It was a prayer that echoed in my mind.

As if Cal could hear my thoughts, he lifted me from the bath. My body still wrapped around his, he climbed the steps out of the tub.

22

CALLEN

Gently, I slid Elyria onto my bed. I hovered over her panting form, peppering her neck and collar with kisses, wanting nothing more than to hear the way she gasped when my lips hit her skin. Her rapid breaths pressed against me with each inhale, making me slow down enough to take in the moment.

I sat back on my heels to admire her. The sight of this queen in my bed was something I'd envisioned more times than I could count. Reality was so much better.

The damp strands of her dark tresses splayed over the white satin. Droplets of water and oil clung to her chest, glistening like diamonds. Every inch of her glorious skin seemed to radiate light. It stunned me, kicking my heart into my throat and knocking every thought from my mind, leaving only how she looked in this moment. Pink swollen lips tilted into an inquisitive smile. The awe must have been painted across my expression.

How did I get so fucking lucky? I was never the lucky one. And how did I ever convince this goddess to give me her heart after everything I'd said and done? I'd spent centuries feeling unfulfilled, like the world had dulled, fading into a mass of nothingness. I chased every thrill and high in an attempt to bring even a shimmer of excitement into my life. Here, Elyria laid in my bed, absolutely resplendent in the way she lit up my heart.

"Say it again," I said, running a hand down the center of her chest.

"I love you." Elyria teased her lower lip through her teeth, hiding the smile that pulled at the corners.

"Again."

"I love you." She crooked her finger, beckoning me back to her.

I couldn't move. I was spell struck, frozen in stone, marveling at the bliss of this moment.

Elyria, on the other hand, was not frozen. She writhed under my attention, growing more impatient with each passing second. She sat up, looping her arms around my neck and sinking her fingers into my hair. There was a genuine sense of urgency behind the embrace. She pulled at me, trying to force us back down on the bed. I braced my hands on either side of the mattress. With the number of times I had envisioned this moment, I was not about to rush past committing every sensation to memory.

I pressed a hand to her chest, pinning her in place. "So eager, Sunshine. We have eternity before us." I slowly ran my fingers down the length of her form. Descending from her collar, over the curve of her breast, I paused to feel its heavy weight in my palm. Her skin was so soft, and the pulse of energy that followed my touch was addicting. I could spend days just touching her.

"Let me drink you down." I slid my fingers lower, gliding them over the light swell of her stomach and exploring the way her muscles flexed beneath my touch.

Elyria shivered, despite the intense heat radiating off her skin. Several times she tried lifting against my hold, but this was mine to claim. I would do it exactly the way I'd fantasized.

"Cal," her impatient voice warned.

"Be patient." I sank my fingers between her thighs. My mouth watered, remembering exactly how she'd tasted while she came on my tongue. Her hips lifted into my touch, spine arching against the hand pinning her in place.

"Cal, please."

I'd once heard her say please with that exact same whimper. I'd told her to wait, making silent promises to show her what was worth waiting for. Linking her hands into my own, I placed a kiss to the palm of each, then pushed them into the mattress beside her beautifully flushed cheeks.

I wasn't waiting any longer. Tonight there would be nothing stopping me from showing her all the ways we perfectly fit together.

With exquisite torture, I slowly sank back into her. Elyria's mouth parted with an exhaling moan, one I swallowed greedily. Her hips pressed up to mine, drawing me into the tight heat until I was fully seated within her. The moment we fully connected, the gates to her power opened, making my blood sing. It was damn near operatic.

"Elle, Fuuuuck..."

I couldn't finish that sentence. She was everywhere. Around me, clutching me, in my veins, and making my very soul quake. I'd never felt anything like it. The sensation of complete connection was verging on cataclysmic, and we weren't even moving yet.

"I could stay here forever, with you wrapped around me in utter perfection," I tilted my hips to emphasize my point.

With a moan, she snaked her spine, forcing my cock to push against her inner walls. The delicate muscles gripping me rolled, contracting one at a time until it wasn't just her moaning. The air around us shimmered with a rainbow heat wave.

Elyria bit down on my lips in warning. "If you don't start moving again, I might actually die."

"That's not funny," I said seriously, drawing back so that barely my tip remained sheathed.

"Neither is how badly I need you." She dug a heel into my back and hooked another behind my knee. With the exact same undulation I'd seen her do while dangling from a golden hoop, she pulled me into her. The fantasy of having that goddess of sunlight and fire in my bed came full circle.

"There is nothing I wouldn't give you, Sunshine."

I drew back slowly, her tortured cry disappearing on a gasp when I slammed hard against her. Before she could recover, I did it again, and again... and fucking again. Her grip tightened and pressed against mine. Her nails lengthened, biting into the backs of my hands. I didn't relent, only drove harder and deeper. And with each hit, streaks of purple flared in my vision.

A tingling sensation pressed against my ribs. Our power was surging and building at the center of my chest. I grabbed hold of it and locked it deep.

Tonight was not the night to unleash whatever that was into the world.

"Cal," she moaned between gasps. The sound of my name hanging from her ecstasy-laced lips only fueled my intensity. It became her own form of mantra, just as much as whispering hers was my prayer.

Elyria crested into her climax, dragging me with her. I lost myself completely to the feel of her beneath me. My vision splintered. The world around us broke apart, over and over. Shattering until it seemed like she was all that was left in it.

Elyria's eyes opened to stare at me in replete amazement. I drank down every curve and line of her face. The graceful slope of her cheeks, the round fullness of her lips as they curved up into a blissed-out smile. In this moment, there was only her. I ceased to exist. She was my everything, my entire universe.

I released her hands and brushed away the still damp hair. She leaned into the touch.

"I love you," she said. Gods, I would never tire of hearing her say that. My heart clenched, causing the heat of our embrace to ricochet between us.

"In this life and the next, beautiful," I replied.

I brushed my lips over hers. The zing of energy passed between them. She murmured, "Someone who matches my spark." Then gave a dazedout giggle.

She looked completely exhausted. Given the emotional toll of this night, it made sense. I kissed each of her closed lids. Part of me wanted to tangle myself around her and start all over again, but an entire lifetime stretched out before us. There was plenty of time to play. Tonight, I would let her sleep. For now.

I slid down to the mattress, grabbing the satin coverlet, and pulling her back into my embrace. She let out a hum of satisfaction as I fitted her against me.

The world slowly righted itself, and those pieces of us that shattered, reformed into something entirely new and complete.

23

ELYRIA

I woke to the sound of the rushing falls filtering in from the open balcony door. My eyes focused on Cal, looking out over the water while sipping from a teacup. The dainty porcelain was at such odds with the large hands that held it. He wore only loose-fitting linen pants that hung artfully from his hips, like he'd walked right out of my fantasies.

Warmth flashed over my chest, remembering the last time I'd been on that balcony, followed by a cascade of images from the night before. We snuggled in peace for exactly five minutes before he was pushing back into me, and I was asking for more. Weeks of denial created a need that couldn't be sated. The only thing that stopped us was sheer exhaustion. Cal had the stamina of a god, and he'd driven me to my limits last night more times than I could count.

My gaze drifted along his dragon mark and over the sculpted lines of his back. I bit down on my lip, letting my eyes settle just below his hips. Stamina wasn't his only god-like quality.

I pulled the satin sheet around me and sat up. A table had been set with various breakfast foods, and an empty teacup sat beside a steaming teapot. Someone had brought this here, while I slept in Cal's bed, utterly naked. Although, we were essentially sharing apartments, this was probably what everyone expected. I just hoped I hadn't given some unsuspecting courier an eyeful of naked boob.

Cal glanced over his shoulder, spotting me sitting up and awake. His warm smile greeted me. Muscles in my core clenched as he appraised the scene spread before him. He walked directly to me, depositing the teacup on the table as he passed by.

"Good morning, gorgeous. You, disheveled from a night in my bed, might be my absolute favorite thing to see in the morning."

I tightened the fabric around me, feeling my face flush.

Pure mischief pulled at his lips. He leaned down ,and with one hand, grabbed the sheet hanging off the end of the bed, peeling the fabric back. It slowly shifted, exposing me to him bit by bit.

Cal climbed onto the foot of the bed, sliding his hands over my ankles and skating them up my legs as he prowled closer. "There is something I have been dying to do ever since you came walking out of that forest, this blazing temptress surrounded by night."

He placed a kiss on my inner thigh, pushing them wider and forcing a whimper from me. "If Xoc hadn't appeared when he did, then I would have devoured you that night."

My heart galloped an irregular rhythm, making me feel lightheaded.

"Oh?" I said breathlessly. Gods, his hands on my skin forced my brain to cease all function. "If Xoc hadn't appeared that night, I would have let you." I sank into the pillows.

Cal growled low, "Don't tell me these things. I already have so many regrets."

He grazed a hand over my breast, lightly tracing the curve and making them feel heavy. "That night in the Lunar Forest, you melted my mind. No matter how hard I tried, I couldn't stop thinking about it. I've dreamt of it every night since, and then this morning, I woke to see the dream never ended."

His thumb rolled over my nipple. "There was a faint blue glow, right here." Cal dipped his head down, licking at the exact place where the juice had stained my skin. He teased his teeth over the tip before drawing my breast into his mouth. Arching my head back, my leg bent to slide up the length of his golden torso. I opened my body to him, allowing access to whatever he'd been dreaming of doing.

Cal's other hand slid between my legs, teasing my already oversensitized flesh. I lifted my hips into his touch in a greedy demand for more.

He moved to the other breast, biting down and forcing a gasp from me.

"Fuck, I love that. I could spend this entire day learning each sound you make and drawing them from you. One day soon, that is exactly what I plan to do," he said, pushing two fingers into me. As if to prove his point, he curled those fingers, drawing my entire body off the bed with one simple motion.

"But for now, I think I will settle for this." His mouth seized my breast once more.

"Please," I begged, not actually knowing what I was begging for. My body was still too sensitized, too in tune with his power, and the ache that he stirred within me was more than I could bear.

"So polite," he said with a smile against my breast. "Light up for me, Sunshine."

Cal worked me with the same effortless precision that he'd used to manipulate those butterfly swords. He was graceful and elegant with his approach, twisting and pulling at exactly the right angles. Until I was screaming at each flick of his tongue, pull of his fingers, and bite of his teeth.

Fire pulsed like a living current at every place we connected. It rose like a wave pulling back from the shore. Until, with a final stroke of his thumb against my clit, it crashed down over me. Flames exploded out, only to be instantly smothered.

I collapsed, my bones having melted into nonexistent mush. The walls and ceiling swayed. My heart was protesting being caged and doing everything it could to break free.

"Did I blow a hole in the ceiling?"

Finally able to focus my eyes, I stared up at the most beautiful painting I'd ever seen. The ceiling featured a brilliant blue sky, and high amid the clouds flew a gold dragon. The illusion was complete as if the marble of the palace opened up directly above me.

Cal sat at the edge of the bed, lazily stroking from my ankle to knee and back again. He looked like a cat with a bowl of cream. An arrogant cat.

"You climax so beautifully." He leaned in and kissed the back of my knee.

"Cal," I cried, unable to take any more of his attentions, or perhaps I was demanding more. I wasn't exactly sure, probably both.

"And, my name on your lips..." Cal groaned low and deep, a sound that rolled down my spine in a direct line to my clit.

I wasn't sure that I could remember how to speak. My core still throbbed. My power sizzled just beneath the surface. It sent shocks rocketing down to my toes and buzzing along my finger tips.

"Are you hungry?" he asked, slowly caressing the skin of my thigh.

"Famished," I said, and then biting my lip, I added, "For you, mostly."

Lifting my foot, I dragged a toe over each perfectly molded ridge of his abdomen.

He pushed his tongue into the side of his cheek. I could see the desire warring within him. As fast as a cobra striking, he latched onto my foot and nipped at the inside of my ankle. "Behave."

I giggled and tugged my foot from his grip. Kicking out, I moved to hook him. If he wasn't going to crawl down here on his own, then I would have to throw him down.

Cal grabbed me by the knee. With a single twist of his arm, I was flipped onto my stomach. One hand on my shoulder, he pushed my face into the pillow. It was so fast that I was still processing the change in position when his other hand cracked down hard on my ass, sending a spike of arousal and pain shooting through my senses. I arched my back, expecting him to double down on the action. Instead, he got up and walked to a chair where a satin robe laid draped over it. He picked it up and tossed it to me.

"Put this on. Or we're never leaving this room."

"Would that be so bad?" I mused airily.

"Oh, it would be heaven." His hand flexed while his eyes settled on where he'd undoubtedly just left a handprint. "Fuck." He scrubbed his face with his palms. "We have actual things to accomplish today, and I'm sure you'll need to be able to walk for most of them. Remember, bad guy and a world to save."

I pouted and slipped my arms into the oversized robe. He was right. There would be time later to lose ourselves in each other. And that last comment had dowsed me with an icy bucket of reality, fueled mostly by memories of Malvat's sickening grin as Rei stroked him. My fire bubbled.

Around Cal, it was so much harder to keep it locked down, reminding me that it wasn't that long ago that I lost a grip on it. I glanced back to see the damage I'd done in my explosion. But the satin sheets were still perfectly white.

"How did you keep the bed from burning? I felt the tether on my fire release."

I placed a glutinous amount of pastries and fruit onto my plate. Gods, I was starving. No longer consumed by sexual need, now all I could feel was how empty my stomach was. Playing with Cal was dangerous. One second I was forgetting to eat, and the next, I was forgetting to breathe.

"I was ready for it, and removed the oxygen from around you. No air, no fire."

"That explains the not breathing part."

"And last night, I locked down our power before things got too out of control."

I set my plate on a small glass table overlooking the bay.

"You can leash my powers?"

"I don't think so. It wasn't like that. It didn't feel like my fire or your fire, just our fire. I'd be happy to recreate the scenario so you can see what I'm talking about." I perked up. I liked that idea a whole lot. "When we get back from The Vanfald," he added, reaching forward and bringing my hand to his lips.

"For my benefit, of course."

"Of course." He nipped at my finger before letting it go.

"Mmm..." I hummed, remembering this thing he'd done with his tongue that made my soul leave my body. "I suppose that means that we need to get moving soon, then."

"Insatiable," Cal mused. His eyes lingered over my body for a few long seconds. "It's probably a good thing Alessia had this sent up." He glanced pointedly down at the teapot. Beside it were several small containers. I picked up the lid of the canister closest to me. Inside was a white powder and the tiniest spoon I'd ever seen. The second pot held honey, and the third a rust-colored powder that smelled faintly like pepper and cinnamon.

"What is this?"

Cal cleared his throat. "We haven't discussed the future much."

I swallowed hard. A slight panic settled into my chest. I hadn't fully come to grips with how I felt about Cal until last night. I certainly hadn't given myself the time to consider what that would mean for us. He'd put me in the rooms destined for his future bride, but did I actually want to be a queen?

Cal rounded the table, settling his hips into mine. One hand tipped my chin up. "Try not to panic."

I frowned. Was I that easy to read?

He chuckled lightly under his breath. Apparently, I was.

"I only meant that we never discussed the possibility of children."

"Oh. Right." I glanced down at the pots. Putting together what the contents of them must be.

"Ideally, that was a discussion we should have had before I spent the night buried in you. But I've never pretended that I was anything but selfish–" Cal's finger pushed at my chin, bringing my gaze back to him. "--and being with you last night was the greatest moment of my life. So I won't apologize for embracing spontaneity."

"So the tea and powders…"

"Are to prevent pregnancy. I'm sure you've had Silphium root before,"

I nodded. That was the most common method of contraception.

"But this–" He pointed to the pot with the white powder. "--was designed by the Seed Singers in court, along with the healers. It's more potent and can prevent conception for a month at a time. But it only works if we're both taking it."

"I didn't know such things existed."

"Alessia, it would seem, had a keen understanding of our relationship and ordered a fresh batch made for this morning." He laughed, glancing back toward my room. "It takes several days to make."

"Of course she did."

Cal's thumb ran along my jaw. "It's your choice. You don't have to take it if you don't want to."

"Cal? That's… that's a pretty serious thing to say." A baby. That's what he was saying; if I didn't want to prevent pregnancy, then he'd support that. It was either the tea or an eventual royal baby. Because after last night, there was no way I'd have the ability to resist being with him.

Gods. A prince, or a princess. I wasn't ready for this conversation. It was too early. I was too hungry, and my brain was still too sex-addled and oxygen-starved to be determining the future of a kingdom based on a cup of tea.

Cal kissed away my trepidation. "I want you, Elle. I want you, however you'll have me. If you want children, then I want them with you. If you don't and you want to abstain to avoid relying on the concoctions of our healers, then I'd do that too. Although, that seems like a considerably less fun option."

I laughed. "As if you could keep your hands off me."

"I would suffer through it if it meant being with you. Then again, I wasn't the impatient and insatiable one last night, so maybe you should consider the tea's merits." He grinned, all white teeth and mirth.

I lifted my hand to smack him, but my heart wasn't in it, and he snatched it easily from the air. Looping my arm around his neck and sinking a deep kiss to my lips.

Breaking away on a laugh, I said, "I'll take the tea. Children are a conversation best left for rational minds."

"The white powder gets mixed into the tea, followed by a spoonful of the red, and the honey is to take away the bitterness of the mixture. Trust me, you'll want the honey. It isn't the most pleasant tasting."

I mixed it all together. Blowing on the hot contents. The red powder tinged the liquid a deep hue similar in shade to the roses in the garden. Sipping cautiously, I drank down the mixture. It had the bite of ginger and clove, followed by a sour bitterness akin to lemon rinds that didn't mix at all with the flavor that preceded it. Finally, it was finished with the thick flavor of honey. He was right. I was grateful for the honey and drained the last of the contents as quickly as possible.

After finishing his glass, Cal placed a kiss to my temple, his expression entirely unreadable.

Changing the topic to something less lifealtering, I asked, "So, how do we find Aurus?"

24

ELYRIA

We were greeted at the stables by Xoc. He was brushing the hair of a gorgeous black stallion and murmuring to it like he was telling the horse a story. The crazier thing was that I was sure the horse responded, neighing at exactly the moment he finished the punchline.

"Did you just tell that horse a joke?" Cal said, confirming what I'd just witnessed. "Xoc, you don't tell jokes."

"I do. I can't help it if you don't have a sense of humor."

"But the horse does?"

"That's between me and the horse."

A stable hand escorted two more stallions in our direction. The one he brought to me had a long black and white mane. The majority of his body was white, except for a black colored ring around his eye. I ran my hand down his neck.

"You are a magnificent steed," I whispered to him.

"His name is Domino, on account of the black rings around his eyes looking like a domino mask," the boy said, smiling and handing me the reins.

Cal came up behind me. "Or, you could ride with me if you wanted."

"I know how to ride," I replied, raising an eyebrow to him.

"I'm sure you do." He leaned in close to me, whispering so that only I could hear him. "You rode me quite expertly. I especially lik-"

Xoc coughed loudly, slapping against his chest. He held up a hand in apology. "Sorry, sorry. I'd rather hear the sounds of my own hacking over Cal discussing how you ride him."

A Kraavian gleam sparkled in Cal's eyes, snatching one of the straps at my

241

waist and pulling me to him. "What if I want to feel you swaying and rocking against me? Think of all the things I could do to you on that long ride." He ran a hand over the curves of my leather corset.

I twisted out of his grip.

"And that right there is why I need my own mount." A torrent of filthy imagery made me curl my toes in my boots. I winked at him. "But, I like where your mind is at."

"Sunshine, between your thighs is the only place my mind has ever been at." He dropped his gaze over my breasts before adding, "The only difference is that now my daydreams are more... accurate."

I rolled my eyes at him. "Nothing about that is surprising."

"But please, say mount again," he said, scooping up a handful of gravel.

"What?" I pointed at his hand, confused. What did he need a pouch of gravel for?

Dropping the stones into the pouch on his hip, he whispered, "You'll see."

Xoc slung a leg over his horse. He was so tall he practically didn't need the stirrup. "I think I liked it better when she was pissed at you. At least then, I didn't have to listen to all this innuendo. It's bad enough when he is spewing this shit, but Elyria, now you, too."

I smiled at him playfully. "Feeling left out? I bet I know someone who'd be willing to go for a ride of her own."

I climbed onto Domino, giving Xoc a not-so-subtle wink. His scowl was legendary. No wonder Cal loved pushing his buttons.

"You two...it was a terrible idea bringing you together," Xoc grumbled.

"Ah, but terrible ideas are always the most fun," Cal retorted, swinging up onto his own saddle. "You should see all the ways we come together."

"Fucking hells, this was not what I meant when I told you to get your head out of your ass and make it right."

"I'd love to stick around and watch you berate Cal some more, but—" Domino did a small trot around the boys. With a cackle, I called, "I'm about to beat you both to that waterfall." I snapped the reins. Domino let out a whinny, kicking up a cloud of dust as we tore out of the courtyard and down the path that led towards the mountain.

Cal's exuberant laughter chased after us.

Wind whipped through my loose hair. I lost myself to the joy and freedom that coursed through me. It had been too long since I'd been for a ride. As a child, we would sometimes unhitch the horses from the carts and take them along the mountain trails or across the plains. As I got older and Duke got lazier, there was rarely enough free time for the kind of leisure that allowed you to disappear for an entire day. The roar of thundering hooves came rushing up on me. I glanced over my shoulder to see the boys advancing on us, quickly.

Cal and Xoc were neck and neck, their horses straining to outpace the other. Cal turned, hurling pebbles one at a time at Xoc. With each small stone, the giant draken cursed loudly. Cal's laughter looked borderline demonic.

Xoc waved his hand. A massive tree root broke out of the ground, stretching across the path. The stallion he was riding leapt over the hurdle with ease. Cal's barely managed to clear the obstacle.

"Should we show them what a race really looks like?" I said down to Domino. "Heyah!" I clicked my heels against his side and snapped the reins. Domino shot forward with lean, powerful strides. I braced my legs against the motion and shouted victoriously to the sky.

The boys increased the pace of their horses. The path narrowed, and Domino leapt over fallen logs and wove between boulders like the championship steed he was.

Sounds of the waterfall grew stronger as we drove further into the forest. Before long, the sparkling mists of the Vanfald came into view. Cal and Xoc tried to weave around us, but each time we cut them off. Just as I saw the lake, Domino's pace abruptly slowed.

I snapped the reins over and over, clicking my heels and making as many encouraging sounds as I could. "Come on, sweet boy. Don't let the mean men win." Domino neighed in a protest that sounded remarkably like, *"No."*

Cal's horse skidded to a stop beside Domino. He lurched forward, barely holding onto the pummel to keep himself from being launched airborne.

Xoc let out a loud whoop of triumph.

"That cheating asshole. He told our horses to slow down!" Cal said, throwing what was left of his pouch of pebbles at Xoc as he blurred by on his jet-black stallion.

After finishing the last half mile at an agonizingly slow pace, we dismounted beside the base of the falls. Xoc's booming laughter carried over the rush the entire way, seconded only by the sound of Cal's grinding teeth and periodic cursing.

I marveled at the stunningly beautiful waterfall. It was exactly as Cal described. It could be the twin of the one at the top of The Steps. Except this one was nearly double the size of our falls.

"When you meet the dragon, try not to look so beaten," Xoc said with a playful punch to my shoulder.

Cal glared at the large draken, while tying up our horses. "This isn't over."

"A Zardothian slug would have been faster. I don't know what you said to Domino, but he wouldn't speed up no matter what I tried. I even promised him sugar cubes. Cal ended up walking the remaining bit on foot. He practically had to drag his horse to the water's edge."

Xoc snorted. "He had it coming."

"What did he do this time?"

"Nothing, yet, but I'm sure he'll do something. It's still early." Xoc gave Cal a nervous glance. "Elyria, when you go in the mountain, don't let him do anything stupid."

"He wouldn't do anything foolish with a dragon."

"Wouldn't he? Cal has some weak spots, one of which is walking in that lair with him. It only takes one misplaced comment."

I rolled my eyes.

"Don't underestimate him. Cal would fight a dragon if it meant keeping you safe." Xoc sounded so genuinely concerned. How many times had Cal gone on missions without him? From the anxiety rippling through the large man, I knew it couldn't have been many. He had a point. Xoc kept Cal level and dragons didn't exactly have a reputation for being forgiving.

"When it comes to my girl, not even Aurus would stand a chance." Cal laughed off all of Xoc's very valid concerns. "Besides, if anyone here is likely to challenge a dragon, it's Elyria."

Would I? If I was provoked enough? Yeah, I probably would.

"Oh, I trust her just about an inch more than I trust you."

I opened my mouth to protest, but Xoc cut me off. "Impulse control isn't exactly one of your strengths." Well, he had me there.

I wrapped my arms around the big man in a laughably awkward hug. "We'll be back before you know it."

"Good Luck. Try not to get eaten!"

Mist rose from the falls. Fine droplets filtered the light into a veil of rainbows. Xoc's parting words triggered a new level of anxiety.

"Cal, dragons don't eat people, do they?"

"They've gotta eat something." His eyes dropped from my shoulders to my toes and back up again. "You'd definitely make a tasty snack."

Cal stepped in front of me on the narrow path, the filtered light of the forest making already toned musculature more defined. Demons below, that ass should not be allowed in leather. He pointed to the cliff that disappeared beneath the spray of the falls. "This way."

"That way?" I said, looking at the solid stone wall before us. "There's nothing there but stone and water."

"Remember our falls." He looked at my lips. "Just trust me."

An umbrella of air fanned over Cal as he quickly disappeared behind the rush. I paused, waiting to see something happen. Then his hand appeared, floating in the middle of the downstream. He snapped and gestured for me to follow him. Watching the water bend around his air shield, I stepped into a dark tunnel.

A small flame manifested at the tip of his finger. He touched it to the channel that was carved into the wall. With a whoosh, the groove ignited. Fire licked at the stone, casting eerie shadows. It snaked along the wall before disappearing around a bend.

"Ready?"

"As I'll ever be."

An ancient power caressed against my senses, one that almost felt familiar. My breathing hitched at the unexpected intrusion, making me trip down the dark mountain corridor.

"This is normal. Don't fight it," he said, taking my hand in his and giving it a squeeze. "I've only seen him once, when I was young, even though I've tried half a dozen times. If he didn't want us here, then we'd spend days wandering these tunnels and never find anything."

The invisible force guided us down a narrow side corridor that seemed to appear out of nowhere. It opened into a larger inner chamber that looked out over a massive black chasm.

Swaths of darkness extended endlessly before us. I squinted my eyes but couldn't discern anything in the abyss. Something large shifted against the rock at the bottom of the pit. Followed by the unmistakable sound of rustling leather and scraping scales as whatever it was ascended the cave wall.

Cal drew closer to me, his shoulder pushing hard against my chest and blocking me from whatever was looming in the darkness. His heat was the only thing calming my nerves, but I was ready. This was why we came, what I asked for.

A flash of light flickered in the dark, followed by a great golden tail that swung over the platform. I held my breath, overwhelmed by the sublime awe of each glittering scale passing overhead. They looked so similar to my own, only much... much larger.

"My children," a voice from deep in the darkness growled.

My heart leapt into my throat. Beside me, Cal dropped to one knee and saluted over his heart, just as the guards had done for him. I copied his motions, awkwardly kneeling beside him. With a side eye, I took in Cal's knowing grin. I'd never bowed for anyone before, ever, and I'd definitely never saluted someone.

One golden eye emerged from the darkness. Even though I knew I should keep my head bowed, I couldn't look away from its luminous depths. Rich gold, rimmed by a darker amber color, veined with fine lines of black, and a large slit that focused directly on me.

A deep chuckle rattled the ground. Was he amused by our prostrations or by how I knelt in submission but obviously couldn't be submissive?

Slowly the eyes grew, his face entering the light and highlighting the rows of razor-sharp teeth. All of it was surrounded by layers of brilliant scales. The ground beneath my knees rumbled. Clawed feet gripped the edge of the cliff that we stood upon. Each claw was larger than my entire body. For the first time, I doubted if coming here had been wise. This cave could easily become our tomb.

"Elyria," he growled and extended his neck to me.

Aurus breathed in a deep pull of my scent, rumbling his approval. I was knocked to the ground with his hot, rushing exhalation.

I climbed to my feet, knocking centuries-old dust and gravel from my pants.

"You look just like her." An extended talon stroked down my length. The smooth surface grazing my chest, over my stomach, and all the way down to my ankles. It was surprisingly gentle, given his immense size, almost sensuous.

Cal rose tall, hackles rising in an oddly territorial fashion— at a dragon.

I pulled him back, trying to say, 'What the fuck is wrong with you?' with my eyes. This was exactly what Xoc was worried about. Five minutes in the old dragon's presence and Cal was already challenging him.

Aurus's head swiveled, giving me a perfect view of the horns that protruded off the back of a fanned collar. They were an onyx black and curled at the ends with a metallic shimmer.

I gasped. It was just like my raven and gold hair. The scales, the unique blend of colors in his irises that matched my own so closely. I'd been told, but it wasn't until this moment that the gravity of that information really registered. I was part dragon. DRAGON. Not merely an orphan, or some circus girl who could do tricks with fire and played with knives. I was descended from one of the oldest and most powerful creatures to ever walk Venterra. It made me want to weep, or cheer.

"You smell like him, Ariyn's son." Aurus exhaled again and grumbled, not nearly as amused to see Cal as he was to see me. "Tell me why you have disrupted my sleep."

Cal looked at me and then cleared his throat.

"War has come to the shores of Innesvale. It is a war that we believe began long before the founding of our city, one that I hope you may be able to help us understand."

"Tell me everything." The last word came as more of a growl than speech. Flames heated the back of his throat, casting a warm glow on Cal's sharp features.

Cal swallowed hard before saying, "The Iron Draken, Malvat, has begun to infect our people with something we call The Shade. It allows him to control people's minds and bodies. He can dematerialize into shadow and form poisonous objects from it."

A deep tremor rattled my bones and shook the stones at our feet. I gripped Cal's arm to steady myself. That didn't seem like a sympathetic reaction, and I braced for the torrent of flames or the swipe of those massive claws. Cal, to his credit, straightened his spine and continued his explanation.

"And for some reason, he has directed all of this horror on Innesvale, on me–" Cal ran a hand over my cheek "--and Elyria. She's been targeted multiple times at the most malicious level. It's why we've come. I need to understand what may have happened five thousand years ago between you and Ferrus, the Iron Dragon."

Aurus's rumble deepened at the mention of Ferrus. He pulled back into the darkness, his claws leaving deep gouges in the ground before me.

My heart sank. Was that it? A mention of his brother and Aurus was gone.

Just as my hope ran out, a man emerged from the dark. Golden hair and eyes, but his face was familiar. He bore a striking resemblance to Cal. If I didn't know better, I could have believed them to be brothers.

"It's easier to speak with you in this form," he said with a deep voice that carried a sultry accent I didn't recognize. "To understand, I must tell you my story from the very beginning." He motioned for us to follow him, opening the door to a sitting room with rich velvet lounges. The chamber was lined with treasures. Vases, crowns, candle sticks. A millennia of offerings all lined neatly against the walls.

The dragon's hoard. It was like I'd walked directly into one of Duke's stories. How many people had seen this trove? It couldn't have been many; perhaps we were the first.

"My brother was always jealous of me." Aurus sat on a lounge, plucking a coin from the bowl beside the seat. It tumbled over his fingers in the exact manner I'd always done to calm my nerves. Gold quieted my anxiety in ways I could explain. It satisfied a hunger that ravaged my nerves. Watching that golden coin tumble, it was blindingly clear that I'd always had dragon traits. I just never recognized them for what they were.

"This will help with the gold lust. When in concentrated amounts, the gold can alter your senses if you don't satisfy it." Aurus flicked the coin to me. I snatched it from the air while he continued his story, "As the eldest child, I was often given privileges that the younger members of our brood were not. Ferrus, the second born, spent his entire life trying to outdo me, and yet he never could. Not in speed, not in strength, nor intelligence. I was larger and stronger than my brother, more gifted with my abilities, and capable of outthinking him strategically."

Cal ran his finger along the rim of the large vase sitting beside him. Aurus's golden eyes narrowed on the action. Did Cal not realize what he was doing? He had to know the stories of what happened to stupid princes who dared to touch a dragon's hoard.

"He would lay traps and challenges for me, and each time I bested him. Every time he tried to claim some bit of prestige, I surpassed him. It served to make his envy that much richer. Eventually, I grew tired of our games."

Aurus walked to the vase and slid it out of Cal's reach. Cal at least had the common sense to look sorry. I understood the draw to the glittering mass of treasure surrounding us, but he needed to exert at least a little self-control. I slipped the gold coin Aurus had gifted me into his hand.

"It was nearly two thousand long years of out-maneuvering him, and I was bored. So, like many of my other siblings before me, I retreated from the world and made a home for myself in this beautiful mountain." He walked to the shelf carved into the cave wall. Carefully he opened what looked like an ancient box. From it, he pulled a glittering chain with a single pearl drop hanging from the center. It was stunning. The pink hue of the pearl reminded me of the sky at sunrise.

"It drove him mad. I refused to play and removed myself from the game. Knowing that he could never prove himself ate away at his sanity, piece by piece. He was too consumed by his own envy to see the bigger picture."

Aurus clasped the chain around my neck and gently cradled my face. My power came to attention, rolling to the surface until it felt like my skin was glowing beneath his touch.

"Then, one day, I fell in love. She looked—" Aurus's features tightened, his molten eyes vibrating. A spiral of emotion clouded my vision. Flashes of lips and hands caressing flesh, followed by ashes blowing in the wind. Lust, love, and loss. Cal let out a breath that sounded pained. "—just like you. Elyria, you inherited more than just her name. You could be her mirror. Beauty and grace, with a heart as pure as sunlight. Raven black hair and pearl white skin."

Aurus's thumb ran over my lower lip.

"My soul was threaded with hers in a way that even death wasn't able to truly separate. She is still a part of me, as surely as I was a part of her."

I could feel Cal's eyes on me. What Aurus described felt a hell of a lot like what I'd experienced last night. My soul had twined around his, and I could still feel that piece of him connected to me now.

"I loved her more than anything, or at least until she bore our children. That was a love that could carve out universes. They were twins, a boy, and a girl." Aurus closed his eyes. A tear slipped from beneath long metallic lashes.

He turned away from us to stare at his reflection in a golden chalice. With a roar that sent my heart into my throat, Aurus hurled it at the far wall. With a loud clang, it smashed against stone with enough force to flatten the opulent cup. What was happening? Duke told me many stories about dragons as a child. Everything I knew said that a hoard was sacred to a dragon. Aurus had just crumpled that chalice. I wasn't sure what to do. Do you comfort a dragon when he is so full of wrath that his body is rocking with it?

With his back still turned to us, he said low, "Ferrus sent an assassin. Driven insane by his rage, he told the spy to take the treasure I coveted most. Anything to draw me out. He saw the way I loved her and knew that while I had several kingdoms' worth of gold, the true jewel in my life was Elyria."

Aurus stepped over to where the fire ran along the corners of the room. He dipped a finger into the oil. Fire danced in his hands. It enchanted me. Aurus's flames felt so pure. They molded to form an entire diorama. A woman stood beside the falls, wind whipping at her hair. She was me, and yet not me. Her face turned in fear, and she silently cried out.

"One day, I took our children for a night flight. Ariyn would always squeal with delight whenever we dipped, and it was one of my favorite things to do. In those days, I couldn't deny them anything that brought smiles to their tiny faces. While I was busy skimming the skies, Ferrus took Elyria from me. We came home, and all that remained was the stench of dragon fire and ash."

He closed his hand, and the flame extinguished. The girl who was not me disappearing in a puff of smoke. The love of his life had been killed by his brother to settle a petty score.

A palpable wave of sorrow washed over us. I sucked in a breath at the tragedy of what he said. Cal's hand wrapped around mine. The connection to Aurus was intense, and his ability to manipulate my thoughts felt like an invasion at the cellular level. The echo of his memory, and the scar it left on his heart, tremored its way through my thoughts.

Cal's thumb across the back of my hand soothed the broken shards of pain that Aurus's grief left behind. His story must have triggered every fear Cal had been wrestling for the past few weeks. When I looked at the man I pledged my love to, his eyes burned and locked with mine. For a moment, I forgot the ancient standing before us. I loved him in this life and the next, but the possibility of this life being cut short was always looming over us, like a guillotine waiting to fall.

"I knew his envy could never be sated," Aurus continued. "In a decision that still breaks my heart today, I split my children up. I'd already lost one love, and all I had left of her was our children. I couldn't bear to see them taken by my brother's insanity. Selina was sent to her mother's people in Indemira. Ariyn, I gave to the lord and lady of Innesvale. They were good leaders, and fate had cursed them by making her womb barren. As they could have no children of their own, giving Ariyn to them seemed fitting."

He placed a hand on Cal's shoulder. "From the mountain, I watched over him, and over the centuries, I watched his descendants."

"To think, all this time we thought we were watching over you," Cal said with a smile, one that Aurus returned, followed by a long sigh.

"It would seem that Ferrus is back to fulfilling vendettas, and he's poisoned his own line to see it done. I never would have thought him capable of doing such atrocities. But then again, a few millennia being consumed by wrath has a way of twisting your reality."

Cal leaned closer to the dragon, "What about The Shade? Why can Malvat control a power that isn't inherent to him? Light and metal, but not shadow."

"The only shadow magic I know of is much deeper and older than any of us. Ferrus must have figured out a way to tap it from within Mt. Kraav, then used it to contaminate his bloodline. Hope, Callen, that is all he has done, and that he hasn't awoken things that ought never wake."

Cold snaked down my spine. *What things?*

"You're speaking of the Old Magics? Before the time of the attuned. Before even the dragons," Cal said, confused, and speaking over my thoughts. "How are we supposed to defeat Old Magics?"

"You are of my blood. That will make you the strongest of your kind. But, together, the power will multiply. Use that connection, and you will be able to accomplish feats this world has never seen. The light of your fire will burn through shadow and devour darkness."

Aurus walked from the room as he did I saw a golden tail slip around the corner.

I jumped up, running after him. He couldn't leave. I had questions.

"Aurus!" I yelled into the darkness. Sharp panic made my yell sound desperate.

The dragon reemerged with just his head forming in the light.

"My parents. What can you tell me of them?" I needed to know they cared. I needed to know that even though I'd killed them, they'd loved me in the time that I was theirs. If he left, I might never get the answers I longed for.

"When you were a baby, they brought you to me. Your father was heir to the Aschen Queen and your mother was mortal. Their love came with a cost."

"A cost?"

"They were cast out from Indemira. But, it was that love that gave them you."

"Is that all you know?" There had to be more. I didn't even have a name.

Aurus blinked his large eyes, something like softness making them rounder. "Is there more that matters?"

I never should have hoped. I knew better than to rely on such a foolish emotion.

"If it's your family you seek, then you will need to go to Indemira."

It wasn't much, barely even information. We knew I must have heralded from the Aschen line.

Aurus lowered his head to me expectantly. I placed my hands along his lower jaw and reached up on my tiptoes to place a light kiss to his muzzle in gratitude, even if he'd barely told or done anything to deserve it.

The disappointment tasted sour. Coming here had been pointless. When Duke told me I was draken, I planned to come here, thinking I would finally feel a connection to family. But this dragon was old and bitter; the only thing he cared about was himself.

Aurus transformed, scale and massive form melting away until it was a man kissing me. The strength of that beast radiated down into my bones, along with a wave of ancient longing and desire. Aurus's hands trembled against my cheeks, and then he released me, leaving me breathless.

Aurus flicked his eyes to a bristling Cal.

"Forgive me. That was a moment of weakness," he said, then ran a finger along my jaw. "I see the ghost of her in you...but with my fire. Go, Elyria, and make the world bend to you. Kneel before no one. For you are descended from the original goddess."

Aurus's resonating emotions were so tangible. I could feel his heart breaking, as purely as if it were my own. It was overwhelming enough that I nearly embraced him.

"Thank you for giving me the gift of seeing her spirit once more."

"Aurus, fight with us," Cal said boldly, tugging on my arm to pull me beside him and out of Aurus's reach.

"Someday, you will see that such things do not ultimately matter. Wars come and go, but in the end, the world endures. The only thing that truly matters is the love you share with those around you. Not the pain that you can inflict upon your enemy, but the love you can give him."

With a last, sad look at me, Aurus leapt into the darkness. How could he say no? This was his fight, as much as it had ever been ours. I'd sacrificed my way of life, my family, and my father to this fight. My entire world has been flipped on its head, and he couldn't be bothered to stand with us?

Rage roared up in me.

"Fuck that," I spat. Cal's eyes went wide at the disrespect, but I didn't care. "I have great amounts of pain that I wish to inflict." A fragment of the energy Aurus had been feeding us forced my voice unusually low, my connection to the dragon blood stronger the longer we remained in the mountain. I let that strength vibrate the tenor of my voice. "He took your wife. He tore away the soul fasted to yours. I felt your rage, your anger. Aurus, I felt your grief, and you speak of showing him *love* in return." I growled again. "I can not and will not. Malvat will die by my hand, Ferrus too, if he is to blame for the carnage he has wrought."

Flames licked along my hands, and the light in the lanterns on the walls flared, making the shadows shrink away until Aurus's massive golden body was fully visible. Wings, horns, and scales all shimmered in the blazing fire. How could he toss aside all that Ferrus was responsible for, all that he had done? He'd killed Elyria, forced him to give up his children. He took the only things Aurus had ever loved. My own rage mingled with all that emotion he'd poured into me.

"Temper, little one. Temper," Aurus said in a patronizing hush. A puff of hot air blew my hair back.

My blood boiled, flaming my vision bright red. I shot a ball of fire straight at him. It broke harmlessly apart against his scales.

Aurus simply chuckled, like I was a toddler throwing a tantrum. "Goodbye, Elyria. Take care of her, Callen. Don't make the same mistakes I did."

Aurus sank back into the darkness. The brush of hot air and the sound of his wings against the stone were the only thing left behind as he disappeared into the mountain.

I looked at Cal, my vision darkening at the edges. "He told us nothing." We were going home with nothing. Not what to do or how to defeat him. "He didn't even tell me who my parents were."

Cal caressed my arms, trying to calm me. "Shhh."

"Old Magics?" I said angrily, pulling from his grip. I replayed the conversation in my mind. "What the fuck does that even mean?"

"Old Magics were the fabric that the world was made from. It was wild magic, one that very few could wield. To be honest, it's more legend than fact. I never considered it to be something that was actually real."

Calling all of the fire from the nearby sconces, I formed a massive dragon, double the size of the beast I'd formed that day in the show—and sent it flying straight into the ceiling until it was smashed against the mountain, reducing into nothing more than sparks.

"Do you feel better?" Cal asked, relighting the lanterns.

"No. I feel like I'm about to explode. What do we do now, Cal? March into the Dead Lands. Hope that we can summon fire hot enough that it can burn the shadows from him, whatever the fuck that means?" I huffed a manic laugh, hurtling a ball of flame into the darkness. "And just wish that Malvat doesn't block it because Aurus, The Great Gold Dragon, says so."

"I think the first thing we should do is test our powers to see what we can actually do with them. We've never tested our limits, Elle," he said, deceptively calm. It was a tone that I knew he was keeping low in an attempt to smother my rage. It made me even more furious. "Then we can make a battle plan."

"And get Rei," I snapped. "We get her out. Cal, I can't leave her there ... with him. I just can't." An ache formed in my chest. The stress of our reality closing in on me like a vice. I'd placed too much hope on Aurus. I'd wanted answers, and the best we got was a story of old pain and vague advice.

"A battle and a rescue plan," Cal said, running his hand down my arm in reassurance.

"Fine," I growled, brushing past him and stomping towards the tunnel. "Let's get out of here. If Aurus is too much of a *coward* to avenge his mate and stand up to his brother, then there is no point in our being here."

I didn't slow to see if my barb struck through that thick dragon hide, but a sharp pang of regret vibrated in my heart. I smirked. That's right, Aurus, choke on your forgiveness because I have none to give.

25

CALLEN

"For someone so small, Elyria can be kind of terrifying." Xoc dismounted his horse and handed the reins to the stable boy who approached us.

She'd spent the entire ride back to the palace seething. With each mile, her thoughts must have spiraled deeper and deeper into her rage. The longer we rode, the lines of her body grew more taught. Until I was sure that if I plucked her, she would sing like a violin—or explode like a grendado.

"Have you ever noticed the way she lifts her chin and arches her back when she's trying to make a point? It presents her breasts like an offering on a sinful plate. Put a knife in her hands and *fuck*." Gods, I shouldn't be thinking about it. I tugged on the waistband of my leathers. Laces and a saddle the entire ride from the Vanfald had been bad enough.

"There is something very wrong with you," Xoc said flatly.

Elyria turned, blazing eyes full of accusation, as if she knew exactly what we were discussing. I walked up to her and ran my hand along the anger-taut muscles of her jaw. My touch didn't melt the ice within her, but only seemed to make her fury more resolute.

"Come on. Let's go down to the grottos and burn off some of this angst. Literally." I extended my hand to her.

Elyria narrowed her eyes. "Fine," she said, pushing me out of the way and heading back towards the castle.

"It's the other way, actually," I yelled at her. I couldn't keep myself from smiling as she growled to the sky. Letting her work that frustration out on me was going to be so damn good.

Xoc snatched Elyria's arm as she stomped by. "Try not to kill him."

She gave him a blank and unamused expression, followed by a blast of power that made my heart stutter. Xoc instantly dropped his hold, shaking out his mildly singed palm.

Easing back to me, he cautiously watched her walk away. "Wow. What exactly did Aurus say to trigger this?"

"He kissed her, then told her to calm down." I laughed, gesturing to Elyria. "Said explosion of rage is the result of being told to watch her temper." Elyria stopped on her warpath and spun towards us.

"Were you going to join me, or just let me figure out the way down to the water on my own."

"Good luck with that." Xoc shifted his serious eyes to me. "I'll come find you later if you're still alive."

I shrugged. "She'll be okay...probably. Or, she might very well kill me." I clapped him on the back. "And then she can be your problem."

Sparkling water and worn arches peppered the shoreline. The Obsidian Cliffs were made from a mix of glassine obsidian and ribbons of black mica. The turquoise waves crashing against the rock made these oft forgotten caves one of my favorite places to escape when I was growing up.

A low stone platform extended beyond the cave walls and soaked up the remaining sunlight. My ancestors built this dock as a hidden exit out of Innesvale, should the royal family ever need to evacuate the grounds in secret. Many of the grottos pushed inward, forming long tunnels. If you followed some of them far enough, they connected with the lowest parts of the palace.

It was the perfect place for children to avoid the watchful eyes of adults. I grimaced at the memory of showing them to Malvat and the childish fun that was now tarnished by the atrocities he committed.

"This is beautiful," Elyria said, gazing out at the blue-green waters. The tide was out, and so the entirety of these beautiful caves and the platform extending beyond them were on full display. She stood just past the mouth of the cave, holding her hand up to shield against the sun hovering above the horizon.

"We have maybe two hours of sunlight left, plenty of time for me to let you beat that anger out," I said, unbuttoning my shirt.

"Let me. It's adorable that you think you let me do anything."

I tossed the shirt onto an out of the way rock. Elyria's eyes lingered on my exposed chest. "We don't know how hot this is going to get. You should discard anything you have that might burn or melt, too."

She ran a hand over the hilts of her blades and pouted.

"Sorry, beautiful. I promise we can play with knives later."

With quick, practiced movements, she removed all of her accessories until she was standing in only her green suede halter and pants. The color was a stunning shade of mossy emerald. Against Elyria's porcelain skin, it was enough to make me want to fall to my knees.

She pulled her hair back with a leather strap and looked at me with her hands on her hips, chest jutting up. I bit back my amusement.

"So, how do you want to go about doing this? Slowly, or just jump right in and try to see how long we can tread water before burning alive?"

"I don't think we can burn alive," I said, in a laugh.

Summoning a fireball, Elyria juggled it before her while maintaining a scowl that could scorch the ground. Fuck, she was sexy. This feral anger only added to the dangerous allure that was like catnip to me. Even with only summoning a tiny bit of fire to play with, I could feel the magnetic pull, and I wanted to drown in it.

Mirroring her, I summoned a flame into the palm of my hand. Mine burned hotter than hers, appearing almost blue against her red. For the first time since arriving at the Vanfald, Elyria smiled. Rolling her shoulders back, she heaved a sigh of relief.

Fire always calmed my nerves, but when Elyria called on them, it was like my soul sat up and took notice. It was a punishing hurt to resist its demand. After all of those torturous weeks by her side, surrendering my magic to the pull was pure ecstasy.

"Catch." I tossed it to her.

The fire spun in and out of her hands. I pressed a fist over my heart in surprise. It was like I was still tethered to my flames. An invisible string pulled at the center of my chest each time she released them.

"Toss it back." I made a gimme motion with my hands. She lobbed both balls with more force than was necessary, but I stopped caring when she sucked in a breath the moment my hands latched onto her magic.

"How about this?" I pushed the orbs together, trying to force them into one.

I've pulled fire from multiple locations many times before, never with the artistry in which Elyria had done it during her performance with Troupe So-laire, but it was easy enough to do. This time, the flames almost repelled each other. They twined together but never consolidated into one as they usually did.

"Interesting," she remarked.

Elyria reached out her hand and pulled back. The fire tried to lurch from my grasp, but I held on. She leveled her stance on me, and instead of pulling merely the small flames sitting in my palms, she pulled the power straight from my core. Intense pressure slammed against the confines of my chest. She yanked harder on that tether, causing a hot burn to flood down my limbs and spark at my fingertips.

"Fuck, Elle!" I gasped for air, squeezing my hands into fists so tightly that my lengthening nails cut into the flesh of my palms.

She let go of the magic, and immediately the pressure eased. Golden scales I hadn't summoned lined the backs of my hands. I rolled my neck, trying to ease the tension that had coiled along my spine.

"Well, this is just plain fun," she said, raking her lip through her teeth. "I didn't even touch you,"

I made a supplicating smile. "Sure, this is fun, in the having your soul torn from your body kind of way."

Elyria raised both hands into an attack stance. I braced myself. From the fiendish gleam in her eyes, whatever she did next was going to hurt.

She pulled with her entire body, rolling from low at her ankles and snaking away from me so that the ending flick of her wrists contained the force of every one of her muscles behind it. If it wasn't for the fact that my heart felt like it was splitting open, I would have been able to appreciate the fluidity of her movements.

Surging power bled every thought from my mind and made my vision go white. Her laughter rang around the cave. I was fully at her mercy, a marionette on her string. The pressure built and grew, raging behind my rib cage. I was going to explode, or implode, or burn from the inside out.

"Come for me, baby," she said mockingly, high on the life force wrapped around her hands.

Blinking away the tears blurring my vision, I looked at her, unable to speak. Her skin was luminous, glowing like a beacon against the ocean waves. I gasped for air, and her radiant look of power quickly shifted to concern.

"Cal?" She released me. "Gods, I'm sorry. Are you okay?"

I bent over, grabbing my knees and gulping down air. Without even looking up, I could sense the bright heat within her. My power thrummed in her veins. I could feel it pulse, feel each beat of her heart, and every breath she took.

"My turn," I said, lifting my eyes to her.

"Oh fuck," she mouthed, but before she could react, I reached out to that heat— and summoned it back. I drew it over and over, reeling it slowly in.

Elyria clutched her chest, crying out a nearly orgasmic moan. I eased the pull a bit, not entirely, but enough that she threw her head back and caught her breath. Her burning gaze focused on me, filled with lust and delicious torment.

I pulled again, harder this time, and she cried out my name. I could see the intensity building within her. Scales slid over her neck and chest, her fingertips glowed white from beneath golden claws. Lines of fire snaked along her arms.

I let the power drift back to her for just a second before pulling a third time and edged that intensity higher. Dropping to her knees, Elyria cried a feral howl of pleasure that was drawn out the longer I held on until, finally, I gave her the release she was crying for.

Yes, we were going to play with this particular trick in much more detail later.

"That–was–intense," she said between gasping breaths.

"I know," I grinned. "Look at you. Have I ever told you how fucking sexy your scales are?"

"I'm not the only one." She pointed at me with a seductive swirl of her finger while climbing to her feet.

I couldn't see myself, but I was sure that I had neared full shift. I even felt the burn at the center of my back that came moments before summoning my wings. Most alluring was the way her magic had felt alive and pulsing in time with my own power. Shifting made the connection easier to control. It felt like that form was the natural one, the one we'd been born to assume.

Like everything about Elyria, her power was both sweet and vicious. Violence and strawberries. Smoke and jasmine. Silk and leather. It was addicting and made me only want to embrace more of the softness, despite the unrelenting burn that ensued— or perhaps because of it. Just like that night in the river, when her power dangled before me as the ultimate temptation, I wanted to coil our flames together and hear her gasp for more.

"Oh, Sunshine." My eyes dropped over the glittering scales covering her chest and stomach. "I just thought of the most delicious idea."

I strolled over to her, lighting my hands up and drinking down the challenge in her eyes. Soft blue flames danced in my palms. She took hesitant steps back, taking my stalking for exactly what it was — a predator closing in on his prey.

She backed up against the cliff until there was nowhere else to retreat and was forced to confront the fire playing in my hands. Using cuffs of hardened air, I pinned her arms to the wall. My little draken wasn't going anywhere. Her chest heaved in sporadic breaths, but she lifted her chin defiantly.

"Let's see," I whispered against her lips. "I believe it was something like this." I ran my hands in tandem up her chest, letting the flames lick over the curves of her breasts and being careful not to touch her. I had a perfect memory of that night in the Lunar River. She had no idea what she'd done to me, or the restraint I'd shown, but she was about to learn.

"Very funny," she said breathlessly. When her hands wouldn't budge, she made a tiny whimper that set my skin crackling.

"Now you understand exactly how tantalizing that display actually was," I purred. "Naked curves lit by excruciating power..." Bringing the temperature as hot as I dared, I added, "and the heat."

Her lips parted, and eyelids dropped so that she could only look at me through those long, gorgeous lashes.

"Do you feel that hum under your skin? Can you feel it building the longer I linger?" Elyria's spine snaked, following the flow of power.

"Are you desperate to feel its burn?" I could hear her need in each panted little breath, one I was completely denying her. The intensity of it pulsed between us.

"Does it feel like you're being devoured by it?"

"Cal, please."

"Please, what?" I whispered into her ear, finally trailing my fingertips down her neck and into the valley of her breasts. Elyria's gasp shifted into a moan the same second the color of my flame transformed from blue into a vibrant purple.

My control over the air faltered as my full attention shifted to the lilac flames flickering against her breasts. These weren't mine. These were more alluring, the same intoxicating power that had threatened to consume us the previous night.

Elyria's eyes opened, the dragon slit pupils blown wide and rimmed by molten gold. Fire rolled up her newly freed arms. She lashed out a whip of flames, coiling it around my torso and pulling me to her.

My fire instantly responded, driving into her vines and claiming control. They circled her neck, forming a purple collar that lit her features, highlighting the way she dragged her pouting lip between her teeth. I breathed a current of violet-tinged heat over that lower lip she so provocatively couldn't stop biting down on.

Her mouth crashed into mine. For the first time ever, I didn't fight the fire, didn't tamp it down, or attempt to contain it. It felt like free falling out of the stars on the back of a comet.

Power rolled between us, bending and transforming into a new and different force. Before even seeing the color of the flames, I sensed the shift. It washed through me in dizzying waves, filling my vision in violent bursts.

A hard pulse of pure energy rocketed out, showering dust and pebbles from the cave wall.

"Woah," I said, my head still spinning. If we kept this up, the cliff would come down on us, palace and all.

Elyria didn't seem to care that the world was spiraling around us or that black mica fragments were clinging to her lashes. Surging forward, she threaded her fingers into my hair, leveraging me down to reclaim my mouth.

I tightened my grip at the nape of her neck. Something was happening, and we needed to slow down long enough to understand what it was before it consumed us both. It took all of my strength to pull away from her, despite the fact that her far more petite frame shouldn't have been able to hold me.

"Wait.. just.. "

Stronger than any siren's call and just as impossible to resist, a tendril of purple flames curled around her lips. "Get back over here."

26

CALLEN

I wasn't sure who moved first. I slammed her body against the cave wall. Her kiss tasted like the darkest levels of Kraav. Between those lips laid the churning embers at the center of the world. I wanted to let it burn me alive.

"*Fuck*, Elle." Summoning the tattered remains of my self-control, I broke away and pushed against her chest to ensure she stayed at arms length this time. "Let me try something."

Ignoring her sexy pouting and keeping my palm over her heart, I concentrated on forming the new flames at the center of my free hand. They crackled and churned in an amethyst ball.

"It's so beautiful," she said, the orb bathing her awestruck expression in violet light.

"Decided to finally pay attention?"

I narrowed my eyes on a rock formation fifty feet from the shoreline. There were two pillars of black, water smoothed stone connected in the middle by a well-worn bridge.

I gave her lips another long draw, inhaling that seductive flame. Then, keeping her body connected to mine, I hurled the fireball at the rocks.

The ball of flames aimed perfectly at the slender extension of stone. It exploded in a star of blinding light, followed by a giant plume of turquoise water that rose high into the air. Droplets rained down on us, causing a brief rainbow to flicker before we were completely engulfed by a thick blanket of steam.

When it cleared, I blinked my eyes. What I was seeing couldn't be real. The rocks were gone. I expected to damage the bridge, but the entire formation had

"My gods," Elyria whispered.

My heart hammered in my chest, or maybe that was her heart hammering. We were so connected at this point that it was getting hard to tell the difference.

"That shouldn't be possible," I said, still stunned by the emptiness before us.

I looked over at Elyria, momentarily awe-struck. She was gilded by the purple light of our fire. *Our fire.* Together, we were literally explosive.

"This was what Aurus meant. This is what can burn away darkness. Beneath this power, even shadows burn."

With an indulgent kiss, I savored the flames lingering on her lips. They tasted like victory, like vengeance. They tasted sweet.

Kicking her head back, Elyria started laughing. "So basically, when we see Malvat again, we just need to start kissing... while on fire–" The skin around her eyes and nose crinkled as she tried to contain her hysterics. "--and then, blamo, we hit him with our sexy flames."

"Blamo?" I said, raising an eyebrow, making her laugh harder.

I put the barest amount of space between us, just enough to break the binding that held us there. The purple flames sputtered before extinguishing in a puff of lavender smoke. The air felt cold and hollow without our power filling it.

"We can do this on command," I said, pressing my lips to her jaw. "And while I could kiss you for days, I'm sure there are other ways to summon it. I've seen these purple flames before. We just need to learn how."

I placed a second kiss against the pounding pulse fluttering along the side of her neck. Elyria's smoke and jasmine scent wrapped around me, accompanied by a sharp thrum of energy that vibrated deep in my chest. The feel of her fire coursing beneath my skin was the most erotic thing I'd ever experienced. I adjusted my stance. This entire experiment of ours had me harder than the rock surrounding us. It was bordering on grueling.

Closing my eyes, I took a deep breath. I could surrender to the flow of her magic and take it all at once, even if it did make my veins feel like they were filled with lightning. Maybe then it wouldn't be such an assault on my senses every time we touched.

Like being drawn by a magnet, I skimmed my fingertips over the patch of skin beneath her halter. *And I absolutely shouldn't be focusing on how each rocketing sensation made me want to start exploring.* I circled her hips, dragging my thumb beneath the leather waistband. Her exhalation brushed warm against my cheek, reminding me exactly how close her mouth was to mine.

We needed to figure out what—

I opened my eyes. Violet flames rolled beneath her golden irises. I hadn't been merely stroking her stomach, had I?

Fuck me. This was a losing battle.

The way she was looking at me. Luminous pools of glowing energy and heat, caged by thick black lashes. Her ravenous gaze roved over my body, feasting on what she saw like a lava cat with a cornered fox.

She ran her hands up my chest, sighing the moment they made contact. Pressure seized around my heart as she drew on my power. "Tell me more of how you'll kiss me for days."

With a single hand, she pushed me—hard.

I flew backwards, soaring over the water and slamming into the stone wall on the opposite side of the grotto. Small stones fell around me, and long thin spider webs of cracks radiated out from the impact. Beneath the stars filling my vision, I caught glimpses of hers flashing bright purple with amusement. The purple bled outward, devouring the gold of her scales.

Before I could process the shift in color, she was on top of me. The sudden nearness and the overwhelming surge of heat that she brought with her was disorienting. My head was still spinning as she bent down to lick a long path from my navel to my collar. In her wake, a trail of purple flames flickered. When she rolled her body back up, she raked a set of gleaming black and amethyst-tipped claws over each ridge and dip of the scales coating my chest.

Something primal glared at me through those purple irises. Elyria reached under my neck and pulled my mouth to hers. My entire torso lifted off the ground as if I weighed nothing. But the shock was quickly forgotten the moment she fitted my body into the curve of hers. Claiming my mouth, she ran her tongue against mine... and...

Fuck it.

We could go back to focusing on how to wield this power after we got this out of our system.

I grabbed her hips. In one smooth motion, I flipped her flat to the ground beneath me.

"Finally." Elyria arched her back. Everywhere we connected pulsed. I stopped resisting it and gave myself over to the rush of heat lighting me up from within.

Violet fire rolled out in waves. It danced as if it were its own living beast. Maybe it was, because I wasn't controlling it at this moment, and from the look in Elyria's lust-hazed eyes, neither was she.

I pulled at the laces of her halter, watching in amazement as my vision streaked. My hands moved so quickly ,they almost seemed to blur. I looked at the web of laces wrapped around my fingers in confusion, not entirely remembering pulling them loose. Elyria's at my waist, were just as quick. One by one, the leather bands snapped away beneath razor-tipped claws.

Kissing her shoulders, I peeled the halter away and tossed it to the side. Amethyst scales arced perfectly over lush curves. The warm plating glittered like the surface of the sun, inviting me to drink deep at the well of magic brimming just beneath the surface. I pulled a shimmering nipple into my mouth, drawing her power into me. Lava flowed over my lips, into my veins, and coiled itself deep in my chest.

I was sinking into the purple abyss of sensation when Elyria hooked a leg around my hip and rolled us. In a heartbeat, she slipped off what remained of our pants. It was so fast that I hadn't even realized what was happening until I felt the tight heat of her muscles gripping me and the hard press of her hips grinding against my pelvis. My entire sense of self was lost. There was only the fire undulating with her movements and the unending surge of power slithering through my veins.

Her dragon mark burned in time with mine, hot against my palms. I dragged my claws down her back. An answering tremor echoed beneath my touch, an earthquake building beneath her skin. It twisted tighter with each punishing hit of her hips.

The demand for more was impossible to resist. I brushed my thumb against her clit. With each rushing stroke, power flowed from my fingertips, not unlike what I had done to her on the balcony. But this time, the surge was completely uncontrolled.

Elyria screamed. Her veins glowed like lightning across the night sky. Arching back, her entire body detonated. Every inch of her burned. Flames curled into the air and exploded in sparks that rained like glitter around us.

"Fuck Elle, you should see yourself."

I sat up to meet her with a kiss that matched the savagery churning beneath my skin, but she laid her palm against my sternum and pushed me back to the ground. The moment her hand hit my chest, a deluge of fire poured through me. The torrent of energy lifted me off the ground and rolled our combined weight back onto my shoulders.

A spider web of lilac light crisscrossed my forearms. I flexed my hands against her waist just as another tumbling wave of energy rolled through me. Claiming her mouth and body as mine, I sent it hurtling back into her. My roar merged with Elyria's scream as the power surge sizzled along our nerve endings.

Fuck. This power. Every cell of my body quaked under its pressure.

A returning wave rocked into me, this one exponentially more intense than the last. I couldn't tell if I was thrusting or if we'd risen off the ground. Pressure tore along my spine and pressed against my ribs, threatening to tear me apart.

The world tipped, and my vision hazed. There was no grotto, no crashing water, no unending cliff of black obsidian. My tether on reality was slipping faster than I could process it.

If we didn't release this power, it would consume us both. Streaks of light wove along her neck and arms, over those perfect breasts, and pointing straight for her heart.

I wrapped my arm tight, and delved into Elle's power. Lifting my hand to the sky, I released all of it. Hers, mine, ours, it poured out.

Elyria screamed my name, gripping the rock behind me to steady herself. I pulled and pulled, letting the power drain until the glow ebbed and her eyes returned to gold. The crackle beneath my skin dulled, and the flames surrounding us retreated until there was only her body moving against mine.

I kissed her slowly until our motion stilled. What we'd just shared was beyond cataclysmic. All of my boundaries had been shattered. I felt connected to this woman on a primal level, and fuck me if I didn't already want more.

Like her bones had liquified, Elyria collapsed, taking me to the ground with her. Faintly in the back of my mind, I registered the sound of the ocean crashing against the rocks.

We pushed that too far, way too fucking far.

"That was..." Her voice trailed off.

Staring at the cliff face, I said, "Elle..."

"Mmm," she murmured against my chest.

"Elle, look up," I said, tapping her shoulder.

"I don't think I can move."

I rolled her off of me and pointed up at the cliff.

A chasm was cut into the rock face. The edges of the torn black stone glowed hot and molten.

"Demons below," she whispered, "Did we do that?"

"Pretty sure. That's what happens when we combine that level of power into one concentrated blast."

I scanned the ground for my pants. Locating them at the far end of the cave, I pulled them on, only to realize that the laces no longer existed. I chuckled, looking over at Elyria. Gods, I loved this woman.

She hadn't moved, but she was glorious. Her naked golden form gleamed against the glittering black stone like a star in the night sky. I lingered for a moment, appraising her, feeling myself already begin to stiffen again. Which could be problematic without being able to lace my pants anymore. Even with everything we'd just endured, it wasn't enough. I was already hungry for more. Of everything. I wanted to feel every bit of her coursing through me. I never wanted it to stop.

I shifted my draken features back and then crawled down on top of her.

"I love you." I kissed her lightly. "I don't think there could ever be a doubt that we were made for each other."

She smiled lazily, not even bothering to open her eyes. Elyria was utterly depleted of all energy. I ran a hand over her scaled breasts one last time. Whispering against them, "Time to put these away, Sunshine."

"Oh..." she murmured, her lids fluttering as she slowly shifted back.

"Let's get you dressed, and I'll carry you back to the palace."

Elyria tried, and failed, to prop herself up on her elbows. A part of me wanted to be proud that I'd so thoroughly sated her, but I knew this was more than that. She poured too much power into me, or I had pulled too much from her. Either way, we pushed things too far.

"I think we need to be very careful with the power drifting. If you give too much, it could consume you entirely," I said, lifting her into a sitting position. "And there was so much power channeling through me, it felt like I was about to combust."

"Mmm..." She agreed. "Is the world spinning?" Elyria reached a hand back to the wall for support.

A laugh rumbled low in my chest. "Holy hells, look at that." I pointed at the wall.

Beside her palm was a perfect imprint of her slender hand—carved into the rock. She must have gripped the wall with such strength that she broke apart the stone itself. Or, from the rounded edges, melted it.

"That's not possible," she said with a whisper.

"I think now, it is." I finished the lacing on her halter. "Can you stand?"

She nodded, and I helped to lift her, sliding one pant leg on after the other.

I gave a last look at the carnage we wrought on the grotto. There were cracks and indents from where she had slammed me into the cave wall. Where Elyria had mounted me, the ground was glassy and still glowing from the intense heat.

I cradled her in my arms. She curled into me, nuzzling into the crook of my neck.

"Where are we going?" she said dreamily.

"Shortcut."

"The fuck happened? Is she alive?" Xoc stood on the balcony of my apartment, eyeing us both. His laughter gave away his true lack of concern. He more than certainly could sense her slow and steady heart rate.

"We.. um.. over-tapped our stores." I laid Elyria's limp body on the bed and brushed the hair from her face. "She fell asleep about halfway back."

"Just watch her for signs of a fever." He closed the balcony doors and drew the drapes. "I was actually starting to get concerned. I've been waiting for over an hour for you to return."

"Yeah, well, things got a little out of hand. You want to have your mind blown? Go take a stroll down to the grottos."

Xoc raised an eyebrow. "And what am I going to find, other than evidence of whatever caused you to misplace the lacing to your pants?"

I laughed, shucking them off and pulling on some loungewear.

"A new level of wreckage." I walked up to him. "Xoc, I carved a damn chasm into the side of the cliff and disintegrated the stone bridge. Elyria burned a handprint four inches deep into the wall."

Xoc gave me a disbelieving look.

"Once we figured out how to combine our power, it became something entirely new. Each time it cycled through us, it grew more powerful. That's how she ended up like that." I pointed to Elyria. "I was able to pull her power from her almost completely. Wielding all of it in a single blow."

"All of her power and yours in a concentrated blast?"

I nodded. "I was barely even aware of what was happening. The power, it's intoxicating. It made us stronger and faster. Elyria threw me into the wall one handed, and cracked the stone." I fisted a hand in my hair. "... and it made my grip on reality slip. Xoc, I can still feel it thrumming in my veins, and I'm already craving more."

"Well...That was the point, right? Why we left to find her in the first place." Xoc nodded, "Question is, do you think it will be enough?"

"I guess we'll find out." I swallowed hard, resisting the urge to look at her. "In the morning, I'm going to call a War Council. I have some thoughts on how we go about doing this." Giving in, I glanced back at the angel lying in my bed. The plan was always to bring her to Kraav with me, but now with the shadow of war hanging over us... I sighed.

"She can take care of herself." Xoc gently placed a hand on my shoulder. "If anything, she'll probably be the one to save your ass."

I tried to find the humor in that, but it fell short. I'd made a similar joke back in Laluna when the boys in the troupe told me to watch over her. That felt like a lifetime ago. I let my eyes skim over Elyria's delicate features, feeling my heart constrict. "Good night, brother."

He nodded in understanding and sent a wave of sympathetic calm in my direction. It wasn't enough. My anxiety pressed in from all sides, crushing me. With each passing second, I moved closer to placing Elyria once more in Malvat's path.

Don't make the same mistakes I did.

Of course, she could hold her own. Duke had given her exceptional fighting skills, especially considering she was a dancer and not a soldier.

If I wanted to mount her to this wall,
then there's nothing either of you could do to stop me.

All of that didn't keep me from wanting to hide her away. I wanted to make a wall of fire so thick and bright that the darkness in this world could never find her.

Promise me you'll keep her safe. Protect her. She's more important than you know. I give you my word.

Joseph's voice and the vow I'd given him repeated on a loop through my mind. *Protect her. Protect her. Protect her.*

I slid Elyria out of her leathers, the green suede now charred and smudged with soot. Slipping into bed next to her, I drew the covers over us both. The satin was cool against my skin, in contrast to how very warm she felt.

Concern drifted over me. Should she feel this hot?

27

CALLEN

"You can't be serious?"

"What I'm saying is, use her fire and fuck her, but you can't marry the girl."

"I can't believe we're discussing this right now. Elyria has been unconscious for five days. She could be dying, Mother!" I slammed my hands down into my desk, feeling the sting of impact radiate back up my arms. "Or have you grown so cold that you've forgotten what it feels like to have a part of your soul torn away?"

Because that's what it felt like when the healer told me she might never wake up. A part of me broke when he said the fever was the first sign of the body giving up as it fought to regain the magic it had lost. Most never survived it.

I did that to her. I'd taken that magic. I'd drained her. Me.

Mother stumbled back a step like I'd slapped her. Served her fucking right.

"I think you're so blinded by emotion that you can't see what really matters." She smoothed the unruffled edges of her gown. It had been a long time since I'd gone toe to toe with my mother. Despite all of my arguments, she still refused to tell me what she knew about Duke, or what their history was. She constantly brought it back to my duties and that Elyria wasn't one of them.

"Like what? I can't see the overflowing Shade rooms, or the reports of how this curse has crippled Innesvale's economy these past six months. I know what's at stake. I know who is relying on me. I can be both a king and a lover."

"Can you? If it was Venterra or her, which would you choose?"

I tightened my jaw until it felt like it was going to pop. I refused to answer her, not because she was so obviously baiting me, but because I honestly didn't know the answer to that. Would I let the world burn to save her?

"Or how about this, after this war is over, what then? Ask yourself, Callen, is she really what's best for this kingdom?"

"Can I say something?" Xoc leaned forward, tapping on the corner of my desk.

"No," my mother and I answered in unison.

"With respect," he continued anyway. This wasn't the first showdown he'd been in the middle of. Xoc was just about the only person in the palace who could speak so freely to my mother. "I just wanted to point out that we're meeting right now to discuss the suggested changes to the fleet, not Cal's marital plans."

Mother spun on him. "Which changes would those be? The ones where you placed an army that I spent centuries commanding in the hands of a pirate? Those changes?"

Xoc cleared his throat and sat back.

My voice dropped a full octave. I was done with her bullshit. "If you don't like it, then leave. Morgan is good for Innesvale. Did you ever think that the reason why our ships keep falling to Astralon's in the North Sea is because we're using outdated methods? This isn't the Covenant Wars, Mother. Technologies change, fighting styles change, command changes. Either change with it or leave."

She opened her mouth to speak, her features going colder than usual. "You think you're ready to lead, then fine. Give this country to pirates and circus performers. I'll start practicing the Norterran salute now."

Mother stormed out of the room. The door slammed shut behind her, making the pictures on the wall crash to the floor.

I exhaled long and slow, letting my body slump down in my chair.

"Well, that could have gone better."

Fisting my hair in my hands, I said, "I don't know what to do, Xoc. My mother blames me for the world imploding. My oldest friend is trying to destroy my kingdom and probably worse. The one good thing left in Venterra is dying in my bed, and it's my fault."

Xoc loomed over me, his shadow making the entire room feel darker. "Sit up."

"You don't command me," I grumbled into my palms.

Ice water ran down my face in a sudden deluge, making me jump. I pushed the plastered strands of hair out of my eyes, scowling up at Xoc and his now empty pitcher.

"She's not dead. This war is not lost. So sit the fuck up."

Xoc rarely used his commander voice on me. "Mal betrayed us all. It hurts me too. Your mother's screams that night will never stop haunting me, but you know as well as I do that there is something bigger at play here. You can't blame yourself for everything. If you ever want to be king, then you are going to have to come to terms with the fact that you can't save everyone."

"I know that."

"Do you? Or is this like when Master Rith told you to climb Mt. Carin with the water buckets, and, to spite him, you chose to do it at a sprint, refusing to stop even after you'd twisted your knee falling down a ravine. The only thing you proved that day was how hard-headed and stubborn you are."

"I was a child then."

"And yet, you are still sprinting up the mountain, Cal."

I stared out the window, watching the boats across the harbor. Several construction docks had been erected, and a dozen ships were being fitted to Morgan's specifications. I still had to work out the details of the naval attack with her. That would probably be another fight. We'd yet to have a meeting that didn't end in someone throwing something.

"What if she doesn't wake up?"

"We'll find a way. That's tomorrow's problem. Let future Cal worry about that."

"I just want one thing to go right. I feel like since the moment my father appeared in the shadows, my entire world has been unraveling. The one good thing that came from this was finding Elyria, and if she dies because I didn't know how to hold back...." Elyria dying would break me. Splintered bits of my soul had already broken free with each day she didn't wake. "I just need one thing to work."

The bell in the corner of the office rang. The small tinkling amid the still chamber sent my heart into my throat.

"There you go. I guess the fates are listening."

28

ELYRIA

The vague sounds of hushed voices drifted in and out of my consciousness. My limbs were too heavy to move, and when I did manage to finally open my eyes, I couldn't get them to focus. Blurry images of Cal caressing my face or the sensation of him rubbing my back would flow over me before I submerged back into the abyss of sleep.

Eventually, I awoke, and the room was in focus. There was a disorienting moment when I couldn't remember where I was. I squeezed my eyes shut and pressed the palms of my hands against them, the pressure at my temples easing.

I counted to twenty. When I opened them again, I remembered.

Cal.

He was the only thing that I could focus my mind on. Sliding my arm over the bed, I felt for him. My hand ran against something sharp, pricking my finger.

"Ow." I brought the pad of my index finger to my mouth, sucking away a small bead of blood. The pain focused my senses. Everything in the marble chamber was still, except for the chiffon drapes shifting in the breeze off of the balcony. Beside me, where Cal should have been, there was a single red rose and a note.

I opened the carefully folded paper. His handwriting had a looping script to it. Like everything he did, it was strong and seductive.

You're beautiful when you sleep.
When you wake up, pull the cord beside the bed.
I love you.
~C

I closed the note and brought it to my lips. The paper smelled like him. Rolling the stem of the rose in my fingers, I looked around. What cord? Beside the bedpost, a thick rope hung against the wall. I pulled on it, but nothing happened. I pulled on it again, thinking that I would hear a bell or something, but the room remained silent. I shrugged. Okay, so that was pointless.

On the bedside table, a pitcher of water and a glass were waiting for me. My throat was drier than the Bone Road. Condensation dripped down the side of the glass, highlighting just how parched I was.

How long was I asleep for? It felt like I hadn't had anything to drink in days.

I swung my legs over the side. The motion sent my head spinning, and I barely managed to grip the side table before landing face first on the marble. A light knock came from the door that connected my rooms to Cal's.

"Elyria?" Alessia's soft voice was barely more than a whisper. She poked her head into the room. "Gods, it's good to see you awake," she said, heaving a sigh of relief and helping me into a chair.

I rose my eyebrows at her. "It is?"

"You've been asleep for nearly five days now. I don't think anyone has ever needed that much time to recover from draining their stores."

"Five days?" I blinked in disbelief. I couldn't have possibly slept that long. Yes, the energy blast had been intense, and the sex legendary, but five days?

"Cal was beside himself. He refused to leave and damn near killed two of the healers when you didn't wake up." I thought of how shaken Cal was that morning on the cliff. I didn't think there was a line Cal wouldn't cross if it meant saving someone he loved. "In the end, he only left after we agreed to rewire the bell-pull to his office."

"So that's what this rope does." I gave the cord a few more yanks. The annoyed image of Cal trying to work dutifully to the sound of an annoying bell made me grin.

"The Master Healer insisted that you'd wake when your magic recovered. And look, he was right. How do you feel?" She put the back of her hand to my forehead. "No more fever, that's good."

"I had a fever?" I said, mildly concerned now.

She nodded her head gravely, making a discontented hum. "Raging. It was high enough to kill the average person. Lucky you're not average, huh, fire girl?"

"I feel a little woozy, and still a bit exhausted, but otherwise, I feel like myself."

"That's probably the dehydration more than anything. You need to drink as much water as possible over the next day or two."

The door to the hallway flew open, the sudden clatter of the wood slamming against the marble wall making me jump. Cal pushed through the doorway, walking to me with long, determined strides. He took my face in his hands and kissed me gently before searching my eyes.

"You scared me," he said, kissing me again.

Alessia snapped at Cal, forcing his attention. "Don't crowd her. She only just woke up. The woman needs to breathe." She shooed him back. "I'm going to send for some food. Nothing heavy, just some toast and jam perhaps. Xoc custom made a tea for you. He said that it would help you recover quicker. I'm going to brew it up, too." Before walking out of the apartment, she turned back to give my prince the most serious glare I'd ever seen from the woman. "I'm not kidding Cal. Ease off."

The door closed with a soft click, leaving us alone. Cal gently wrapped me in his arms, cradling my head to his chest and taking a long deep inhale. I craned my neck as much as he would allow to look at him.

"So, slept for days? You'd think I'd be less tired." I tried to smile, but it was lost under the strong current of concern radiating from Cal. I raised my hand to his hair. "Why are you wet?"

"Fuck, Elle." He kissed me like he was afraid he might never kiss me again. "I thought..." He shook his head. "We're never doing that again." He tightened his hold on me and pressed his cheek into the top of my head.

"I don't even know what 'that' was," I said honestly, remembering flashes of purple fire, golden scales, and bright light.

"You poured all of your power into me. You'd take some of mine back and then pour even more. It felt like I was splitting apart. I released the magic into a single blast, but then the connection between us kept pulling at you, and you just kept giving. It was dangerous, Sunshine." His eyes bored into mine. "*Really fucking dangerous.*"

"I don't remember danger."

"Elle, you almost died."

"I just remember feeling really powerful." Heat bloomed in my chest from the memory. "Like I could devour you whole. Like, I could devour the entire world whole." I rested my hand against his chest, running my fingers over the ridged scar beneath his shirt.

"I won't ever pull power from you like that again. It felt too good, and the cost on you was too much." He pressed his lips to my temple. "I should have been fully drained after the blast, but I barely slept that night with all that energy coursing through my system. At first, I felt this thrill, knowing that it was your power that fed me. The next morning I ran close to twenty-five miles at a full sprint and barely broke a sweat. When I returned, I expected to see you awake, making some kind of alluring joke. But you were still sleeping, and there was the fever. The bed was drenched with sweat. The sheets were slick with it, and you were so hot. It made me sick to know that the rush I felt had cost you everything, and it nearly cost me everything to watch you growing weaker and paler by the day."

He dropped his furrowed brow to mine. "Elle, I can't lose you. I can't know what it means to be whole only to have a piece of my soul ripped away again."

Cupping his cheek, I did my best to reassure him. Cal seemed composed and cavalier, but he worried all the time. "I'm okay. Like the healer said, I just needed time."

I gingerly sat back down at the table. Every muscle and joint in my body ached. It felt like I had been torn apart and then glued back together.

Alessia returned, a tray in her hands. Even from the other side of the room, I could smell the citrus and vanilla scents of the tea. Cal dragged a chair directly next to mine. I looked questioningly at it. But rather than protest, I rested my head on his shoulder. It was nice being able to rely on his strength. Alessia slid a plate with two pieces of bread, a seed I've never seen before lining the crust, and a small dish of jam.

"Can I get you anything?" She said to Cal.

He smiled gently at her. "Maybe some tea, but not whatever concoction Xoc made. Just a regular black tea will be fine."

"I'll be right back."

"Thank you, Alessia."

Cal reached forward and began spreading the jam on the toast. "Strawberry," he said with a smile. "I had it brought specially up from town."

I rolled my eyes at him, "I'm capable of preparing my own toast."

"I know," he said, holding the bread out for me to take a bite. The jam exploded against my tastebuds, sweet and tart.

I reached towards the teapot, but my hand was quickly shooed away. "And pouring my own tea," I added.

"Just shut up and let me take care of you. Twice in as many days, I thought you were going to die, and there was nothing I could do about it but wait. So, let me have this."

I smiled at him from behind my teacup. He was really the sweetest sometimes. "So, what's the plan? When do I get to blast Malvat's face off with our new sexy fire?" I said, taking another bite of my toast.

"We don't need to discuss this right now. Let's just focus on getting you up and moving before we discuss destroying maniacal overlords," he said, placing a hand over mine. The concern in his eyes made my heart swell.

"Giving me something to focus on is a good thing. I've never been idle for a day in my life. I'll go mad without a goal."

Cal grumbled. "Fine. We have a plan to take down Malvat and retrieve Rei."

I gestured for him to go on.

He sighed, then relenting, said, "Morgan is going to sail us to the floating lands. Apparently, she can convert Star Spear into an airship. She's working with our fleet to adapt more of our vessels with the same modifications. We're going to make a frontal assault with Innesvale's armies. Malvat will most likely unleash the Iron Legion."

My spine straightened faster than a stepped on cobra. "The Iron Legion?"

"They're the second largest army, next to the Oers. They almost double our numbers. But it's okay. It won't be for long, and we want to draw him out of the Floating City. A frontal assault will do that. Mt. Kraav Fort is strategically the only place that would make sense for him to be during an attack. Also, it would keep him close to Ferrus and whatever dark energy he keeps poisoning him with. Hopefully, this will minimize the amount of civilian casualties as well, since the majority live on the Floating Islands. Once the fighting reaches a crescendo, and the legion is fully engulfed in battle, you, me, and Xoc are going to slip into the Fort via the Lava Tubes."

"Lava Tubes?"

"Hope you don't mind a little heat," he added with a wink.

Alessia returned. She poured Cal a cup, then poured herself one and sat down next to us.

He glanced at her for a second.

"Continue," she said, smiling.

He shook his head, apparently okay with discussing things in front of her. How much time had they shared together this past week while fretting over me?

"The lava tubes connect to the fort in the same way the grotto tunnels here connect to the palace. They are rather dangerous, so they're never patrolled. We get in, find Rei. Xoc has a plan to get her out before Malvat is aware of our presence. With a little luck, he'll be too preoccupied with fending off an invasion to even notice that we've infiltrated the fort at all."

"You know he expects you to go right for Rei," Alessia said, interrupting. "Invasion or no, he'll be waiting for you."

"I have to agree," I said, leaning back in my chair. "I'm sure it's why he took her, to assure I'd come running. We'd be walking straight into a trap."

"I've got that covered. It's partly why we need to lure him down to the Fort. After Rei's safe, then, my little pyromaniac draken, we will rain down unholy fire upon him."

"Good. The only way I plan on walking out of that fort is over the smoldering cinders of his corpse. I hope that bastard gets to feel his soul shredded apart while serving his eternity in the deepest level of Kraav." I drained the last of my tea and stood up. Strength flooded back into me, and I rolled my shoulders.

Alessia eyed me warily. "Brutal."

I gave her a saccharine smile.

"And he'll deserve every second of it," Cal added, not necessarily in commiseration but more to soften the extreme nature of the curse I'd so blatantly declared.

"So, when do we leave?" I said, pulling my leg behind me to stretch my quadriceps. Cal's eyes drifted down my legs to where his large tunic hung loosely just below my hips. He must have dressed me in it while I slept.

"End of the week." Realizing he had let them drift, Cal flashed his eyes back up to me. "We need to be sure you're fully recovered before we attempt this. We're already risking enough. I won't have you marching in there with half a charge." He pointed at my bent knee. "Should you be doing all of that?"

I shrugged. "To be honest, I feel great. Xoc, really knows his tea. Energy is already returning to me. I feel like I could run to Suman and back right now." I gave a little bounce on my toes, followed by a quick spin. The dizziness, the pain in my joints, they all seemed to have vanished. I flashed him an enlivened smile. "I just feel tight, like my muscles and joints need to stretch." Without even thinking, I pulled my leg high behind me before rotating it to my side in an acrobat's stretch I'd done millions of times.

Cal raised an eyebrow, attention dropping deliberately along the leg I held extended beside me. His fingers toyed with the tunic that had gathered at my hip. The heat of his gaze had a flush running over my chest almost immediately. Slowly, I released my ankle and dropped my leg.

"I'm going to go," Alessia said slowly. "I'll send some provisions along later. Something tells me you'll still be here."

It was like Cal hadn't heard her. He didn't acknowledge her comment or her movements. He steadily rose out of his chair. His hands braced against the table, eyes tracking the increasing rhythm of my breaths.

"I think I can help with limbering you up. Loosening tight muscles is a specialty of mine." His eyes flashed with predatory intent, and his fingers tightened along the edge of the table. "When I'm done with you, you'll be practically boneless."

Squirming under the intensity of his gaze, I bit down on my lip. I really wanted what those eyes were promising. The door latched behind Alessia, leaving us once more alone. Cal caught the movement of my eyes and then pounced.

I squealed and leapt into the air towards the balcony in a weak attempt to flee. Cal plucked me mid-leap, seizing me around my waist and hauling me back into him. With one motion, he spun me, sliding the loose shirt over my shoulders and locking his lips onto mine.

Cal threw the shirt behind him and then lifted me into the air. Lips moving feverishly over mine, one hand running up my side as he laid me back on the bed. Then unexpectedly, he paused and brushed the hair from my face. The dark expanse of his golden flecked irises glimmered down at me, dazed, as if he'd sunk into the depths of my eyes and lost himself there.

"What?" I said breathlessly. An amused smile playing at my lips.

He dipped down and pressed a soft, reverent kiss to my jaw, following it up with another to my mouth. "I've just never felt this way before."

"Oh?" I said beneath the pressure of his lips.

"Elle, I am so fully consumed by you that I can't even tell if it is my heart pounding or yours. The bright heat of your soul has seared itself around mine and merged so completely that it's left me awestruck by the beauty of it. Desire and love pale in the shadow of this new emotion. It's left me stunned and terrified out of my fucking mind."

"You were thinking all of that?" He kissed me harder this time, and I melted against him.

"Mmm...but mostly I'm thinking that I'm going to fuck you so hard that the stars that fill your vision won't disappear until they're replaced by the ones in the night sky."

I laughed against his lips. "But, it's morning."

29

CALLEN

After spending days in exhausted worry over Elyria, it was comforting to be able to laze about the apartment with her. Twice messengers had come to my rooms demanding my attention, and I shooed them away as quickly as they had come. She was awake and healthy, and one hundred percent mine.

The future was so uncertain, but the one thing I knew was that, for the next twelve hours, I wasn't leaving her side or the blissed-out hazy bubble that cocooned around us. The rest of the palace could just deal with it.

Elyria would glide out of the bed, only to find me pinning her to the wall beside it... Or the balcony, or the floor, the desk, the table...I couldn't stop touching her, rolling her over in my arms, and feeling her wrapped around me. The magnetic pull grew stronger the longer we laid there. Her power nestled against my soul, refusing to relinquish control over me. I didn't want it to. She could take as much of me as she needed.

With laughter on her lips and ecstasy shining in her eyes, in those quiet, heady hours, she became my whole world. Having finally given myself permission to indulge, I lost myself there, fully seated in the rising addiction that was Elyria.

It wasn't until late in the night that the charge of energy between us finally abated, although I don't think that driving need would ever be fully sated. Elyria pulled the bedding onto the balcony, creating a small sea of satin and feather pillows. With the smooth curves of her naked body pressed into the length of mine, we watched the clouds drift across the moon. The stars blinked in the distance, and the lights of the harbor reflected off of the wide expanse of the black unending sea.

I pressed my face into the soft slope of her neck. The silken strands of her hair drifted in the air current I grazed over her flushed skin. Her sweet and smokey smell wound its way through me, and the sound of the water rushing from the spouts on either side of us blanketed the moment with pure serenity. For the first time in my life, I might actually be content. I'd be perfectly happy to live in this moment forever, and committed every second of it to memory—tucked it away deep in my heart for safekeeping.

The first rays of light shone off of the pure white marble, rousing me from sleep. Elyria's raven hair was splayed against the pillow we had pilfered from our bed. Because after last night, I'd never spend another night apart from her. There might not be a ring or a formal declaration, but what was mine was now hers, in every sense.

Her hand was delicately placed against my chest, having fallen asleep to the beat of my heart.

I gently rolled her onto her back, deciding that trailing kisses down her body was the preferred way to wake her. I was just reaching the divot of her hip as she began stirring, and the sleepy murmurs of awareness slipped into cries of passion the lower I dipped, and the longer I explored.

Her body was still trembling with orgasmic aftershocks when Elyria's eyes refocused on me. "We probably can't stay in this room pretending the rest of the world doesn't exist, can we?"

I prowled up her body, taking my time to wish good morning to each individual freckle along the way.

"No," I kissed the ridge of her collarbone, gliding a hand along her stomach. Then sighed. "No, I still have an invasion to coordinate."

As if on cue, a knock rapped against my door. I growled and then kissed Elyria soundly before climbing out of our nest. "Stay here."

"And what, just wait for you?"

"Yes. That would be ideal," I said with a wink.

The knock came at the door again, more insistent this time, and I scowled over my shoulder at it.

I picked up a pair of discarded linen pants. From the corner of my vision, I caught Elyria wrapping the blanket into a makeshift dress. When I laughed at her, she stuck her tongue out at me and slipped into the bathroom. I should have known better than to try to give her any kind of a command.

I smiled at the closing door. Fuck, I was happy. Had I ever actually been happy before? Because this elation was unlike anything I've experienced in my long life. Elyria's smiling face flashed in my mind. Just the thought of that shining smile had my heart racing again. How quickly could I make whoever this was go away?

The knock came a third time, rousing me from my daydream. I pulled the door open with an annoyed, "What?"

Mattias walked into the room, not waiting for an invitation. "Good morning, Your Highness."

I narrowed my eyes. "Your timing is something else, Mattias."

"Quite, although it would seem that there was no separating you and Miss Solaris. So I'm not sure it's an issue of timing."

I shrugged. "Get on with it. If you dragged yourself up to the apartments, it must be serious."

"You hardly left me a choice. You sent the last two of my messengers back to me with the simple message of "go away.""

"Actually, what I said was 'fuck off', but you didn't come to argue semantics." I chuckled. "Besides, we were preoccupied."

Mattias pursed his lips, but his judging eyes showed a hint of amusement. "Captain Sangrior is waiting in the War Room. She was quite—" He hesitated for a second, raising a hand to rub at a small mark sliced into the side of his throat. "—*persistent* that I bring you to meet with her. The preparations to the fleet have been completed, and I believe she is ready to discuss the embarkment plans."

I ran a hand through my hair. So this was it. We'd be leaving, and soon. An icy bath of reality washed over me, rinsing away the warm feeling of contentment that filled the apartment. An old and too-familiar weight slammed back onto my shoulders, one that was now tinged with a raw fear for the woman who so securely snared my heart.

Elyria peeked her head out of the bathroom, wrapped in a warm robe. She spotted Mattias and looked at me. The unspoken question of decorum flitting between us.

"It's okay, my love." I raised my arm, gesturing for her to come into the room. It was only Mattias, and there was nothing his keen eyes missed, anyway.

She flushed bright red as she slipped into the crook of my arm.

"Good Morning, Miss Solaris. It looks as though you have recovered."

"Hello, Mattias. I'm feeling much better. Thank you." Her body tightened against mine, connecting in an unbroken line from my shoulder to the floor. After last night, I'm sure she's feeling much, much better.

I leaned down to press a soft kiss on her crown. If the tenderness shocked Mattias, he didn't show it. He'd seen me in my most rakish days and escorted more than a few ladies out of the royal apartments, but he didn't seem the least bit surprised by my candor. Although I barely recognized the man I had become, Mattias seemed almost as if he had been waiting for this day.

"Tell Commander Xoc that Elyria and I will be joining Captain Sangrior in the War Room in twenty minutes. We just need time to dress."

"Of course. Is there anything else you require?"

I squeezed Elyria's hip. "There are many things I require, but as you have so politely stated, I have responsibilities to see to."

30

ELYRIA

"Destroying their fleet will cut off their ability to carry out a counter-attack! Or can your tiny little mind not understand that?" Morgan's sharp voice echoed off the stone walls.

Cal slammed his hand on the table, the sound shooting straight to the back of my eyes.

"And then everyone will be looking right at your monster of a ship as we try to slip *undetected* into the floating lands. Brilliant. Why don't we just ask Malvat on board for tea while we're at it?"

It had been hours. A non-stop assault of Cal and Morgan flinging insults and arguments over strategy. My head throbbed from the way they kept moving in circles. Her tiny cyclone of power bounced off the hard wall of his resolve, and nothing was getting accomplished. I was starting to miss the coma. They were probably the two worst people to put in a room together and expect any kind of resolution to come about.

Morgan wanted the primary attack to come by sea, and Cal wanted the main approach to be over land. Innesvale only had so many forces to deploy, and we were outnumbered. We needed every advantage that could be afforded to us, which meant a carefully planned strike at the unsuspecting Iron Legion. Something Malvat couldn't ignore, but somehow didn't leave Innesvale vulnerable. Morgan insisted that Star Spear would have an easier time slipping by the forces if it was one of many ships. Which made sense. Cal seemed to think that it wouldn't matter if the Iron Legion was focused on the Lava Fields.

Xoc stood by the window, staring out at the gardens and listening to their bickering. Now and then, he would voice an obvious point of contention, but

Cal would make some smart-ass comment that would send Morgan right back into a rage.

On and on it went.

In a moment of peak frustration, Morgan hurled a pitcher at Cal. He blew the carafe against the wall, spraying ceramic shards around the room. Morgan retaliated by making the falling water fly in a blade straight for him.

I threw up a fireball, making the spike of water evaporate with a hiss.

"Enough." I rolled my shoulders. "You two are worse than children with a new toy." I rubbed at my temples. "I wish Aurus had agreed to help us. Then, maybe, none of this would be necessary."

"Is that actually an option?" Morgan asked, genuinely intrigued. "Because that would change—"

"It's not an option. He refused to involve himself." I rolled my shoulders, trying not to fall back into all of my frustration against the dragon. "Explain to me, again, why can't we do both? Send ground forces and airships over the Lava Fields and a second armada by sea. Split the Iron Legion's focus to two fronts."

"We don't have the people for dual fronted attack. It wouldn't be sustainable, and after Malvat decimated our forces, Innesvale would be undefended. That would invite an entirely different sort of attention from some of the less friendly neighbors."

"That's true," added Xoc. "Astralon is always looking for an opportunity to march South."

I chewed on my lip in contemplation. "You're thinking too long term."

"Sunshine, war is long term."

"But, we don't need a lasting force. Like you said, it's a quick strike."

Cal shook his head. "We'd be sacrificing everyone we sent over the Lava Fields."

"No, we wouldn't. They just need to hold out for one quick attack. When I kill Malvat, the power will shift."

"*If* you take down Malvat." Morgan's sapphire eyes pierced mine.

I squared my shoulders at her. "When. There is no way that bastard sees daylight. Mark my words, I will kill him, and the Iron Legion will fall from the sky."

"When *we* kill him. I'll be right there with you." Cal put a reassuring hand on my shoulder, the heat from his palm making my skin tingle with awareness. "Always."

Xoc spoke up, looking away from the window. "It's a good plan."

"Thank you."

"We do it in tiers. I can send an extra battalion by land for a short and targeted attack, then retreat to reinforce our city walls. We'll be exposed for a short time, but..." Xoc walked over to the battle map and shifted the figures around, adding more to the ground plane. "It will force all attention to shift to the Lava Fields the way Cal wanted. Malvat would need the full might of his forces on the ground and out of the fort. We would have enough men to keep the Iron Legion fully engaged, if for a short time."

Morgan perked up. "Then, we send just enough ships to be a distraction and force Malvat's forces to shift and scatter. Star Spear will simply slip through in the chaos."

"While the majority of the land forces pull back to our walls." Xoc's eyes flashed to me with what felt a hell of a lot like pride. "And if something goes wrong, our forces pull back entirely, and we shore up our borders to prepare for retaliation."

"It won't come to that," Cal said with far too much hubris.

Morgan tapped her hand against her hip, running her fingers along the delicate guard of her saber. "It'll work. I promise my airships will be impossible to ignore, and the eyes of the Iron Draken won't be anywhere near you. Then, when the opportunity presents itself, you drive that blade deep and twist."

I smiled. "That, I can do." I arched my back, stretching the muscles that stiffened from sitting in the hard wooden chairs.

Morgan panned an unamused glare at Cal. "We set sail day after tomorrow, mid-day. See you are there before then. I don't care to wait on spoiled princes who feel like a good fuck takes precedence over winning a war."

Cal opened his mouth to argue. Morgan turned for the door without bothering to wait for his rebuttal and dismissing him in that way only she could pull off.

I stretched my arm across my chest. "Listening to the two of you has me wanting to punch something." I looked at Cal. "Feel like going a couple of rounds in the training ring? I promise not to stab anyone, probably."

Cal raised an eyebrow at me.

To my surprise, Xoc spoke up. "Actually, if the three of us are going into that fort in two days, then it would be wise to practice fighting together beforehand. Cal has sparred with you before, but I have next to no experience with your fighting style."

Cal tilted his head to the side. He looked intrigued but unconvinced.

A broad smile spread across my face. "Unless you're worried, I'm just going to kick your ass again." I bounced on my toes, ready to burn off the pent up energy brought on by sitting still for too long.

"Sunshine, I'm never going to turn down a chance at a few rounds with you. We can do round, after round... after round." He licked his lips and let his eyes scan down the length of my body.

"Gods Cal, a full day of fucking around, and your mind is still only on your dick."

"If you'd had the same day I just had, your mind would be on your dick too."

31

ELYRIA

I ran my finger along the perfectly spaced stitching, staring at the most exquisite bit of leatherwork I'd ever seen. Alessia left this glorious wardrobe of death on the bed for me, the armor at odds with the delicate satin comforter. But, it's not like the bed was getting any other use, so it might as well serve as a staging area.

For the three days since I'd woken, Cal wouldn't let me out of his arms long enough to make it to my apartment. Even now, he only reluctantly let me over here because I needed to dress for our mission.

The halter had a built-in sheath and boning along the spine for the Sun Serpent Dagger to be held discreetly in place. It was expertly tooled and matched perfectly with each of the other equally deadly parts. The pants were seamed along the joints with a lightweight silk that stretched to provide maximum flexibility.

"Excellent," I whispered into the quiet room. Beside the clothing sat a set of bracers with straps to hold darts along the top and two flat throwing knives along the underside. Next to them was a sheath to keep my throwing knives along my waist and an upgraded version of my boots, knife straps included. I grinned. This was like Solstice morning and my birthday combined.

I quickly slipped them on, flexing my arms and legs to test the leather and the stretch of the silken inserts. The armor was perfection. I did a high back kick in place, spinning into an aerial return kick. The leather shifted with me effortlessly, almost like a second skin. It was obviously made for me, and my style of fighting. Elation spilled from me in a little whoop of excitement. This armor made me feel strong, invincible.

Cal leaned against the doorway, watching me. Those dark eyes followed each and every one of my movements.

"You look like a goddess of violence." He chewed on the knuckle of his hand, lightly running it over his bottom lip before slowly looping in his belt.

"Maybe I am. What would you pray for?" Bending forward, I kicked into a handstand and allowed my legs to spread wide.

He sucked in a breath while walking closer. "Deliverance."

Cal's eyes glowed; a fire in them licking around his irises, making the gold bleed outward. Images of us wound in purple flames flashed through my mind. I licked my lips. There was nothing like that rush.

"When we get back..." Keeping my balance centered over my hands, I looped one knee behind his neck and another around his waist. I pulled until he was forced to come flush with my body. His cheek brushed my inner thigh. Each barely controlled breath rocked the hard ridge of his cock against my back. His hands easily found my hips.

I sat up, my hands leaving the ground and trusting my legs to support me. Cal kept his grip on my hips steady as I curled upright. It was a move similar to what I would do when hanging from the hoop by my knees and switching into a seated position. Except, this time, I had a leg looped over Cal's shoulder, and I wasn't sitting on anything as boring as a hoop. "When we get back, you can bend me into any position you want."

"Fuck me, Elle," he moaned out, biting the juncture of my hip while dropping his hands to cup my ass.

"That too." I slid down his torso, smiling innocently back at him. "I'll even keep the knives out."

Cal groaned, taking a step away from me and adjusting his pants, the bulge of his erection unmistakable. "Do you have any idea how uncomfortable these fighting leathers are with a hard on?"

I bit my lip, fully enjoying the anguish on his face. This was the best distraction from my anxiety yet. Closing the space between us, I surged forward, barely managing to brush the taught leather before Cal reacted. Snatching my wrist, he quickly spun me so that my hands were pinned between my lower back and his stomach. The force of the impact sizzled desire along each of my nerve endings. His breath was hot against my ear and fanned the tiny hairs along my neck. In the past two days, there was no part of my body he hadn't explored, and yet the simple feel of his breath had me melting into a puddle of wanton heat.

His palm coasted between my breasts, circling my throat to angle my face towards his. I pointlessly tugged against his hold. His grip was as firm as a pair of iron manacles.

Cal's voice rumbled against my back. "The next time you are begging for me to make you come, and I deny you that release, I want you to remember this moment."

A power laced kiss pressed beneath where his fingers still circled my throat. When I shuddered against him, I could feel his smile stretch against my skin.

"Let's go," he said, releasing my wrists and slapping my ass for emphasis. "Morgan will have my balls if we're late."

Just before he opened the door, Cal stopped, turning to me. "Oh, and Elyria, when we get back— there is no surface in this palace that I won't bend you over. When I'm done with you, even the stone will be singing my name." He smiled, seemingly pleased with the flush blooming over my neck and chest. "And that's if you're lucky, because I'm fairly certain I will never be done with you."

32

CALLEN

That woman was going to be the death of me. Probably literally. I was going to be too busy dreaming about her writhing beneath me to notice an attack flying straight at my face. It was impossible not to, not when I could still sense her lingering on every part of me. Elyria had imprinted herself in the best way possible.

As we approached the gates, Xoc hurried to catch up to us while lacing his bracer. It was beyond bizarre. Xoc was never late for anything. He was the king of punctuality, and Elyria had ensured that our trip took twice as long as it should have to get down here. Not that I was complaining.

"You're late."

"I needed to see to something before we left."

I leaned to the side to peer around him. "Were you coming from the Southern gardens? And why are you still dressing?"

Xoc glanced at the row of lemon blossom trees separating the garden from the gatehouse. "Shortcut."

"Shortcut from where? The pond?"

"It's not important. Look, Alexander is already here."

A line of five men and one woman stood at attention. A medallion with a dagger impaling an eye hung from a cord around each of their necks. The head of their unit didn't move as I approached, but I noticed Alexander's dark eyes flick to Elyria.

Alexander and I spent more than one evening hustling tail in the lower end of Innesvale. That was until he met his husband, the tall blonde standing beside him. The corner of his mouth twitched. I'm sure he was remembering the night he told me he'd proposed to Petros. It was the same night I drunkenly proclaimed that would never be me, and when it was finally forced upon me, any marriage I chose would be a political alliance, not love. I was so naïve. That was a hard fact to swallow, one the man before me would make sure to shove down my throat the first opportunity he could find.

I tilted my chin slightly toward Elyria in confirmation. The idiot who made those declarations never could have anticipated what it meant to be thoroughly consumed by someone. Alexander had known, and I had laughed.

Choking back what I really wanted to say, I gestured to the rigid line of soldiers. "Elyria, this is Innesvale's most elite fighting unit; they are known to Venterra as The Undying."

"The Undying. That sounds so... formidable." Elyria's eyes scanned each of them, smiling in appreciation when she noticed Alanea. The Seed Singer's cinnamon colored hair was braided into an intricate pattern down her back, revealing the red warrior's tattoo marking her neck. It matched the one on Xoc's brow. When Xoc returned with me to Innesvale, he immediately enlisted to join our ranks. He and Alanea were the only Oerish members of their training class. Five years later, when they were both awarded a Captain's position in the guard, the pair had the red markings inked to celebrate. They might not live under the jungle canopy anymore, but the tattoos were a constant reminder of where their journey began.

"That's because they are," Xoc added smoothly. The Undying were Xoc's own personal pet project. They answered directly to him. He oversaw their training, scouted their unique abilities from the ranks of Innesvale's armies, and hand-picked each member to work together as a flawless unit.

On this mission, they would fill in the missing gaps among Morgan's ranks onboard Star Spear. It was one of many issues of contention between us. Morgan didn't want anyone who wasn't one of her's on board. She made no small point of saying that suffering me was already enough of an allowance, but this wasn't something I was willing to budge on. I needed skilled fighters to flank us on our approach to the Lava Tubes, people that could ensure a clear path and not get mowed down in the process. Also, Morgan's ship would need all of their attuned to keep us aloft once we passed over land. Should we get boarded, which was likely, I couldn't let the Captain's pride put the mission in jeopardy. Just two of the Undying would be enough to take out any boarding party. All six were, well, there was a reason they were called The Undying.

Elyria skimmed a finger over Alexander's shoulder plates. The light seemed to be absorbed by the black leather armor as she traced the cresting waves set into the shoulder piece. Elyria didn't know it, but that was a symbol very few ever got to wear. The Undying were as unending as the ocean and just as impossible to stop.

"Leather?" she questioned, "I mean, I know I'm in leather because of the weight and fire, but I would have thought our forces would be wearing proper armor,"

Our forces. Fuck, why did that make me hard?

"Don't let our Leather Smith Brok hear that," I chuckled. Alexander's silent eyes met mine. He was doing a shit job of suppressing his smirk. I was going to get a serious earful the moment we were free.

Elyria started comparing the construction to her own suit. They were similar, although hers was lighter and more suitable for her level of agility. In fact, each set of armor Brok created was tailored to the needs of each individual soldier. Some featured back holsters for long swords or boning along the knuckles for maximum impact, spring-loaded short arrows along bracers, hidden knives in boot soles. The possibilities for customization were endless. Brok was particularly good at reading a person's style and matching their equipment to it. It's why he'd been making my sets for years, and why I had him design one for Elyria, too.

Her eyes glittered as she took in the variety of weaponry, even going as far as to pull the obsidian short sword from Petros' scabbard. Alexander made an amused grunt when she began swinging it, testing its balance and giving it a loping toss into the air. Elle had to be the only person who would think to toss a sword like that. I loved that about her.

When she finally made it to the Alanea, Elyria paused with an inquisitive cock of her head. "Is that a slingshot, no knives or swords? What are you going to fight with?"

Alanea's responding smile would be sweet, if not for the feral excitement crinkling her eyes. "I can do more damage with one shot of this..." She tapped the top of the wooden handle, then tilted her chin down the line of men. "Than any of those morons can do with their swords. They're all so precious about it, but they know the true threat of our group is me." Alanea winked before straightening back to attention. Elyria's expression lit up, a resonating kinship already forming between the two women. I groaned.

"It's because of the Iron Legion." Xoc directed her attentions away from the line, probably thinking the same thing I was. Elyria already walked the fine line between gorgeously lethal and recklessly uninhibited. The last thing my girl needed was another savage friend encouraging her to run headfirst into a fight. "We can't send our forces in with metal armor. It's already enough of a risk to send them with metal weapons."

Elyria looked over her shoulder at Petros' stone sword. He raised his eyebrows, willing her to connect the dots. "Why?"

"With an army covered in steel or iron, a skilled singer could level an entire battlefield with one swipe of his hand," Xoc explained.

I blinked away the image of Elyria falling on the lava fields with a sword in her back. I laced my fingers into hers, needing to feel the buzz of our connection. She looked so ready for a fight, and it was causing a tempest of conflicting emotions to riot in my gut. I'd sailed into battle countless times. There was always a sort of eager anticipation that came before embarking, but with Elyria in my life, everything was different. This conversation, against the backdrop of warships, sharpened the worry that I'd been biting back for days. I knew she could handle herself. Elyria was as capable as anyone boarding Star Spear, but that didn't make my panic any less potent. If she was taken by Malvat... I couldn't even bring myself to imagine the horrors he could inflict or what nefarious plans were worth sending his shadows all the way to Laluna.

"But, I..." Elyria's wide eyes scanned her very metal knives.

"Don't worry." I ran a finger over the throwing knives at her waist. "Most of the Iron Legion won't be proficient enough to control the metal in such small quantities. And if you need it, those darts–" I tapped the top of her wrist "--are made of Earth Singer obsidian, as are the throwing knives on your hip and the one in your right boot. They're stronger and sharper than any steel blade."

"Ooo," she said, bouncing on her toes with enthusiasm and slipping a black dart between her fingers. With a quick flick, she sent it flying, embedding the projectile in the floorboards—an inch from Morgan's feet.

The Captain was mid-word, halting the commands she was issuing. Her tattooed brow rose as she gave the dart a cold look, then slowly lifted her attention to Elyria.

Elyria, to her credit, laughed. "Want to try dodging knives next?" She spun one of the stone daggers in her palm before smoothly re-sheathing it into the bracer.

"You could try..." Morgan retrieved the dart from the ground and tossed it lightly in her hand. "But then again, you'd never get the chance to loose one." A fiendish smile curled her crimson lips.

Was that her idea of a joke? In almost unison, both women chuckled darkly. I looked between them and then to Alanea, who was smiling like she was somehow in on the joke, too. These women. If they ever had the opportunity to fight at each other's back, they would be terrifying. I might very well get that chance today.

Morgan's smile vanished when she directed her blue piercing eyes at me. "Sails up in ten." Any levity that had been in the moment vanished with those four simple words. "I hope you're ready. The vanguard set off an hour ago."

There was no changing our minds now. War had begun.

The vanguard would be approaching via a dead strip of desert that stretched between our kingdoms. By now, they would be nearing the edge of the lava fields. The magnetic force of the land picked up at the shift, and the Iron Legion would use that to their advantage. With the extreme magnetism and the Metal Singers they'd have in their ranks, iron airships could easily skim over the lava fields, avoiding all the dangers that came with them. Our forces will have a trickier time navigating those fields, but still possible—for as long as magical reserves hold out.

That lava would be our saving grace and Malvat's undoing. The shores held long tunnels of ocean cooled lava. They wove deep into Mt. Kraav, and the foundation of the fort was built atop them. Not unlike Malvat using our grottos to gain access to the castle, we would use the Lava Tubes to infiltrate the fort. The difference being that we would need to avoid not only the rivers of molten lava that sometimes spilled into the tubes but also the lava cats that made their dens deep in the tunnels. There was a reason Venterrans referred to Kraav as a place of death, demons, and eternal damnation. No sane person would approach this way, and that was where I hoped we would have the advantage of surprise.

"Did the aerial division have any difficulties with their ascension?" Xoc asked.

"No, smooth take offs, all of them. The additions I made worked perfectly, of course. I retained a dozen smaller speeders to fend off the attack fliers."

I flicked my eyes discreetly at Elyria. She was thumbing the stone knife again, flipping it back and forth in her hand before sliding her thumb along the hilt. Either it was her nervous need to fidget or her way of learning the intimate nature of a new blade. Probably both. Either way, the fluid, unthinking nature of her movements was sexy as hell.

Morgan strode up the gangplank with determined, thumping steps. Swiveling with a backward step onto the main deck of Star Spear. "Were you just going to stand there with your band of unnecessary muscle behind you, or were you actually going to join in on this little war we're waging?"

Trudging down the dock, Elyria said, "If a certain spineless dragon was here, then we could just fly over and burn the whole damn mountain to the ground. We wouldn't need an armada." She looked back towards the Vanfald, holding up a middle finger. Petros, standing directly in her line of sight, did a double take. Turning to see nothing but the mountain behind him, he looked back at Elyria with an offended and possibly hurt expression.

It took everything I had not to break into laughter.

Pushing Elyria up the ramp, Xoc remarked, "Try not to insult the men who will be watching our backs only hours before we go into battle."

With a mock whisper and a glance over my shoulder to be sure he was paying attention, I added, "Plus, Petros is sensitive, and it's hard to fight when his panties are all in a twist."

Pete's indignation turned down into an outright scowl. Alexander, on the other hand, looked like he might start cackling.

Morgan didn't wait for us. The second she stormed the main deck she began shouting orders. "I want guns and all hands at full alert. Signal the rest of the fleet on first sign of approaching enemy forces. Archers, grenadiers, you do not need command to fire. You see an opportunity to bring something down. You take it."

A chorus of "Aye, Captain" rang out along the deck. Several stomped their feet or slapped the outer deck with their swords.

The advancements we had discussed were visible everywhere. From the dock it had looked like the same ship, but standing amid the rigging, I could spot the changes everywhere. Mounted crossbows now lined the outer decks and looked like the spikes running along the dragon's spine. The bolts for each were roughly the size of my arm. Not only would these tear a man apart, they might just be able to take out an entire airship if they were stupid enough to buzz anywhere near Morgan's air space. With a quick glance at the other ships readying to sail beside us, I could see they were all similarly outfitted. It was amazing what she managed to accomplish in such a short span of time.

A team of Sea Singers moved into formation on the quarter decks with hands raised. The ship lurched beneath us, and I reached out to steady Elyria against me. Rows of attuned soldiers lined the starboard bows of the ships flanking us. Their combined force pushed the fleet from the harbor, sailing as one. Morgan and Bein had done their job well. Their timing was a perfect machine.

My heart rate increased as we left Innesvale behind. The coil of barbed nerves at the center of my chest slowly began winding itself tighter with each moment we moved towards the distant volcanos.

I reached down and gripped Elyria's hand in mine. She gave me three small squeezes. Together we watched the Guardians as we sailed past, Innesvale's sentinels with swords raised, and the water that crested over the sides in two great waves. The rainbows shimmering in the mist felt like the universe was wishing us luck. We would see them again.

"This will work," Xoc said resolutely, reading my mind.

I looked at them, at the brother who has had my back during every battle, and at the woman who gave me a reason to hope.

"It has to."

33

CALLEN

The distant glow on the horizon grew, along with the rumble of tumbling rock and the hiss of lava along the shores. To the west, the lava fields extended in an unending expanse. The lingering smoke clouds blocked the intermittent rays of sunlight, turning the sky an ominous red. It was no wonder Venterrans believed this place to be cursed.

A horn blared, the same horn that announced a call to battle stations. I ran my hands over Elyria's shoulders, feeling a light tremor there. Scales shifted beneath my fingers, covering her velvet skin in armor. She looked over her shoulder at me. Her eyes were bright, fire sparkling around their edges. Of course, she was shaking in anticipation and not fear.

I leaned down, claiming her mouth with my own, our kiss a silent prayer to every god I knew to keep my girl safe. My hair fell forward, brushing her cheek. She lifted her hand to the now golden strands, then caressed the scales forming along my collar. I would never tire of feeling her hands on me.

"You're not waiting until we're alone?"

"I'm not taking any chances, not with Malvat in the wind and you here beside me. It's easier to control my power when I'm fully shifted. The Undying are sworn to me, and Morgan's men would never dare betray her command." Gods only know what she does to traitors. A shiver prickled along my neck imagining it. "And, any of the Iron Legion who get close enough to identify us, won't live long enough to speak of it. Our secret is safe."

Elyria glimmered in the grey light, a radiant beacon atop the perilous sea. Ash floated in the air, landing in Elyria's dark hair like snow. Beyond her, buzzing similar to an agitated hive of bees drew my focus to the quickly growing spot on the horizon.

A black streak buzzed by us, followed by four more dark metal ships falling into formation with the lead flyer. Perched on top of the wings of each ship were a line of Legionnaires, balanced and poised to drop on us. Xoc spotted them too and called out a command to The Undying. His voice was almost lost amid the growing sound of engines.

The airships circled back around, centering their approach to the bow. The bowmen lining Star Spear's decks tracked their movement. Before anyone could fire, the airships disappeared into the cover of the grey clouds.

Morgan's cutting voice called out, "Fire."

Beside me, five grenadiers pulled back on their catapults. The deadly blue orbs shone in their catches. I didn't know what they could be aiming at, but perhaps they didn't need to make direct contact with them. The grenade just needed to be close enough for the shrapnel to take them down.

One by one, they released into the clouds. The dull buzzing filled my ears until a concussive boom rocked the sky and sent our ship rolling. I held on to Elyria's shoulders, keeping her firmly to my chest. Explosions echoed across the sky, and two fiery airships spiraled down into the water, a trail of thick black smoke following behind them.

Movement caught my eye. Elyria and I looked up together. Our escorting fleet of speeders zipped in and out of the clouds to the sounds of ricocheting projectiles and clashing metal. They must have been waiting for our initial attack. Once it was clear, they zoomed in to pick off the survivors. Each was small, barely more than the size of a man, but they were fast. They would be impossibly hard for the opposing force to track and shoot down. The twang of bow strings sang above us. The speeders were equipped with small preloaded crossbows. Bolts of what almost looked like lightning shot across the sky, aimed straight for the remaining airships.

The buzzing on the horizon mutated into dull roar. An armada of massive airships, more than double our own ranks, emerged from the clouds. I scanned the boats sailing on either side of us, watching as they worked to eliminate the speeders still zipping around our airspace. We'd left Innesvale with every barque and schooner we could spare, but despite our efforts, we didn't have near the numbers to fend off ships of this size and quantity. For the first time since we began discussing our attack, I questioned if we would even make it to the lava tunnels to begin with. As I watched the large envoy approaching, I realized lives may never leave the deck of this ship.

"Demons below. What in the hells of Kraav are those?"

A deep blaring horn echoed over the clouds, loud enough that I felt it in my chest. In unison, each of the massive warships broke apart, splintering into dozens and dozens of smaller ones. They blotted out the sky as they descended on our fleet. Several broke away, zeroing in on Star Spear to circle around on us. With one of our speeders hot on their tail, two of the new vessels streaked overhead, dropping two dozen men onto the deck of Star Spear. The action seemed suspended as everyone processed what was happening. And then, fighting exploded everywhere, all at once.

"Hello, pretty-pretty," one of the men said in a low, gravely voice that didn't sound remotely human. Elyria stuttered in her step, taking in the same nightmarish details that I was.

In place of the Legionnaire's armor, a skeletal set of plates were embedded into their flesh. Scarred skin gripped metal ridges that resembled a macabre version of a ribcage. Similarly, puffy, inflamed skin wrapped around the edges of a skull-like mask, showing only white eyes beneath. Malvat hadn't even spared his own people from the Shade.

An unwanted shiver ran down my spine. What had he done to his forces? The Mal I knew growing up, the man I called brother, cared about every single person under his care. He never could have inflicted this level of abuse. As I studied the patinated metal impaling the man before me, my chest ached with the memory of my father's knife piercing it. Each bit of weathered metal made them look more like monsters than men. These were once good people, too.

Was the entire Iron Legion now more undead than living flesh? I glanced towards where *I had sent* the majority of our forces. The weight of their lives felt heavier than ever. Were they all facing people as unstoppable as Andros and Andromeda had been? How were we supposed to fight an unrelenting army who were oblivious to their already dying bodies?

Elyria pulled her shoulders from my grip and flashed me eyes sharper than the daggers strapped to her body. They glowed brighter than I had ever seen, a nearly ethereal gold, flames crackling at the center of her irises.

"I've got this." She licked her lips. "The only thing worth fearing on this deck right now is me."

Elyria pulled out a throwing knife and sent it whizzing into the air. It embedded itself into an iron clad warrior, right in the throat. He fell instantly with an unceremonious thud.

The twitching man twisted into an impossible contortion while crawling back to his feet. He should have been dead. With a slow drag, the throwing knife tore free of his throat, slicing through tendon and baring the entire left side of his esophagus. A wet raspy sound that might have been laughter gurgled from him, the exposed muscles flexing as he tried to swallow. Torrents of blood poured from the grotesque wound and down his chest before death finally claimed him.

"Gross." Elyria grimaced.

Defying all my instincts, I put space between us and brandished my short sword. Light flashed as Elyria unsheathed both Butterfly blades. I wasn't ready for the rush of pride that came over me, knowing that I was fighting with her by my side. But feeling that spark and connection between us now, nothing had ever felt so right.

For each Legionnaire that fell, two more seemed to drop out of the sky. They were definitely targeting Star Spear. In the back of my mind, the nagging 'I knew it' rang. I shot a bitter glare in Morgan's direction.

The air became thick with smoke, both from the nearing volcano and the exploding wreckage of each airship Morgan's crews shot down. Explosions lit up the hovering smoke cloud with flashes of light. The sounds of men jumping into the ocean mixed with the clatter of machinery and swords.

Two Legionnaires came straight at us. I moved to engage them, but Elyria spun, cutting off my attack. Two brilliant streaks of silver cut through the air. Sparks flew off of the butterfly sword as they connected with an iron ribcage. She dropped below the counter strike of the man and used the motion to swivel behind him. Elyria swung low and with precision. This time the blades connected with flesh, severing the tendons and muscles along his ankles. The Legionnaire's white eyes showed no reaction and continued to advance, but with muscles no longer functioning, he dropped to his knees.

Anticipating the man's fall, Elyria crossed the blades, letting his own gravity and motion drag the blade across his throat. Blood spluttered from his mouth, spraying across her chest before his head thunked to the floor.

The second man stepped over the headless corpse. Elyria caught the motion and pulled out a throwing knife. It hurtled at the second man, flashing red in the firelight—Until it wasn't. The metal knife spun, suspended in the air before her. My muscles tensed, ready to halt the blade should it fly back. The Legionnaire's iron-clad hand extended towards the blade. The knife disintegrated into thick shining drops that splashed against the ground.

The Legionnaire bellowed a laugh. "Silly girl thinks she can play with knives."

"Well, that was a mistake," I said, lowering my sword and leaning against the railing to watch the show. Elyria would eviscerate him. It was going to be a glorious thing to watch.

Elyria growled at the man. "Fucking Metal Singers, I only had two of those left, you asshole." Fearless and wild, she leapt into the air, pouncing on the man like a cat. She drove her foot deep into his throat with a gruesome-sounding crunch. Her weight toppled them to the deck followed by the sound of several bones cracking and muscle tearing apart beneath razor-tipped claws.

Wondering why I even bothered to brandish the thing, I sheathed my unnecessary sword.

After wiping the blood from her hands with the tails of the man's tunic, Elyria stood up, one foot still on top of the man's flattened throat. Her hair flipped behind her, the golden tips gleaming crimson in the lava light.

"You are the most beautiful kind of violence." I gripped the holster strapped beneath her blood-splattered breast and pulled her to me while she simultaneously yanked on my collar to bring my lips down to hers. The adrenaline pounding from her heart flooded into mine, radiating down into my fingertips with a seductive power that only she could give.

A battle cry, followed by the concussive blast of a pistol firing, echoed from behind us. Feeling a tug on my shoulder, I broke my lips from Elyria's and turned. A shorn bit of leather fell to the ground at the feet of a man stumbling forward. The iron sword replacing his hand dropped limply to his side. I only looked at the mutilated limb for a moment before my attention zeroed in on the rosette blooming over his heart.

"This isn't a brothel." Morgan hollered from the plank that ran along the edge of the quarterdeck. She was parrying with the long thin saber she always kept at her hip. The small pistol attached to her blade smoked slightly. With a spin, the sword plunged straight through the man. "I can't keep saving your life." Pushing the dying man off of her blade with her foot, he tipped over the edge and crashed into the water. She was the exact vision of every battle story and merciless tale I'd ever heard. I knew in this moment they were all true, and none of them exaggerated.

"I knew you liked me," I called back.

"I like your money. You're barely tolerable."

On the deck behind her, Bein swung a giant battle ax. The stories of Morgan's first mate were nearly as notorious as her's. Whilst Morgan was all commanding grace, Bein was sheer brawn and brute force. The flat side of the axe swung through the air, shattering the bones of his attacker, who instantly melted to the ground in a heap. Bein reached down, grabbing the man by the throat and tossing him as if he wasn't anything more than a scrap of paper. The limp body arced over the railing, soaring directly into the airship that was buzzing by. In a violent shower of sparks, the man, the ship, and the five men perched on its wings all went spiraling down into the water.

A sword dragged over the scales lining my arm, drawing my attention back to our immediate surroundings. I spun, an airblade rocketing from my hand. The heated edges sliced through the man, sending the severed segments of his body to the ground before his face could even register that I'd turned.

Xoc was several paces away from us. Claws extended, he tore out the throat of one Legionnaire while swiping his other hand and gutting a second. Two more men dropped from the sky on top of him. A high-pitched whistle, like a bird's cry, cut through the din of battle. There was a flicker of recognition before something small zinged past Xoc's cheek, embedding into the eye of the man closest to him. What was once an eerie white eye exploded with ivy vines. Xoc tightened his grip, sending the mass of vines writhing like tentacles to ensnare the other Legionnaire. A muffled cry fell from the man before he was suffocating under the mass of leaves that shoved their way into his throat.

Xoc lifted his chin to the rigging where Alanea was perched, slingshot in hand, flinging her seeds at man after man. She winked while simultaneously plant life tore from the chests and mouths of Legionnaires on every part of the deck, shredding their metal skeletons like wet tissue paper. I'd seen her use this technique before, but that didn't make the image of thorns piercing a man from the inside out any less nightmare inducing.

The Undying effortlessly cut through the Iron Legion, killing them within minutes of dropping onto our ship. The iron-plated head of one attacker went rolling across the deck before me. Petros reached down, grabbing a fist full of the severed head's hair, and flung it into the cranium of the man before him. The strike came with such force that both skulls broke apart like melons in a shower of blood and bits of iron.

It was almost laughable. Despite the numbers of Legionaries that besieged us, the ship clearly never left Morgan's control. As quickly as the battle descended on us, it abated. Stragglers fighting for their lives found swift deaths, and the sound of bodies being heaved overboard replaced the sounds of clashing blades. A quick survey of the other ships showed that they'd also maintained their ranks. Morgan had trained our men well. Once we got Rei back, I'd owe her a thank you for introducing the Captain to us.

I looked past the dragon head at the bow of the ship to the approaching shore. In the distance, a second fleet of airships was moving in our direction. It wouldn't be long before this next offensive wave reached us. Thankfully, we were nearly to the lava torn shores of the Dead Lands. By the time this next wave descended Xoc, Elyria, and I will have disappeared into the depths of Kraav.

From the helm, Bein's loud voice bellowed, "Wings."

Star Spear shuttered along with the gears grinding beneath my feet. The dragon's wings, artfully carved into the side of the hull, unfurled. Black sails draped over skeletal boning spread wide. Wind Singers took position at the port and starboard sides of the ship. Seconds before we would have run aground, Star Spear took to the air. The dragon's wings flapped, gaining altitude. Elyria and I leaned over the edge. Dark, broken earth and rivers of lava skimmed beneath us, curtained by the plumes of steam rising from where each lava flow touched the ocean.

Morgan strode over to us, her dark skin and flaming red hair an echo of the savage earth around us, but it was her expression that caused my spine to straighten. She looked uncharacteristically grim for someone who had commanded the decisive victory of the past hour. Morgan pushed a long, jagged sword of black metal before me. "Have you seen this before?"

Xoc leaned over my shoulder. Laying in Morgan's petite hands was a blade straight from my nightmares, a black-green liquid coating the edge and dripping from the tip. Every person who was given even a knick from one of these swords would succumb to the same bleak end as Duke.

Xoc growled, and I felt the muscles of my neck tighten with matching outrage. Once again, Malvat was not fighting fair. He didn't need superior numbers or possessed soldiers. This wicked curse would be enough to take down the entirety of our forces. A renewed sense of urgency gripped at my gut. We'd be at the openings for the Lava Tubes soon. We had to destroy Malvat before there was no one left to fight.

"It took down one of my men," she said, pointing over to a sailor who was writing on the deck. Anger sharpened Morgan's features. The skin of the young pirate howling in pain was quickly turning black.

Elyria dug her fingers into my arm. She took a step back and fell into me. I slipped an arm around her waist to support her. Morgan's keen eyes drifted over Elyria's face, and her expression softened, if only for a moment.

"It's a shadow poison... a curse." I said, meeting Morgan's icy blue eyes. "It's fatal for most. You'd be better to put that man down now rather than to let him succumb to the effects." I glanced at Elyria, flashes of the night Duke died filling my mind. "It would be a mercy."

The Captain grimaced. It was then I truly saw how much she cared for her crew. Morgan turned to Bein and soundlessly shook her head. Her second moved without question, quickly slicing the throat of the fallen man. Within a second, his trembling ceased, and his cries silenced. Elyria tucked her face into my side.

"Toughen up girl." Morgan tightened an intense gaze on Elyria. "That won't be the last of the death you see today, and those fools you dropped earlier won't be the last you ravage. Fear is useful only as far as it heightens your senses." Letting her blood-stained nails sink into Elyria's chin, she roughly pulled her face until it was inches from hers. "Never let it command you. When fear bares its fangs, you roar back and make it submit to your will."

Elyria tightened her jaw against Morgan's fingers. Her intense golden eyes flamed and refused to back down from The Captain's blue ones. Elyria released me, standing tall.

"You're right."

"Of course I am." Morgan released her grip, expression deadly serious. She turned towards me. "We're going to drop you over there and then circle back to the water before that second fleet can make it to us. I'll continue fighting until you're ready for me to come and fetch you, but I'm not coming back until I see the Iron Legion fall from the sky. Failure is not an option."

"I'm going to get her out," Xoc said, placing a hand on her shoulder.

Morgan shifted her eyes to him. Standing so close, Xoc nearly doubled her size. Wind whipped at his long green hair. Tied up high on his head, it only added to his height. Blood streaked the side of his face and chest, contrasting intensely against his green scales.

The Captain was furious when Xoc told her of Rei's capture. After destroying her quarters, she channeled her warring emotions into making our attack streamlined and effective. While she portrayed a cold and emotionless exterior to her crew, we knew just how personal this fight was for her.

Morgan's lips pressed into a thin line. "Make it hurt." She looked over our heads, then abruptly strode away.

A passing shadow bathed Star Spear in darkness. The first of the floating islands sailed overhead. Smoke clouds drifted in and out of craggy black earth, and above it, the lights of a city filtered through. More islands peppered the sky, the largest showing the spires of the Floating Palace.

The same intense magnetism that the Iron Legion exploited to fly over the Dead Lands kept the ore-laden islands afloat. While the land below was teaming in lava rivers and sulfur pools, the land atop the islands was lush and vibrant, a blend of rich vegetation and mechanical marvels you could only find among those who were attuned to its element. A part of me loved that city and all its technical wonder, but that wasn't where we were going. We were sinking into the bowels of the earth, straight into a hell so foul even the land tried to get away from it.

The ship slowed. Not even a mile off, the clash and din of battle raged. The land forces must have been pushed farther east than we expected. Malvat probably saw through our attempt to split his focus and drove our forces to the shoreline.

Xoc leaned over the railing, surveying the carnage. "Looks like we'll be wading through the fight after all. The tube entrances are right in the middle of that hornet's nest."

"We knew this was a possibility." It was why I wanted The Undying with us. I'd just hoped that it wouldn't be necessary.

Two Innesvalen speeders buzzed past, clearing the few people at ground level that might have intercepted us. For the next few minutes, the ground would be clear. It was now or never.

I turned to Elyria, tightening my hand at her waist. "You ready?"

She looked over the edge, the glow of the lava lighting her beautiful features with the promise of violence. Looking back at me, she smiled with that same glimmer in her eyes that I saw that day in The Crooked Crow. It was the gleam of gods surrendering to demons, the burning gaze of a woman who would devastate anyone in her path.

"Morgan said make it hurt. So, let's go get this bastard. I have some pain to deliver." Elyria grabbed a coiled bit of rope, kicking up and dropping over the edge of the ship in an artful spin. Gods damn me, if she wasn't the most alluring creature on this earth. There was nowhere I wouldn't follow her.

"Nobody is surprised she leapt first." Xoc hopped on the railing and dove into the open. As soon as he hit the air, his wings manifested. The green leather caught the updraft, and he circled back around to land next to Elyria.

"Show off," I shouted.

"Stop stalling," he called back. "Get down here."

I exhaled and forced my own wings to manifest. The dragon mark on my back burned. I breathed through the pain until the breaking of my spine tore through my skin, and two large wings slid between the slats of my crisscrossing armor. I flexed them. The leather stretched taut just as the air current pulled at their heavy weight, making me hyper-aware of each inch of the newly exposed flesh.

Fuck this felt good. I grinned at the sensation. It had been ages since I felt their pull. We needed to teach Elyria how to manifest hers. I bet they were as sexy as every other one of her assets. It would be something to soar through the air with her by my side. I closed my eyes to picture the fantasy. With the wind hitting my face, it was easy enough to envision.

Xoc and I used to sneak away to the Obsidian Cliffs to fly. Those moments were fleeting and not something I cared to indulge in after The Shade decided to change our entire world. With Elyria it would be different. This was something I could share with her that Malvat couldn't take away.

I extended my wings, snapping them to their full width. Elyria was about to lose her damn mind. I stood on the railing, throwing one last glance at Morgan and Bein. They didn't seem the least bit surprised by our wings. But then again, the Captain was rarely surprised by anything. Bein lifted a fist in his own form of a salute.

I flapped and summoned a gust to pull me up before soaring straight at where Elyria and Xoc waited. I landed lightly beside Elyria. Her eyes were wide with disbelief.

"Exactly when..." she said, running a hand along the outer ridge of the wing closest to her. "...were you going to tell me that you can manifest wings, too?"

A single finger drifted over the central membrane, forcing my wings to tremble. I rolled my neck, trying to shake off the feeling. It'd been a long time since I'd had wings, and they'd never—never been touched by anyone else. Not like that, not ever.

The sparkle of amusement glittered in her eyes. She licked her lips like she was savoring the taste. "You know, Xoc told me once that wings are very sensitive." She breathed a single column of flame over the golden leather.

"Fuck, woman."

"Hmmm," she hummed contemplatively.

I swear she enjoyed pushing those buttons just to watch me snap. Standing straighter, I roughly pulled her to me. Elle tripped over my feet, landing hard against my chest. I hissed into her ear. "This is not the time to play, Sunshine." I raked my teeth over the bit of skin I could still see poking out behind her ear. "And when we return, we are going to have a long conversation about why you know Xoc's wings are sensitive."

A hard whack knocked my head into hers.

"Knock it off. I understand the woman has a leash around your dick, but it's like marching into battle with a couple of cats in heat. Only if you were cats, you'd listen to me when I told you no."

Elyria looked sidelong at Xoc. With a playful push, she spun out of my grasp. "So, when do I get to manifest wings?"

The sound of a dozen boots hitting the ground thudded behind me. I tilted my head to a smirking Alexander.

"A full shift makes it easier to harness your power," Xoc explained. "It might

334

be sooner than you think."

"Let's just worry about surviving the next twenty-four hours, and then we can talk about wings," I said and signaled for Morgan to leave, only to realize she was already ascending.

A half dozen Legionnaires lay dead a few feet from where we stood. The closest man sat up like a discarded doll, his neck twisted at an awkward angle.

"What happened here?" Alexander asked, pointing at the metal-clad dead man.

"Oh, you know, just another man underestimating me," she replied, walking towards the volcano in the distance, a dagger spinning in her palm.

Petros chuckled. "She's feisty. I like her." He and Alexander took up a position to my right.

I met his eyes, and he quickly went back to the impassive man they had been trained to be. In fact, now that I was looking, they were all watching her walk away. That tight ass stretching the leather with every dip of her hips, knives gleaming in the lava light. Part of me wanted to rip their eyes from their sockets for daring to look at my girl, but it was pride, not jealousy, that warmed my chest. Walking across this savage wasteland, silhouetted by the volcano's glow, Elyria looked like a dark goddess of death. Despite their hungry gazes, this goddess was mine alone to worship.

"Let's move," Xoc commanded. "Last thing we need is that crazy, little draken leading the charge."

A blast of fire rocketed from Elyria's hand, reducing the man who had been running towards her to a charred husk of burnt flesh and melted metal.

"I'm not sure feisty quite covered it, Pete," Alexander added, stepping over the body. "Though I can see the appeal."

Mt. Kraav sputtered hot and red, the acrid smell of sulphur suffocating every breath. It didn't take long for dual shadows to pass overhead. The lead fliers of Malvat's second wave closed in on Morgan's dragon.

Her ship banked hard. With a booming explosion, two airships plummeted to the ground, alarmingly close to us. Petros threw up his arm. A hard shield of ice domed over us, deflecting debris from landing on our small company.

Our landing didn't seem to go unnoticed. The small group of soldiers that Elyria and Xoc had disabled was nothing compared to the battle quickly shifting towards us. It would be only a matter of moments before the fighting bled onto the path we needed to take. Maybe this was a good thing. Maybe this would help to keep our approach unnoticed.

Xoc took the lead, Petros and Alexander in position on either side of him. Alexander reinforced the ground as we wove between the channels of hot lava. Which was lucky,because without him, it was likely our trip would have taken double the time to navigate.

An arrow whizzed by my shoulder. A pulse of energy flared, sending what felt like a concussive blow outward. The thick iron bolt was frozen in the air, mere inches from Elyria's side. The projectile trembled and then crumpled under the force of the power surrounding it.

I gave a grateful look at Kai. The Metal Singer nodded his head, sending his long locks shaking around his shoulders, then flicked his eyes to the thick cloud above us. With a snap of his wrist, the twisted ball of iron went zinging back in the direction it came. There was a loud crack, echoing around us like thunder. "They're coming." That was the only warning we had before chaos descended on us.

Like ghosts appearing in the night, an entire platoon dropped from a near-silent airship. I flung up my hands, sending a hard spiral of air outward.

It pushed several of the men falling away from us, but there were too many to just blow them away.

Alexander yelled, "Save your magic! This is why you brought us." He smiled wickedly, curling his arms like he was lifting a massive weight. The earth beneath our feet began rolling like waves. I pulled Elyria close and braced for whatever was about to happen. The leader of the Undying punched his fists into the air, causing the ground to open beneath the approaching soldiers.

Lava rose from the cracks, forming into two molten hands. The smoldering fingers curled around the men, making the skin they came in contact with instantly char and bubble. They pulled down dozens of ghostly-eyed Legionnaires before once again reforming into hard, solid ground.

Elyria gripped my arm. "What the fuck was that?"

"An Earth Singer," I answered in stunned reverence. Her wide eyes were full of all the shock I was feeling. I'd been in battle with Earth Singers before, but never on the Dead Lands. What Alexander had just done was absolutely terrifying. The ground itself was deadlier than any sword, ending a person in the most horrific way imaginable.

A second group of Legionnaires sprinted at us. Alexander huffed a laugh, "They just don't learn." Once again, he opened the ground before us. This time, the Legionnaires hurled themselves into the air, jumping the impossible distance over the river of lava. "Ok, so maybe they learned a little bit." He rose a second hand, cresting the wave of lava. It swung into the air like a whip. Small drops of liquid rock flung wide. I bubbled Elyria and I in a wall of air. The lava whip wrapped around the men sailing over the river. Just as quickly as the lava struck out, it tore through men. Those in its grip landed at our feet, torn in two.

"That was incredible," she gasped, pushing out from under my wing.

"Let's move," Xoc called.

More men dropped from the sky, mixing with the battle which had spilled onto the plain before us. Soldiers with skin turning black littered the ground, falling faster than any of us could have anticipated. We needed to get out of this area before we were completely outnumbered.

The Undying cut a path toward the volcano. They moved as a perfect machine, never allowing anyone within fifteen feet of our party. Eventually, a deep, dark hole opened into the earth.

"That's it."

A tunnel formed a long slide that disappeared into the scorched earth. Hopefully, a river of lava wasn't waiting for us at the base.

"Be safe, my friends." Alexander's hand fanned over his heart in salute. "Nothing will follow you. I swear it. We'll keep the entrance secure."

Petros shot an icelance over my head. A Legionnaire dropped from the sky and landed with thud, only a few feet from us.

I saluted back. "Thank you for everything, Alex. If the war turns, get your team out. Go home, protect the walls, and keep everything within them safe."

"May death be blind and never find you," Alexander said, kissing the medallion around his neck. With a nod, he rejoined the line Petros and the others were forming around the tube entrance. Alanea quick fired dozens of seeds. Thorny bushes sprouted from the center of the iron men closest to us, momentarily giving us cover.

"I'm going first," I said, forming a protective barrier beneath me. The barrier wouldn't do much to cushion the ride, but it would keep me from being boiled alive, if there was a bubbling lava bath waiting at the base.

The slide felt unending. Pock-marked stone scraped against my scales and tore at the leather of my wings until, finally, my feet landed on solid ground, and I was thrown forward. Only my barrier of air kept me from breaking my face against the opposite wall. The total darkness of the underground was disorienting. For one dizzying moment, I wasn't sure which way was up except for the brush of my hair against the low ceiling.

A scrabbling sounded, followed by an "Umph" that knocked directly into me. I barely had enough time to wrap an arm around Elyria before we were thrown into the air shield. Forming a small flame in my hand, the tunnel brightened. The dark expanse of the lava tube pushed endlessly deeper. I tried to banish the eerie memories of that tunnel I'd peered down in The Steps. They felt entirely too similar, but I knew for certain that these weren't formed by leviathan worms. Only molten, fiery earth that would dissolve flesh and bone with a single misstep.

Xoc brushed the dirt from his pants and shook his wings out as he stood to almost his full height. The low ceiling kept him from being able to stand completely. "Into hell," he said. "I always knew you'd drag me here."

Xoc pulled a torch from that mystical rucksack of his and tilted it towards Cal for a light.

The air was thick with heat. I gripped at my chest, pulling on the straps of my holster in a feeble attempt to loosen them. It felt like drowning slowly, without the water.

"You'll adjust to the air," Cal said. "It's hard to breathe now, but you'll get used to it. Try not to panic."

I nodded and took in a shallow breath, trying to focus on our task. Spiraling tunnels branched off in several directions. I peered down the closest one. "How will we know we're going the right way?"

"You know how I showed Malvat the grottos?"

I nodded.

"Well, he showed me these. Once. When we were young, dumb, and bored. We were attacked by the lava cats and were never stupid enough to try it again." He winced at the memory, and a flurry of worry twisted in my stomach. "All the tubes connect to the volcano. As we get closer to the Fort, we will see the tunnel take more of a man-made shape. Then we begin climbing back up. For now, we just follow the heat." He pointed into the darkness. "This way."

I took a tentative step after him and stumbled, the hot hand of fear locking me in place. It drove the oxygen from my lungs, making the already hard to breathe air even harder to suck down. It was easy to feel brave when facing down men with swords. I could see them, feel my blade slicing flesh, and see the light fading from their eyes. But this looming darkness and the unknown danger lurking in its depths was terrifying. After Duke's death, I don't think I'll ever be comfortable in the dark again. The only thing keeping me steady was the buzz of Cal's presence. Blood pounded in my ears with each step he took away from me.

Xoc's heavy hand rested on my shoulder with a subtle squeeze. A cool, rushing calm slithered down my spine and released the cage around my lungs. I took a breath, my courage coming back to me in one long exhale.

"Thank you."

"I don't know what you're talking about." He winked at me, then gently urged me forward.

Cal glanced backwards. "Everything okay?"

"Yeah." I stood up a little taller. "Let's go find this bastard."

We wove our way through the labyrinth, moving deeper and deeper into the mountain. Eventually, the tunnel before us turned, and I could see a faint glow ahead of us.

"Lava?" I questioned. "Are we getting close?"

Xoc held up his hand, and we all stopped.

"What is it?" I whispered, not able to shake the image of the last time he'd halted our movements—moments before a leviathan worm burst through the side of a cliff. Whatever was around that bend wasn't good.

A shadow drifted across the mouth of the tunnel, blocking out the light. My heart rate immediately increased. The shadow was so... large. Sounds of scuffling drifted down the tunnel, followed by a high-pitched yowl that echoed off the walls. The little hairs on my body all stood on end, and a charge of acute awareness tingled down my spine. There was nowhere to go in this tunnel, nowhere to hide.

The call of the first beast was answered by multiple yips. So many yips.

"Lava cats," Xoc whispered.

"This might be a bad time to ask," I whispered nervously, "But what are lava cats?"

Moving close enough that his chest brushed my back, Cal breathed a laugh, "Nothing good."

The scratching of claws on stone grew louder.

"The stories of the demons that live beneath Kraav, they aren't exactly stories."

"Cal, light up the tunnel. I need to see exactly what I'm dealing with," Xoc commanded with a deep whisper.

"Can do." Cal pushed past me and hurled a firebolt down the tunnel.

Jagged walls lit up as the small ball of fire traveled into the dark. The fire broke apart, rolling harmlessly off a large armored form. This wasn't any cat. This was a beast. A monster covered in hard armored plates, with paws the size of dessert plates and glowing red eyes.

It growled low, and then more cats joined in. The rumble resonated in the thick air, bouncing off the surface of the tunnel. Cold sweat dripped down the back of my neck.

"You've fought these things before?" I said, barely recognizing my panicked voice.

"You know that scar that runs down my side."

"You said that was from an animal attack. My gods, I thought you were joking," I hissed at him.

"Don't worry, Sunshine. You should know by now I'm not above cheating the game. This time we came with an ace up our sleeve," he said, pointing to Xoc.

Two bright red eyes glowed alarmingly close to us. From this distance, I could smell its foul breath. The growl trembled the air, becoming deeper with each breath the animal took. Four more sets of eyes appeared behind him.

Being able to talk and command animals was one thing, but I've seen that power fail him before, and it seemed like the pack multiplied with each heartbeat.

"Guys," I said, taking a step backward into the hard wall of Cal's frame.

He whispered into my ear, "It's going to be okay, breathe."

Xoc kneeled down, tucking his wings tightly behind him and shrinking his considerable size as much as he could.

"What are you doing?" I squeaked, completely panicked now.

Xoc started making a purring sound. "Here, kitty-kitty," he cooed low and lovingly.

"Kitty, kitty?" I hissed.

Oh gods. We are going to die. This is how I die, as some demonic creature's midnight snack. The growling ceased. I held my breath. Was this when they pounced?

A small chirping noise came curiously from the nearest cat. The pointed ears were pinned back, with small tufts of hair peeking out from beneath each of the plates. His long whiskers flicked in the air before him as he tentatively sniffed the air.

Xoc repeated the purring noise, mimicking them with surprising accuracy. The beast cocked his head to the side, listening.

I think my heart stopped beating. With each step he took, the cat grew in size until he dwarfed Xoc's kneeling frame. Then something I never in my life thought I would see happened. The great beast walked in a circle and flopped down on the ground before Xoc. He rolled onto his back and presented his stomach to him.

A completely inappropriate giggle burbled up from me.

"I'm sorry. Did he just ask you for belly rubs?"

The cat purred a deep rumble. The pent-up tension eased.

"Yeah, that is not how my last encounter went," Cal said in an unusually high pitch.

I looked up at him. He'd seemed so calm and sure, but the relief in his voice just then said otherwise. There was a part of him that really thought we were going to have to fight our way through a pack of feline monsters.

Xoc stroked the soft underbelly while a second walked right up to me. This cat was smaller than the first, and his red eyes held an almost orange light to them. Closer now, I could see that his black plates were really more of a dark purple, with glittery, red streaks that reminded me of bonfire sparks flashing against a night sky.

Like a sweet house cat, he wove in and out of my feet, rubbing the hard edges of his plates against my ankles. Warmth radiated in waves from the creature, unlike anything I'd experienced before, almost like he was generating his own heat source.

"This is unreal." I laughed and bent down to scratch him behind the ear. My fingers sank into the soft downy fur beneath the outer plate. The vibrating rumble in his throat increased, so deep and resonant I could feel the thrum in my bones.

"He likes me." The absurdity of what was happening made a strange kind of joy bubble up in me. "I'm going to call you Sparky," I cooed at him, unable to suppress my laughter. "You aren't so scary. Are you, baby?"

Sparky put his paws on my chest, nearly knocking me over. A hot puff of sulfur breath blew the hair back from my face. "Errg, we need to get you some mint to chomp on."

I glanced over my shoulder at Cal. He was leaning against the rough pumice wall, looking equal parts perplexed and amused.

"Up on the surface, a battle is raging, and down here, you are playing with one of the deadliest wild cats known to man. You are utterly perfect, you know that?"

"You said it yourself. We don't play by the rules." I flashed Cal a self-satisfied smile, dropping to sit cross-legged on the ground. I patted my lap, and Sparky dutifully curled into a heap of hard plates and warm soft fur. His massive bulk covered me completely and was a lot heavier than I was ready for, forcing me to brace myself to keep from tipping over.

My new pet placed two enormous paws on my shoulders, roughly licking at my cheek with his sandy tongue. "Yelch," I laughed, trying to avoid having the skin of my face rubbed off.

The deep, contented rumble of his purr shook the ground. He was so sweet, a big furry baby.

"Do you think we-"

"No."

I pouted at Cal.

"You can't keep him."

"I've never had a pet, and Gregory's cat Lucky doesn't count." That old cat may have tolerated me, but he was never truly mine. "Do you think lava cats shed?" I blew at the fur that kept trying to get into my mouth, smoothing my hands down his side. The wall of powerful muscle shifted with each of the cat's breaths. "Besides, Sparky likes me."

"Sunshine, I'd give you the world if it made you happy, but you can't have a pet that might eat the palace staff." He laughed. "Now, if you're done, we do have a maniacal draken to end." Cal took a step towards me.

Sparky's muscles went taught. His ears pinned back to his head, followed by a low, vicious growl that promised violence. This might have been funny if I wasn't so worried that he was going to claw Cal's face off—and I was rather partial to that face.

Slowly, Cal moved back to his position on the wall.

"Elyria," he said in warning.

"Aww. Don't be jealous, baby." I scratched under Sparky's chin.

"I'm not jealous. Elle, that's a lethal *wild* cat."

I gave him a side-long glance. "I wasn't talking to you."

"Sparky, baby, don't be jealous of mean, old Cal," I hushed. Immediately, Sparky perked back up and lapped at my cheek, the pebbles vibrating with his returning purrs.

"This is ridiculous. Xoc, say something."

I smirked. "I don't think he heard you." Xoc was too busy wrestling with the first giant cat on all fours, playing what looked like it might have been a game of tug-of-war with an old femur.

"When did I become the rational one?" Cal let out a deep breath and then stepped forward again. As if being more assertive would somehow remedy the situation. Sparky's eyes glowed bright with menace. That rumbling growl returned, deeper this time.

"Elle!" Cal said again, this time with more urgency.

"He's right, Elyria," Xoc added, climbing up to his feet. "We need to keep moving."

"Fine, fine. I suppose it would be nice to kill Malvat while it's still dark enough to see the light leaving his eyes." I gave Sparky a kiss on his nose before standing. "Hey, pretty kitty. Can you take us to the Fort?"

"That is actually a brilliant idea, Elyria," Xoc said.

"It is?"

"It is." He flicked his hand. All the cats, including Sparky, looked at him with red unblinking eyes. With a unison howl loud enough that I had to cover my ears, they took off down the tube.

"Why did you call them to you first, if you could just do that?" I said, brushing the paw prints from my leathers.

"Doing it this way showed them we should be trusted. Otherwise, the second I broke control, they would have turned on us. That's not a risk I wanted to take. But now, we are part of the pride," he explained flatly.

"So wait." I swallowed hard, pointing frantically to where we were just sitting. "You weren't controlling them just then."

"No," Xoc said, amused. "You definitely just let Venterra's most fearsome predator lick your face."

My jaw went slack. "But, it's okay. The moment he shifted his mood, I would have stopped him. Most likely before he took a bite out of you."

"Most likely?"

As if our conversation had summoned him, Sparky circled back to my side. "Maybe he recognized that I wasn't prey and belonged among predators." The torch light shone off of the plates along his back. I dipped my hand down, letting my fingertips brush each one while we walked. "Why the plates? Why not just the fur?"

"They absorb heat and protect from the lava when they come in contact with it. Lava cats need extreme temperatures to survive. During the day, the cats will lie on the surface and soak up the heat from the sun, but at night they retreat deep into the tunnels where it is warmest. The plates absorb that heat and keep them warm through the night." Xoc said, pointing to them. "I'm sure you noticed how warm he was."

Sparky chirped, pushing his nose into my hand. The tunnel climbed, and the craggy stone around us transitioned into a polished wall.

"We must be getting close."

Cal nodded, wary eyes still on the cat beside me.

One of the lava cats yipped. Sparky ran ahead, joining his motionless pride, waiting for their next command. It was actually creepy, not a whisker twitched. But what were they staring at? There was nothing here but a brick wall.

"They must have bricked it off. What do we do now?" I said, looking between them. "I could blast it."

"Woah, fire child." Xoc grabbed my rising hands.

"Did you just call me child?"

"As much as I love a good explosion, all that would do is announce our arrival."

Cal pushed between us. "Don't worry. I expected this. All of the tunnels are walled up, but there's a trick. Just like a woman, if you find the right spot to stroke, she'll open wide." Cal slid his hand down the seam of the bricks. Before I could refute that claim, he pressed down on a single stone, exclaiming, "Ah-ha."

With a click, the wall soundlessly moved to the side, revealing a dark corridor. Cal swiveled around, giving a smug bow. So fucking pleased with himself that he might as well be daring one of us to punch him.

"Stop showboating," Xoc said, smacking him with the long staff that he materialized from nowhere. "She's already riding your cock every chance you get. You can stop trying so hard now."

Cal swatted at the end of the spear that Xoc was still badgering him with. "Feeling left out, big man?"

I leaned against the wall. "Don't let him fool you. It takes more than a single touch."

"Careful, Sunshine, that sounds an awful lot like a challenge."

My heart skipped, even as I rolled my eyes. Because I knew he could detonate me with a single brush of his fingertips. What's more, he definitely knew it, too.

35

ELYRIA

C al moved to push through the now open doorway but was yanked back. Xoc shook a finger, "No."

Almost immediately, there was the click of heels on stone. We slunk into the shadows of the tunnel, disappearing from view just as a patrolman in a high collared uniform walked by. He slid to a stop, scratching his beard in bewilderment before the open doorway. This man, unlike the Legionnaires, wasn't white eyed, just a regular soldier. It would seem Malvat didn't waste his time possessing the regular guard, only his attack dogs.

I put a hand over my mouth to stifle the laugh that almost bubbled up. The man looked so perplexed. He mentally walked his fingers along the route, muttering to himself as he tried to rationalize its existence.

At my feet, the largest of the cats, the one that had led us to the wall, growled. It was a menacing, deep rumble. The patrolman's eyes went wide, shaking with instant recognition. He fumbled at his waist to draw his weapon, but he never got to retrieve it.

With a single long leap, the lava cat latched his large jaws on the side of the man's cheek, knocking him to the ground. A pained, muffled yell slipped from the man, quickly replaced by the wet sound of his jugular being torn apart and the lapping of a tongue. It all happened so fast. That the man was dead before he got a chance to finish his scream. Blood pooled at our feet. I hopped into the hall to avoid stepping in it.

"Good kitty," Xoc cooed as the largest feline dragged the man back into the tunnel. Xoc pointed to the body, and the remaining cats all pounced on the corpse, tearing off pieces of flesh and swallowing them whole. I could feel the blood draining from my face. For some reason, seeing a man being eaten was so much harder to watch than seeing one torn in half.

"Yep, that's what you were just whispering sweet nothings to," Xoc said with a laugh.

Cal shared an amused glance with him. "And she wanted to keep one as a pet." He moved me to the side, then walked to the end of the hall, making sure there weren't any surprises ready to jump out at us.

"We probably want to go this way," Cal pointed down the corridor. "This should lead towards the upper floors."

Xoc closed his eyes, his brows creasing in concentration. "There are two men around the corner, another in a nearby room...and...." His voice drifted off. "Rei."

"What?" I said, pulling on the strap across his chest.

Xoc opened his eyes. "Or, I think it's Rei. It's hard to tell," he said, tilting his head to the side and closing his eyes again. "But I think she's alone. Three floors up."

"What about Malvat?" Cal said, his eyes narrowing with predatory focus.

"Harder to tell. He has his essence spread over so many people. The strongest signature is on the central terrace." Xoc pointed behind us. "Just as we planned. That's where he'd have the best vantage point for the battle."

"Let's go. There's an iron set of shoulders that needs to be relieved of a head," I said, spinning the butterfly swords in my hands. I wanted his blood so badly I could almost taste the copper tang on my tongue. "You say there are two more around the corner?"

Xoc nodded, "They're heading this way."

I licked my lips. An anticipatory buzz vibrated beneath the surface of my skin. The fire sparked within me, ready for a fight. Cal's golden eyes flashed bright. Had his eyes always flared in response to my own rising power? It seemed so obvious now.

"You two hang back. I've got this."

"Elle..." Cal started, but I didn't wait to hear whatever bullshit reasoning he was about to hit me with.

I stepped into the adjacent corridor just as two men turned the corner at the end of the hall. "They say she has a massive..."

The guardsman on the right stopped, sticking a hand out to pause his partner. They seemed completely stunned by my sudden appearance.

"She has a massive what? Intellect? I bet it was intellect, wasn't it? Please don't stop on my account," I said sweetly. Then I sprinted towards them, which only seemed to confuse the guards further. They scrambled at their waists for their hilts. I kicked up into a flip, vaulting over them while slicing in a windmill. Each blade rotated, carving into their still shocked expressions.

The first man dropped to his knees. Blood coated the walls in a spray. He howled in pain, staring at the arm that now laid discarded and sliding down the grey stone. He opened his mouth to scream, but I sliced across his throat before he could so much as moan.

"Innesvalen bitch," The second man spat, his hand clutching at the gash crossing his cheek.

"Aww is that how you speak to a lady?" I gave the butterfly blades a twirl, sending twin streams of blood in a criss-crossing streak across the man's already bloody face and chest.

"You're going to regret doing that." The remaining guardsman grinned at me like he held every ace in the deck. He held up a hand, causing the swords to fly from my grip.

Fuck. So much for most won't be able to manipulate metal that small.

The man grabbed the blades from the air, and grinned at me.

"Those don't belong to you," I gritted out.

"Neither do you... and yet." The man's grin spread wider, causing the blood pooling in the cut on his cheek to spillover. He crooked his finger at me. I tilted my head to the side in confusion. If he thought I was going to come to him like some kind of pet—

A sharp tug yanked at my waist. I let out a noise of surprise. The metal of my throwing knives lifted higher. My feet left the ground, and I kicked into the empty air. With a simple flick of his hand, I drifted towards him. The hilt of the Sun Serpent dagger cut into my back as it was clutched by the web of his magic. I wriggled against the unstoppable pull. I hadn't expected this.

"I bet you thought you'd sneak in here and cut us down. Stupid woman. Those weapons are useless here. And to think I was angry that I wouldn't get any action tonight. All that fun happening down on the fields and being forced to stay in the Fort on worthless patrol." He sucked in a breath, eyes stripping me and making note of each blade strapped to my body. The dagger at my ankle tugged, and my boot lifted into the air, followed by the buckles on my forearms. I gave my left ankle a roll, grateful that I had switched out the metal blades for the obsidian ones on that foot. "But then, here you are, splayed helpless in the air before me. Wrapped up in metal like a pretty little present."

The man gripped my hips, pushing between my legs and grinding roughly against me. He leaned in, sending foul, hot breath drifting against my neck. I swallowed the rising bile. He continued his exploration, gripping my ass and waving his hand over the dagger strapped to my thigh, forcing my legs wider.

I could feel Cal approaching. The anger that pulsed off of him made the blood in my veins quicken. Holding up a finger, I signaled for him to wait. This moron had no idea he'd just forfeited his life.

"Your first mistake," I said in a sultry tone that lured him closer. He licked his lips, staring at mine, "is to assume I'm helpless."

I wrapped my free leg around his throat, pinning his jugular against the hard bone of my other knee, and squeezed. Every muscle in my body contracted, pushing down on the nerve that I knew would knock him out. His eyes fluttered as he scrambled wildly against my legs to get free. Now, barely conscious, the tether he held on the metal I wore released. I leaned into the gravity, using the momentum to arch backwards. My hands landed firmly on the ground. I whipped my legs up, keeping them hitched around the patrolman and throwing him down the hallway behind me.

With a spluttering whimper, he slid straight into Cal'd feet. Flaming rage roiled in his eyes as he looked down at the man. He lifted the man by the sides of his head.

"You're lucky we have somewhere to be, or I would flay every part of you that just touched her." With a clean and efficient twist, Cal snapped the man's neck and unceremoniously dropped the now limp body.

"That was fun," I said, picking up the discarded butterfly blades and watching Cal prowl down the hall to me.

"No. What that was, was too damn close," he said, still angry.

"I was completely in control the entire time."

"You're lucky you didn't have metal buckles or knives on the other leg as well."

"But I didn't, on purpose, I might add. Come on, my blood is pumping. Let's go cut something." I flipped my hair over my shoulder.

"I knew you liked a good fight, but I didn't realize just how blood thirsty you were," Cal said to me, his eyes heated. "I can't decide if it's turning me on or terrifying me right now."

"Knowing you, both," Xoc said, walking past us and turning the corner. While passing me, he extended an arm and produced a thick wooden spear from the space beside him. The polished point was sharpened into a jagged blade, framed on either side by sloping hooks and a bamboo tube sliding along the shaft. It didn't look like anything I'd seen before. Even in practice, this wasn't something he'd used.

"What's the tube for?" I asked, looking to Cal for an answer.

Xoc spun the spear, the long rod sliding with ease through the tube and back to a ready position in a fraction of a second. It was so fast the entire movement happened in a blur. My eyes barely had time to register it. Adding speed with his size and that reach, enemies would fall long before they ever made it within striking distance.

Cal pulled on my shoulder, slowing me down to put space between us and Xoc. "The Ironwood Yari is an ancient Oerish weapon. Most in the Wood prefer a closer form of combat, but Master Rith was particularly fond of this one. That..." He pointed to the spear spinning in the palm of the giant draken. "...heirloom was his gift to Xoc before we left for Innesvale. They say the ironwood absorbs the blood of those it slays, making the wood stronger, and that spear has seen hundreds of battles."

A door opened to his left. Without slowing or even looking, he struck it out, spearing the yari directly through the center of the man who emerged. The guard dropped to the ground, Xoc's pace never faltering.

"And you call me blood thirsty," I muttered.

We ascended the stairs of the tower at the north end of the building. A large window was cut into the wall of the stairwell, giving me my first real look at the main battle. Smoke billowed up from the Dead Lands. The lava fields were littered with wreckage. The din of battle drifting on the wind, carried with it the wails and battle cries of the men below.

The sound of running feet echoed up the staircase.

"I think they've found your trail of carnage." Cal laughed at me.

"My trail?" I placed my hand on my chest in disbelief. I'd dismembered a few men. That was barely a head count compared to the demonstration Xoc had given of exactly what that fancy spear of his could do. "I'm not the one who impaled every man who entered the hallway." We exited onto the third floor, the pounding of feet growing closer.

"Ten," Xoc said. He tossed the wooden spear to Cal, who effortlessly snatched it from the air.

"My turn," he said, giving me a peck on the cheek. "Can't let the two of you have all the fun. "

"True, your ego would never survive it," Xoc chuckled low, tilting his chin towards the door. "Five seconds."

In exactly five seconds, ten armed guards tumbled from the stairwell. Cal spun, slicing them down one by one. Bodies carpeted the hallway. Seeing his hands flex around the slide, the muscles of his arms and shoulders shifting beneath his scales, gracefully applying all of that strength into every single movement, was enough to make my entire body feel tight. He made the entire fight look effortless as if thrusting a wooden spear through a man's heart was second nature to him.

When he was done, he wiped at the blood streaked across his brow with the back of his hand. Sweat clung to his neck, making the tendrils of his hair curl. I wanted to wrap my fingers in that hair. Cal flashed me a smug look that said he knew exactly what I was thinking. Goddess slay me, this man was unfairly sexy.

Flinging out the spear, the hooked end snared under my arm. Fuck, that thing was fast. With a hard yank, Cal threw me to the wall. The point pinned my shoulder in place. Slowly Cal descended on me, the tube along the shaft sliding him closer to me with ease. He pulled the spear free, replacing the weapon with his palm and gliding it up to my throat.

"There's something wrong with us." I bit down on my lower lip. I was dying to taste him.

"Funny, I was just about to say the same thing," Xoc remarked, pushing past us. "If you two are done panting all over each other, Rei is at the end of the hall."

I closed my eyes, shaking away the wave of lust. "Is she still alone?"

"Yes."

"Are you ready? We won't have much time. We can't allow her to disappear, or Malvat appearing when we aren't ready for him," Cal said, all playfulness gone. His hand caressed down my jaw. "And don't stray too far from me. If he does show, I need to be able to get to you."

I nodded, taking a deep breath.

"Elle..." His voice was tight, choked by emotion. My eyes flashed up to meet his. Flames flickered into their reflection. The edges of his brows drew together in what could almost be misconstrued as pain. "I love you."

Fuck, we were really doing this. Tight anxiety closed around my chest as I lifted my lips to his. This was going to work. I refused to let that be the last time I ever heard those words.

Xoc produced a thin syringe. The sharp end of the needle shone in the torchlight, a small bead of liquid clinging to the tip. "Let's just get this done. Save the 'I love yous' for after."

The chamber she was kept in was surprisingly spacious. It was decorated in lavish fabrics and ornate wall coverings. Deep maroon drapes hung by the window. A velvet spread was mussed up on the bed as if whoever used this bed had just risen. It was more fit for a royal guest than a prison. Above a fireplace was a large hanging portrait of a tall handsome man with sculpted features and carefully styled corn-silk hair. Malvat. That's when it hit me. These rooms weren't just opulent they were royal.

This was Malvat's personal room.

Anger boiled within me. I tried to convince myself that the display he put on at the palace was all for show. That it was just something to rile me, but he was keeping her here. I could only think of one reason for that. My heart ached for my friend.

The telltale purple glow of her tattoos cut through the darkness. Rei stood motionless, her hands gripping the railing of the terrace before her. The glowing, molten light from the lava fields below made her tawny skin look nearly red. Through some stroke of luck, she hadn't noticed the door opening. My nervousness eased some. That was the first hurdle.

Xoc crept around the edge of the room with silent steps. It was impressive how quiet the giant could be. Cal and I approached from the other side.

Exiting the shadowy chamber, red light spilled onto the side of Xoc's features. The needle glowed in his extended hand. The syringe was only inches from her neck.

I held my breath. One second. It was all he needed. One second, and she

Xoc stretched, a bead of liquid clinging to the tip of the needle. Just as his fingers should have latched on to her throat, she stepped away. Rei turned, not towards him, but towards me. Despite the shadows that hid me, her white eyes cut through the darkness, latching me in their vice-like grip.

How had she known we were here? Xoc froze, assessing the situation.

"I've been waiting for you, little mouse," she said in a velvety purr that sounded nothing like her carefree lilt. Hearing his words from her lips turned my stomach.

A low growl rumbled beside me. This was entirely different from the purrs and yips of the lava cats. Xoc's focus shifted to the sound, his brows knitting together in confusion. Cal stiffened against my back. Whether he realized he was doing it or not, he pressed closer to me.

An inky black wolf padded across the room. Shadows bled from its fur, dripping and pooling beneath his steps like ethereal blood. It snarled, green eyes glowing with menace. Rei raked her nails through its misty form as the phantom beast circled around her.

Cal grabbed my hand pulling me behind him at the same time a harsh wind gusted over the balcony. The wolf's form shifted in the breeze, solidifying just as quickly as it vanished. She hadn't acknowledged Xoc yet. There was still a chance. He was so close to her. Deciding that the risk of the vanishing wolf was worth it, Xoc lunged.

A wall of shadow slammed between them. His large form buckled against the railing, one of his wings bending awkwardly in the wrong direction. The syringe flew from his hand, tumbling end over end through the air.

Cal reached out, halting the needle in the air with his magic. For a second, I thought maybe... just maybe this was it, until a dark, iron-scaled hand wrapped around the glass.

Malvat.

He looked at the vial, studying it. His long claws tapping against the surface. He was shirtless. Iron plates protruded like blades from his arms and shoulders, each surrounded by brown, glittering scales. Dark tendrils curled along his neck until they disappeared beneath where his brown scales shifted into a color so dark I didn't think you could even classify it as black. They seemed to obliterate every ray of light, giving back only nothingness.

The syringe twirled between his fingers, but those grotesque eyes stayed trained on me while he spoke. "Smart, Xoc. I suppose this was how you planned to get her out of here." He prowled closer, not like a predator. He was something more, a creature in the night that feasted on the predators. The ink of his eyes bled down into his cheeks, even more black now than they had been at the ball. Pure evil resided in their depths, and the ice of his glare was focused solely on me. I would do anything to keep that focus on me, despite the way Cal kept pace with him to ensure that he remained between us.

"I'm sure this was one of your finer concoctions." Malvat continued, crushing the vial in his hands. My hope shattered along with glass. "Although, I never really had a taste for your mixes." Tiny pieces showered down, making the sound of tinkling glass fill the room. He dusted off his hands, seemingly bored by our rescue attempt.

I blinked, and Malvat was instantly on me, his claws biting into the flesh of my neck as he circled my throat. "I've waited longer than you can possibly fathom for this." He took a long, slow inhale up the side of my face, his cold lips brushing my cheek in a mockery of a kiss. "You smell fucking delicious."

I steeled every ounce of anger into ice. My mind was screaming to fight. I wanted to claw and tear at the naked skin of his hand, even as it flexed, forcing my pulse to pound against my temples.

Instead, I shrank, abandoning my warrior instincts and letting his body envelop me. I just needed him to fall for the bait, coming close enough for me to sink my dagger into his black, dead heart. Doing my best to pretend that fear and not rage were what kept me motionless, I let my lip quiver and my eyes go wide, heaving tortured breaths, knowing that each one made my breasts swell and catch the light.

"You're a stunning little actress." Tendrils of shadow coiled around my arms and snaked between my legs, immobilizing me in a way that I hadn't anticipated. "That plump lip trembling so sweetly, I could almost believe that you were afraid, but my dear, you've never tasted true fear. I'd smell its intoxicating perfume. You will see. Think of how those golden eyes will shine with tears and how your flawless ivory skin will glow when it's stained in blood." Over the rush of my pulse, I heard the wolf growling a threat at Cal.

Malvat's nose brushed my cheekbone. I pulled futilely at my shadow bindings, doing my best not to panic. His lips rested at my ear, adding, "You'll be drenched in the fragrance of fear when I am through with you." The shadow coils tightened, forcing my body to press against his, pulling my thighs apart to make space for the leg he ground against me. The claws of his other hand trailed over my cheek, pressing deep enough to break the skin and cause my blood to well in the marks. Turning my bloody face towards Cal, he added. "Do you think if I can make your screams loud enough, he will hear us and come running?"

Fire lit up the chamber. It rolled up Cal's arms, exploding out in waves.

Malvat didn't even bother looking at him. He simply twitched his free hand, and the shadow beast howled a warning, loud enough to make me jump.

"Be a good boy and stay." Malvat's whisper trickled over my neck, "Maybe Calico needs a reminder of his place. Shall we show him where he belongs, pet?"

The feet of distance separating us felt more like miles. The wolf's sharp black fangs and long razor claws glistened with the same black-green hue as the spider that killed Duke. He didn't need to eviscerate Cal to kill him. All it would take was a single scratch.

Our eyes met, and I pleaded with him not to do something rash. I couldn't watch him fall to the same fate that took Duke. He shook his head. The obstinate ass was going to get himself killed for me. Cal's limbs went taught, ready to spring into action. The shadows surrounding the room swelled or the corners of my vision were starting to lose focus under the pressure of Malvat's grip. It was almost as if, to my right, I could see a shadow stalking us.

"Careful, Calico, I need her body," Malvat warned. "But that doesn't mean that I care if she dies." One iron claw carved along the swell of my breast, leaving a deep groove in the scales covering it. "It would be a pity, though. She won't be nearly as much fun to play with then."

A wild roar rattled the chamber. Sparky leapt out of the darkness, teeth bared and dark plates shining molten in the light. He latched onto the shadow wolf and pinned him to the ground. Gnashing teeth and snapping jaws clashed at one another. The shadow wolf's claws slid harmlessly off of my beautiful beastie's plating.

Malvat looked stunned like this was the first thing tonight he hadn't expected, and didn't know how to respond. It was all the distraction we needed.

Xoc leapt up from where he was waiting on the balcony. He grabbed Rei around the waist. She bucked and yelled, but before she could wriggle free, he manifested another needle and sank it deep into her neck. The scream rattling her vocal cords died as her body went instantly limp. With Rei tucked close to his chest, Xoc looked at us for only a second of confirmation and then jumped from the balcony. There was a flash of green wings as he banked, dipping only for a minute as he favored the uninjured wing. A streak of fire shot through the sky, aimed directly for them. Xoc twisted, avoiding the strike. That was the last I saw of him before directing my attention fully to the embodiment of pure evil.

Malvat growled in frustration. That was his leverage flying away.

Cal used the moment to roll across the ground and thrusted the wooden spear directly for his chest. Throwing me like I weighed nothing, I flew across the room. Malvat blocked, the iron blades in his arm shearing off a piece of the ancient wood.

Cal didn't relent. He flipped the staff over, bringing the clubbed end down hard on Malvat's shoulder. There was a loud, *CRACK.* I couldn't be sure if it was wood or bone splintering, but it sounded like victory. Cal spun again, the bladed end swinging across the Iron Draken's unguarded throat.

A trickle of black blood dripped over the scales decorating his chest. It may have cut him, but before Cal could recoil the spear, Malvat grabbed the end with a smug chuckle. Changing tactics entirely, Cal leapt. Using the spear as leverage, he spun over the tip. One foot connected with the side of Malvat's head, forcing it to snap hard to the side. His grip loosened just enough that Cal was able to wrench the spear loose. The rod rotated in his hand, landing an impressive hit to Malvat's side, followed by his head, and finally, Cal sunk the bladed end into his stomach.

Malvat fell backwards, the spear clattering noisily to the ground. My heart jumped into my throat. *Was this it?*

Malvat looked dazed. His eyes spun wildly around the room. He tried to get to his feet, slipping and falling away from me. His hand went to his stomach. Shock ricocheted across his face as he took in the black blood that dripped through his fingers. The bitter taste of that expression was the sweetest thing I'd ever experienced. I threw my head back and sighed.

Cal advanced on him, fueled on by pure and unrestrained wrath. His eyes blazed bright gold, and flames trailed from his fingertips. This was our moment. I stepped towards them. Ready to relish in our victory, I drew all of my power into the palm of my hand.

With one knee on the ground, Malvat lifted his head. His black eyes tightened—and then, he smiled, making my instincts scream. How many times had I tried to hit him that night on the balcony? This had been too easy. He'd taken that spear to the gut on purpose. I knew it with every fiber of my being.

Fire lined Cal's arms. It lurched in my chest, my power fueling the flames in his hands. It wouldn't be enough to simply stab Malvat again. Cal had too much fury to settle for simple defeat. No, Cal's rage would demand he come in close enough to feel his life-force drift away—and Malvat knew it.

Power vibrated around Cal, pulling from my heart and surging through him. Golden fissures of light streamed over the curves of his cheekbones. Currents of air and fire shimmered like a halo of pure elemental force around him.

He was too lost in his emotions to see that Malvat was not wounded, not truly.

I screamed. *"CAL!"*

37

CALLEN

That bastard was going to die right here, right now. He touched her, fucking placed his lips to her face, marked her. I pulled the primal rage and fire from my core and channeled every scrap of power I could scrounge into my fist. My mind flashed an alternating rhythm of Elyria's panicked tremble and my father's cold unfeeling face as I laid dying. It was all because of Malvat, because of this demon-possessed man. To think that I once trusted him, thought of him as a brother. That he would try to take from me everything that I loved. To take Elyria.

Malvat rose onto one knee. Then he smiled at me. As if this broken form of his somehow had the upper hand. He was already dead. He'd signed his death certificate the day he decided power trumped friendship and came for me in the shadows.

No. This was ending. Right. Fucking. Now.

I released the fire into a single blast, moving my body along with it. All the power I never let out of its cage focused into a single blow.

Malvat's smile grew, and then he flickered.

Time slowed. My fist passed right through his iron smile and straight into the stone floor beneath him. My knees followed, and I landed with all that momentum hard against the ground.

Reality sped back up the second my face slammed into the slate floor. Gods, I should fucking know better. Faintly, I remembered Elyria screaming my name before I struck. Now I was practically kneeling while Malvat stood tall above me with that long, jagged saber.

I pulled my short obsidian sword just in time to avoid that black blade slicing across my outer wing. Redirecting my movement, I drove the hilt of my sword into his wounded side. He didn't even react to what should have been a crippling blow. My eyes flicked to his abdomen. Where there was once raw flesh, now there was a patch of knitted black skin. Fuck me, the darkness was healing him. My mother was right. In a fight alone with Malvat, I was never going to win.

As if she could hear my thoughts, the flash of Elyria's butterfly swords cut through the air. I moved low and hard, forcing him into the line of her attack. Her blades struck against his scales.

Malvat's eyes met mine, and he looked—amused.

I wanted to obliterate every one of those shining metal teeth. My fire boiled over, spilling from my hands in a blinding stream. Elyria raised her palms. With a battle cry, she unleashed all of her fury, blasting white fire at him from both sides.

As quickly as the light flared, it was smothered. A wave of shadow rolled towards us, taking with it every stray ember. The shockwave of power meeting power sent Elyria flying back. As if she were merely a spider hanging from a thread, she twisted mid-air, landing on her feet and springing back into action.

From every direction, streaks of black sliced through the air. I spiraled fiery blades of air around us, barely managing to stop them. Malvat laughed, a deep belly laugh like he was having the time of his life. Thorned wire unspooled from where it was sitting next to the wall. It snaked directly for Elyria. I fired blast after blast to slow them down, but the thin surface of the wires simply cut through all of my counter currents.

Fearless as always, Elyria jumped into the air, both arms raised high above her head.

Malvat's laughter continued. He didn't so much as bother raising a hand to block her. The wires lashed out, binding her raised wrists. With a flick of Malvat's hand, Elyria was pulled off her feet and was sent hurtling back towards the wall.

Her boots scrabbled against the smooth floor, but she was helpless against the force.

The wires looped into rings bolted high on the wall, proving that he'd planned for this all along. The panic squeezing at my stomach tightened. How had we ever thought this would work? We knew we were walking into a trap, and my arrogance brought the one good thing in my life to him. I might as well have shackled her myself. The leather of her bracers fell away beneath the razor wire, exposing her golden arms to the thickening metal reshaping itself into seamless cuffs. Long, thin spikes slithered down her arms. She pulled and fought against the bindings, with each motion embedding the spikes into her flesh.

The pained cry that came from her was one I would never forget. She tried to bite back the sound, but as the spikes embedded themselves deeper, she couldn't keep the wail contained. How the hells were we going to get out of this? My eyes flicked between Elyria and Malvat, torn between wanting to free her and take him down.

"Wait your turn, little mouse." Malvat hissed at her. He lazily raised his hand, directing the wires to lift her high against the wall, completely suspended. Gritting her teeth against the barbs circling her wrists, Elyria pushed off the wall as much as they would allow. She twisted and spun in a useless attempt to free herself.

"Malvat!" I growled at him. I raised my obsidian sword and struck, hitting wall after wall of hard shadow, never making it within a foot of him.

Malvat re-sheathed his sword. "Now, now, Calico. I don't know that we need that anymore."

Shadow vines snapped out, my sword went flying from my hand, and to my horror, it went soaring through the air straight for Elyria. I moved forward without thinking and slammed my entire body into the wall of shadow that separated us. I sent every ounce of air at the blade. Anything to keep it from sinking into her perfect flesh.

The sword met stone with a loud crack. It echoed in the chamber. Tiny fissures spider webbed out from where my blade was embedded in the wall, just above her shoulder and entirely too close to her neck.

The growl that came from me was something primal, the roots of my dragon lineage making my wings flex and the fire in the room flare. "Release her."

"Manners," he tsked, and then she screamed. Not like before, where you could see her fighting back the pain. Elyria's face twisted in an agonized cry. The kind of howl that only came from a person being torn apart. The sound of her suffering echoed off the walls in an unending loop.

"Stop. STOP!" I shouted and started at a run for her, but that fucking wall of shadow kept pace with every step I took. It caged me in—forcing me to endure her screaming.

"Scales are a fascinating trait." Malvat leaned against the side of a burrow, legs crossed at the ankles, and casually inspecting his nails.

Elyria's scream became louder before being ominously cut off. I spun, unable to keep myself from seeing the second wire wrapping its way between her breasts and around her throat. It was happening again. I was going to have to watch her die, and there was nothing I could do about it.

"Did you know they are impossible to cut through? Stronger than iron."

A muffled sound wheezed from her lips, "Fuck you, asshole."

"But have you ever had one of your scales removed? During a full shift, the flesh under them is soft, extra tender. It's actually quite easy to do if you know how to apply the correct pressure." He pushed off the burrow, striding towards the love of my life.

"Right now, my razor wire is weaving its way beneath those beautiful golden scales." He dragged his index finger through the blood dripping from her wrists, using it to paint her breasts. "Every time she pulls against her restraints, my thorns cut deeper into that vulnerable, sensitive skin." Licking the crimson drops from his fingertip, he turned to me. "And every time you move, I will send a new thorn beneath another scale."

Her life force dripped steadily from her arms and down her neck, pooling beneath her. I had to do something, but the moment my weight shifted her muffled scream called out again. I stopped. Fucking helpless.

"You coward. Come at me. Stop hiding behind your wall of shadow and fight me. You want to hurt someone, then get over here and fight me. *Hurt me.*"

"Oh, Calico. I am hurting you. You think I don't know that it's your heart that's beating in her chest? Each of her screams is as good as a sword in your side."

I growled in frustration. This wasn't over. I didn't need to move to kill him. The surrounding air vibrated, charging with sparks of desperate power. It spiraled around the room, pulling every object into a massive funnel. In moments, the entirety of the chamber was swirling around us. The air pulled at Elyria, still tethered to the wall. She screamed, and guilt tore at my heart, but I wasn't giving up now.

Chairs, vases, tables, pictures from the walls, irons from the fire, even the fucking water basin and pitcher. Everything took to the air in one massive funnel. They careened at Malvat, object after object. From every angle. Whips of shadow lashed out, slicing through stone and wood alike.

The last of the debris settled to the ground. Bits of metal and glass sparkled in the moonlight like a macabre treasure chest, but Malvat hadn't sustained so much as a scratch. The Iron Lord brushed the dust from the back of his arms as if the tornado I'd summoned was nothing more than a tantrum.

Desperation sank in my heart, driving me to my knees. The sounds of the battlefield drifted in from the balcony, mixing with Elyria's cries. The flaring light of an Innesvalen airship exploded in the sky, lighting up the chamber—highlighting our defeat. The finality of this moment drove the air from my chest.

The tips of Malvat's boots moved into view, stopping only inches from where my hands gripped the stone floor. I couldn't bear to look up and see the victory in his expression.

"Aww," he crooned, his patronizing tone rubbing salt into my bleeding heart. "She was mine this entire time, Calico." The toe of his shoe pressed under my chin, tilting my face up. "You were only the delivery boy, and there's nothing you can do about it."

Nothing I could do. The thought hollowed me out because it wasn't true. There was one option my arrogance hadn't dared consider until now. I'd lied to myself. This whole time, I believed that he was targeting Elle only to hurt me. The diabolical truth was he *needed* her. Mal's nightmare of a wave reducing

Venterra to a world of bones suddenly felt too possible.

My shoulders shook under the weight of the only option left. I might not be able to kill Malvat, but I could still stop whatever he was planning. Images of my sister smiling at the ball flashed in front of my eyes, my mother still in her mourning gown, and the countless lives depending on the fate of this night. If I bottomed out the last of my power, I could take this entire chamber with me. Then, gods willing, I would find Elle in the next life. Maybe our deaths would give Venterra a fighting chance.

Like it was torn open, my chest burned, the revelation shredding my heart to ribbons. The broken promise I'd made to Joseph in The Bullseye echoed in my ears. Not only couldn't I save her, but her death would be by my hand. The blood pooling beneath Elyria was my doing. I'd brought her here, I'd failed to protect her, and now I was about to kill the only good thing I'd ever known. I couldn't breathe. Pain seared the center of my chest, making my vision go white. What the fuck was happen—

Realization put its hooks into me, her voice on the battlefield drifting through my memory, *"Just another man who underestimated me."* That wasn't defeat driving the air from my lungs; it was power surging against my ribs. Elyria saved me in more ways than she'd ever known, but she never needed me to save her. Before Malvat figured out what was happening, I moved for the discarded spear and ignored the pressure squeezing my heart like a vice.

Malvat grinned, a long sword materializing in his hand at the same time the wall of shadow fell to the ground in a shimmering curtain of black dust.

"And here I thought you were about to give up. It's good to see you still have some fight left in you." The crystal blade spun in his palm, the lava light from the balcony making his green-black blade look blood red. "Perhaps we need ambiance. Sing for me, pet."

Elyria howled a string of barely intelligible curses, all colored by pain, frustration, wrath—and power.

Malvat drove forward, and I spun, deflecting his attacks while indirectly pushing him back. Each strike moved him into position. I let him believe he'd gotten the upper hand. He was so sure of his superiority, and that was his greatest weakness. Elyria knew it when she pretended to fear him. A few more feigned attacks, and he would be exactly where we needed him.

Malvat swung, perhaps too close, as his sword sliced away a chunk of leather from my chest.

My eyes flashed to Elyria in time to see her entire blood streaked form wreath in a blaze nearly too intense to look at.

38

ELYRIA

The pain. The pain. The pain.

Like the beat of Solaire's war drums, it flared through my body in a cadence, demanding that I let the dragon out.

The wire at my throat cut off my screams. It lanced across my vision, infiltrating every one of my thoughts. Anger and frustration made my tears steam.

Fucking careless. Stupid. I was so focused on the shadow power that I forgot Malvat was a Metal Singer, and each inch of that stupidity was tearing beneath my scales. The thorns sank into my flesh and carved grooves against my bones. Each scrape cleaved away at my confidence, replacing it with fear just as he'd promised. Scream after scream burned up my throat, only to be cut off by the wire noose.

In the haze of pain, I was distantly aware that the curtain of shadow that separated me from Cal fell to the ground. I forced my eyes to focus, gritting my teeth and slowing my breaths until I could make sense of what was happening before me.

The crystalline sword in Malvat's hands slashed in a brutal arc. Cal flipped and kicked, spinning the spear to move the blade away from his body, then returning the blow with one of his own. My heart seized each time the blade swung dangerously close to cutting something vital. With each faltering beat, the realization that our time was running out sank in. Cal wouldn't be able to sustain fighting like this. He was already beginning to slow down. Malvat would win.

I frantically pulled at my bindings. I wasn't going to hang here and watch the

GENEVA MONROE

other half of my existence be cut down by the same man who'd stolen my father
from me. Our souls were irrevocably entwined. That connection couldn't be
severed now that I'd finally accepted it.

The wires tightened, sending fresh rivulets of blood down my arms and
splashing into my eyes. I pulled hard at Cal's power, letting it fill me until I
was brimming with it. Malvat had underestimated me. Just as I always knew
he would. Continuing to struggle against the wires, I knew the sound of my
scrabbling and screaming would make Malvat think he still had the upper hand.
Cal drove him nearly within arm's reach, and then I summoned every bit of
magic I had running through me.

The reservoir of power was strong enough that it felt like my skin was made
of pure energy. I focused all of the heat within me to my arms and wrists. The
metal binding me dripped to the ground. Molten ore mixed with the pools of
my blood.

I landed nimbly on my feet, ignoring the way my legs shook and the woozi-
ness in my head from the blood loss. Silently, I unhooked the rope dart from
my hip. Snapping the fuse at the center of my heart, I ignited. This monster
was going to die. Now. I cracked the now flaming whip. The leather grabbed
Malvat's arm just as he swung across Cal's chest, a shorn piece of armor falling
to the ground. Malvat let out a startled sound of alarm, his crystal sword
evaporating into mist.

Cal took several lunging steps, our fingers brushing for the barest of seconds,
before a wave of shadow threw him into the adjoining room. Malvat tried to
wiggle the burning whip free of his arm. I snapped the leather again, cracking
it sideways to make the hooked blade rotate. The braid circled Malvat's throat
twice before the hook latched onto one of the iron blades protruding from his
shoulder. I spun, twisting and tugging the leash until his arms were pinned to
his lower back in a net of burning leather.

Brandishing the onyx dagger at my thigh, I drove it into the tender space
between his collar and shoulder. It sank into his flesh with a satisfyingly slick
sound, deeply imbedding itself into the bone, a perfect handle for me to leverage myself on to him. Ignoring the iron scraping against the raw and exposed

376

scaling, I wrapped my arm around his throat. I dug deep into the pure well of our power, sending heat pluming out from my palm and directly over Malvat's heart.

For the first time, the Iron Lord's resolve wavered. I could see it in the black shaking abyss of his eyes.

His tongue flicked against his iron teeth. "You think a little fire and a blade can stop me?" He swung his body, trying to dislodge me. "I was born in the heat of a dying star." Shadows flickered along his skin as he fruitlessly tried to dissolve. I wasn't sure if it was the power that I was funneling into him, or the blade. But he didn't get to just vanish this time. I dug my feet into his hips and held on. Beneath my heat, the iron blades decorating his shoulders melted, running down his arms like blood.

Malvat gritted his teeth against the pain but fell to his knees all the same. It was better than I'd fantasized. At the same time, I barely registered Cal falling to the ground.

"You feel that?" I hissed into his ear, intensifying the burn deeper. "I'm going to incinerate your heart inside its iron cage. That stench you smell isn't fear. It's your death."

Smoke billowed around us, and I didn't know if it was from my fire or if Malvat's shadows were crying out in protest.

Meeting Cal's gaze from where he kneeled on the ground, he nodded to me. This was our moment. I reached for what was left of his power, a warm, pulsating heat as familiar to me as my own. I let my power caress those flowing tendrils. Cal released his hold on it. Immediately, the rush of power flowed to me, becoming part of me. My vision bled with purple light.

Streaks of pure energy crackled down my arms and poured into my palms, causing my veins to glow. Malvat twisted and bucked against me. It wasn't enough. I needed more, pulling harder on the flow of energy.

Cal cried out from the force, making my focus momentarily flicker. "Keep going," he yelled, one hand gripping the slate floor. "I can take it."

I intensified the draw, turning the fire to a brilliant red-purple. Cal sank lower, gripping at his chest, but despite the pain, his eyes stayed strong. He was giving me his strength, and I would not waste it. Pressing both palms flat to the chest of my enemy, I focused the torrent of power into a single concentrated flow.

Malvat didn't just scream. The sound that left his lips reduced him to his basest nature. No longer brave and malevolent, just a man crying out. A man who knows his death is imminent.

Beneath my palms, his heart pumped erratically out of time. Malvat's body crumpled, but still, I held on until he was supported only by my arms. If not for the raging purple flames, one might think that I held him in a lover's embrace.

I brought my lips to his ear. "This is for the lives you stole and the horror you wrought upon the innocent. They deserved better, and you deserve nothing. When the fires of Kraav sear the flesh from your bones, I want you to think of me and know that even the flames are more kindness than you deserve."

The thorns of my power branched out, snaking around his heart and cutting deep. I was going to tear the black lump of flesh from his chest. I wanted to see the second it failed to beat.

Malvat loosed another scream, but all I could hear was a rasping breath, one I knew better than my own. Cal's silhouette was barely visible through the flames. He was on his stomach, limp wings folded over him. He wasn't moving, not even the subtle rise and fall of his breathing.

Panic seized me, my need for vengeance warring with my love for the one man who really saw me. Fucking fate was handing me an impossible choice. I could kill Malvat, but he would take Cal with him.

Fire and blood pounded in my ears in a roar. I couldn't lose him. I couldn't. I wouldn't.

Letting go of the tether, his power snapped back. The air crackled between us, and Cal took a deep breath. I heaved a relieved sigh. I needed to get closer to him, to touch him so that we could access the kind of power needed to end this madness, before it was too late. Cal was breathing, but he could barely lift his head to look at me. The distance felt impossible.

Malvat had kept us separated this entire time on purpose, knowing I'd never be able to pay the price of his sacrifice. My entire body trembled with rage. We were so close, and yet...

Malvat chuckled, laughter mixed with a wet, pained sound. I twisted the knife in his shoulder, and that demented laughter shifted into a moan.

"Accept it, little mouse. If you want my death, then you will kill him, too. Finish me now. Feel his life fade as you squeeze at my heart. Hear the sweet sound of my screams mixing with his. You won't get another chance."

My heart pounded in my ears. Tears flowed down my cheeks.

"No."

"Elle, do it." Cal's voice sounded so weak.

"No!"

There were other ways to kill a man. I reached behind my back for my Serpent Dagger.

"Too late," Malvat whispered.

He ripped the knife from his shoulder and threw me down. I toppled over his shoulder, landing hard against the stone. The newly freed dagger tumbled from my grip. Faster than I could process my upturned reality, Malvat snatched the Sun Serpent and lodged it in my thigh. The golden dragon and sun gleamed crimson with blood, my blood.

I screamed in frustration as much as in pain.

Malvat winked at me—and vanished.

39

ELYRIA

"With my own damn knife."

I pulled the dagger from my leg and slipped it back into its sheath. At least the leather kept the blade from cutting too deep. Favoring the uninjured leg, I hopped up and closed my eyes against the throbbing in each of my limbs. This was barely an echo of what those thorns had done while I hung from the wall. Honestly, it was a miracle I was even standing. Only Cal's power and my wrath were keeping me on my feet. Drawing on my draconic roots, I pushed forward. My will was stronger than anything Malvat could dream up. The beast in me would not submit to a little pain and blood loss. There would be time for licking wounds later, if we managed to survive the night.

On the far side of the room, Sparky's dark mass laid unmoving. I couldn't bring myself to look at my sweet boy. He'd sacrificed himself to save us, one more body for Malvat to atone for. The gathering shadows crept inward, swallowing his too still form.

"Be ready," Cal said, picking his spear back up with shaky hands. He was swayed slightly, but I could see the strength coming back to him with each passing second.

I palmed two of the obsidian daggers. The hum of energy still coursed through me, making my fingers prickle with awareness.

Darkness thickened around us, almost a tangible thing in the room. It blotted out the light of the lava fields, smothering the room and closing the space around us.

I sprinted for Cal, releasing my daggers straight into the darkness forming at his back. I didn't know how I knew. Maybe my instincts were singing, or it stood to reason that Cal was the greater threat between us. I was a fraction too slow. Malvat appeared, the swipe of his sword grazing one of Cal's golden wings. One obsidian blade sank into Malvat's shoulder, the second into his side.

Pulling the stone free with a snarl, he threw them away. Cal buckled forward. Ignoring the pain, he spun around, grabbing Malvat's arm and flinging them both through the darkness toward what was once the terrace.

For a heart stopping second, it was silent. Then, the clang of Cal's spear on the sword rang out. I took the shadow at a run, leaping through the mist and praying that it didn't solidify as I passed through it.

Cal drove the bladed end of the spear into Malvat's already wounded shoulder. Then whipped it back around to slam it into the knife wound on his side.

Malvat bellowed with rage and pain.

"Block this, you shadow jumping son of a bitch." I pulled the darts free of my bracer and flung all five at Malvat.

Startled by my sudden appearance, Malvat flashed a glare in the direction of the thin deadly blades heading straight for him. He raised a hand, but the shadow tendrils were only able to deflect two of the darts. One sank into his neck, the others landing in his torso. Malvat spluttered and scrambled to remove them.

It gave us the opening we needed.

Cal's hand gripped mine, the instant charge like a lightning bolt between us. All the power I'd stored flowed back into him. It swirled between us, his power caressing my own and merging into an unstoppable force. Flames burned back the wall of shadow, turning richly purple against the darkness. This was a strength to burn away the night.

Malvat's black eyes churned with rage.

I flung out a dagger from my hip, slicing across his hand and forcing him to drop his sword. Malvat curled his hands into fists, making the darkness in the room vibrate. Black blood oozed from his wounds and dripped from the corner of his eyes. The wood and stone of the terrace rattled and groaned under his dark power.

"You should have surrendered to me when you had the chance." His voice was layered with dissonance. This was more than just a lord gone mad with power. There was something darker beneath that voice.

A beam of purple fire shot from my hand straight for Malvat. The shadow surrounding him solidified and glittered black-green against our blast. Power cycled between us, growing stronger with each pulse. The world resonated with us, becoming an audible vibrating hum.

Cal raised his hand, adding a second beam. Black mist and purple flame collided, repelling off each other before clashing again. Like a wave from the shore, the darkness reared back, rallying the full force of Malvat's power.

Cal's purple eyes flashed with recognition. We needed more power when Malvat attacked, or we wouldn't survive it.

Stopping the flow of fire, Cal pulled me into his arms, making the world go momentarily dark. The inky shadows pressed in, scraping at my scales with a million tiny blades and whispering nightmares in my ears. I closed my eyes, ignoring the pitch black terror and focusing on the man enveloping me in the safety of his arms.

Cal's hand settled over my heart, igniting a supernova in the center of my soul. Every cell in my body was set aflame. This didn't feel like when we'd power drifted before. It was so much more than his fire merging with mine. Cal's essence funneled through me, binding us in a way I didn't think was possible. Just when I thought the universe was disappearing beneath the force, I sent it all back. I poured everything I had into the flow. The grief over Duke's death, the fear of losing Cal, the uncertainty of our future, and the overwhelming love. It all went careening back.

Daring to open my eyes, I was awestruck by the man who held me. Cal's skin crackled with purple light. His veins pulsed, and his wings glowed. My head fell back in delicious surrender. I lost myself in the bliss of our souls converging into a singular source of power.

The shadow recoiled, forming a protective shield around Malvat.

Cal murmured against my lips, "In this life and the next, Sunshine."

With one devastating release, Cal directed all of our power at Malvat. Raw energy flowed into the darkness. The light flared until it was too bright to see anything but the pure radiance. My legs weakened with the last sparks of energy that drained out of me.

Everything stopped. The flames. The shadows. My heart. My breath. The feeling of becoming one with the fabric of Cal's soul. Everything.

"I've got you, Elle."

Time sped back up. My vision slowly returned, revealing the shadowy form of a man, the stones around him glowing brightly with residual heat. My hope shattered. He was still there. Malvat still stood.

"We need to leave before he recovers." Cal's arms scooped me up. His wings beat, preparing to take flight. The gust from his wings swirled the residual smoke in the room, and then the shadowy form of Malvat crumbled in a shower of black, glittering dust.

Silence fell over us like a heavy blanket. The clang and din of battle on the fields ceased. Streaks of red light fell from the sky—airships. Legionnaire speeders were falling from the sky.

"Holy gods. Did we do it?" I whispered.

I looked at the void where Malvat had stood.

At the center of the dark, crystalline pile was a pale, ivory body. Seeing him there should have filled me with satisfaction, but I felt only fear. What if it wasn't enough? What if this nightmare wasn't over? I needed to wrap my hands around his cold flesh and know that he was dead.

Slipping from Cal's arms, I tried to be steady on my feet. Walking felt like trudging through quicksand, but I still managed to stumble to his body with clumsy steps.

Malvat looked like a ghost in a bed of black ash. His features, once harsh and full of evil, looked almost angelic.

"I hope you're screaming in hell." Tears fell from my eyes and landed in thick splashes against his chest.

And then, he moved— a slight raise to his chest made my tears roll down his sides as he took in a breath. It had to be some kind of cruel joke, a trick of my tear-blurred eyes. But then his chest rose again... and again. A rasp leaked from his lips.

"He's still fucking alive," I choked. Anger and wrath turned my vision red. I gave everything, including my last breath, and he still lived.

I dropped to my knees and straddled him. With whatever strength I had left, I wrapped my fingers around his throat and shook. I scraped at the edges of my power.

Malvat's eyes fluttered beneath his lids. The iron bits once imbedded in his skin were no longer there. The dark brown scales were gone. All that was left was pale skin with a thin sheen of sweat clinging to his brow.

I tightened my hands, making his windpipe flex beneath my fingers.

"Die already. You took EVERYTHING I had, and still, it wasn't enough. *JUST DIE.*"

Malvat moaned and wheezed. His eyes still fluttering wildly beneath their lids, mocking me with their ceaseless movement.

"Elyria," Cal said hesitantly.

I couldn't hear it. I wouldn't. This man, this monster, would perish here and now. By my hand, I would claim his death.

"No, Cal. His blood will coat my fingers as I carve his heart from his chest."

I reached behind me and pulled the Sun Serpent dagger from my back. Clutching it in both hands, I raised it high above me, mustering whatever I could from within me. Deep in my core, something cracked, particles of my soul splintering and turning to flame. They wreathed the dagger in light. I didn't care if it killed me to summon more magic. All I cared about was seeing the life drain from him before it did. The fire at my hands burned hotter.

"Elle, Sunshine. It's done. You have to stop."

"*NO!*"

I exploded. A detonation of fire burst from me in every direction, an inferno devouring everything in its path. The stone surrounding us disintegrated until only the ash covered sky remained. The day my father found me, I was the only living thing in a sea of destruction. If this was how I died, I would do it taking everything with me again, including the monster beneath me.

I swung the blade down. Cal grabbed my wrist. The point of my dagger stopped a hair's breadth from Malvat's pallid chest.

"Not everything, Sunshine," he said softly. "He didn't take everything. You still have me, and I won't let you do something you'll regret later."

"Regret?" I ground out, pushing against Cal's hold. "The only regret I have is that I was too weak to do this properly the first time."

"Elle, look at him. That's not the monster. That's what the monster left behind."

I blinked away the rage in my eyes and really looked. The light of my dagger flickered over his features. The blackened skin around Malvat's eyes was gone. As if I had summoned his awareness with my scrutiny, they fluttered open. In place of the black cold eyes that haunted my dreams, I saw only pale blue struggling to comprehend the dagger held above his heart.

Cal was right. Whatever poison had taken over him was gone, leaving only this shell. I dropped my hand; the dagger slipping from my fingers along with what little power bled into it.

Tears came on hot and fast. Wracking my body. It was done.

"Let's go." He said, pulling me into his arms. "Let's go home."

A wave of chills swept over me, forcing my entire body to shake. My heart thumped out of time. I twisted my eyes in confusion. The taste on my tongue turned to ash.

"Cal?" I whispered. What was happening? "Something's wro-"

The world spun, a grey haze narrowing my vision. My head lolled back against Cal's arm...and then I was falling.

"Fuck. *No!*" Cal said, laying me down on the ground. "Elyria, open your eyes." Slowly, I obeyed. His irises were still purple. They were so beautiful, despite the growing panic within them. I tried to raise my hand to touch his cheek, but my arms felt numb and unresponsive. My vision tunneled again, and I closed my eyes, feeling the ground beneath me shift and spin.

"Elle. Stay with me, Sunshine." Cal shook me, my back slamming violently against the stone. *"FUCK!"*

Cal's fingers shook as he ripped at my leather halter. Or maybe it was the world shaking? "Not again. Don't do this to me." My eyes fluttered open enough to see him tossing the leather aside. His palm glowed white hot as he placed it against my bare chest. It hurt, like a vice crushing heart.

"Come on, my love. Open to me. Take what I'm giving you. *Please*."

The abyss of unconsciousness seemed so warm. A deep pool that I could just float away on. Not like the pain trying to force its way into me.

"Elyria!" Cal slammed my hand against his chest.

That was my name. He sounded so far away. Why did he sound like he was miles from me?

Tears fell from his eyes, coating my cheeks. "*Please don't leave me.*"

Why was Cal crying? I crawled my consciousness back from the abyss, cracking my eyes open.

"I refuse to let this be where we end." His hand flashed brighter, washing the entire room in white, blinding light. My body bowed off the ground. Searing pain clawed at my chest, snapping me from the blissful pool and forcing its way into my veins. Feeling returned to my numb limbs, causing a tingling sensation at my fingertips.

I took a deep breath. It both burned and cooled my lungs as if that was the first breath I had ever taken. My eyes focused on Cal. The purple had faded from his irises.

He loosed a sobbing breath. "Thank the gods." He wrenched me to his chest, squeezing me so tightly I nearly stopped breathing again. Strength surged back in me, faster even than it had bled out.

"I'm okay," I said, blinking my eyes. I pushed at his hands. "You can let go of me. I'm fine."

"The fucking hell you are! Gods, Elle, I swear you just died in my arms."

I untangled myself from him and climbed back to my feet. I swayed for only a second, but the world shifted from liquid to solid in the matter of a breath.

Cal was still kneeling, looking up at me with desperate eyes. With the backs of his hands, he brushed away the tears that were still falling.

"Well, I'm not dead anymore." In truth, my body felt like I'd been sent through a meat grinder. Even breathing hurt, but I wasn't going to let him know that. Cal would only worry and insist on doing something absurd, like carrying me all the way back to Innesvale. I looked around the ruined chamber. What little remained was crumbling and charred. My gaze drifted to the spot Rei was standing when I'd last seen her. Had Xoc made it back to Star Spear? Was she freed from Malvat's thrall?

With a whine, a warm nose pushed into the palm of my hand. My shock tilting up into I smile, I beam down at the beautiful cat. Sparky rubbed against my legs, purring his deep rumble. Killing the darkness in Malvat must have saved him too. A new kind of relief tugged at me. I hadn't acknowledged how much it hurt seeing his prone form, but the relief was palpable. "I'm okay, baby beastie. You don't need to worry. Cal is overreacting. I only died a little. I'm fine now."

"Elyria, you were-" Cal started, his tone shifting from concern to anger.

"Save it." I cut him off, picking up the discarded laces to my halter. I didn't need a lecture right now. Tying the leather shut, I said, "Get me out of this cursed place. You can lecture me on poor choices later." I started walking towards what was left of the door, Sparky padding alongside me. When I didn't hear his following footsteps, I turned back.

Cal was standing over Mal. A conflicted expression shadowing his face. "We need to bring him back to Innesvale, lock him up until we can make sense of what happened."

I knew he was right. I didn't want to spend another second in his presence, but Malvat had a lot of crimes to answer for.

Cal picked him up, wrapping an arm around his shoulder.

"*Cal*," he croaked.

On instinct, my hand tightened into a fist.

"Yeah, it's me, asshole," Cal said gruffly and adjusted Mal's weight against him.

"Just leave me to die. I don't deserve your mercy," he rasped. "I *deserve* to die."

"You do," Cal said. "Just not today."

With a heave, he pulled Mal higher on his shoulder and shuffled to the door.

He grimaced in pain. I'd forgotten the strike Cal took to the back. The extra weight must be excruciating.

I took a deep breath, swallowing the nausea, and wrapped Mal's other arm over my shoulder.

"Together."

Cal nodded. "Always."

We carried him down the stairs and out of the central courtyard. For each patrolman we passed, Malvat ordered them to stand down, those who didn't backed away the moment they caught sight of Sparky. He didn't even need to growl. Most were already shocked by the dozens of Legionnaires who had fallen to the ground. Those poor souls were in a trancelike state, unmoving and staring at the hands covered in iron armature and blood.

We slowly started making our way to the edge of the lava fields, in the direction of the tiny blue dot growing larger on the horizon. Morgan.

That was when hell opened around us.

The earth shook, causing great cracks to splinter across the ground. Bubbling magma oozed up in a deadly spiderweb.

"Now would be a really good time to have Alexander here," Elyria said, pushing closer. That beastly cat of hers forced his way between my feet. I was barely able to keep Mal upright, and Sparky wasn't helping.

"Now would be a really good time to be anywhere but here," I added, swiveling my head to try and find a stable route out of this mess.

A deep rumble drew our attention back to the mountain. Elyria clutched at the arm wrapped under Malvat's shoulders.

"Tell me I'm not seeing what I'm seeing." Elle's voice was broken by panic.

At the base of the mountain, the Iron Dragon uncurled from his resting position. His dark brown hide camouflaged perfectly with the stone of the mountain. He prowled down from his perch, and with each step he took, more fissures opened in the ground.

"Fuck." I swallowed. "That's the Iron Dragon." Ferrus's full attention was on us. The gravity of what we'd done settled on me. Ferrus was responsible for corrupting Malvat. Of course, he wasn't just going to let us leave. I glanced back. Morgan's ship was still too far away. She was picking up speed but still not approaching fast enough.

Ferrus stretched his back and shook out his massive wings, letting out a roar loud enough to rattle my bones.

"That's not Ferrus," Mal croaked, standing upright.

"What?" Elyria yanked back on his shoulder. "What's that supposed to

"I killed Ferrus. That's not him."

"You?.. Killed a dragon?" She scoffed in disbelief.

Ferrus thumped onto the paved ground of the Fort's central court.

"He looks pretty alive, Mal," I said to him.

"That's not him. We need to move."

"Move where? We're surrounded by lava. Fissures the size of chasms are literally opening beneath our feet. And, oh, there's a dragon that could snatch us from the air in a heartbeat," Elyria said with wild hysteria.

Mal was right, but I couldn't look away from Ferrus. His hide shimmered. The image of a dragon flickered in the light from the volcano. A concussive wave of rippling black-green power flowed from him, knocking us down like pins in a game. My hand landed only inches from the lava pool. Elyria's fall forced the earth to splinter like ice beneath her. It would be only moments before there wasn't anything left to where we stood.

The dragon flickered again, melting from its form. It turned and twisted before us. My mind struggled to make sense of what I was seeing. A second wave of power made the cracks in the ground grow wider, filling with even more lava. The heat and sulphur overpowered the air, making it hard to breathe. I tugged Elyria to me just before the clay where she was standing melted away.

Lava pooled along the edge, threatening to overflow on the small patch of rock that we were left standing on. Mal and Elyria pressed into me. We couldn't stay here. If the dragon didn't kill us, this lava surely would.

I looked over the top of Elyria to where Mal was barely standing upright. "Can you fly?"

"I don't know," he said in a rasp. His features tightened, straining in pain. A smattering of discolored scales covered his chest, followed by two russet wings unfurling from his too-white skin.

"So what? Just everyone but me gets wings?" Elyria said in a huff.

"Present dangers, my love. Worry about wings later." I looked down at Elyria's pet. What was I going to do about the cat? Elyria would be heartbroken if anything happened to him now. I could see it, she was attached, and he did save my life. As if he could read my thoughts, Sparky took off with an impressive leap, jumping the twenty feet from our island to the next. The lava that he'd landed his front paws on didn't seem to bother him at all. To think I'd worried for a second. This hellish landscape was home for him.

The waves of power were coming more regularly, each one shaking the world and drawing the borders of our tiny island closer. But that wasn't what was really making me panic. Ferrus had melted down into the shape of a man. Unlike when Aurus had shifted, Ferrus barely resembled a human. Black, ink-like essence dripped from him with every step. Long hair, black like an oil slick, drifted in the wind. With each step, his body dripped away, then reformed. Step by step, he became more solid.

"Is he melting?" Elyria, just like me, was trying to make sense of the nightmare vision before us.

"Cal, we need to leave now," Mal said, bracing his hands against his knees to hold himself up. "You can't let him get her."

"It was never you who wanted her." I stared at the monster at the gate. What did he want with Elyria? Thinking about it made my skin go cold, despite the heat suffocating us.

"Get me?" Elyria said, pulling Mal hard enough that he nearly tipped over.

"Fuck this." I scooped her into my arms and kicked off the ground. I narrowed my vision on Morgan's ship. She wasn't too far off. I refused to acknowledge the way my strength was waning, and I'd long since grown numb to the throbbing pain that sliced through my back muscles. Mal, on the other hand, I wasn't sure could take to the air. But, between him and her, it was going to be her. It would always be Elyria.

My wings beat hard, straining against my torn muscles. We weren't moving fast enough. I called for the air to speed us along, but I'd given Elyria the last of my magic to save her life. There was nothing left, not even a wisp. Whatever that nightmare was, it watched us, his head cocked to the side in calculation.

Mal came up beside me, trying to catch the updraft to spare energy. He looked like he might fall from the sky at any second. The dark mass of Sparky kept pace below us, jumping from island to island.

Another wave of energy bolted through the air. It knocked me to the side, causing my weak wing to give way. Elyria and I did a full double spiral before I was able to right myself. The hard yank of the air on my wings jolted her loose from my arms. Elyria screamed but managed to grab my leg before falling into the ocean of lava beneath us. Mal, on the other hand, was plummeting towards the ground.

"Hold on to me, Sunshine," I said, yanking her up and changing our trajectory into a sharp dive. I reached out my arm, snatching Mal's hand at the last second. Hot lava sprayed up around us. Elyria howled with pain as it hit her legs and ate through the leather of her pants.

I beat my wings harder, trying to climb against the weight.

Morgan's ship was there, barreling down on us. I just had to get us to it.

A deafening boom shook the air. The side of the mountain cracked open, spewing ash into the air. Torrents of lava rolled over the mountainside, devouring the fortress at its base. Comets of molten earth streaked through the sky. The troops on the fields screamed as one, trying to run away from the onslaught. I knew I should look away, but I couldn't.

A roar, like that of a tornado, echoed over the Dead Lands. A thick beam of green power shot directly at us and clipped my right wing, disintegrating the delicate membrane instantly. A howl of pain tore from my lungs, but it was quickly swallowed by Elyria's panicked screams. I strained every muscle against gravity's vice. The ground was coming up at us too fast.

Malvat splayed his fingers wide, calling the Sun Serpent dagger from Elyria's back. It melted in his hand, reforming into a thin sheet beneath our feet. The magnetic polarity of the ground pushed against the steel, slowing our descent.

"NO!" An ear-splitting wail tore from Elyria. Gold-tipped claws swiped at Mal with vengeful fury. Scales formed in a scattered pattern across his arm, blocking most of her attack.

We hovered a few feet from what would have been our certain death. It was quick thinking on Mal's part. His face was pale, and sweat rolled down his brow. Even that small bit of magic had taken its toll on him. It was necessary, but Elyria would never stop mourning the loss of that dagger.

I folded my wings behind me, the mangled one not fully able to sit flush to my spine. I couldn't stop the hiss that pushed through my teeth.

"Your wing," Elyria said, gently brushing mutilated flesh.

"It's nothing. We have bigger issues." I gestured with my chin back towards the lava-submerged fort. The demon was hovering over the smoldering rubble on a cloud of ash. With a single gesture, a wall of black shadow flowed out of the man. A great tidal wave of power charging for us. I looked back at Morgan's ship. We would never make it in time.

"Cal." Elyria's panicked hands turned my face to meet hers. Tears rolled from her eyes. "Kiss me. If I'm about to die, I want it to be with your lips on mine."

She was right. That wave would be the end. I grabbed Elyria and pulled her into me. I covered as much of her as I could with my body, wrapping my ravaged wings around us. She pulled my face to hers. The salty taste of her tears mixed with the sweetness of strawberries and the burn of spice. Our hearts pounding as one, we waited for the inevitable wall of power to slam into us.

One heart beat.

Two heart beats.

A roar shook the earth—from behind us.

Elyria's confused gaze met mine. I peeled back my wings and was momentarily blinded by the wall of flame that shot over us. The fire crashed into the shadow wave, pushing it back. The ash-strewn sky disappeared, replaced by a flood of golden scales soaring over our heads. Reflected light gleamed down in rainbows around us.

"My gods! He came!" Elyria cried out. Fresh tears streamed from her eyes.

Wings stretched out to touch the horizon, each beat sending a cyclone of air across the scorched earth. Aurus's lip curled back, sounding a second roar in warning. A torrent of liquid flame slammed into the cascade of black shadow.

Elle's parting words to him must have stung more than we'd realized, or had he sensed our distress through the dragon bond? I'd experienced his anguish in the Vanfald as purely as if it had been my own. Could Aurus feel what happened tonight, Elyria's pain while being tortured, and my desperation as she laid dying in my arms? Was the image of losing Elyria again more than he could bear?

For each blast of inky night, Aurus fought it back with more powerful dragon fire. Wave after wave collided against one another. Tendrils of razor-tipped darkness lashed out at us, but Aurus stomped and snapped them away. His long tail snaked back and forth, protectively caging us in.

Deep laughter echoed over the Dead Lands. "It's been a long time, nephew."

The shadow power retreated, crawling like a swarm of bugs over the lava torn land. It enveloped the few people who still remained, and from the writhing mass of darkness came bone-chilling screams. They filled the air, growing into a crescendo of torment.

"Cal!" Elyria shrieked, her trembling hands covering her mouth. Horror sluiced through me as the full view of the scene unveiled itself. Where once there were men running for their lives, now there were only blackened, shriveled-up skeletons. Bright green light drifted in streams from the corpses and twisted into the thickening mass of black ink.

The mass of energy fed directly to the man standing before the gates, the powers of those he consumed lighting him from within. The demonic man shifted into dragon form, larger than before. Black-green scales and thick rows of crystal spikes ran down his back. Massive emerald wings unfurled against the red glow of the erupting volcano. Taking to the sky, they shimmered with each deafening beat.

Kicking off the ground with a spray of lava rock, Aurus gave chase, soaring like a bullet into the dark night sky. His angry roar hit so deep that for a moment, I thought I felt a second heartbeat. The two dragons collided in the air, clawing and snapping at each other. Golden fire burst from Aurus, met in the sky with a plume of equally black flames.

"That fire," Elyria whispered. "It's like anti-flame. That's what the healer used to push back Duke's curse. It didn't last long, but it's what made him wake up."

"How in the Kraav did a healer in Laluna get those flames?"

"I have no idea. How do those flames exist at all?"

"They're unnatural," said a voice as second to me as my own. The beat of Xoc's wings tossed Elyria's raven locks into the air.

"You're alive." Her expression immediately shifted to relief, wrapping her arms around his waist. "Is Rei-"

"She's alive, too. Let's get out of here before that changes." Xoc grabbed my arm and started hauling me over his shoulder.

I yanked it from his grip. "Get Elyria, I'll manage."

"Like hell you can. Have you seen your wings? Don't be a baby," he said, re-tightening his hold on me.

Aurus' massive body plummeted out of the sky, wings pinned close to his back so that he rocketed directly towards us. He swooped low, circling our patch of lava and snapping his jaws to prevent the dark dragon getting too close. An answering wave of black, anti-fire poured from the demon's mouth. The ancient dragon's golden hide took the brunt of the attack, protecting us but blanketing the rest of the scorched earth with that bizarrely cold heat.

Baring glistening fangs, Aurus bellowed another battle cry, unbelievably louder than the last. Aurus was livid. I could feel his wrath seeping into me, no doubt Elle could too. For all his posturing in the cave, there was a potent serving of deadly intent flooding my system.

"Fucking hells," Xoc yelled in awe, the wind off of the beast's wings knocking him back and nearly taking me down with him. Ascending into the sky, the spines on Aurus's tail skimmed the lava field, kicking up bits of molten rock and ore. I threw up a hand to block us, only to have the air refuse my call. I covered what I could of Elyria with my body, preparing for the sting of lava.

The spray passed through a powerful jet of water, cooling the pieces so that they rained down as harmless pebbles and sand.

"You lot plan on watching the end of the world from down there, or do you think we could get out of this hell?" Morgan leaned over the railing of the approaching ship, dropping a ladder for us. "When I die, it's going to be with the salt of the open ocean on my skin, not hovering amid the stench of sulphur and death."

A dragon roar, this time from the dark dragon, shook the skies as both monstrous forms cut above the cloud layer.

"I've never been so happy to see this ship." Despite the pain and exhaustion, I smiled up at her. Morgan was coated in blood. It tinged her skin an ominous shade of crimson, only intensified by the fiery glow of her hair. A thick slash curved its way around her arm. Had she been cut, before or after we'd burned the curse from Malvat? Either way, we were lucky she made it here when she did.

Mal uncurled the fingers I hadn't realized were gripped defensively around Elyria's forearm. To Xoc he said, "Take him up, I'll get Elyria. But I can't raise this disc with his weight, too."

"That's not necessary. SHE can take care of herself." Elyria grabbed the bottom of the rope ladder and deftly began climbing.

Xoc's eyes flashed with annoyance and concern.

Elyria shouted, "Wait, Sparky." She whistled loud. The massive cat leapt onto the metal disc, forcing it to tip with the unbalanced weight.

I cursed, gripping Xoc to keep my balance. "Sunshine, the demon cat does not come with us."

Elyria yelled, "He's coming. Mal, bring him up, or so help me, I *will* go back to cutting your heart out."

"I'm sorry, Cal, but Elyria—" The look on Mal's face told me it didn't matter what I was about to say.

"Fine," I relented, wrapping an arm around Xoc's shoulders. "But Elyria, you get to explain the beast to my mother."

Clashing dragon fire lit up the sky in streams of gold and green, giving me a perfect view of her elated face. For all she had lost, maybe letting her keep the cat was a small concession. We kicked off the disc, slowly rising with each beat of Xoc's wings. It was uneven flying thanks to his also injured wing.

"So, we're just taking him with us? Back to Innesvale?"

"You saw how attached she is to that beast. You try telling her no."

"Not the cat, Malvat. What happened to the whole dagger to the chest plan?" Xoc asked.

"I'll explain on the sail back."

"The fact Elyria doesn't have a knife shoved in his throat is enough for me. "

"Trust me. She tried," I said.

"Besides, it's Morgan you're going to have to win over. He'll be lucky if she doesn't hang him from the mizzenmast."

Bein reached over the edge of the ship. He grabbed the straps of Elyria's halter and hauled her up.

"I can climb over on my own." She slapped at his hands. Which was almost laughable, given how much larger his hands were than hers.

"She says she's fine, but she's not," I said to him.

He gave my wings one look. "And what about you?"

"I'll manage." Xoc and I tumbled onto the deck, followed by Mal. His metal disc clanged hollowly against the wood.

Elyria sank to her knees before it, her entire body shaking for what was once her most beloved possession. Sparky circled around Elyria, nestling his head into the crook of her neck in sympathy.

"Bring it back around. All singers on deck. Get us the FUCK OUT OF HERE," bellowed Morgan.

The wood of the ship and the sails groaned in protest of the hard gust of air that hit us, and then we were soaring back towards the shoreline. The Captain eyed Sparky wearily. "Is that what I think it is? "

"Unfortunately." I nodded in affirmation.

"If he eats any of my crew, I'm throwing it and her overboard."

"It won't come to that," Xoc said, saving me from having to threaten Morgan minutes after she saved our asses.

The rolling thunder of the dragons' roars tumbled through the sky as they swooped around the Floating Islands. I was still wrapping my mind around the fact that Aurus came to our rescue. I thanked every god I could think of for it. Without him, we never would have made it off those fields.

I pulled Elyria into my arms, holding her tight. It felt like the earth's axis was tilting. The world, and how I understood it, suddenly defied logic, and the fear it left in its place drove my breath away like a punch to the gut.

Green fire cut across the sky like lightning, illuminating the entire ship and the army of skeletons littering the lava fields.

"Hope that is all he has done, and that he hasn't awoken things that ought never wake."

Over my shoulder, I studied Mal. Really looking at him for the first time. His face was blanched of all color, muscles emaciated, cheekbones and jawline more pronounced. It was as if that darkness had been feeding off him, and it only left this shell behind. Mal's cornflower eyes met mine.

"When the dust settles, you have a lot to tell me." I said low, "A lot to answer for."

Mal opened his mouth to say something, but a soul splitting yowl rang out from the volcano.

The black dragon's jaws were locked around Aurus's throat, and his claws were hooked into his back along the wing joint. Phantom pain sliced down my back. Elyria dropped to her knees, wrapping her arms around her torso with a choked scream. Part of a golden wing tore free, falling from the sky like a leaf on the wind. Aurus spun violently, twisting like a tornado and trailing a thick plume of smoke. With a final whip of his tail, he shook the black dragon loose.

Aurus snapped fiery jaws, closing around smoke and air. I could feel his anger and confusion crackle across the void separating us. The deep foreboding it called forth twisted at my gut.

Mal's hands tightened on the railing. His knuckles looked like they were going to crack. He closed his eyes, head lowered like he knew what was coming and couldn't bear to watch. And that, more than anything we'd seen tonight, had me worried. *What if Aurus lost?*

I'd seen the fading to smoke trick plenty over the past weeks, but unlike the fight with Mal, this time the smoke turned into a black-green oil. It coated Aurus's luminous golden scales, enveloping him completely. The ancient dragon thrashed at the viscous intrusion, his momentum driving them into the ash cloud.

Everything went quiet, leaving only the creaking of the ship as we all stared at the sky...waiting.

"Cal?" Elyria's plea broke and echoed in the silence. Her nails dug into my hand.

I dipped my face into her hair and tightened my eyes, instincts preparing me for what I knew was inevitable. Searing pain lanced at my heart, like being torn in half. Elyria trembled against me, and I knew she felt it too. She gripped her chest and cried out in an anguished sob. Whatever was happening to Aurus in that cloud, it wasn't good.

"I'm sorry. I'm so fucking sorry," Mal murmured. He slumped to the ground in a pathetic mass of sorrow and regret.

My vision went white. At first, I thought I might be blacking out from the pain until I realized the sky was illuminated with an all-consuming burst of light. Intense green flames shot through the ash, lighting the clouds on fire. The pillowing surface smoldered and glowed as the inferno ate through the atmosphere.

BOOM!

A wave of concussive energy hit the back of the ship, sending us into a spiral. People flew in all directions, sliding across the deck, the unlucky few tipping over the sides to their deaths. Bracketing Elyria's body to the railing, I held on with the last of my strength.

Morgan and Bein cried out commands. Star Spear skidded out over the ocean, splashing down. The right wing severed on impact, sending a plume of seawater raining down on us.

The ocean waves rose, threatening to overturn the ship. Sea Singers shouted commands, the water splashing the deck on all sides as they fought for control. But I wasn't watching them, or the deadly swells.

I was transfixed by the streak of gold falling from the sky. A trail of flames cascaded behind it, making him look more like a shooting star than a dragon plummeting towards the earth.

"Fly, Damn it. Fly! Why isn't he flying?"

Aurus' unmoving form sank directly into the heart of the volcano, a wave of lava enveloping him.

Elyria's mouth opened on a scream, but I couldn't hear anything above the roar of my pulse pounding in my ears. It felt like a critical part of my soul was being carved away. Her trembling body collapsed in my arms, and I knew exactly what the pain searing its way into her heart was.

Aurus was dead.

The green-black smoke cloud swirled in the air, before rocketing to the ground in the form of a man. Long black hair whipping in the wind, his body silhouetted by the river of lava behind him.

Star Spear cut through the water faster now that she was in her element.

I stared down the thing at the mountain, watching as his body disintegrated into mist.

If Aurus, the largest and most powerful of the dragons, couldn't defeat whatever that was, then what chance was there for Venterra?

Xoc was unmoving, still staring at where that thing had just disappeared.

"What in the *depths of Kraav* was that nightmare?" Elyria rasped against her tortured vocal cords.

Mal rose to his feet with steady seriousness, his pale eyes unwavering.

"That was Caedrin, Sovereign of Lifeblood, God of Chaos and Destruction, and he will devour this land in a wave of death, leaving only bones in his wake."

End of Volume 2

Cal, Elyria, and Xoc will return in *Silver Shard, Sun Serpent Saga Vol. 3*
coming 2024

AUTHOR'S NOTE

So, how about that third act? Are you still there? Nerves still intact? Do you need to take a breather? I'd understand if you do. I threw a lot at you in the end of this book. Lulling you in with the sweet romance, and then, BAM!

Was your heart breaking right along with Cal's? The poor guy is on a never-ending emotional roller coaster. Elle keeps finding her way to death's door like she's got a skip-the-line pass. They're probably going to need to discuss that death wish of her's. But, when he falls to his knees and accepts defeat, that was a particularly low point for the golden boy. Luckily, our girl isn't the waiting to be saved type.

Did you miss Xoc in this book? Don't worry Xocians, Xocettes, Xocophiles... I'm gonna have to work on a name for you all. So much of Star Spear was about Cal and Elyria's relationship, there just wasn't room for the big guy. He made it pretty clear, he didn't want to be in the middle. We asked, he said no...emphatically. Xoc wasn't made to be a third wheel, he's really got more *main character* energy.

Surprise! Dragon fight before the end of the book! Did you read that last line of chapter 39 and say, "Whaaat?" So cool though, right, except for the whole Aurus dying thing? Can't win them all. But hey, I brought back Sparky for you. Don't pretend you didn't cheer when he popped back up. You can only use the resurrection power so many times before it loses full potency, and our girl is already on her what, third...fourth life? Chapter 40 was one of the first scenes I thought of when I sat down to write Sun Serpent. I had the image of Cal wrapping Elle in his wings, then peeking out to see the flood of scales whooshing over them and Aurus's fire beating back Caidren's death wave. And the fall into the volcano, epic.

Lastly, DO YOU KNOW HOW HARD IT'S BEEN KEEPING CAIDREN A SECRET! Sorry for the shouty caps, but seriously, do you have any idea? I'm terrible at keeping secrets, TERRIBLE. This was a big one. Caidren is one sadistic, scary-ass god. That's right folks, we just leveled up to a god tier fight. I'm so excited for the next book. Tighten your titty straps, because now the story really gets to start.

If you enjoyed this book, then please drop me a review on Amazon and/or Goodreads. Let the world know how many times you cursed my name and wanted to throw your Kindle at the wall, or about that time I got you to laugh so hard you snorted. Reviews are the lifeblood of an indie author. Sorry, don't tell Caidren I said that, he is Sovereign of Lifeblood after all. Here's a handy link to post a review.

Dying to talk about the book, after that ending? I wouldn't be surprised if you were. Join us online at Geneva Monroe's Pretty St@bby Readers. I'm not going to say I have the best fans in the world. Fuck it, yes I am. I have the best fans. They're all over on Facebook, chilling in the group. Be sure to check out the Star Spear spoiler chat.

I'll be back soon, sooner if you subscribe to my newsletter. Subscribers get a Sun Serpent bonus chapter, *That One Time at Joseph's*. If you like exclusives, then the newsletter is where you want to be. I share everything from sneak peeks, fan and character art, to bonus content. After all, Xoc and Rei were up to a whole lot while Cal and Elyria were busy getting busy. Keep your eyes on your email.

XOXO,

Gen

ACKNOWLEDGMENTS

My author dreams are only possible with the immense support and love of my husband. His pride drives me forward and makes me strive more than anything to make the next one bigger and better. Thank you for being my everything, in this life and the next.

To my writing wifey and editor, Alessia. Your dreams are big, and the fact that making mine come true is one of them makes this book what it is. Star Spear's success belongs to you just as much as it does to me. Thank you for the late-LATE nights tearing this book apart and helping me put it back together. Now, I just need to figure out how to ocean jump for espresso breaks.

This book is barely a shadow of the first draft written nearly two years ago. The fact that she glows today, is in massive part due to the work of my beta team: Shelby Gunter, Anka Lesko, Lindsay Bliss Raab, Jessica Jordan, Erica Karwoski, Mandy Slaughter, Nova Lateuere, and Chelisse Redman. I seriously can't wait for you all to see the finished product. I love you.

Reanna Breaux, thank you for making this book shine like the Solstice sun. Someday I will learn where a comma goes. I swear.

Chelisse, thank you for listening to every single chaos fueled idea that pops into my head. You're my person in the chair, the Thelma to my Louise, the sugar in my coffee. Everything's better with you in it.

Erica, Thank you for letting me pay you in hotdog gifs and talking me off the self-doubt ledge more times than I can count. I'm so glad I put a dragon on my cover and was brave enough to ask you to read my book that day.

This book is largely dedicated to the love and support of my parents. There are fans, and then there are your parents with full war paint screaming from the sidelines. If you decide to skip the shmexy times, I'll understand.

To my soul sister, Lara, I love you...wait 'til the next book. There's a reason Xoc always grows lavender.

Lastly, thank you to every single person who took a chance on a debut author and stuck around for the chaos party. Things only get crazier from here. Thank you for the shares, the reviews, the videos. Everytime I feel like a fraud, or like I don't know what in the depths of Kraav I'm doing, one of you says that my book made you feel something and that gets me through it. These books are for you. So is the next one... and the one after that.

I love my aunties. You know who you are.

STAR
SPEAR

SUN SERPENT SAGA VOLUME 2

Made in United States
Troutdale, OR
10/02/2023

13363397R00257